For Uwe Weitendorf

DRAGON RIDER

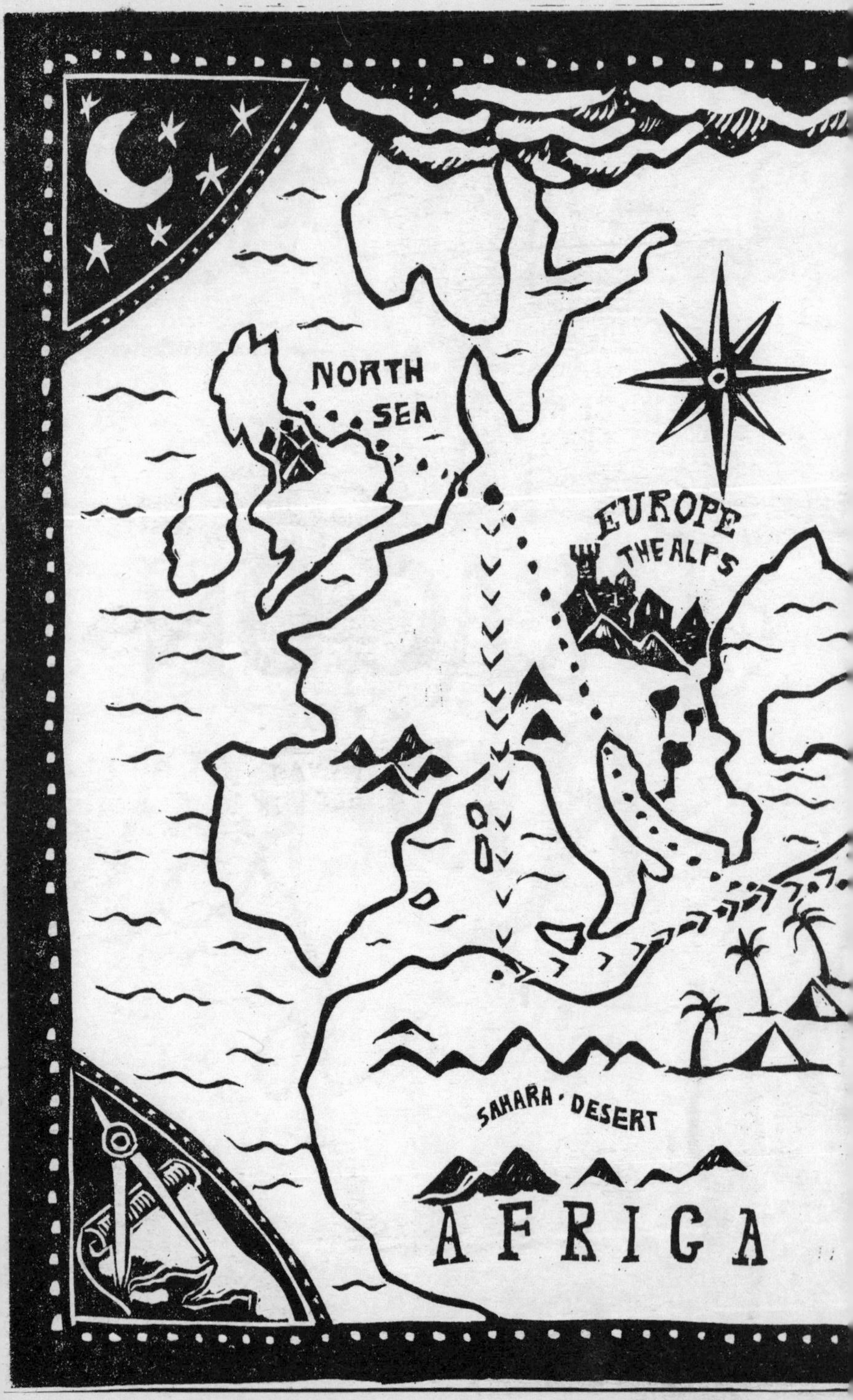

NORTH SEA
EUROPE
THE ALPS
SAHARA · DESERT
AFRICA

MAP MADE BY
GILBERT
GREYTAIL.

TIEN SHAN

PLATEAU
OF
TIBET

THE HIMALYAS
RIM OF HEAVEN

ARABIAN
PENINSULA

WADI
JUMA'AH
GORGE

ARABIAN
SEA

A MESSAGE FROM CHICKEN HOUSE

DRAGON RIDER is the very first dragon adventure from the legendary Cornelia Funke. I fell instantly in love with this thrilling tale of a boy and a dragon – and I think you will too. Turn the pages, and embark on a dangerous, magical and unforgettable journey. What's it like to fly on a dragon's back? This story holds the answer . . . So what are you waiting for? Climb aboard and hold on tight!

BARRY CUNNINGHAM
Publisher
Chicken House

WRITTEN AND ILLUSTRATED BY

CORNELIA FUNKE

2 Palmer Street, Frome, Somerset BA11 1DS

Original text © Dressler Verlag 2000
Original English translation © Oliver Georg Latsch 2001
First published in Germany as *Drachenreiter* by Cecilie Dressler Verlag, Hamburg, 1997
This translation by Anthea Bell © Chicken House 2004

Cover illustration © Laura Ellen Anderson 2017
Map © Alexis Snell 2017
Inside illustrations © Cornelia Funke 1997

First published in Great Britain in 2004
This edition published in 2017
Chicken House
2 Palmer Street
Frome, BA11 1DS
United Kingdom

www.chickenhousebooks.com

Cover design by Steve Wells
Typeset by Dorchester Typesetting Group Ltd
Printed and bound in by CPI Group (UK) Ltd, Croydon, CR0 4YY

The paper used in this Chicken House book is made from
wood grown in sustainable forests.

3 5 7 9 10 8 6 4 2

British Library Cataloguing in Publication data available.

ISBN 978-1-911077-85-5
eISBN 978-1-909489-14-1

CHAPTER ONE

Bad News

All was still in the valley of the dragons. Mist had drifted in from the sea nearby and was clinging to the mountains. Birds twittered uncertainly in the foggy damp, and clouds hid the sun.

A rat came scuttling down the slope, fell head over heels, tumbled down the moss-covered rocks and picked herself up again.

'Didn't I say so?' she muttered crossly to herself. 'Didn't I tell them?'

Snuffling, she raised her pointy nose, listened, and made for a group of crooked fir trees at the foot of the highest mountain.

'I knew before winter,' murmured the rat. 'Oh yes, I knew before winter, I could smell it coming, but they wouldn't believe me, no, not them! They feel safe here. Safe! Huh! I ask you!'

It was so dark under the fir trees that you could scarcely see the gaping crevice in the mountainside that swallowed up the mist.

'They don't know anything,' the rat continued peevishly,

'that's their problem. They know absolutely nothing about the world. Not the least little thing.'

She glanced warily around again, and then disappeared into the crevice in the rock. There was a large cave behind it. The rat scurried in, but she didn't get far. Someone grabbed her tail and lifted her up in the air.

'Hi, Rat! What are you doing here?'

The rat snapped at the furry fingers that were holding her tight, but all she caught was a mouthful of brownie hairs, which she furiously spat out.

'Sorrel!' she hissed. 'Let go of me this instant, you brainless mushroom-muncher! I don't have time for your silly brownie tricks.'

'You don't have time?' Sorrel placed Rat on the flat of her furry paw. She was still a young brownie, no bigger than a human child, with a spotted sulphur-yellow coat and bright, catlike eyes. 'How come, Rat? What's the big hurry? Need a dragon to protect you from hungry cats, or what?'

'This has nothing to do with cats!' hissed Rat angrily. She didn't care for brownies herself, although all the dragons loved them and their furry faces. When the dragons couldn't sleep they would listen to the strange little songs the brownies sang, and when they felt sad, no one could cheer them up as well as those sharp-tongued brownie layabouts.

'I've got bad news, if you want to know. Extremely bad news,' grumbled Rat. 'But I'm not telling anyone except Firedrake. Certainly not you!'

'Bad news? Oh, festering fungus! What sort of bad news?' Sorrel scratched her stomach.

'Put – me – down!' snarled Rat.

'If you say so.' Sorrel sighed and let Rat hop down to the stony floor of the cave. 'But he's still asleep.'

'Then I'm waking him up!' spat the rat, making her way further into the cave, where a fire burned blue, keeping the darkness and damp away from the heart of the mountain. Beside its flames the dragon lay asleep, curled up with his head on his paws. His long tail with its spiny crest was coiled around the warmth of the fire. The flames brought a glow to his scales and cast his shadow on the cave wall. Rat scurried up to the dragon, climbed on his paw and tugged his ear.

'Firedrake!' she shouted. 'Firedrake, wake up. They're coming!'

Sleepily, the dragon raised his head and opened his eyes.

'Oh, it's you, is it, Rat?' he murmured in a rather hoarse voice. 'Has the sun set already, then?'

'No, but you must get up all the same! You have to wake the others!' Rat jumped off Firedrake's paw and scuttled up and down in front of him. 'I warned you, I really did – I warned the whole bunch of you, but you wouldn't listen, oh no!'

'What's she talking about?' The dragon cast an enquiring glance at Sorrel, who was now sitting by the fire, nibbling a root.

'No idea,' said Sorrel, munching. 'She just keeps nattering on. Well, there's not much room for sense in a little head like hers.'

'Oh, really!' Rat gasped indignantly. 'Honestly, I ask you, I—'

'Take no notice, Rat!' Firedrake rose, stretched his long neck and shook himself. 'She's in a bad temper because the mist makes her fur damp.'

'Pull the other one!' Rat cast Sorrel a venomous glance. 'Brownies are always bad-tempered. I've been up since sunrise, running my paws off to warn you. And what thanks do I get?' Her grey coat was bristling with anger. 'I have to listen to her silly fur-brained fancies!'

'Warn us of what?' Sorrel threw the nibbled remnants of her root at the wall of the cave. 'Oh, putrid puffballs! Stop winding us all up like this or I'll tie a knot in your tail!'

'Quiet, Sorrel!' Firedrake brought his claw down angrily on the fire. Blue sparks flew into the brownie girl's fur, where they went out like tiny shooting stars.

'All right, all right!' she muttered. 'But the way that rat carries on is enough to drive anyone crazy.'

'Oh, really? Then just you listen to me!' Rat drew herself up to her full height, planted her paws on her hips and bared her teeth. '*Humans* are coming!' she squeaked, so shrilly that her voice echoed all round the cave. 'Human beings are coming! You know what that means, you leaf-burrowing, mushroom-munching, shaggy-haired brownie? Humans are coming – coming *here*!'

Suddenly all was deathly quiet.

Sorrel and Firedrake looked at each other as if they had been turned to stone. But Rat was still trembling with rage. Her whiskers were all aquiver, and her tail twitched back and forth on the cave floor.

Firedrake was the first to move.

'Humans?' he asked, bending his neck and holding his paw out to Rat. Looking offended, she scrambled on to it. Firedrake raised her to his eye level. 'Are you sure?' he asked.

'Perfectly sure,' replied the rat.

Firedrake bowed his head. 'It was bound to happen some day,' he said quietly. 'They're all over the place these days. I think there are more and more of them all the time.'

Sorrel was still looking stunned. Suddenly she jumped up and spat into the fire. 'But that's impossible!' she cried. 'There's nothing here they'd want, nothing at all!'

'That's what you think!' The rat bent over so far that she almost fell off Firedrake's paw. 'Don't talk such nonsense. You've mingled with humans, right? There's nothing they don't fancy, nothing they don't want. Forgotten that already, have you?'

'Okay, okay!' muttered Sorrel. 'You're right. They're greedy. They want everything for themselves.'

'They do indeed.' The rat nodded. 'And I tell you, they're coming here.'

The dragon-fire flared up, and then the flames burned low until the darkness, like some black animal, swallowed them. Only one thing could extinguish Firedrake's fiery breath so fast, and that was sorrow. But the dragon blew gently on the rocky ground, and flames flickered up once more.

'This is bad news indeed, Rat,' said Firedrake. He let Rat jump up on to his shoulder, and then went slowly towards the mouth of the cave. 'Come on, Sorrel,' he said. 'We must wake the others.'

'And won't they just be pleased!' growled Sorrel, smoothing down her ruffled fur and following Firedrake out into the mist.

CHAPTER TWO

A Meeting in the Rain

Slatebeard, the oldest dragon in the valley, had seen more than his memory could hold. His scales no longer glowed, but he could still breathe fire, and whenever the younger dragons were at a loss they would come to ask his advice. Once all the other dragons had assembled outside Slatebeard's cave, Firedrake woke him. The sun had set. A black and starless sky lay over the valley, and it was still raining.

When the old dragon emerged from his cave he looked gloomily up at the sky. His bones ached from the damp, and the cold weather made his joints stiff. The others respectfully made way for him. Slatebeard looked around. None of the dragons were missing, but Sorrel was the only brownie present. The old dragon moved through the wet grass, with heavy steps and dragging tail, towards a rock that rose in the valley like a giant's head covered with moss. Breathing hard, he climbed up on it and looked round. The other dragons gazed up at him like frightened children. Some of them were still very young and knew nothing but this valley, others had come with Slatebeard himself from far, far away, and remembered that the world had not always belonged to mankind. They all scented misfortune, and they hoped he would deal with it. But Slatebeard was old and tired now.

'Come up here, Rat,' he said in a hoarse voice. 'Tell us what you saw and heard.'

The rat scampered nimbly up the rock, climbed Slatebeard's tail and crouched on his back. It was so quiet under the dark sky that only the sound of the rain falling and the rustle of foxes out hunting by night could be heard. Rat cleared her throat. 'Humans are coming!' she cried. 'They've roused their machines and fed them and sent them on their way. They're already eating a path through the mountains only two days' journey from here. The fairies will hold them at bay for a while, but they'll get here some time or other – because it's this valley of yours they're making for.'

A groan ran through the ranks of the dragons. They raised their heads and pressed closer round the rock where Slatebeard stood.

Firedrake was a little way away from the others, with Sorrel perched on his back, nibbling a dried mushroom. 'Oh, terrific, Rat,' she muttered. 'Couldn't you have put it a little more tactfully?'

'What does that mean?' one of the dragons called out. 'Why would they want to come here? Surely they have all they want where they are.'

'Humans never have all they want,' replied Rat.

'Let's hide until they go away again!' suggested another dragon. 'The way we've always done when one of them loses his way and turns up here. They're so blind they only see what they expect to see. They'll think we're odd-looking rocks, same as usual. Or dead trees.'

But the rat shook her head.

'Look here!' she shrilled. 'If I've told you once I've told you a hundred times, those humans are making plans. But big animals don't listen to little animals, right?' She looked around her, crossly. 'You hide from human beings, but you aren't interested in what they're up to. Rats aren't so stupid: we go into their houses, we eavesdrop on them. We know what they're planning for your valley.' Rat cleared her throat again and stroked her grey whiskers.

'Here she goes again, winding up the suspense,' Sorrel whispered into Firedrake's ear, but the dragon ignored her.

'What are they planning then, Rat?' asked Slatebeard wearily. 'Come on, tell us.'

Rat fiddled nervously with a whisker. It was no fun bringing bad news. 'They – they're going to flood the valley,' she replied, her voice faltering. 'Soon there'll be nothing here but water. Your caves will be flooded, and none of the tall trees over there,' she

said, pointing one paw at the darkness, 'none of them will be left. Not even the treetops will show above the water.'

The dragons stared at her, speechless.

'But that's impossible!' one of them exclaimed at last. 'No one can do a thing like that. Not even us, and we're bigger and stronger than they are.'

'*Impossible*?' Rat laughed sarcastically. '*Bigger*? *Stronger*? You don't get it at all. You tell them, Sorrel. Tell them what human beings are like. Maybe they'll believe *you*.' With an injured expression, she wrinkled her sharp nose.

The dragons turned to Firedrake and Sorrel.

'Rat's right,' said the brownie. 'You've no idea.' She spat on the ground and picked at a piece of moss stuck between her teeth.

'Human beings don't go about in suits of armour these days, like they used to when they hunted you dragons, but they're still dangerous. More dangerous than anything else in the world.'

'Oh, nonsense!' said a large, stout dragon scornfully, and turned his back on Sorrel. 'Let the two-legs come! Rats and brownies may be right to fear them, but we are dragons! What can they do to us?'

'What can they do to you?' Sorrel threw her nibbled mushroom away and sat up very straight. She was angry now, and an angry brownie is not to be trifled with. 'You've never set foot outside this valley, dimwit!' she said. 'I expect you think human beings sleep on leaves like you. I expect you think they do no more harm than a fly because they don't live much longer than one. I expect you think they've got nothing in their heads but eating and sleeping. But they aren't like that. Oh no, not these days!' Sorrel was practically gasping for air. 'Those things that sometimes fly across the sky – being so stupid, you call them noisybirds – those things are machines built by humans for travelling through the air. And human beings can talk to each other when they aren't even in the same country. They can conjure up moving, talking pictures, and they have cups made of ice that never melts, and their houses shine at night as if they've trapped the sunlight, and, and . . .' Sorrel shook her head, 'and they can do wonderful things – terrible things too. If they want to flood this valley with water then they will. You'll have to leave whether you like it or not.'

The dragons stared at her. Even the one who had just turned his back. Some of them looked up at the mountains as if they expected machines to come crawling over the black peaks any moment.

'Oh, drat it!' muttered Sorrel. 'Now he's gone and made me

so cross I threw my delicious mushroom away. It was an oyster mushroom too! You don't find those around here very often.' In a thoroughly bad temper, she scrambled down off Firedrake's back and started searching the wet grass for her titbit.

'You heard, all of you!' said Slatebeard. 'We have to leave.'

Uncertainly, their legs heavy with fear, the dragons turned to him again.

'For some of you,' the old dragon continued, 'it will be the first time, but many of us have had to flee from human beings before. Although now it will be extremely difficult to find a place that *doesn't* belong to them.' Slatebeard shook his head sadly. 'It seems to me there are more and more of them with every new moon.'

'Yes, they're all over the place,' said the dragon who had been mocking Sorrel a moment ago. 'It's only when I fly over the sea that I don't see their lights beneath me.'

'Then we must just try living in harmony with them,' suggested another dragon.

But Slatebeard shook his head. 'No,' he said. 'No one can live in harmony with human beings.'

'Oh yes, they can.' Rat stroked her wet coat. 'Dogs and cats do, and mice and birds, even us rats. But you,' she said, letting her gaze roam over the dragons, 'you're too big, too clever and,' she added, shrugging her shoulders, 'too *different*! You'd frighten them. And when something frightens human beings they—'

'They destroy it,' the old dragon said wearily. 'They almost wiped us out once before, many, many hundreds of years ago.' He raised his heavy head and looked at the younger dragons one by one. 'I'd hoped they would at least leave us this valley. It was a foolish hope.'

'But where are we to go?' cried one of the dragons in despair.

'This is our home.'

Slatebeard did not reply. He looked up at the night sky, where the stars were still hidden behind clouds, and sighed. Then he said, huskily, 'Go back to the Rim of Heaven. We have to stop running away some time. I'm too old. I shall crawl into my cave and hide, but you younger ones can make it.'

The young dragons looked at him in surprise. The rest of them, however, raised their heads and looked eastward, their eyes full of longing.

'The Rim of Heaven.' Slatebeard closed his eyelids. 'Its mountains are so tall that they touch the sky. Moonstone caves lie hidden among its slopes, and the floor of the valley in the middle of the mountains is covered with blue flowers. When you were children we told you stories about the Rim of Heaven. You may have thought they were fairy tales, but some of us have actually been there.'

He opened his eyes again. 'I was born there, so long ago that eternities lie between me and that memory. I was younger than most of you are now when I flew away, tempted by the wide sky. I flew westward, on and on. I have never dared to fly in the sunlight since. I had to hide from humans who thought I was a bird of the Devil. I tried to go back to the Rim, but I could never find the way.'

The old dragon looked at his young companions. 'Seek the Rim of Heaven! Go back to the security of its peaks, and then perhaps you will never have to flee from men again. They aren't here yet,' he said, nodding towards the dark mountaintops around the valley, 'but they will come soon. I have felt it for a long time. Don't linger. Fly! Fly away!'

All was perfectly still again. Drizzling rain as fine as dust fell from the sky.

Sorrel hunched her head between her shoulders, shivering. 'Oh, thanks a million,' she whispered to Firedrake. 'The Rim of Heaven, eh? Sounds too good to be true. If you ask me, the old boy dreamed it up.'

Firedrake did not reply, but looked up at Slatebeard thoughtfully. Then he suddenly stepped forward.

'Hey!' whispered Sorrel in alarm. 'What's the idea? Don't do anything silly.'

But Firedrake took no notice. 'You're right, Slatebeard,' he said. 'In any case I'm tired of living in hiding, never flying outside this valley.' He turned to the others. 'Let us look for the Rim of Heaven. Come on, let's set out today. The moon is waxing. There'll be no better night for us.'

The others shuddered as if he had taken leave of his senses. But Slatebeard smiled for the first time that night. 'You're still rather young, Firedrake,' he pointed out.

'I'm old enough,' replied Firedrake, raising his head a little higher. He was not much smaller than the old dragon, but his horns were shorter and his scales shone in the moonlight.

'Here, hang on! Wait a mo!' Sorrel scrambled hastily up Firedrake's neck. 'What's all this nonsense? You may have flown beyond these hills all of ten times, but,' she said, spreading out her arms and pointing to the mountains around them, 'but you've no idea what lies further off. You can't just fly away through the human world, looking for a place that may not even exist.'

'Be quiet, Sorrel,' said Firedrake crossly.

'Won't!' spat the brownie girl. 'See the others? Do they look as if they want to fly away? No! So forget it. If human beings really come, I'm sure I can find us a nice new cave!'

'Yes, listen to her,' said one of the other dragons, moving

closer to Firedrake. 'There's no such place as the Rim of Heaven except in Slatebeard's dreams. The world belongs to men. If we hide here they may leave us in peace. And if they really do come to our valley, well, we'll just have to chase them away.'

At this, Rat laughed. Her laughter was shrill and loud. 'Ever tried turning back the tide?' she asked.

But the dragon who had spoken did not answer her. 'Come on,' he told the others, and he turned and went back through the pouring rain to his cave. They followed him one by one, until only Firedrake and the old dragon were left. Slatebeard, his legs stiff, climbed down from the rock and looked at Firedrake. 'I can see why they think the Rim of Heaven is only a dream,' he said. 'There's many a day when it seems like a dream to me too.'

Firedrake shook his head. 'I'll find it,' he said, and looked round. 'Even if Rat is wrong and the human beings stay where they are, there must be some place where we won't have to hide. And when I have found it I'll come back and fetch the rest of you. I'll set out tonight.'

The old dragon nodded. 'Come to my cave before you leave,' he said. 'I will tell you all I can remember, even though it isn't much. But now I must get in out of the rain, or I won't be able to move my old bones at all tomorrow.'

With difficulty, Slatebeard trudged back to his cave. Firedrake stayed behind with Sorrel and Rat. The brownie girl was perched on his back, looking fierce. 'You idiot!' she said quietly. 'Acting the big hero, right? Off to look for something that doesn't exist. I ask you!'

'What are you muttering about?' asked Firedrake, turning his head to look at her.

This was too much for Sorrel. She lost her temper. 'And who's going to wake you when the sun sets?' she demanded. 'Who's going to protect you from human beings? Who's going to sing you to sleep and scratch you behind the ears?'

'Yes, *who*?' asked Rat sharply. She was still sitting on the rock where the old dragon had stood.

'*Me*, of course!' Sorrel spat at her. 'Tedious toadstools, what else can I do?'

'Oh no you don't!' Firedrake turned so abruptly that Sorrel almost slipped off his wet back. 'You can't come!'

'And just why not?' Sorrel folded her arms, looking offended.

'Because it's dangerous.'

'I don't care.'

'But you hate flying! It makes you airsick!'

'I'll get used to it.'

'You'll be homesick too.'

'Homesick for what? You think I'm going to wait here till the fish come and nibble my toes? No, I'm going with you.'

Firedrake sighed. 'Oh, very well,' he murmured. 'You can come. But don't blame me afterwards for taking you along.'

'She will,' said Rat, chuckling as she jumped off the rock into the damp grass. 'Brownies are never happy without something to complain about. Well, now let's go and see the old dragon. If you're going to start tonight there's no time to waste. Certainly not enough time to finish your quarrel with this dim-witted mushroom-muncher.'

CHAPTER THREE

Advice and Warnings

Slatebeard was lying at the mouth of his cave listening to the rain when they arrived. 'You haven't changed your mind?' he asked when Firedrake lay down beside him on the rocky ground.

The young dragon shook his head. 'But I won't be alone. Sorrel's coming with me.'

'Well, well!' The old dragon looked at Sorrel. 'Good. She may come in useful. She knows human beings, she has a quick mind, and brownies are more suspicious by nature than dragons. Which won't be any bad thing on this journey of yours. Her big appetite could be a problem, but no doubt she'll soon get used to eating less.'

Sorrel looked anxiously down at her stomach.

'Listen, then,' Slatebeard began again. 'I don't really remember very much. These days, the pictures get more and more muddled in my mind, but I do know this: you must fly to the highest mountain range in the whole world. It lies far away in the east. And when you get there, you must find the Rim of Heaven.

Look for a chain of snow-covered peaks encircling a valley like a ring of stone. As for the blue flowers growing in the valley,' he added, closing his eyes, 'their fragrance hangs so heavy in the cold night air that you can taste it.' He sighed. 'Ah, my memories are faded now, as if they were lost in the mist. But it's a wonderful place.' His head sank to his paws, he closed his eyes, and his breath came more heavily. 'There was something else,' he murmured. 'About the Eye of the Moon. But I don't remember what.'

'The Eye of the Moon?' Sorrel leaned towards him. 'What's that?'

But Slatebeard only shook his head sleepily. 'I don't remember,' he murmured. 'But . . . beware,' he said, his voice so soft that they could hardly hear it, 'beware of the Golden One.' Then a snore emerged from his muzzle.

Firedrake straightened up, looking thoughtful.

'What did he mean by that?' asked Sorrel anxiously. 'Come on, we'd better wake him up again and ask him.'

But Firedrake shook his head. 'Let him sleep. I don't think he can tell us any more than he's said already.'

They left the cave quietly, and when Firedrake looked up at the sky, the moon was visible for the first time that night.

'Oh, good,' said Sorrel, holding her paw up in the air. 'At least it's stopped raining.' Suddenly she clapped herself on the forehead. 'Oh, fearsome fungi!' She swiftly slipped off Firedrake's back. 'I must pack some provisions. How do we know there won't be mushroom shortages where we're going? Back in a moment. And don't you dare,' she added menacingly, wagging a furry finger in Firedrake's face, 'don't you dare even *think* of starting without me.'

With that, she disappeared into the dark.

'Now listen, Firedrake,' said the rat anxiously, 'you really don't know much about what you're looking for. You're not used to navigating by the stars, and Sorrel's mind is usually so full of mushrooms that she could get north and south mixed up and confuse the moon with the evening star. No, it won't do.' Rat stroked her whiskers and looked at the dragon. 'You need help, believe you me! As it happens, a cousin of mine makes maps. Very special maps. He may not know exactly where the Rim of Heaven is, but he can certainly tell you where to find the highest mountain range in the world. Stop off and see him on the way. I have to admit, visiting him isn't entirely without its risks,' said the rat, wrinkling her brow, 'because he lives in a big city. But I think you ought to chance it. If you set off soon you can be there in two nights' time.'

'City?' The indistinct figure of Sorrel emerged from the mist.

'For goodness' sake, *must* you scare me to death?' asked Rat. 'Yes, that's right. My cousin lives in a human city. When you've left the sea behind you, keep flying eastwards inland, and you can't miss it. It's huge, a hundred times larger than this valley, and full of bridges and tall buildings. My cousin lives in an old warehouse on the river.'

'Does he look like you?' asked Sorrel, stuffing a few leaves into her mouth. She was carrying a bulging backpack which she had brought back from one of her excursions into the world of men. 'Yes, of course he does, you rats all look the same. Grey, grey and grey again.'

'Grey is a very practical colour!' spat the rat. 'Unlike your silly spots. As it happens, however, my cousin is white. Snow-white. He wishes he wasn't.'

'Do stop squabbling,' said Firedrake, looking up at the sky. The moon was now almost at its height, and if they were to set out that night, it was time to leave. 'Climb aboard, Sorrel,' he said. 'Shall we take Rat too, to give you someone to quarrel with?'

'No thanks!' Rat took a couple of small steps backwards in alarm. 'There's no call for that kind of thing. I'm perfectly happy to know the world at second hand. It's a lot safer.'

'I never quarrel with anyone anyway,' Sorrel mumbled with her mouth full as she clambered up on to the dragon's back. 'Pointy-nosed persons are over-sensitive.'

Firedrake spread his wings, and Sorrel hastily clutched one of the large spines on his crest.

'Look after yourself, Rat,' said the dragon, bending his neck to nuzzle the little animal affectionately. 'It's going to be some time before I'll be back to keep you safe from wild cats.' Then he stepped back, took off from the damp ground and rose into the air, beating his wings powerfully.

'Oh no!' groaned Sorrel, clinging on so tight that her furry fingers hurt.

Firedrake rose higher and higher into the dark sky, and a cold wind whistled round the brownie girl's pointed ears.

'I'll never get used to this,' she muttered. 'Not unless I start growing feathers.' She peered cautiously down at the valley below. 'None of them,' she grumbled. 'Not a single one has so much as put his neck out of his cave to say goodbye. They probably won't come out until they're up to their chins in water. Hey, Firedrake!' she called to the dragon. 'I know a nice little spot over there beyond those hills. Why don't we stick around here instead?'

But Firedrake did not reply.

And the black hills rose between him and the valley where he had been born.

CHAPTER FOUR

A Big City and a Small Human Being

'Oh, pestiferous parasols!' grumbled Sorrel. 'If we don't find somewhere pretty quick they'll catch us and put us in the zoo.'

'What's a zoo?' asked Firedrake, raising his muzzle from the water. He had landed in the big city an hour ago, in the darkest part of it they could find, far from the streets that were full of noise and light, even now when night had fallen. Ever since, he had been swimming from one dirty canal to the next looking for a place to hide during the day. But, hard as Sorrel strained her catlike eyes and raised her sensitive nose to the wind, they couldn't find anywhere that was large enough for a dragon and didn't smell of human beings. Everything smelled of humans here, even the dark water and the rubbish adrift in it.

'You mean you don't know what a zoo is? Oh, I'll explain later,' muttered Sorrel. 'Although come to think of it, they're more likely to stuff us. Bother, it's going to take me hours to wash this filth off your scales.'

Firedrake was swimming like a silvery snake in the dirty canal, under bridges, past the grey walls of buildings. Sorrel kept glancing uneasily at the sky, but there was no sign yet of the treacherous sun.

'There!' the brownie suddenly whispered, pointing to a tall building. The water of the canal lapped its windowless brick walls. 'See that hatch? If you make yourself as thin as you can, you might fit through. Swim over there. I'll sniff around a bit.'

The dragon cautiously let himself drift towards the wall. A large loading hatch just above water level gaped open. Its decaying wooden door hung loose from the hinges. With one bound Sorrel jumped off Firedrake's back, got a handhold on the rough-cast wall, and put her head through the opening, snuffling.

'Seems okay,' she whispered. 'There hasn't been a human being in here for years. Nothing but mouse droppings and spiders. Come on.'

In a flash she had disappeared into the dark. Firedrake hauled himself out of the water, shook his scaly body and forced it through the hatch. He looked curiously around him at this structure, the work of human hands. He had never been inside a building before, and he didn't like it. Large wooden crates and rotting cardboard cartons were stacked by the damp walls. Sorrel sniffed everything with interest, but she couldn't pick up the scent of anything edible.

Wearily, Firedrake dropped to the floor in front of the hatch and looked out. This was the first time he had made such a long flight. His wings ached, and the city was full of frightening sounds and smells. The dragon sighed.

'What's the matter?' Sorrel sat down between his paws. 'Oh,

I see. Who's homesick now, then?' She opened her backpack, took out a handful of mushrooms and held them under his nose. 'Here, get a noseful of these. They'll drive the stink of this place out of your nostrils. I expect our friend the rat would like it just fine here, but you and I had better get out as soon as we can.' She patted Firedrake's dirty scales comfortingly. 'Get some sleep now. I'll have a bit of a nap too, and then I'll be off to look for Rat's cousin.'

Firedrake nodded. His eyes closed. When he heard Sorrel singing softly to herself, it was almost like being back in his cave. His tired limbs relaxed. Sleep was laying soft, soothing fingers on him ... when Sorrel suddenly jumped up.

'There's something in here!' she hissed.

Firedrake raised his head and looked round. 'Where?' he asked.

'Behind those crates!' whispered Sorrel. 'You stay here.' She crept towards a stack of crates that towered up to the ceiling. Firedrake pricked up his ears. Now he could hear it too: a rustling, a scraping of feet. The dragon raised himself.

'Come on out!' said Sorrel. 'Come out, whatever you are!'

For a moment all was quiet. Very quiet. Except for the noises of the big city drifting in from outside.

'Come on out!' spat Sorrel again. 'Or do I have to fetch you?'

There was some more rustling, and then a human boy crawled out from among the crates. Sorrel retreated in alarm. When the boy rose to his feet he was a good deal taller than she was. He stared incredulously at the brownie girl. And then he saw the dragon.

Firedrake's scales still shone like silver in spite of the canal water, and in this small space he seemed enormous. Neck bent, he was gazing down at the boy in astonishment.

The dragon had never seen a human being at close quarters before. From everything that Rat and Sorrel had told him, he had imagined them as looking different – very different.

'He doesn't smell of humans at all!' Sorrel growled. She had recovered from her fright, and was inspecting the boy suspiciously, although from a safe distance. 'He stinks of mice,' she added. 'That's why I didn't smell him. Yes, that'll be it.'

The boy took no notice of her. He raised his hand – a bare hand with no fur growing on it – and pointed at Firedrake. 'It's a dragon!' he whispered. 'A real live dragon.'

He gave Firedrake an uncertain smile.

The dragon cautiously stretched his long neck out towards the boy, and sniffed. Sorrel was right. He did smell of mouse droppings, but there was something else as well. A strange smell, the same smell that hung in the air outside – the smell of human beings.

'Of course it's a dragon,' said Sorrel crossly. 'And what are you?'

The boy turned to look at her in surprise. 'Oh, wow!' he exclaimed. 'You're quite something too! Are you an extraterrestrial?'

Sorrel proudly stroked her silky coat. 'I'm a brownie. Can't you see that?'

'A what?'

'A brownie!' repeated Sorrel impatiently. 'Typical. You humans may be able to tell a cat from a dog, but that's about all.'

'You look like a giant squirrel,' said the boy, grinning.

'Very funny!' spat Sorrel. 'What are you doing here anyway? A little titch like you isn't usually out and about on his own.'

The grin vanished from the boy's face as if Sorrel had wiped it away. 'A thingummy-whatsit like you isn't usually out and about here either,' he pointed out. 'If you must know, I live here.'

'Here?' Sorrel looked round, raising an eyebrow.

'Yes, here.' The boy glared at her. 'For now, anyway. But if you like,' he added, looking at the dragon, 'if you like, you can stay here for the time being.'

'Thank you,' said Firedrake. 'That's extremely kind of you. What's your name?'

The boy pushed his hair awkwardly back from his forehead. 'My name's Ben. What about you?'

'This,' said the dragon, nuzzling Sorrel gently in the stomach, 'is Sorrel. And I am Firedrake.'

'Firedrake. That's a good name.' Ben put his hand out tentatively to stroke the dragon's neck, as if he feared Firedrake would disappear the moment he was touched.

Casting the boy a suspicious glance, Sorrel went over to the hatch and looked out. 'Time to go and look for that rat,' she said. 'You – human – can you tell me where the dockland warehouses are?'

Ben nodded. 'Less than ten minutes' walk from here. But how are you going to get there without being captured, or stuffed and put on show in a museum?'

'You can leave that to me,' growled Sorrel.

Firedrake put his head between the two of them, looking anxious. 'You mean it's dangerous for her?' he asked the boy.

Ben nodded. 'Of course. Well, looking the way she does I bet she won't get ten metres from here. The first little old lady to spot her will call the police.'

'Police?' asked Firedrake, baffled. 'What kind of thing is police?'

'I know what the police are,' muttered Sorrel. 'But I have to reach those warehouses, so it's just too bad.' She sat down and was about to let herself drop into the dirty canal water when Ben grasped her by the arm.

'I'll take you there,' he said. 'I'll give you some of my clothes to wear, and then I can smuggle you past somehow. I've been living here a long time. I know all the back alleys.'

'Would you really guide her?' asked Firedrake. 'How can we ever thank you?'

Ben went red. 'Oh, it's nothing. Really,' he muttered.

Sorrel was not looking so enthusiastic. 'Human clothes,' she growled. 'Yuk. Dismal death-caps, I shall stink of human beings for weeks.'

But she put the clothes on all the same.

CHAPTER FIVE

Gilbert the Ship's Rat

'Which warehouse is it?' asked Ben. 'If you don't know the number we could have a long search ahead of us.'

They were standing on a narrow bridge. Warehouses lined both sides of the canal: strange, narrow buildings of red stone, with tall windows and pointed gables. The harbour of the big city wasn't far away, and a cold wind was blowing from that direction, almost tearing the hood away from Sorrel's pointy ears. A great many humans were pushing past them, but no one stopped and stared at the small figure with Ben, clutching the balustrade of the bridge. The sleeves of Ben's sweatshirt, which were much too long for her, hid Sorrel's paws. His jeans, turned up twice at the bottom, hid her legs, and her catlike face was hidden in the shadow of the hood.

'Rat said it's the last warehouse before the river,' she whispered. 'And her cousin lives in the cellar.'

'Rat? You don't mean a real rat, do you?' Ben looked at Sorrel doubtfully.

'Of course she's real. What do you think? Don't just stand there looking stupid. Not that you don't do it well, but we've got more important things to do.' She impatiently pulled Ben along after her. The bridge led to a narrow road running beside the bank. As they hurried along the pavement, Sorrel kept looking anxiously around. The sound of motor traffic hurt her ears. She had been in small towns before, stealing fruit from gardens, exploring cellars, teasing dogs. But there were no gardens here, no bushes where you could crouch down and hide in a hurry. Everything in this city was made of stone.

Sorrel was greatly relieved when Ben guided her into a narrow alleyway which led back to the canal between the last two warehouses. There were several doors in the red walls. Two were closed, but when Ben pushed the third, it opened with a slight creak.

They hurried in. An unlit stairway lay before them. Daylight filtered in through a narrow, dusty window, and revealed one flight of steps leading up and another down.

Ben looked suspiciously down the dark steps. 'There'll be rats there, that's for sure,' he whispered. 'The question is, can we find the right one? How will we recognise it? Does it wear a collar and tie or something?'

Sorrel did not answer. She pushed back her hood and scurried down the steps. Ben followed her. It was so dark at the foot of the steps that he took the torch out of his jacket pocket. A cellar with a high vaulted ceiling lay before them, and once again he saw any number of doors.

'Huh!' Sorrel inspected the torch and shook her head scornfully. 'You humans need your little machines for everything, don't you? Even to look at things.'

'It's not a machine.' Ben swept the beam of the torch over the doors. 'What are we actually looking for? A mousehole?'

'Don't be silly.' Sorrel pricked up her ears and twitched her nose. Still snuffling, she moved slowly from door to door. 'Ah, here we are.' She stopped in front of a brown door that was slightly ajar. Sorrel pushed it open just far enough for her to slip through the crack. Ben followed.

'My goodness!' he murmured.

The tall, windowless room they entered was stuffed with junk up to the ceiling. Among shelves full of dusty folders stood stacks of old chairs, tables piled on top of each other, cupboards without doors, mountains of index-card files and empty drawers.

Sorrel raised her nose, sniffing, then shot purposefully away. Ben banged his shin following her. He had already lost track of the door they had come through. The further they went the more chaotic the clutter became. Suddenly some shelving units barred their way.

'That's it then, I suppose,' said Ben, letting the beam of his torch wander round the place. But Sorrel ducked, crawled through a gap between two shelves – and disappeared.

'Hey, wait for me!' Ben cried, and pushed his head through the gap.

He was peering at a small study. A study just the right size for a rat, barely a metre away from him and underneath a chair. The desk was a book propped on two sardine cans. A coffee mug turned upside down did duty as a chair. There were card-index files full of tiny slips of paper, empty matchboxes stood everywhere, and the whole place was lit by an ordinary desk lamp standing on the floor beside the chair. But whoever it was who used this study was nowhere to be seen.

'You stay here,' Sorrel whispered to Ben. 'I don't think Rat's cousin will be particularly pleased to see a human being.'

'Oh, come off it!' Ben crawled through the gap and straightened up. 'If it doesn't get a fright at the sight of *you* it won't mind me either. Anyway, it's living in a human building. I don't suppose I'll be the first human it ever saw.'

'*He!*' hissed Sorrel. 'It's a he, and don't you forget it.'

She looked around her, curiously. As well as the little study area under the chair there was also a human-sized desk, a huge chest of drawers, and a large old globe of the world hanging at an angle on its stand.

'Hello?' called Sorrel. 'Anyone at home? Oh, drat it, what was his name again? Giselbert – no, Godfrey – no, Gilbert Greytail or some such.'

Something rustled above the desk. Ben and Sorrel looked up and saw a fat white rat looking down at them from his perch on top of a dusty lampshade.

'What do you want?' asked the rat in shrill tones.

'Your cousin sent me, Gilbert,' said Sorrel.

'Which one?' asked the white rat warily. 'I've got hundreds of cousins.'

'Which one?' Sorrel scratched her head. 'Well, we always just call her Rat. Wait a moment . . . I remember! Her name's Rosa. That's it!'

'You've come from Rosa?' Gilbert Greytail let a tiny rope ladder down from the lampshade and quickly clambered down it. He landed on the big desk with a thump. 'Oh, well, that's different.' He stroked his whiskers, which were white as snow, like his coat. 'What can I do for you?'

'There's this place I'm looking for,' Sorrel told him. 'Well, it's a mountain range really.'

'Ah!' The white rat nodded, looking pleased with himself. 'You've come to exactly the right person. I know all the mountain ranges on this planet, large, small and medium. I know everything about them. After all, my informants come from all over the world.'

'Your informants?' asked Ben.

'Yes, ship's rats, seagulls, the sort of folk who get around a lot. And I have a large extended family.' Greytail went over to a big black box standing on the desk, raised the lid and pushed a knob on its side.

'That's a real computer!' said Ben, surprised.

'Of course it is.' Greytail hit a couple of keys and looked at the screen, frowning. 'A laptop, all the bells and whistles. I sent off for it to help me get my files into some kind of order. But the fact is,' he sighed, and tried some more keys, 'the fact is it's always giving me grief. Right, what mountain range was it you wanted?'

'Er, well,' said Sorrel, scratching her stomach. She was itching horribly under the human's clothes. 'It's supposed to be the highest there is. The highest mountain range in the whole world. With a chain of mountains somewhere in the middle of it called the Rim of Heaven. Ever heard of it?'

'Oh, that one, is it? The Rim of Heaven. Well, well.' Greytail looked curiously at the brownie. 'The valley above the clouds, home of the dragons. Not so easy.' He turned round and hammered busily away at the keyboard. 'The place isn't really thought to exist at all, you know,' he said. 'But one hears odd things now and then. What's your interest in it? A brownie girl and a human boy! They say even the dragons have long since forgotten where the Rim of Heaven lies.'

Ben opened his mouth, but Sorrel gave him no time to speak. 'This human has nothing to do with it,' she said. 'I'm on my way to find the Rim of Heaven with a dragon.'

'A dragon?' Gilbert Greytail looked at Sorrel in surprise.

'Where've you hidden this dragon, then?'

'In an old factory,' Ben answered quickly before Sorrel could open her mouth. 'Not far away. He'll be safe there. No one's been in it for years.'

'Aha!' Gilbert nodded his white head sagely.

'Well, what about it?' asked Sorrel impatiently. 'Do you know where the Rim of Heaven is? Can you tell us how to get there in reasonable safety?'

'One thing at a time,' replied the rat, twirling his whiskers. 'Nobody knows where the Rim of Heaven lies. There are a few vague rumours about it, that's all. But the highest mountain range in the world is the Himalayas, no doubt of that. All the same, it won't be easy to find a safe route for a dragon to take. Dragons,' he pointed out, chuckling, 'aren't exactly inconspicuous, know what I mean? And their horns and claws are in great demand. Quite apart from the fact that anyone setting up as a dragon-slayer could be a big star on TV for weeks. I'll admit I wouldn't mind taking a look at your friend myself, but,' he said, shaking his head as he turned back to the computer, 'but I never go further than down to the harbour. Far too risky for me with all those cats prowling about. And there's other dangers too,' he added, rolling his eyes. 'Oh, you wouldn't believe the half of it! Dogs, great big clumsy human feet, rat poison. No thank you very much!'

'But I thought you'd been all over the world?' said Sorrel in surprise. 'Rosa said you were a ship's rat.'

Gilbert tugged at his whiskers, looking embarrassed. 'Well, yes, so I am. Learned the trade from my granddad. But I get seasick as soon as a boat casts off, even a little rowing boat. On my first voyage I jumped overboard while we were still in harbour. Swam back to the bank and never set paw on one of those swaying sardine cans again. Ah.' He leaned so far forward that his sharp nose touched the screen. 'Here we are. The Himalayas. Also known as the Land of the Eternal Snows, Roof of the World and all that. You've a long journey ahead of you, friends. Follow me.' Paw over paw, Gilbert Greytail made his way along a cord stretched right across the room from the desk to the big globe. He sat on top of the heavy wooden stand and kicked the globe with his hind paws. Squealing, it moved slightly, and Gilbert brought it to rest with his paw again.

'Well now,' he murmured. 'What have we here, then?'

Ben and Sorrel looked inquiringly at him.

'See that little white flag?' asked the white rat. 'It more or less marks the spot where we are now, but the Himalayas,' said Gilbert, swinging himself over the stand and tapping the other side of the globe, 'the Himalayas are here. And the Rim of Heaven, so the old stories say, is somewhere in their western parts. Unfortunately, as I was telling you, no one knows any details, and the area we're talking about is unimaginably large and extremely inaccessible. It gets bitterly cold by night – and by day,' he added, grinning at Sorrel, 'by day you'd probably be perspiring heavily in that fur coat of yours.'

'It's a terribly long way off,' murmured Ben.

'Indeed it is!' Gilbert Greytail leaned forward and traced an invisible line on the globe. 'By my reckoning your journey ought to go something like this: a fair stretch south first, then turn east.' He scratched his ear. 'Yes. Yes, that's it. I think the southern route is best. The humans are at war with each other again in the north. And I've heard some very nasty stories about a giant.' Gilbert leaned so close to the globe that his nose was pressed against it. 'See that place? The giant is said to be at large there, in the Tien Shan mountains. No, no, take my word for it,' continued Gilbert Greytail, shaking his head, 'you'd better take the southern route. You may get your fur baked in the sun now and then, but look on the bright side: there probably won't be much rain at this time of year. And rain,' he said, chuckling, 'I've heard that rain makes dragons melancholy. Is that right?'

'Usually,' replied Sorrel. 'But where we come from they've had to get used to it.'

'Correct, I'd forgotten. You're from the wettest part of Europe, aren't you? But let's get on with it.' Gilbert gave the globe another little push. 'Where was I? Oh yes. Up to here,' he tapped the map with his paw, 'I can offer you first-class information. By the time you reach this spot you ought to have most of the journey behind you. But the region beyond . . .' Gilbert sighed and shook his head. 'Zilch, zero, nix, nought, nothing, total radio silence. Even a tourist party of Buddhist temple mice I met down by the harbour last year couldn't tell me anything useful about it. And I'm afraid that's exactly where the place you're looking for lies – if it really exists. I'm planning to ask a relation of mine to survey the area some time soon, but until then,' he said, shrugging his shoulders regretfully, 'until then you'll just have to ask your way – if you get that far. I've no idea who or what lives around there but I'll bet,' he said, stroking his white whiskers, 'I'll bet there are rats. We rats go everywhere.'

'That's a great comfort, I'm sure,' muttered Sorrel, looking gloomily at the globe. 'Looks like there's a long-haul flight ahead of us.'

'Oh, it's even further to New Zealand,' said Gilbert, swinging paw over paw back along the cord to the desk. 'But I'll admit it is a long way, even for a dragon. Long and dangerous. May I ask what put the idea of such a journey into your minds? I know from Rosa that you dragons have quite a comfortable life up there in the north.'

Sorrel looked at Ben and cast the rat a warning glance.

'Oh, I see.' Gilbert Greytail raised his paws. 'You'd rather not say in front of this human. Of course. We rats have had some bad experiences with humans too.' Gilbert winked at Ben, who was standing there feeling embarrassed and not sure where to look. 'Nothing against you personally, understand?' Greytail went back to his computer and began typing again. 'Right, here goes. Destination: Himalayas. Travel party: 1 dragon, 1 brownie. Travel options: calculate safest route, danger spots, places to avoid at all costs, best travelling time. Enter.'

The rat stepped back, looking pleased with himself. The computer hummed like a captive bumblebee, the screen flickered – and went black.

'Oh no!' Gilbert Greytail jumped on the keyboard, hammering at it frantically, but the screen did not respond.

Ben and Sorrel exchanged anxious glances. Gilbert leaped up, swearing, and slammed the lid of the laptop down over the keyboard.

'Like I told you,' he said crossly. 'Nothing but trouble. Just because a little salt water got into it. I mean, do *you* stop working if you happen to drink a sip of salt water?' Furiously, he jumped off the desk to the chair that sheltered his little study, slid down one of the chair legs, and began rummaging around in the matchbox index files.

Ben and Sorrel lay down on the floor and watched. 'You mean you can't help us after all?' asked Sorrel.

'Yes, yes, I can.' Greytail was fishing tiny fingernail-sized cards out of the files and flinging them down on the desk. 'If that stupid thing won't work I'll just have to do it the old-fashioned way. Can one of you great big giants open the third drawer down in the chest of drawers there?'

Ben nodded. When he opened the drawer a large quantity of maps fell out: maps large and small, maps old and new. It took Gilbert Greytail some time to find the one he was after. It looked odd, quite different from the maps Ben knew, more like a small book folded up over and over again, with narrow white ribbons dangling from the pages.

'A map?' said Sorrel, disappointed, when Gilbert proudly spread this oddity out in front of them. 'You mean all you have for us is a map?'

'Well, what did you expect?' Looking offended, the rat put

his paws on his hips.

Sorrel didn't know what to say. Tight-lipped, she stared down at the map.

'Look at that, will you?' Gilbert passed his paw lovingly over the seas and mountains. 'This map's got half the world on it. And very few blank spots – only those places I couldn't discover anything about. But unfortunately, as I was saying, most of those do happen to be where you're going. See these ribbons?' He beckoned the two of them over and pulled one of the ribbons. Part of the map immediately unfolded, and another map came into view.

'Cool!' exclaimed Ben.

But Sorrel just made a face. 'What's that in aid of?'

'This method,' said Gilbert, proudly twirling his whiskers, 'is my own invention. By pulling the ribbons you can see each part of the map again on a larger scale. Useful, don't you think?' Looking pleased with himself, he closed the map again and tugged at his ear. 'Now, what else? Oh yes. Just a moment.' Gilbert took a little tray from his desk. On it stood six thimbles full of inks, each one a different colour. A bird's feather with its quill sharpened lay beside them.

'I'll write down the meaning of the different colours for you,' said Gilbert portentously. 'I expect you know the usual: green for lowland country, brown for mountains, blue for water and so on and so forth. Everyone knows that, but my maps tell you rather more. For instance, I'll use gold,' he said, dipping the pen into a thimble of bright gold paint, 'for my recommended flight path. And red,' he added, carefully wiping the pen on the leg of the chair and dipping it into the red ink, 'to shade in places you ought to avoid because the humans there are fighting each other. Yellow means I've heard strange stories about those parts, and misfortune clings to them like a snail trail, if you take my meaning. Yes, and grey means this would be a good place to rest.' Gilbert wiped the pen on his white fur and looked up at his two customers. 'All clear?'

'Yes,' growled Sorrel. 'All clear.'

'Excellent!' Gilbert put a paw in his jacket pocket, brought out an ink pad and a tiny rubber stamp, and thumped it down on the bottom corner of the map as hard as he could. 'There!' he said, closely inspecting the mark left by the stamp and then nodding, satisfied. 'Easily recognisable.' He dabbed at the mark with his sleeve, folded the map up with care, and looked expectantly at Sorrel. 'So now we come to the matter of my fee.'

'Fee?' said Sorrel, taken aback. 'Rosa didn't say anything about any fee.'

Gilbert immediately put a protective paw down on the map. 'Oh, didn't she? Typical. Well, customers have to pay me. *How* they pay is something I leave to them.'

'But I . . . I don't have anything,' stammered Sorrel. 'Only a few roots and mushrooms.'

'Huh! You can keep those,' said Gilbert scornfully. 'If that's all you've got then the deal's off.'

Sorrel tightened her lips and stood up. Gilbert Greytail came only up to her knee. 'I've a good mind to shut you in one of your own drawers!' hissed the brownie girl, leaning over him. 'Since when do people ask to be paid for a little friendly help? You know something? If I wanted to I could just snatch that map from under your fat little ratty bum, but I don't want to. We'll find our way to those Himble-layers – or whatever they're called – without it, see? We'll—'

'Just a moment,' Ben interrupted. He pushed Sorrel aside and knelt down in front of the rat. 'Of course we'll pay,' he said. 'It must have been an awful lot of work making that map.'

'I should say so!' squeaked Gilbert, still sounding affronted. His nose was quivering and his long white tail was agitatedly tying itself in knots.

Ben searched his trouser pocket, took out two pieces of chewing gum, a ballpoint pen, two rubber bands and a small coin, and laid them all on the floor in front of the rat. 'Which do you fancy?' he asked.

Gilbert Greytail licked his lips. 'Hmm. A difficult choice,' he said, examining everything very thoroughly. Finally he pointed to the chewing gum.

Ben pushed it over. 'Okay. Now let's have the map.'

Gilbert removed his paw from the map, and Ben put it in Sorrel's backpack.

'Give me the ballpoint too,' squeaked the white rat, 'and I'll tell you something else that could be useful.'

Ben pushed the pen over to Gilbert and put the other things away. 'Go on,' he said.

Gilbert leaned slightly forward. 'You're not the only ones looking for the Rim of Heaven,' he whispered.

'What?' gasped Sorrel, taken aback.

'Ravens have been turning up here for years,' Gilbert went on, still in a whisper. 'Very peculiar ravens, if you ask me. They ask questions about the Rim of Heaven, but what they're really interested in is the dragons said to be hiding there. Naturally I haven't told them anything about the dragons in my dear cousin Rosa's part of the world.'

'Are you sure?' asked Sorrel, suspiciously.

Looking offended, Gilbert drew himself up to his full height. 'Of course I'm sure. What do you take me for?' He wrinkled his nose. 'They offered me lots of gold. Gold and pretty precious stones. But I didn't care for those black birds.'

'Ravens?' asked Ben. 'How come ravens? What have they got to do with dragons?'

'Oh, they don't want the information for themselves.' Gilbert Greytail's voice sank again. 'They're acting on behalf of someone else, but I haven't found out who yet. Whoever it is, your dragon had better be careful.'

Sorrel nodded. 'The Golden One,' she murmured.

Gilbert and Ben looked at her curiously.

'What did you say?' asked the boy.

'Oh, nothing.' She turned thoughtfully and made for the gap between the shelves.

'Thanks, Gilbert, and goodbye,' said Ben, following her.

'Give Rosa my love if you ever get back again!' the rat called after them. 'Tell her to come and see me again some time. There's a ferry quite close to your home, and they don't put rat poison down on it.'

'Oh yes?' Sorrel turned back once more. 'And what will you give me to deliver your message?' Then, without waiting for Gilbert's answer, she disappeared between the shelves.

CHAPTER SIX

Dragon-Fire

'Well, we could have saved ourselves the trouble!' said Sorrel crossly once they were out in the street again. 'We come to this stinking city purely to find that stuck-up rat, and what does he give us? Oh, stinking sticky-bun fungus! A map, that's all. Scribbles on a bit of paper! Huh! I could have found that heavenly brim thing just by following my nose.' She imitated Gilbert's voice. '"*So now we come to the matter of my fee.*" I ought to have tied that silly fat podge to his globe with his own tail.'

'Calm down, will you?' said Ben, pulling the hood up over Sorrel's ears before he led the way along the street. 'It's not a bad map. There are some things your nose won't tell you!'

'You don't know anything about it,' muttered Sorrel, plodding crossly after him. 'You humans use your noses for nothing but sneezing.'

For a while the two of them walked on in silence.

'When are you going to set out again?' Ben asked at last.

'As soon as it gets dark,' replied Sorrel, almost colliding with a fat man whose dachshund was sniffing its way along the pavement. The dog raised his head in surprise when the scent of brownie reached his nostrils, and tugged at his lead, yelping. Ben quickly drew Sorrel away and into the nearest alleyway.

'Come on,' he said. 'There's not so much going on here. Anyway, we're nearly back.'

'Stones everywhere. Nothing but stones!' Sorrel looked uneasily up at the walls of the buildings. 'My tummy's rumbling louder than those machines with their engines. I'll be glad to be out of here again.'

'It must be really exciting to go on such a long journey,' said Ben.

Sorrel wrinkled her forehead. 'I'd rather have stayed in my cave. Much rather.'

'But just think of going to the Himalayas!' It sounded so exciting to Ben that he started walking faster. 'And flying on a dragon's back! Oh, wow!' He shook his head. 'I'd be bursting with happiness! It sounds like a thousand adventures rolled into one!'

Sorrel gaped at the boy, shaking her head. 'Don't be so daft. What sort of adventures? It sounds to me like cold and hunger. It sounds like danger and fear. We were very well off at home, take my word for it! Rather too much rain, maybe, but what does that matter? You know something? It's all because of you humans we're going on this crazy journey. Because you won't leave us alone. Because we have to find somewhere your nasty furless noses will never come poking in! Oh, why do I bother telling you all this? You're one of them yourself. We're escaping from human beings and here I am hanging around with one. Now that really *is* crazy!'

Ben did not reply. Instead he hastily shoved Sorrel into the dark doorway of a building.

'Hey! What's the big idea?' She looked at the boy, irritated. 'Are you angry with me now, or what? We have to cross the street, right? The factory's on the other side.'

'Exactly. Can't you see what's going on there?' whispered Ben.

Sorrel peered over his shoulder. 'Humans!' she breathed. 'Lots and lots of humans. And they've got machinery with them too.' She groaned. 'Speak of the devil—'

'You stay here,' Ben interrupted her. 'I'll go over the road and find out what's up.'

'What?' Sorrel shook her head vigorously. 'No, that's no good. I have to warn Firedrake. At once!' And before Ben could stop her she was out in the street. She dodged between the hooting cars and clambered over the low wall round the factory yard.

Cursing, Ben ran after her.

Luckily there was so much else going on in the yard that no one noticed the two of them. A couple of men were standing beside a large digger, talking to each other. Ben saw Sorrel hide behind the big scoop of the digger to eavesdrop. Hastily he ran across and crouched down beside her.

'I can't make out what they're saying!' Sorrel whispered. 'At least, I can hear them all right, but I don't understand the words. They keep talking about blowing something up. What do they mean?'

'Nothing good!' Ben whispered back. 'Come on, quick!' He pulled her to her feet and ran towards the factory building. 'We must find Firedrake. We have to get him out of there somehow. Fast.'

'Hey, you two! What are you up to?' someone called after them.

They swiftly disappeared into the dark shelter of the tall building, but within seconds they heard footsteps following them down the stairs. Heavy footsteps. 'That's the way they went!' someone called. 'Couple of kids, it was!'

'Damn it! How could a thing like this happen?' replied someone else.

Ben and Sorrel ran on through the empty, dilapidated factory basement. Their footsteps echoed down the long corridors, giving them away. But what else could they do? They had to warn the dragon before anyone discovered him.

'Suppose we're too late?' gasped Sorrel. As she ran the hood slipped off her pointy ears, and she quickly pulled it up again. 'Maybe they've already found Firedrake. Maybe they've already gone and stuffed him!' she sobbed.

'Rubbish! Come on!' Ben took her paw, and they ran on side by side. The footsteps behind them were coming closer and closer. Sorrel's legs were trembling, but it wasn't far now to Firedrake's hiding place. Then Ben stopped suddenly, gasping for breath.

'Wait a minute – why didn't I think of it before? We must lead them *away* from Firedrake. You go on. Tell him to follow the canal to safety. The two of you must swim as far away from the factory as possible. This whole place is about to go up in smoke.'

'What about you?' panted Sorrel. 'What will you do?'

'I'll be okay,' Ben managed to say. 'Go on, run! You must warn Firedrake!'

Sorrel hesitated for a split second, then turned and ran on. The stairs were quite close now. She rushed round the corner and into the room where she had found Ben. The dragon was lying asleep by the hatch.

'Firedrake!' Sorrel jumped between his paws and shook him. 'Wake up, we've got to get out of here. Quick!'

The dragon sleepily raised his head. 'What's the matter? Where's the human boy?'

'I'll explain later!' whispered Sorrel. 'Quick, through the hatch and into the canal.'

But Firedrake pricked up his ears. He rose and went slowly towards the corridor down which Sorrel had run. He heard human voices: two deep male voices, and Ben's as well.

'So what d'you think you're doing in here?' snapped one of the men.

'Looks like a runaway to me,' said the other man.

'No, I'm not!' cried Ben. 'Let me go! I haven't done anything – nothing at all!'

Looking anxious, the dragon stretched his neck further forward.

'Firedrake!' Sorrel tugged desperately at his tail. 'Firedrake, come on! You have to get out of here.'

'But the boy may need help.' The dragon took another step. The men's voices grew harsher and Ben's more and more uncertain. 'He's afraid,' said Firedrake.

'He's a human!' hissed Sorrel. 'And they're humans too. They won't eat him. They won't stuff him either, but they'll stuff you and me if they catch us and no mistake! So will you, for goodness' sake, come on?'

But Firedrake wouldn't move. His tail was lashing the floor.

'Hey, watch out, he's trying to make a break for it!' yelled one of the men.

'I'll get him!' shouted the other.

Feet scuffled on the ground and there was a sound of running footsteps. Firedrake inched a little further forward.

'Got him!' shouted the man.

'Ouch!' cried Ben. 'Let go! Let go of me, you great toad!'

Then Firedrake sprang. Like an enormous tiger, he shot across the cellar of the factory. Sorrel ran after him, cursing under her breath. The human voices grew louder and louder, until the dragon suddenly saw two men standing with their backs to him. One of them was holding the struggling Ben.

Firedrake uttered a low growl. Deep and threatening.

The man whipped round – and dropped Ben to the floor like a sack of potatoes. He scrambled up in terror and ran towards Firedrake.

'You were supposed to get out of here!' he shouted. 'I . . .'

'Climb on,' the dragon interrupted, without taking his eyes off the two men. They were still standing there as if rooted to the spot. Ben, his legs trembling, clambered up on to Firedrake's back.

'Go away,' the dragon commanded. 'This boy is mine!' His low voice echoed through the dark cellar.

The men staggered and fell against each other in alarm.

'I'm d-dreaming!' one of them stammered. 'That's . . . that's a dragon!'

But still the pair of them didn't move. Then Firedrake opened his mouth, roared, and spat blue fire. His dragon-fire licked over the dirty walls, the black ceiling, the stone floor, and filled the room with leaping flames. Terrified, the men retreated, and ran away screaming as if the Devil himself were after them.

'What's up? What's going on?' Out of breath, Sorrel caught up with Firedrake.

'Quick, the canal!' cried Ben. 'If they come back they'll bring twenty more with them.'

'Climb on, Sorrel!' Firedrake said, listening uneasily to the fading echoes of the men's footsteps. When Sorrel was finally on his back, the dragon turned and strode back to their hiding place.

Bright sunlight was still pouring through the open hatch. Cautiously, Firedrake put his nose outside.

'It's too light!' Sorrel moaned. 'Much too light. What are we going to do?'

'Come on!' Ben grabbed the brownie's hand and pulled her off the dragon's back with him as he clambered down. 'Firedrake must swim alone. That way he can dive beneath the surface and they won't see him. We'll take my boat.'

'What?' Sorrel flinched away from the boy distrustfully and pressed close to Firedrake's scales. 'Must we really separate again? How will we find each other?'

'There's a bridge.' Ben turned to the dragon. 'Swim down the canal on the left and you can't miss it. Hide under it until we arrive.'

Firedrake looked at the boy thoughtfully. Finally, he nodded. 'Ben's right, Sorrel,' he said. 'Take care of yourselves, both of you.'

Then he forced his way through the hatch, dived deep into the murky water, and disappeared from sight.

Sorrel watched him go anxiously, and without turning her head she asked, 'Where's this boat of yours, then?'

'Here.' Ben went over to the stacked cartons and pulled them aside. A red-painted wooden boat came into view.

'Call that a boat?' said Sorrel, horrified. 'It's not much bigger than a toadstool!'

'If you don't like it you can swim,' said Ben.

'Oh, drat it all!' Sorrel listened. She could hear agitated voices far, far away.

Ben quickly crawled behind the stack of crates where he'd

been hiding when they'd first met, and came out again holding a large backpack.

'Coming?' he asked, and pushed his boat over to the hatchway.

'We'll drown, that's what,' Sorrel muttered, staring with disgust at the filthy water.

But she helped the boy to launch the boat on the canal.

CHAPTER SEVEN

Waiting for Dark

No one saw Firedrake as he made his escape along the canal. Twice, boats came towards him, but they were chugging through the water so noisily that Firedrake could hear them a long way off and was able to dive in good time – deep down to the bottom of the canal, where rubbish got stuck in the mud. As soon as the dark shadows of the boats had passed over him and disappeared, the dragon came up again and let himself glide on. Gulls circled over his head, screeching, until he shooed them away with a soft growl. At last he saw a bridge beyond some tall willow trees. Their branches hung low, floating on the water.

Broad and massive, the bridge spanned the river. Traffic noises drifted down from it, but the shadow it cast was as dark as the mud on the bottom of the canal, and offered the dragon shelter from prying eyes. Firedrake raised his head from the water and looked around. There was no one in sight on either the water or the bank. The dragon crawled up on land, shook the dirty water off his scales and settled among the blackberry bushes growing in the shade of the bridge.

He licked his scales clean and waited.

Before long, he was half-deafened by the noise above, but even worse was his anxiety for Sorrel and the boy. Sighing, Firedrake laid his head on his paws and looked at the water, which reflected the grey clouds overhead. He felt lonely. It was an unfamiliar feeling. Firedrake had not been alone often, and never in such a strange, grey place. Suppose Sorrel didn't come? The dragon raised his head and looked back along the canal.

Where could they be?

It was odd. Firedrake let his head drop to his paws again. He was missing the boy too. Were there many human beings like Ben? Firedrake thought of the two men who had grabbed the boy, and the tip of his tail twitched with anger.

Then he saw the boat.

It came drifting down the canal towards him like a nutshell. The dragon quickly stretched his long neck out of the shadow of the bridge and breathed a shower of blue sparks on the water.

When Sorrel saw him she hopped about in such excitement that the boat swayed perilously, but Ben paddled it safely to the bank. Sorrel jumped out on to the slope and ran to Firedrake.

'Hey!' she cried. 'Hey, there you are!' Flinging her arms round his neck, she nipped his nose affectionately. Then she dropped to the grass beside the dragon with a sigh. 'You've no idea how awful I feel!' she groaned. 'All that rocking about! My tummy's churning as if I'd eaten a death-cap mushroom.'

Ben tied the boat up to a tree and shyly came closer. 'Thank you,' he said to the dragon. 'Thank you very much for chasing those men away.'

Firedrake bent his neck and gently nuzzled the boy. 'What are you going to do now?' he asked. 'You can't go back there, can you?'

'No.' Ben sat down on his backpack, sighing. 'That factory won't be left standing much longer. They're going to blow it up.'

'Oh, you'll find somewhere else to hide!' Sorrel looked round, snuffling, and picked a few leaves from the bramble bushes. 'I know, why not move in with Rat's cousin? He's got plenty of room.'

'Rat's cousin!' cried Firedrake. 'With all the excitement, I'd entirely forgotten about him. What did he say? Does he know where we must look?'

'Well, sort of!' Sorrel stuffed the leaves into her mouth and picked herself another handful. 'But we'd have found that out for ourselves anyway. One thing's for sure, we have a long journey ahead of us. Are you certain you don't want to change your mind?'

But Firedrake only shook his head. 'I'm not turning back, Sorrel. Exactly what did the rat say?'

'He gave us a map,' said Ben. 'The map shows it all. Where to fly, what to watch out for, everything. It's great!'

Excited, the dragon turned to Sorrel. 'A map? What kind of a map?'

'Well, just a map.' Sorrel took it out of her backpack. 'There you are.' She spread it out in front of the dragon.

'What does all that mean?' Firedrake looked at the tangle of lines and marks, baffled. 'Can you read it?'

'Of course,' said Sorrel, looking important. 'My granddad was always drawing things like that. To help him find his way back to his mushroom stores.'

The dragon nodded. 'Good.' He put his head on one side and looked up at the sky. 'Which way do I fly first? Straight east?'

'Um, east? Wait a mo.' Sorrel scratched behind her ears and bent over the map. Her furry finger traced Gilbert's golden line.

'No, I think we go south. First south, then east, he said. Yes, that's exactly what he said.' She nodded. 'I'm certain he did.'

'Sorrel,' said Firedrake, 'are you *quite* sure you understand what these scribbles mean?'

'Of course I do!' Sorrel looked offended. 'Oh, bother these human clothes!' Crossly, she pulled Ben's sweatshirt over her head and slipped out of the trousers. 'I can't think properly with this stuff on.'

The dragon looked at her thoughtfully. Then he stretched his neck and looked at the sky. 'The sun's setting,' he said. 'We can start soon.'

'Thank goodness!' Sorrel folded up the map and put it in her backpack. 'About time we left this city. It's no place for a dragon and a brownie.'

Ben picked up a couple of stones and chucked them into the dark water. 'I don't suppose you'll be coming back, will you?'

'Why on earth would we want to?' Sorrel stuffed a few extra bramble leaves into her backpack. 'I certainly don't want to see that conceited white rat again.'

Ben nodded. 'Then I'll wish you both luck,' he said, throwing a final stone into the water. 'I hope you find this Rim of Heaven place.'

Firedrake looked at him. Ben returned the dragon's glance.

'You'd like to come too, wouldn't you?' asked Firedrake.

Ben bit his lip. 'Of course,' he muttered, hardly knowing where to look.

Raising her head, Sorrel pricked up her ears uneasily. 'What?' she said. 'Come with us? What are you two going on about?'

Firedrake took no notice of her, but just looked at the boy. 'It will be a dangerous journey,' he said. 'Very long and very dangerous. You may never come back. Wouldn't anyone here miss you?'

Ben shook his head. 'I'm on my own. I always have been.' His heart beat faster. Hardly daring to believe it, he looked at the dragon. 'Would you . . . would you really let me come too?'

'If you like,' replied Firedrake. 'But think about it carefully. Sorrel often gets very bad-tempered, you know.'

Ben felt weak at the knees. 'Oh, I do know!' he said, grinning. He was feeling quite dizzy with delight.

'Hey, hang on half a sec!' Sorrel pushed her way in between them. 'What's got into you, Firedrake? He can't possibly come.'

'Why not?' Firedrake playfully nuzzled her furry stomach. 'He's been very helpful. We can use all the help we can get, don't you think?'

'Helpful?' Sorrel was so indignant she almost fell over. 'He's a human! A human being! Only pint-sized, but still a human being. And it's the humans' fault we're not at home in our nice warm cave. It's their fault we're off on this crazy quest! And now you want to take one of them along?'

'Yes, I do.' Firedrake rose, shook himself, and bent his neck so low that the brownie girl had to look him in the eye. 'He's helped us, Sorrel. He's a friend. So I don't mind whether he's a human being, a brownie or a rat. What's more,' he added, looking at Ben, who was standing there hardly daring to breathe, 'what's more, he doesn't have a home now any more than we do. Isn't that true?' He looked enquiringly at the boy.

'I never did have a home,' muttered Ben, looking at Sorrel.

The brownie bit her lip and dug the claws of her toes into the muddy bank. 'Oh, all right, all right,' she murmured gruffly at last. 'I'll say no more. But he sits behind me. I insist on that.'

Firedrake nudged her so firmly with his nose that she fell backwards into the dirty grass. 'He sits behind you,' Firedrake agreed. 'But he's coming with us.'

CHAPTER EIGHT

Flying Off Course

When the moon had risen above the city rooftops, and a few lone stars were appearing in the sky, Firedrake came out from under the bridge. Sorrel was up on his back in an instant, but Ben didn't find it quite so easy. Sorrel watched with a scornful grin as he laboriously clambered up Firedrake's tail. When he finally reached the dragon's back he looked as proud as if he had climbed the highest mountain on earth. Sorrel took his backpack, buckled it to her own, and hung them like saddlebags over Firedrake's back.

'Hang on to the spines of his crest,' she told Ben. 'And lash yourself to them with this strap, or the first gust of wind will blow you off.'

Ben nodded. Firedrake craned his neck round to look at the two of them. 'Ready?'

'Ready!' said Sorrel. 'Here we go. Fly south!'

'South?' asked Firedrake.

'Yes, first south, then after a while turn east. When I tell you.'

The dragon spread his shimmering wings and took off. Holding his breath, Ben clung tight to the spines of Firedrake's crest. The dragon rose higher and higher. They left the noise of the city behind. Night enfolded them in darkness and silence, and soon the world of men was no more than a glitter of lights far below.

'Well, how do you like it?' Sorrel called to Ben when they had been flying for some time. 'Do you feel sick?'

'Sick?' Ben looked down to where roads wound through the darkness like gleaming snail trails. 'It's wonderful! It's – oh, I can't describe it!'

'Personally I always feel sick to start with,' said Sorrel. 'The only thing that helps is eating. Take a look in my backpack and hand me a mushroom, will you? One of the little black ones.'

Ben did as she asked. Then he looked down again. The wind was roaring in his ears.

'Wonderful!' said Sorrel, smacking her lips. 'A following wind. This way we'll be in the mountains before daybreak. Firedrake!'

The dragon turned his head to her.

'Time to turn east!' Sorrel called. 'Eastward ho!'

'What, already?' Ben looked over her shoulder. Sorrel had the rat's map on her lap and was tracing the golden line with her finger. 'But we haven't reached the right place yet!' cried Ben. 'We can't have.'

Putting his hand in his jacket pocket, he brought out a little compass. His torch, his penknife and his compass were his chief treasures. 'We have to go further south first, Sorrel!' he called. 'It's too soon to change course yet.'

'No, it's not.' The brownie patted her stomach happily and leaned back against the spines of Firedrake's crest. 'Here, see for yourself, cleverclogs.'

She handed Ben the map. It fluttered so much in the wind that he could hardly hold it. Anxiously, he scrutinised the lines the rat had drawn. 'We really do have to go further south!' he called. 'If we turn east now we'll end up in that patch of yellow!'

'So?' Sorrel closed her eyes. 'Good thing if we do. That's where Gilbert said we should stop and rest.'

'No, he didn't!' cried Ben. 'You mean grey. It's in the grey parts he told us to rest. He warned us against yellow. Look.' Ben switched on his torch and shone it on the words at the bottom of the map. 'Gilbert wrote it down here. *Yellow = danger, bad luck*.'

Sorrel swung round crossly. 'I knew it all along!' she spat. 'You humans always think you know best. Honestly, you're the end! We're flying in exactly the right direction. My nose tells me so. Understand?'

Ben could feel Firedrake slowing down.

'What's the matter?' the dragon called back to them. 'What are you arguing about?'

'Oh, nothing,' muttered Ben, folding up the map and putting it in Sorrel's rucksack. Then he peered anxiously out into the night.

Day dawned very slowly, and in the grey twilight Ben saw mountains for the first time in his life. Their dark shapes emerged through the morning mist, with their rocky summits outlined against the sky. The sun made its way between the peaks, dispelling the twilight and painting the grey rock in a thousand bright hues. Firedrake sank lower, circled among the steep slopes in search of a landing site, and then made for a small patch of green that lay just below the treeline, surrounded by stunted firs. The dragon glided towards it like a huge bird, beat his wings powerfully once or twice until he was almost stationary in the air, and then came down gently among the trees.

Their legs stiff, Ben and Sorrel climbed off Firedrake's back and looked around. A mountain towered high into the sky above them. The dragon yawned and looked around for a sheltered place among the rocks, while his riders made their way cautiously to the rim of the plateau.

The sight of cows looking no bigger than beetles on the green slopes below made Ben feel quite dizzy, and he quickly took a step backwards.

'What's the matter?' asked Sorrel sarcastically, venturing so close to the edge of the chasm that her furry toes were over empty space. 'Don't you like mountains?'

'I'll get used to them,' replied Ben. 'You've had to get used to flying, right?' He turned to look back at Firedrake, who had found a good place and was coiled up in the shadow of a projecting rock, muzzle on his paws, tail tucked around him.

'Flying is terribly tiring for dragons,' Sorrel whispered to Ben. 'If they don't sleep it off they get melancholy. So melancholy you can't do a thing with them. And if it rains as well,' she added, rolling her eyes, 'oh, my word! But luckily,' she decided, looking up at the sky, 'luckily it doesn't look at all like rain. Or do you want to argue about that too?'

Ben shook his head, and looked around.

'The way you gape at everything I guess you've never been in the mountains before, have you?' asked Sorrel.

'I once went tobogganing downhill on a rubbish tip,' said Ben, 'but it was no higher than that tree over there.' He sat on his backpack in the grass, which was wet with dew. He felt extremely small among the tall peaks – as small as an insect – but all the same he could hardly get his fill of all the rounded and craggy summits rising against the horizon. On one peak far, far away Ben saw the ruins of a castle. It towered black into the morning sky, and although it seemed not much bigger than a matchbox, it still looked menacing.

'Look.' Ben nudged Sorrel. 'See that castle over there?'

The brownie yawned. 'Where? Oh, that.' She yawned again. 'What about it? There are lots of those where Firedrake and I come from. Old human dwellings. *You* ought to know about them.' Opening her backpack, she stuffed into her mouth some of the leaves she had picked under the bridge. 'There we are!' She threw her pack down on the short grass. 'One of us can have a snooze now while the other keeps watch. Shall we toss for it?'

'No, that's okay.' Ben shook his head. 'You lie down. I couldn't sleep at the moment anyway.'

'Whatever you say.' Sorrel marched over to the place where Firedrake was sleeping. 'But don't go falling off anything, will you?' she called back over her shoulder. Then she curled up beside the dragon, and next moment she too was asleep.

Ben took a spoon and a can of ravioli out of his backpack, opened the can with his penknife, and sat down with it on the grass at a safe distance from the precipice. As he ate the cold pasta he looked around him, remembering that he was on watch. He glanced at the castle. There were tiny specks circling in the clear sky above it. Ben couldn't help thinking of the ravens Gilbert Greytail had mentioned. Oh, come off it, he thought. I'll be seeing ghosts next.

The sun rose higher and higher, driving the mist out of the valleys and making Ben feel drowsy, so he rose to his feet and walked up and down for a while. When Sorrel began snoring loudly he went over to her, looked in her backpack and found Gilbert Greytail's map.

He opened it carefully and took the compass out of his pocket. Then he pulled one of the dangling ribbons and had a closer look at the mountains where they must have landed. Next he anxiously examined the entries made by the rat. 'Oh wow!' he murmured. 'I thought so! We've landed in one of those nasty yellow patches. We're too far east. I don't like this at all.'

Suddenly there was a rustling sound behind him.

Ben raised his head. There. There it was again. Perfectly clear. He turned round. Firedrake and Sorrel were still asleep; only the tip of the dragon's tail twitched in his dreams. Ben looked round, feeling uneasy. Were there snakes in these mountains? Snakes were about the only thing he was really frightened of. Oh, come on, he thought, probably just a rabbit. He folded the map, returned it to Sorrel's backpack and—

Ben could hardly believe his eyes.

A small, fat man had emerged from behind a large, moss-grown rock scarcely a pace away from him. This apparition, hardly bigger than a chicken, wore a huge hat on his head, which was as grey as the surrounding rocks. He was also holding a pickaxe.

'No, it's not him,' said the little man, looking Ben up and down.

'How do you know, Stonebeard?' Three more stout little fellows came out from behind the rock. They were inspecting Ben as if he were some strange animal which, to their astonishment, had landed on their mountain.

'Because our scalps wouldn't be prickling if he was, that's how I know,' replied Stonebeard. 'This is a human being, can't you see that? Only a small one, though.' The dwarf glanced in all directions, evidently worried. He even glanced up at the sky. Then, looking determined, he made for Ben, who was still crouching on the ground, bewildered. Stonebeard stood right in front of him, clutching the pickaxe in his little hands as if it would help him to face a giant human. His three companions stayed near the rock, watching their fearless leader with bated breath.

'You, human!' whispered Stonebeard, tapping Ben on the knee. 'Who else is here with you?'

'Wh-wh-what?' stammered Ben.

The fat little man turned to his friends and tapped his forehead. 'A few teacups short of the full set!' he informed them. 'But I'll have another try.' He turned back to Ben. 'Who – else – is – here – with – you?' he asked. 'An elf? A fairy? A brownie? A will-o'-the-wisp, or what?'

Without meaning to, Ben glanced swiftly at the place where Firedrake and Sorrel were sleeping.

'Ahaaa!' Stonebeard stepped to one side, stood on tiptoe . . . and gasped for breath, awestruck. His eyes were as round as marbles. He took off his huge hat, scratched his bald head, and put the hat back on.

'Hey, Leadengleam, Gravelbeard, Graniteface!' he called. 'Come out from behind that rock.' He added, in devoutly hushed tones, 'You're never going to believe this. It's a dragon! A silver dragon!'

Slowly, still on tiptoe, he crept towards the sleeping Firedrake. His friends came hurrying after him in a state of high excitement.

'Here, wait a minute!' Ben had finally recovered his powers of speech. He jumped up and moved between Firedrake and the little men. They might not be much bigger than large lemonade bottles, but all the same they raised their hammers and pickaxes and stared grimly up at him.

'Make way there, human!' growled Stonebeard. 'We only

want a look at him.'

'Sorrel!' Ben called over his shoulder. 'Sorrel, wake up! There's a bunch of funny little men here.'

'*Funny little men*?' Stonebeard took a step towards Ben. 'Do you by any chance mean us? Did you hear that, brothers?'

'What's all this racket?' grumbled Sorrel, yawning as she crawled out from behind the sleeping dragon.

'A forest brownie!' cried Leadengleam in alarm.

'Mountain dwarves!' said Sorrel. 'Well, fancy that. You're never safe from them anywhere.' With one leap she had jumped in among the little men and picked Leadengleam up by the collar. The dwarf dropped his hammer in alarm and kicked his crooked little legs in the air. His friends instantly made for Sorrel, but the brownie girl effortlessly fended them off with her free paw.

'No need to get all worked up,' she said, relieving the dwarves of their hammers and pickaxes and chucking them over her shoulder. 'Don't you know you must never wake up a dragon? Suppose he'd eaten you for breakfast? You look really juicy. Nice and crunchy too!'

'Huh! Silly brownie talk!' said Stonebeard, scowling at Sorrel, but even so, he took two tiny steps backwards to be on the safe side.

'Dragons don't eat anything that breathes,' said the fattest dwarf, taking cover behind a rock. 'They live on moonlight. All their strength comes from the moon. They can't even fly when it isn't shining.'

'Oh, very clever, aren't you?' Sorrel put the struggling Leadengleam back on the grass and leaned over the others. 'So tell me how you knew we were here? Have we been stupid enough to land right on your doorstep?'

The four of them looked anxiously up at her. Stonebeard nudged the smallest of them. 'Go on, Graniteface,' he growled. 'Your turn now.'

Graniteface stepped forward hesitantly, fingered the brim of his hat, and looked uneasily up at the two giant figures facing him. 'No,' he said at last, his voice trembling, 'we live a good way further up the mountain. But our scalps were prickling this morning. Usually they only do that when we're near the castle.'

'And what does that mean?' asked Sorrel impatiently.

'Our scalps prickle when there are other fabulous beings somewhere near,' replied Graniteface. 'Humans and animals don't have the same effect.'

'Which is lucky,' sighed Leadengleam.

Sorrel looked suspiciously at the four of them.

'You said something about a castle just now.' Ben knelt down in front of Graniteface and looked enquiringly at him. 'Do you mean the castle up there?' he asked

'We don't know anything!' called the fattest dwarf from behind his rock. 'Not a thing!'

'Shut up, Gravelbeard!' said Stonebeard.

Graniteface looked at Ben like a frightened rabbit and hastily retreated to join the others. But Stonebeard took a step towards the human boy.

'Yes, that's the castle we mean,' he grunted. 'It makes our scalps prickle so hard it's unbearable. That's why we haven't been there for years, even though the mountain where it stands has such a strong smell of gold it's enough to lift the hat off your head.'

Ben and Sorrel looked up at the castle.

'Who lives there, then?' asked Ben, not liking the sound of this.

'We don't know!' whispered Graniteface.

'No, no idea,' muttered Gravelbeard, giving Ben and Sorrel a nasty look.

'And we don't want to know either,' growled Stonebeard. 'Evil things happen up there. We don't want to know, do we, brothers?'

The four all shook their heads again and drew rather closer together.

'Sounds as if we should fly on as soon as possible,' said Sorrel.

'I told you we ought to avoid yellow!' Ben looked with concern at Firedrake, but he was still sleeping peacefully, and had merely turned his head over on the other side. 'We didn't fly far enough south. But you wouldn't believe me.'

'Yes, all right, all right!' Sorrel pensively chewed her claws. 'Nothing to be done about it now. We can't leave this place before sunset, and Firedrake needs to sleep all day or he'll be too tired to fly tonight. Right.' She clapped her paws. 'This is a good chance to stock up with provisions. How about it, boys?' She leaned down to the mountain dwarves. 'Know where to find any nice tasty roots or berries?'

The four little men whispered to each other. Finally Stonebeard stepped forward looking important, cleared his throat, and said, 'We'll show you a place, brownie, but only if the dragon will pick up the scent of the rocks for us.'

Sorrel stared down at the dwarf in surprise. 'What good would that do you?'

Here Gravelbeard stepped forward too. 'Dragons can scent treasure,' he whispered. 'Everyone knows that.'

'Really?' Sorrel grinned. 'Who told you so?'

'It says so in the old stories,' replied Stonebeard. 'Tales of the time when there were still dragons here.'

'There used to be lots of them here, lots and lots, but,' added Graniteface, sadly shrugging his shoulders, 'but they all went long ago.' He glanced admiringly at Firedrake.

'My grandfather,' whispered Leadengleam, 'my maternal grandfather, that is, he used to ride one. The dragon found him gold and silver, quartz and tourmaline, rock crystal, yellow lead ore and malachite!' The dwarf rolled his eyes in ecstasy.

'All right,' agreed Sorrel, shrugging her shoulders. 'I'll ask the dragon when he wakes up. But only if you show me where to find something really tasty to eat.'

'Come along, then!' The mountain dwarves led Sorrel to a place where the mountain fell steeply into a valley, and they began to scramble expertly down the rock face.

Sorrel retreated from the precipice in alarm. 'You want me to go down there?' she asked. 'Not likely! I don't mind a bit of climbing on mountains when they're all rounded and soft like a cat arching its back, but I'm not going down there, no way! Suppose you boys go down on your own and find me something? I'll wait here and call you when the dragon wakes up. Okay?'

'Just as you like,' said Leadengleam, disappearing into the depths. 'But you *will* call, won't you?'

'Brownie's honour.' Sorrel was shaking her head as she watched the little fellows go. They were jumping from rock to rock as nimbly as fat flies. 'I hope they know what brownies like to eat,' she muttered.

Then it was her turn to go on watch.

Unfortunately she never noticed Gravelbeard, the fattest of the dwarves, part company with the others and disappear inconspicuously beneath the branches of a fir tree.

CHAPTER NINE

Nettlebrand, the Golden One

The dwarves were right.

The castle near the place where Firedrake had landed by mistake was a sinister spot – and far more dangerous for a silver dragon than for a few mountain dwarves. Its occupant took no more interest in dwarves than he did in spiders or flies. But he had been waiting for a dragon for over a hundred and fifty years.

Rain had long ago eroded the castle walls. The towers were in ruins, the stairways overgrown with thistles and thorn bushes. But that didn't bother the castle's owner. His armour was proof against rain, cold and wind. Nettlebrand, the Golden One, lay in the deep, damp vaults far underground, longing for the return of the good years when the castle roof was intact and he had enjoyed himself chasing the only prey he liked to hunt – silver dragons.

Nettlebrand's own scales still shone like pure gold. His claws were sharper than splinters of glass, his teeth had a keen cutting edge, and he was mightier than any other living creature. But he was bored – consumed by boredom. It made him wild and savage, more ferocious than a chained dog, and so bad-tempered that he had long ago eaten most of his servants.

Only one of them was left, a spindly little manikin called Twigleg. Day in, day out he polished Nettlebrand's armour, dusted the spines on his back, cleaned his gleaming teeth and sharpened his claws. Day after day, from sunrise to sunset, Twigleg worked while the golden dragon lay in his ruined castle, hoping one of his countless spies would bring him the news he had been waiting for so long – news of the last dragons, so that he could go hunting again.

On the morning when Firedrake was sleeping among the rocks only a few mountain peaks away, two spies had already come back – one of Nettlebrand's ravens from the north and a will-o'-the-wisp from the south. But they had nothing to tell him, nothing at all, only silly stories about a couple of trolls here, a few fairies there, a sea serpent and a gigantic bird – nothing about dragons. Not a word. So Nettlebrand ate them for breakfast, even though he knew that raven feathers always gave him terrible indigestion.

He was in a shocking temper when Twigleg, armed with cleaning cloths and brushes, bowed low before him. As usual the manikin clambered up on to Nettlebrand's huge body to polish the golden scales of his master's armour from head to tail.

'Careful, you bone-brained homunculus!' Nettlebrand spat at him. 'Ouch! Don't tread on my stomach, for goodness' sake! Why didn't you stop me eating that wretched black bird?'

'You wouldn't have listened to me, master,' replied Twigleg. Picking up a green bottle, he poured into a bucket of water some

of the polish specially made by the mountain dwarves for his master's scaly armour. That polish was the secret of buffing the scales to such a shine that he could see his reflection in them.

'Correct,' growled Nettlebrand.

Twigleg dipped his cloth into the bucket and set to work. But when he had cleaned only three of the scales his master groaned and turned over. Twigleg's bucket fell off and landed on the ground.

'That will do!' bellowed Nettlebrand. 'You can leave the polishing for today! It makes my stomach ache worse. Get on with sharpening my claws!' And he blew Twigleg off his back with his icy breath. The little creature tumbled head first to the cracked flagstones of the castle floor. Without a word he picked himself up again, took a file from his belt and got to work on the dragon's black claws.

Nettlebrand, disgruntled, watched him. 'Come on, tell me something,' he growled. 'Tell me about my heroic deeds of old!'

'Oh no, not that again!' muttered Twigleg.

'What did you say?' growled Nettlebrand.

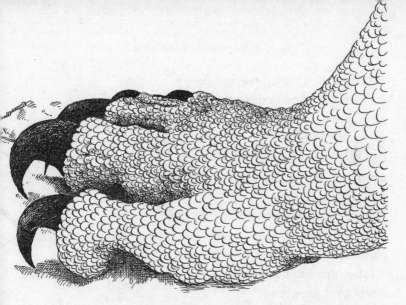

'Oh, nothing, nothing,' replied Twigleg hastily. 'Right, master. Just a moment. How did it go? Oh yes.' The manikin cleared his throat. 'One cold, moonless winter night in the year 1423—'

'1424!' snarled Nettlebrand. 'How often do I have to tell you, beetle-brain?' He struck out angrily at the little man, but Twigleg nimbly avoided him.

'One cold, moonless winter night in the year 1424,' he began again, 'the famous alchemist Petrosius Henbane created the greatest marvel the world has ever seen, the mightiest being, the—'

'The mightiest and most dangerous being,' Nettlebrand interrupted. 'Get it right, can't you? Or I'll bite your spidery legs. Carry on.'

'. . . the mightiest and most dangerous being,' Twigleg obediently recited, 'ever to set claw on this earth. He made it from a creature whose name no one knows, and he added fire and water, gold and iron, hard stone and the dew that falls on the leaves of lady's mantle. Then he took the power of lightning and with it he breathed life into his creation, and he named his great work

Nettlebrand.' Twigleg yawned. 'Sorry, 'scuse me.'

'Carry on,' growled Nettlebrand, closing his red eyes.

'Carry on, yes, sir. At your service, sir!' Twigleg stuck the file under his arm and moved over to the next paw. 'That same night,' he continued, 'Petrosius made twelve homunculi, little manikins, the last of whom sits here filing your claws. The others—'

'Skip that bit,' growled Nettlebrand.

'Would you like me to tell you how our creator Petrosius perished between the teeth of your noble jaws?'

'No, that's not interesting. Tell me about my hunt, armour-cleaner, my great hunt.'

Twigleg sighed. 'Soon after his creation, the magnificent, invincible, ever-shining Nettlebrand, the Golden One, set out to remove all other dragons from the face of the earth. He planned to polish them off in one fell swoop.'

'Polish them off?' Nettlebrand opened one eye. 'Polish them off? What do you mean? That doesn't sound very heroic.'

'Oh, do I usually put it some other way, master?' Twigleg rubbed his pointed nose. 'It must just have slipped out. Oh dear, the file's broken.'

'Fetch a new one,' growled Nettlebrand. 'But hurry up, or you can join your eleven brothers in my belly.'

'No thanks,' whispered Twigleg, jumping up. But just as he was about to run off a large raven came hopping down the stone steps that led to the hidden vaults of the castle.

Twigleg was not surprised to see the raven. Those black-feathered birds were Nettlebrand's most industrious and faithful spies – even though he was in the habit of eating them from time to time. But today a fat mountain dwarf was sitting on the raven's back, and it was unusual for the dwarves to venture up here.

They didn't even deliver the armour polish themselves; one of the ravens was always sent to collect it.

The dwarf held his outsize hat on tight as the raven hopped down the steps. His face was red with excitement. At the foot of the steps he hastily climbed off the bird's black back, took a couple of steps towards Nettlebrand, then prostrated himself on the floor in front of him.

'What do you want?' asked Twigleg's master, grumpily.

'I've seen one!' uttered the dwarf, without raising his face from the floor. 'I've seen one, Your Goldness!'

'Seen one what?' Bored, Nettlebrand scratched his chin.

Twigleg went over to the dwarf and bent down to him. 'You'd better get to the point instead of squashing your fat nose flat,' he whispered. 'My master has a truly terrible temper.'

The dwarf scrambled up, looked nervously at Nettlebrand, and pointed a trembling finger at the wall behind him. 'One of those,' he breathed. 'That's what I saw.'

Nettlebrand turned round. There was a tapestry on the wall, a tapestry woven by human beings hundreds of years ago. Its colours were faded, but even in the darkness you could make out what it showed – knights hunting a silver dragon.

Nettlebrand suddenly sat up. His red eyes stared down at the dwarf. 'You say you saw a silver dragon?' he asked. His voice boomed through the ancient vaults. 'Where?'

'On our mountain,' stammered the dwarf, straightening up. 'He landed there this morning. With a brownie and a human. I flew straight here on the raven to tell you. Will you give me one of your scales now? One of your golden scales?'

'Quiet!' growled Nettlebrand. 'I must think.'

'But you promised!' cried the dwarf.

Twigleg pushed him aside. 'Quiet, stupid!' he hissed. 'Haven't you got any sense under that big hat of yours? You can count yourself lucky if he doesn't eat you. Climb back on the raven and get out of here. It's probably just a big lizard you saw.'

'No, it isn't!' cried the dwarf. 'It's a dragon! His scales look as if they were made of moonlight and he's big, very big.'

Nettlebrand looked at the tapestry. He stood there motionless. Then he turned.

'It'll be the worse for you if you're wrong!' he said in a deep voice. 'I shall squash you like a cockroach if you've raised my hopes only to dash them again!'

The dwarf bowed his head.

'Armour-cleaner, come here,' growled Nettlebrand.

Twigleg jumped. 'The new file, the file, yes, master!' he cried. 'I'll fetch it at once. I'll hurry, I'll fly like the wind.'

'Forget the file,' spat Nettlebrand. 'I have more important work for you to do. Get on the raven's back and fly to the mountain where this idiot came from. Find out what he saw. And if it's really a dragon, then find out why he's alone, where he comes from, and what the human and the brownie are doing with him. I want to know everything, you hear? Everything.'

Twigleg nodded and ran over to the raven, who was still waiting patiently at the foot of the steps.

Disconcerted, the dwarf watched him go. 'So what about me?' he asked. 'How am I going to get back?'

Nettlebrand smiled. It was not a nice smile. 'You're going to sharpen my claws while Twigleg is away. You're going to polish my armour and dust my spines, clean my teeth and pick the woodlice out of my scales. You're my new armour-cleaner! That's my reward for your good news.'

The dwarf looked at him, horrified.

Nettlebrand licked his lips and grunted with satisfaction.

'I'll make haste, master,' said Twigleg, mounting the raven. 'I'll be back soon.'

'Oh no, you won't,' said Nettlebrand crossly. 'You'll send me news by water, understand? That's quicker than flying back and forth all the time.'

'Water?' Twigleg made a face. 'But it could be difficult to find water on the mountain, master!'

'Ask the dwarf where to look, beetle-brain,' spat Nettlebrand, turning round. Treading heavily, he lumbered slowly over to examine the tapestry with its shimmering silver dragon. Thousands of threads had gone into its weaving. Nettlebrand stood very close to it.

'Perhaps they really are back,' he murmured. 'After so many long years. I knew they couldn't hide from me for ever! From human beings, perhaps, but not from me.'

CHAPTER TEN

The Spy

Twigleg looked back uneasily as the raven took off from the ruined castle walls and rose into the sky. The little homunculus had only ever left the castle when Nettlebrand's hunting instincts took him down to the valleys to prey on sheep and cows. And even then they travelled by way of underground passages, for Nettlebrand was a flightless dragon, whose heavy golden armour would have made it impossible for him to rise from the ground. Instead, he swam along underground rivers deep beneath the earth, and if he came up to the surface it was only at night, under cover of darkness. But now the sun, high in the sky, was bright and hot and Twigleg had only a raven for company.

'Is it much further?' he asked, trying not to look down.

'It's the mountain over there!' croaked the raven, streaking like an arrow towards it. 'The one with the stump-shaped peak.'

'Do you have to fly so fast?' Twigleg dug his thin fingers into the raven's feathers. 'This wind is almost blowing my ears off.'

'I thought we were in a hurry,' replied the raven, without slowing down. 'You're not half as heavy as that dwarf, even though you're not much smaller. What are you made of, air?'

'Good guess.' Twigleg was shifting uncomfortably back and forth. 'Air and a few other choice ingredients. But the recipe's lost.' He peered ahead. 'There! There's something shining in the grass!' he exclaimed suddenly. 'Oh, sacred salamanders!' His eyes opened very wide. 'That stupid dwarf was right. It *is* a dragon.'

The raven circled over Firedrake where he lay coiled up among the rocks. A few metres away from him Ben and Sorrel were bending over the map, with three mountain dwarves standing beside them.

'Let's land on that rocky ledge,' Twigleg whispered to the raven. 'Just above their heads, where we can eavesdrop on them.'

When the raven landed on the ledge Sorrel looked up suspiciously.

'Fly away now,' Twigleg whispered to the bird. 'Hide in that fir tree until I give you a signal. The brownie won't notice me, but you seem to worry her.'

The raven rose in the air again and disappeared among the dark fir branches. Twigleg cautiously moved right out on the ledge.

'Okay, I'll admit it,' the brownie was saying. 'So we did lose our way a bit, but it doesn't really matter. We'll reach the sea tonight all the same.'

'The only question is *which* sea, Sorrel,' said the human. He was only a small human, still a boy.

'You know something, cleverclogs?' hissed the brownie girl. 'You can do the steering tonight. Then at least I won't have to put up with your sniping if we go the wrong way again.'

'Where are you going, anyway?' asked one of the dwarves.

Twigleg pricked up his ears.

'We're looking for the Rim of Heaven,' said Ben.

Sorrel gave him such a hefty nudge in the ribs that he almost fell over. 'Who said you could tell any old chance-met dwarf that, eh?'

The boy went very quiet.

Twigleg moved yet a little further forward still. The *Rim of Heaven* . . . what on earth could that be?

'He's waking up!' one of the dwarves announced suddenly. 'Look, he's waking up.'

Twigleg turned his head – and there he stood. The silver dragon.

He was much smaller than Nettlebrand, and his eyes were not red but golden. The dragon stretched his beautiful limbs, yawned, and then looked in surprise at the three little creatures hiding behind the human boy.

'Ah, dwarves!' he said, in a voice with a faint rasp that sounded like the lick of a cat's tongue. 'Mountain dwarves.'

The boy laughed. 'Yes, they absolutely had to meet you,' he said, urging the dwarves to venture out from behind him. 'This is Stonebeard. This is Graniteface. This is Leadengleam. And this—' Ben looked around in surprise. 'Where's the fourth of you? I don't know his name.'

'Gravelbeard,' said Stonebeard, looking up at the dragon in awe. 'I've no idea where he is. Gravelbeard's a bit peculiar.'

Up on the ledge, Twigleg could hardly keep from chuckling. 'Gravelbeard's an idiot,' he whispered, 'and right now he's hard at work cleaning Nettlebrand's armour.' A pebble came loose as the manikin moved even closer to the rocky edge. The wretched stone fell right on the brownie's head. She looked up suspiciously, but Twigleg had hastily withdrawn his long nose.

'These dwarves think you can pick up the scent of treasure, Firedrake,' said the boy. 'They want you to try doing it on their mountain.'

'Treasure?' The dragon shook his head. 'What kind of treasure? Do you mean gold and silver?'

The dwarves nodded. They looked hopefully at the dragon. Firedrake went over to the mountainside and put his nose against the rocks, drawing in the scent of them. The dwarves crowded excitedly around his legs.

'It smells good,' said the dragon. 'Different from the mountains I come from, but good. Yes, it really does. But with the best will in the world I can't tell you exactly what it smells of.'

The dwarves looked at each other, disappointed.

'Are there more dragons where you come from?' asked Graniteface curiously.

'I'd like to know that too,' whispered Twigleg, up in his lookout post.

'Oh yes,' replied the dragon. 'And where I'm going as well, I hope.'

'That's enough of that!' said the brownie girl. Just when things were getting interesting! Twigleg felt like spitting on her head. She placed herself between the dwarves and the dragon and shooed the little people back. 'You heard what Firedrake said. He doesn't know whether there's any treasure in the mountain, so fetch your hammers and pickaxes and find it for yourselves. Firedrake has to rest again now. We still have a long way to go.'

And that was it. Over the next few hours Sorrel ensured that Twigleg heard nothing else of interest. Instead, the dwarves told Firedrake stories of the good old days when their grandparents used to ride on dragon-back, and Stonebeard gave the dragon an endless lecture on quartz and silver ore.

It was infuriating. Twigleg was yawning so hard he almost fell off the ledge.

When the sun was sinking low over the mountains, Twigleg left his hiding place, signalled to the raven to follow him, and laboriously clambered up the rocks to the spring that Gravelbeard had described to him. It was easy to find. The water bubbled out of a crevice in the rock and fell into a pool. The dwarves had set gleaming semi-precious stones into the rim of this natural basin. The raven settled on the spot and pecked at the beetles lurking between the rocks. But Twigleg climbed up on to the largest boulder – and spat into the clear water.

The smooth surface of the pool rippled. The water turned dark, and the image of Nettlebrand appeared in it. Gravelbeard was standing on the Golden One's back, dusting the spines of his crest with a large soft brush.

'At last!' Nettlebrand growled at Twigleg. 'Where've you been all this time? I almost ate this dwarf out of sheer impatience.'

'Oh, don't do that, master,' replied Twigleg. 'He was right. A dragon did land here. Silver as moonlight and much smaller than you, but definitely a dragon.'

Nettlebrand stared incredulously at the manikin.

'A dragon!' he whispered. 'A silver dragon. I've had the whole world searched for them, every last grubby nook and cranny of it, and now one lands almost on my doorstep.' He leered and licked his lips.

'See?' said Gravelbeard, so excited that he dropped the brush. 'I found him for you! I did it! Will you give me my scale now? Maybe even two scales?'

'Shut your gob!' Nettlebrand snapped at him. 'Or I'll give

you a spectacular close-up view of the gold fillings in my teeth! Carry on cleaning!'

Gravelbeard slid off the dragon's back in alarm and retrieved the brush. Nettlebrand addressed his old armour-cleaner again. 'Tell me what you've found out about him! Are there any more of his kind where he comes from?'

'Yes,' replied Twigleg.

Nettlebrand's eyes were gleaming. 'Aaah!' he sighed. 'At last! At last I can go hunting again.' He bared his teeth. 'Where do I find them?'

Twigleg rubbed his pointed nose and looked nervously at his master's reflection. 'Er, well,' he said, hunching his head between his shoulders, 'I don't exactly know, master.'

'You don't know?' Nettlebrand bellowed, so loud that Gravelbeard fell head first off his back. 'You don't know? What have you been doing all this time, you useless spidery creature?'

'I can't help it! It's all that brownie's fault!' cried Twigleg. 'She makes sure the dragon doesn't say anything about where he comes from. But I know what he's looking for, master!' Eagerly, he bent over the dark water. 'He's looking for the Rim of Heaven.'

Nettlebrand straightened up and stood motionless. His red eyes were turned in Twigleg's direction, but he was looking right through him. Gravelbeard knocked the dent out of his hat and climbed back up the spiny tail, swearing.

The homunculus cleared his throat. 'Er – do you know where that is, master?' he asked quietly.

Nettlebrand was still looking straight through him. 'No one knows where it is,' he growled at last. 'Except the dragons who have been hiding there for over a hundred years, ever since they escaped me. I searched for the Rim of Heaven until my paws were bleeding. Sometimes I was so close I thought I could smell it. But I never found the dragons, and that was the end of my great hunting days.'

'You can hunt this dragon, though!' Gravelbeard called from Nettlebrand's back. 'The one who was stupid enough to land in front of your nose.'

'Huh!' Nettlebrand said scornfully, slapping a paw down on a passing rat. 'And then what? No, the fun would be over too soon, before I'd even discovered where he comes from. I'd never find out where the others are either. No, I have a better idea. A much better idea. Twigleg!'

The homunculus jumped in alarm. 'Yes, master?'

'You must follow him,' grunted Nettlebrand. 'You must follow him until he leads us to the others – either the dragons he's looking for or the dragons he left behind.'

'Me?' Twigleg beat his thin chest pitifully. 'But why me, master? Aren't you coming too?'

Nettlebrand hissed. 'I'm not planning to run my paws off till they're sore again. You'll report to me every evening. Every evening without fail, do you hear? And when he's found the Rim of Heaven I'll join you.'

'But how, master?' asked Twigleg.

'I have powers at which you cannot even guess. Go away now and get to work.' And Nettlebrand's image in the pool began to blur.

'Wait! Wait, master!' cried the manikin. But the water in the basin grew clearer and clearer until Twigleg was looking into the eyes of his own reflection.

'Oh no!' he whispered. 'Oh no, oh no, oh no!'

Then, with a heavy sigh, he turned and went in search of the raven.

CHAPTER ELEVEN

The Storm

The mountain dwarves had long ago fallen asleep in their caves when Firedrake prepared to set off. This time Ben clambered up on his back to sit in front, holding his compass. He had spent hours studying the rat's map, memorising every detail: the mountains around which they would fly, the rivers they should follow, the cities they had better avoid. First they had to go several hundred miles further south, making for the Mediterranean. If they were in luck they'd land on its shores before dawn.

With a few powerful wing-beats the dragon rose into the air. The sky was clear above the mountains. The waxing moon hung bright among a thousand stars, and only a light wind blew towards them. The world was so silent that Ben could hear Sorrel munching a mushroom behind him. Firedrake's wings rushed through the cool air.

When they had left the mountains behind them Ben turned to take one last look at the black peak. For a moment he thought he saw a large bird in the darkness, with a tiny figure sitting on its back.

'Sorrel!' he whispered. 'Look behind you. Can you see anything?'

Sorrel put down the mushroom she was nibbling and looked over her shoulder. 'Nothing to worry about,' she said.

'But it could be a raven!' Ben whispered hoarsely. 'The rat warned us against ravens, didn't he? And isn't there something sitting on it?'

'Yes, there is.' Sorrel returned to her mushroom. 'That's why there's no need to worry. It's an elf. Elves love flying in the moonlight. We only have to feel suspicious about ravens *without* riders, and even they can't keep up with a dragon in flight for very long unless they have magic powers.'

'An elf?' Ben looked round again, but the bird and its rider had disappeared as if the night had swallowed them up.

'They've gone,' murmured Ben.

'You bet they've gone. Probably on their way to one of those silly elf-dances.' Sorrel threw the bitter remains of her mushroom into the darkness below and wiped her mouth. 'Mmm! That horn of plenty was delicious!'

During the next few hours Ben frequently looked back over his shoulder, but he never saw the figure riding the bird again. Firedrake was flying south faster than the wind. Ben kept asking Sorrel what her keen brownie eyes could see on the earth below, for he himself could make out nothing in the darkness but the rivers and lakes that reflected the moonlight in their waters. Working as a team, the two of them steered the dragon past cities and other dangerous places, just as the rat had advised.

When day dawned they found a place to rest in an olive grove near the Greek coast. They slept all day, surrounded by chirping cicadas, and set off again at moonrise. Firedrake turned southeast towards the Syrian coast. It was a mild night, with a hot southerly wind blowing over the sea. Before dawn, however, the weather changed.

The wind that had been blowing towards them all this time grew stronger and stronger. Firedrake tried to avoid it. He rose higher and then dropped lower, but the wind was everywhere. The dragon was finding it more and more difficult to keep going. Clouds towered like mountains ahead of them. Thunder rolled, and lightning flashes lit up the dark sky.

'We're swerving off course, Firedrake!' cried Ben. 'The wind is driving you south!'

'I can't make any headway against it!' the dragon called back. He braced himself against the invisible enemy with all his might, but the wind carried him away, howling in his ears and forcing him down towards the foaming waves.

Ben and Sorrel clung desperately to the spines on Firedrake's crest. Luckily Sorrel had tied herself firmly in place too, for without the straps holding them they would have slipped off Firedrake's back and fallen into the depths below. Rain lashed down from the towering clouds. Soon the dragon's spines were so slippery that his riders found it difficult to hold on, and Sorrel had to cling to Ben's back. The sea was raging down below. A few islands lay among the waves, but there was no other land in sight.

'I think we're being blown towards the coast of Egypt!' Ben yelled.

Sorrel clung to him even tighter. 'Coast?' she shouted back. 'A coast sounds good, never mind what coast. Just so long as we don't get blown into the briny down there.'

The sun was rising, but only as a pallid light behind dark

clouds. Firedrake was in difficulties. The storm forced him down towards the waves again and again, until Ben and Sorrel could feel the surf spraying into their faces.

'Does that brilliant map of yours say anything about the weather in these parts?' Sorrel shouted to Ben.

Ben's hair was dripping wet, and his ears hurt from the noise of the storm. He could tell that Firedrake's wings were growing heavier and heavier. 'The coast,' he called, 'the coast where the storm's driving us,' he wiped water out of his eyes, 'it's full of yellow patches. Covered with them!'

They saw a ship tossing like a cork on the foaming water below. Then a strip of coastline suddenly emerged from the mist.

'There!' cried Ben. 'Land ahoy, Firedrake! Can you get that far?'

With the last of his strength the dragon steeled himself against the wind and slowly, very slowly, approached the safety of the shore.

Beneath them, the sea was lashing low cliffs where palm trees were bowed by the wind.

'We're going to make it!' shouted Sorrel, digging her little claws through Ben's pullover. 'We're going to make it!'

Ben saw the sun rising higher among ragged clouds. The sky was slowly brightening. The storm slackened, as if lying down to sleep as the day dawned.

With a couple of final wing-beats, the dragon left the sea behind, descended even lower and landed, exhausted, on fine, soft sand. Ben and Sorrel undid their sodden straps and slid off Firedrake's back. The dragon had laid his head on the sand and closed his eyes.

'Firedrake!' cried Sorrel. 'Get up, Firedrake! We have to find a place to hide. It's soon going to be as bright here as if we were inside a fairy hill.'

Beside her, Ben was looking around anxiously. Only a stone's throw away, palm trees lined the banks of a dried-up riverbed, their fronds rustling in the wind. Behind the palms rose sand dunes, and in the morning light the travellers saw fallen columns, ruined walls – and a large camp full of tents.

No doubt about it, there were people in those tents.

'Quick, Firedrake!' Sorrel urged the dragon as he got up wearily. 'Make for the palms over there!'

They ran over the sand, crossed the dry riverbed, and climbed the rocky slope of the bank where the palms grew. The trees stood close enough together to hide Firedrake from prying eyes for the time being, but the place wouldn't do as a hideout for the whole day.

'Maybe we can find somewhere in the hills,' said Ben. 'A cave, or a dark corner among the ruins.'

He took the rat's map out of his trouser pocket, but it was so wet that he couldn't unfold it. 'Bother,' he muttered. 'We'll have to dry it in the sun or it won't be any use.'

'What about those humans over there?' asked Sorrel. 'The place is swarming with them.' She peered anxiously through the palm trees at the distant camp. 'They *are* humans, aren't they? I never saw so many humans living in canvas houses before.'

'With all those tents, I think it must be an archaeologists' camp,' said Ben. 'I once saw a camp just like that in a movie.'

'Archaeolojiwhats?' asked Sorrel. 'Is that a particularly dangerous sort of human?'

Ben laughed. 'No, archaeologists are people who dig up old temples and vases and so on.'

'What for?' asked Sorrel, wrinkling her nose. 'Those things

must have got broken ages ago. Why bother to go digging them up?'

Ben shrugged his shoulders. 'Out of curiosity. To find out how people lived in the past, see?'

'Oh,' said Sorrel. 'And what do they do then? Do they repair the buildings and the vases and everything?'

'No.' Ben shook his head. 'Sometimes they stick the shards of pots back together, but mostly they leave things the way they find them.'

Baffled, the brownie girl looked at the broken columns. The sun was rising higher, and the people in the camp seemed to be starting work.

Firedrake brought Sorrel out of her thoughts and back down to earth.

He yawned, stretched, and arched his neck wearily. 'I'll just lie down under these funny-looking trees,' he murmured drowsily. 'The rustling of their leaves is sure to tell me wonderful stories.'

He lay down, sighing, but Sorrel hauled him up again. 'No, no, Firedrake, it's not safe enough here!' she cried. 'I'm sure we can find somewhere better. Ben's right, it really doesn't look too bad up in the hills. We just have to find a place far enough away from the humans' camp.'

She was pushing the dragon further into the palms when Ben suddenly clutched her arm.

'Hey, wait, Sorrel!' He pointed back to the beach. 'Look at that!'

They had left clear tracks in the damp sand behind them, leading across the dry riverbed and then up the slope.

'Oh, bother, how could I be so stupid?' said Sorrel crossly. She hastily climbed the trunk of a palm tree and pulled off a long frond. 'I'll see to the tracks!' she hissed down to Ben. 'You find a good hiding place for Firedrake and I'll catch up with you. Go on, get moving!'

Reluctantly, the dragon turned, while Sorrel jumped down into the riverbed and began sweeping the palm frond over the sand to cover their tracks.

'Come on,' Ben told Firedrake, putting the backpacks over his shoulders.

But the dragon did not move. 'Shouldn't we wait for you, Sorrel?' he called anxiously. 'Suppose the humans turn up?'

'Well, even if they do come this way, I'll hear them from a long way off!' replied Sorrel. 'Go on, get out of here.'

Firedrake sighed. 'Very well, but hurry up.'

'Brownie's honour,' promised Sorrel. She looked round, pleased. The tracks on the slope and in the riverbed were already gone. 'If you happen to pass any mushrooms, think of me!'

'We will,' said Ben, and he followed the dragon.

They found Firedrake a hiding place, a cavern among the rocky foothills, half hidden by tangled thorn bushes and at a safe distance from the human camp. There were carvings of ugly faces in the rock round the entrance, and in one place the stone was covered by writing in a strange script. In fact the place looked rather eerie. But the coarse, prickly grass around it grew tall, and no path had been trodden through the thick undergrowth. To Ben's relief, it looked very much as if the archaeologists weren't interested in this cavern.

'I'll go and see what's keeping Sorrel,' he said, when Firedrake had made himself comfortable in the cool cave. 'I'll leave the backpacks here.'

'See you later,' murmured Firedrake, already half asleep.

Ben unfolded the rat's map as well as he could, weighted it with small stones, and left it to dry in the sun. Then he ran back to join Sorrel as fast as possible. On the way he obliterated Firedrake's tracks. His own human footprints weren't likely to arouse much suspicion, but where he could he walked over the stones and remains of walls that rose out of the sand everywhere. The sun wasn't very high yet, but it was extremely bright as it blazed down from the sky. Wet with perspiration and breathless, Ben reached the dry riverbed. It was cooler here under the palms. He looked around.

Sorrel was nowhere to be seen. He raced down the slope, crossed the riverbed, and ran to the place on the beach where Firedrake had landed. But there was no sign of Sorrel there either, only the dragon's tracks. His huge paws had sunk deep into the sand, and the long mark left by his tail dragging behind him was clearly visible too. Why hadn't Sorrel finished getting rid of all those tracks?

Ben looked round anxiously. Where *was* Sorrel?

The camp was swarming with people now. Vehicles were driving in and out, and there were men digging in the hot sand among the ruins.

Ben went over to the spot where Firedrake's tracks appeared as if out of nowhere. Sorrel had clearly only got this far. Ben crouched down to look at the sand. It was all churned up as if a great many feet had been scuffling in it. He could hardly make out Sorrel's paw-prints among the tracks of all the human boots that had trampled around in the sand. His heart thudding, Ben straightened up again. There'd been a vehicle standing not far off, and the prints of the boots led to it. But Sorrel's paw-prints didn't show up again anywhere.

'They took her with them,' muttered Ben. 'Those horrible

people just took her away with them.'

The tyre tracks led straight to the camp. Ben set off for it at a run.

CHAPTER TWELVE

Captured

There was hardly anyone in or around the big tents when Ben slipped into the camp. Most of the people staying there were out in the ruins, freeing ancient walls from the sand in the morning heat and dreaming of secret burial chambers where mummies slept. Ben looked longingly past the tents to the place marked out by ropes where the excavation site lay. It must be thrilling to climb down the ruined stairways where the archaeologists were scraping desert sand off the steps.

The sound of excited voices brought Ben out of his dreams. Cautiously, he followed the noise, creeping along the narrow alleys between the tents, until he suddenly came to an open space. Men in long, billowing robes, and a few others wearing pith helmets, were crowding around something that stood in the middle of this space in the shade of a large date palm. Some of them were waving their arms about, others seemed to have been struck dumb. Ben thrust his way through the crowd until he could see what they were so excited about. Several cages, both large and small, stood under the palm tree. There were chickens in some of them, and another held an unhappy-looking monkey. But the largest cage contained Sorrel. She had turned her back on the gaping humans, but Ben recognised her at once.

The men around him were speaking a variety of different languages – Arabic, French, English, German – but Ben could pick up a phrase here and there that he understood.

'In my opinion it's a mutant monkey,' said a man with a big nose and a receding chin. 'No one can doubt it.'

'I do doubt it, though, Professor Rosenberg,' said a tall thin man standing not far from Ben.

Professor Rosenberg groaned and raised his eyes to heaven. 'Oh, please! Don't start on about those fabulous creatures of yours again, Greenbloom.'

But Professor Greenbloom only smiled. 'What you have there, my dear colleague,' he said quietly, 'is a brownie. A Spotted Forest Brownie, to be precise – which is distinctly surprising, since the species occurs chiefly in the highlands of Scotland.'

Ben looked at him in surprise. How could the man know that? Sorrel was obviously listening to the conversation too, for Ben saw her prick up her ears. However, Professor Rosenberg just shook his head pityingly.

'I don't know how you can keep making such a fool of yourself, Greenbloom!' he said. 'I mean, you're a scholar. A professor of archaeology, a doctor of history and ancient languages and I don't know what else besides. Yet you insist on putting forward these ridiculous theories!'

'In my view it's the rest of you who are making fools of yourselves,' replied Professor Greenbloom. 'A monkey! Oh, come on! Did you ever see a monkey like that?'

Sorrel turned to look angrily at the pair of them. 'Fly agarics!' she spat. 'Death-caps, yellow stainers, destroying angels!'

Professor Rosenberg retreated in alarm. 'Good heavens! What extraordinary sounds it's making!'

'It's calling you names, didn't you hear it?' Professor Greenbloom smiled. 'It's calling you mushroom names, and it seems to know a good deal about fungi! Fly agaric, death-cap, yellow stainer, destroying angel – those are all poisonous species that make you feel sick, and I expect we're making this brownie feel pretty sick ourselves. What terrible human presumption it is to catch other living creatures and hold them captive!'

Professor Rosenberg merely shook his head disapprovingly and moved his large paunch a little closer to the cages.

Ben tried to give Sorrel an inconspicuous signal, but she was far too busy muttering angrily to herself and rattling the bars of the cage to notice. She didn't even see him among all the tall grown-ups.

'And what kind of a creature would you say *this* is, my dear colleague?' asked Professor Rosenberg, pointing to a cage next to Sorrel's.

Ben stared in surprise. The cage contained a little manikin with his face buried in his hands. He had untidy carroty-red hair and very thin arms and legs, and he was wearing strange knee-breeches, a long, close-fitting jacket with a large collar, and tiny pointed boots.

'I expect you think it's another mutant,' said Professor Greenbloom.

His fat colleague shook his head. 'Ah, no, this must be a very complex little machine. We're trying our hardest to find out who lost it here in the camp. It was discovered among the tents this morning, wet through, with a raven pecking at its clothes. We haven't yet found out how to turn it off, so we put it in the cage there.'

Professor Greenbloom nodded, and looked thoughtfully down at the little man. Ben couldn't take his eyes off the strange creature either. Only Sorrel didn't seem interested in the manikin. She had turned her back on the humans again.

'You're right on one point, Rosenberg,' said Professor Greenbloom, coming a little closer to the tiny captive. 'What we have here is not, in fact, a natural creature like the brownie. No, this is an artificial being, although not, as you believe, a little machine, but a creature of flesh and blood made by human hands. The alchemists of the Middle Ages had great skill in the manufacturing of such creatures. Yes, no doubt about it.' He stepped slightly backwards again. 'This is a genuine homunculus.'

Ben saw the little man raise his head in alarm. His eyes were red, his face as white as chalk, and he had a long, pointed nose.

But Professor Rosenberg laughed, such a loud, booming laugh that the chickens flapped round their cages and the monkey began chattering in alarm. 'Greenbloom, you're priceless!' he cried. 'A homunculus! You know something? I'd like to hear what crazy explanation you have for those curious tracks down on the beach. Come along, let's take a look at them together, shall we?'

'Well, I was about to go back to that basilisk cave I found.' Professor Greenbloom cast the captives a final glance. 'I discovered some very interesting hieroglyphs there. But I can spare a few minutes. How about it, Rosenberg – will you set these two free if I tell you what creature made the tracks?'

Professor Rosenberg laughed again. 'You and your jokes! Since when do people set such valuable specimens free?'

'Since when, indeed?' murmured Professor Greenbloom. Then he turned, with a sigh, and went away with his fat colleague. He towered more than a head over him. Ben watched them go. If this man Greenbloom knew that Sorrel was a brownie he'd probably recognise the dragon tracks too. It was high time they got back to Firedrake.

Ben looked anxiously round. A few people were still lingering near the cages. He crouched down in the dust beside the tall palm tree and waited. It seemed an eternity before everyone went back to work again. When the open space was empty at last, Ben jumped up and hurried over to Sorrel's cage. He looked cautiously around once more. There was only a skinny cat prowling about. The little man had buried his face in his hands again.

'Sorrel!' hissed Ben. 'Sorrel, it's me.'

The brownie girl swung round in surprise. 'And about time too!' she spat. 'I thought you wouldn't come until these revolting stinkhorns had stuffed me and put me in a museum.'

'Okay, calm down,' said Ben, investigating the lock of the cage. 'I've been here for ages, but how could I do anything while they were standing around wondering whether or not you were a monkey?'

'One of them did know what I was,' hissed Sorrel through the bars. 'I don't like that at all!'

'Do you really come from Scotland?' asked Ben.

'Mind your own business.' Sorrel cast him an anxious glance. 'Well, can you get that thing open?'

Ben shrugged his shoulders. 'I'm not sure. It doesn't look easy.' He took his penknife out of his trouser pocket and stuck the point into the lock.

'Hurry up!' whispered Sorrel, looking around in alarm. Luckily there was still no one to be seen among the tents.

'Most of them are down on the beach looking at what you left of Firedrake's tracks,' murmured Ben. 'Oh, bother, this thing is impossible.'

'Excuse me, please!' someone suddenly said in a timid voice. 'If you get me out of here I might be able to help you.'

Ben and Sorrel turned round in surprise. The homunculus was standing close to the bars of his cage, smiling at them.

'As far as I can see, the lock on my prison here is an easy one to pick,' he said. 'They probably thought a simple lock would do because I'm so small.'

Ben glanced at the lock and nodded. 'You're right, this one will be a doddle.' He took his knife and was applying it to the lock when Sorrel grabbed his sleeve through the bars of her cage.

'Wait a moment, not so fast!' she hissed. 'We don't know what kind of thing this is.'

'Oh, nonsense.' Ben shook his head impatiently. With a

sudden jerk, he cracked the lock of the homunculus's cage, opened the tiny barred door and lifted the little man out.

'My most grateful thanks!' said the tiny creature, bowing low to the boy. 'Pick me up and hold me steady in front of the other lock, will you? I'll see what I can do for your bad-tempered brownie friend.'

Sorrel gave him a nasty look.

'What's your name?' asked Ben, curiously.

'Twigleg,' said the manikin, putting his spindly fingers into the lock of the cage and closing his eyes.

'Twigleg!' muttered Sorrel. 'Suits you.'

'Could you please keep quiet?' said Twigleg, without opening his eyes. 'I know brownies enjoy a good natter, but this isn't the right moment.'

Sorrel tightened her lips. Ben looked round. He could hear voices – some way off still, but coming closer.

'Quick, Twigleg!' he told the homunculus. 'There's someone coming!'

'Nearly done it,' replied Twigleg. The lock clicked. With a satisfied smile, the little man removed his fingers. Ben quickly put him on his shoulder and opened Sorrel's cage. Muttering crossly, she jumped down into the powdery sand.

'Twigleg,' said Ben, carrying the homunculus over to the sad monkey's cage, 'could you pick this lock too?'

'If you like,' said the homunculus, setting to work.

'What's he doing?' hissed Sorrel. 'Are you two crazy? We have to get away from here.'

The monkey chattered excitedly and retreated to the farthest corner of its cage.

'We can't leave the poor monkey here,' said Ben. There was another click. Ben opened the cage door, and the monkey ran rapidly away.

'Come on, for goodness' sake!' complained Sorrel.

But Ben stopped to open the chickens' cages as well. Luckily they were only bolted and not locked. Perched on Ben's shoulder, Twigleg watched the boy with surprise. The voices were coming closer and closer.

'Almost done!' said Ben, opening the last cage. A startled hen stretched her scrawny neck towards him.

'How do we get out of here?' asked Sorrel. 'Quick, which way should we go?'

Ben looked helplessly around. 'Oh no! I've forgotten which way I came,' he groaned. 'And these tents all look the same.'

'They'll be here soon!' Sorrel tugged at his sleeve. 'Where's the way out?'

Ben bit his lip. 'Never mind,' he said, 'the voices are coming from that direction, so we'll have to go the other way.'

Taking Sorrel's paw, he hauled her along after him. No sooner had they disappeared among the tents than a hue and cry broke out behind them.

Ben darted right, then left, but people were coming towards them from every direction, trying to catch the fugitives and barring their way. It was only thanks to the homunculus that Ben and Sorrel escaped. Twigleg had scrambled up on to Ben's head as quick as a scurrying insect, sat there like a sea captain on the bridge of his rolling ship, and steered them out of the camp with his shrill commands.

Not until they were a safe distance from the tents did they slow down, making their way through tangled thorn bushes and staying under cover. A few lizards scurried away in alarm when Sorrel and Ben finally dropped to the ground, panting. Twigleg climbed out of Ben's hair and sat down on the sand beside the boy, looking pleased with himself.

'Well done,' he said. 'You two are quick on your feet. I could never have kept up. But I have a quick brain. A person can't have everything.'

Sorrel sat up, breathing heavily, and looked down at the little man. 'And you're not the faintest bit conceited either, are you?' she said.

Twigleg just shrugged his narrow shoulders.

'Take no notice of her,' said Ben, peering through the branches. 'She means no harm.' There was no one in sight. Ben could scarcely believe they had managed to shake off their pursuers. For the time being, anyway. Relieved, he let himself drop back on to the sand.

'We'll take a breather here for a little while,' he said. 'Then we must get back to Firedrake. If he wakes up and finds we're not there he might go looking for us.'

'Firedrake?' Twigleg brushed the sand off his jacket. 'Who's that? A friend of yours?'

'None of your business, midget,' spat Sorrel, and she stood up. 'Thanks for the help, one good deed deserves another and all that, but our ways part here. Come on,' she said, pulling Ben to his feet. 'We've had enough of a rest.'

Twigleg bowed his head and sighed deeply. 'Right, you two go your own way!' he whispered. 'I understand entirely. I expect the vultures will eat me now. Yes, I expect that's what they'll do.'

Ben looked at him in consternation. 'But where do you come from?' he asked. 'Don't you have a home? I mean, you must have lived somewhere before they caught you.'

Twigleg nodded sadly. 'Oh, yes, but I don't want to go back there ever again. I had a master who made me work day in, day out, polishing his gold, doing handstands, telling stories till my head was in a whirl. That's why I ran away. But I have such terrible luck. No sooner had I escaped my master than a raven picked me up and carried me away. It dropped me from its claws last night in the storm – and where did it let me fall? Right above the camp we've just escaped from. Such terrible, awful luck. I always have rotten luck.'

'A very nice story too,' said Sorrel. 'Come on, time we were off.' She tugged at Ben's arm, but he stayed put.

'We can't just leave him here,' he said. 'All alone like this.'

'Oh yes, we can,' Sorrel whispered, 'because I don't believe a word of his touching tale. There's something wrong about this little titch. I mean, it's rather odd the way he turns up here at the same time as us. What's more, he's too friendly with ravens for my liking.'

'You were the one who said ravens were only suspect on their own,' Ben whispered back.

Twigleg pretended to take no notice of their whispering, but inched slowly closer to them.

'Oh, forget that!' whispered Sorrel. 'Okay, I often do talk dreadful nonsense.'

'Like now, for instance,' said Ben. 'You're forgetting how he helped us. We owe him.' Ben held his hand out to the homunculus. 'Come on,' he said. 'We'll take you part of the way with us. We're sure to find somewhere you'd like to stay, okay?'

Twigleg jumped up and made a deep bow. 'You have a kind heart, Your Honour!' he said. 'It is with the greatest gratitude that I accept your offer.'

'Oh, for heaven's sake!' groaned Sorrel. She turned angrily, and said not a word on the way back to the cavern.

As for Twigleg, he sat on Ben's shoulder dangling his legs.

CHAPTER THIRTEEN

The Basilisk

Firedrake wasn't bothered about anything. He was fast asleep. Outside the sun burned down, growing hotter and hotter, but it was cool in the cavern, and the dragon was dreaming of mountains, of dwarves climbing up his tail, and of the dirty canal flowing through the great human city.

Suddenly he raised his head. Something had roused him from sleep. A horrible stink rose to his nostrils, washing over him like the dirty water in his dream just now. Outside the mouth of the cave, the leaves of the thorn bush went limp and drooped.

The dragon sat up uneasily. He listened.

A hiss came out of a crevice in the darkest corner of the cavern. Feathers rustled, claws scraped over the stony ground. And suddenly the most monstrous creature Firedrake had ever seen emerged from the darkness.

It looked like a gigantic cockerel with yellow feathers and broad, spiky wings. The monster's staring eyes were blood-red, and it wore a circlet of pale spines like a crown on its horrible head. Its tail coiled like the scaly body of a snake and ended in a claw, which was snatching at invisible prey.

The monster stalked slowly towards Firedrake.

The dragon could scarcely breathe. The dreadful stench was making his head swim. He retreated until his tail became entangled in the thorny tendrils outside the cave.

'Aaargh, you woke me!' croaked this ghastly creature. 'A dragon! A fire-worm! Your sickly-sweet smell made its way into my darkest dreams and disturbed them. What are you doing here in my cavern?'

Firedrake wrenched his tail free of the thorns and took a step towards the monster. The stink surrounding it still made breathing difficult, but he was no longer frightened of the strange creature's horrible appearance.

'I didn't know this cavern was yours,' he replied. 'Forgive me, but if you don't mind I'd like to stay here until nightfall. I don't know where else to hide from human beings.'

'Human beings?' hissed the monster. It opened its curved beak and laughed. 'You took refuge from human beings in *my* cave? That's a good one! That's a really good one!'

Firedrake looked curiously at the ugly cockerel-headed creature. 'What are you?' he asked. 'I've never heard of anything like you before.'

With a shrill cackle, the monster spread its spiny wings. Dead beetles and spiders dropped out of its plumage. 'Don't you know my name?' it screeched. 'Don't you know my name, fire-worm? I am the worst nightmare in the world, and you have woken me from my sleep. You are the light, but I am the deepest darkness, and I shall swallow you up. The two of us cannot be in the same place, any more than night and day can ever exist together.'

Firedrake stood there as if rooted to the ground. He tried to move. He wanted to breathe dragon-fire and drive the horrible cockerel-headed creature back into the crevice in the rock from which it had crawled, but he simply could not move at all. The monster's eyes began to flash. The spines on its head quivered.

'Look at me, fire-worm!' whispered the yellow monster. 'Look – deep – into – my eyes.'

Firedrake wanted to turn away, but those red eyes held him spellbound. They were filling his head with a black fog that was smothering everything he knew.

Suddenly a sharp pain roused him from his daze. Someone had trodden on his tail – hard. Firedrake whipped round and saw a man standing in the cave entrance, a man as thin as a rake and wearing shorts. He was holding a large, round mirror high above his head.

Firedrake heard the monster behind him beat its wings.

'Move aside, dragon!' the man called. 'Quick! Move aside, and don't look at it if you value your life!'

'No, look at me, fire-worm!' screeched the cockerel-headed monster, lashing the rocks with its snaky tail. 'Look at me!'

But Firedrake looked at the man instead, stepped aside – and the monster saw its own reflection.

It uttered a shriek so terrible that the sound echoed in Firedrake's ears for days to come. Then it flapped its wings until the entire floor of the cavern was covered with poison-yellow feathers, puffed itself up so that the spines on its head touched the roof of the cavern . . . and burst into a thousand pieces.

Incredulously, Firedrake looked at the place where the monster had just been standing.

The man beside him, exhausted, lowered the mirror.

'My word, that was a close shave!' he sighed, propping the mirror against the cave wall.

Firedrake, still dazed, stood staring at the remains of the monster. Nothing was left of it but feathers and stinking dust.

The man cleared his throat, and cautiously approached the dragon. 'May I introduce myself?' He bowed slightly. 'Barnabas Greenbloom, Professor of Archaeology, special subject Fantastic Phenomena of every kind. It's an honour to make your acquaintance.'

Firedrake nodded. He still felt numb.

'May I ask you,' Barnabas Greenbloom continued, 'to breathe a little dragon-fire over the remains of that terrible creature? It's the only way we can prevent the cave from being contaminated for hundreds of years. What's more,' he added, holding his large nose, 'it would get rid of this disgusting smell.'

Firedrake was still staring at the man in some amazement, but he did as he was asked. When he breathed blue fire on the monster's remains they crumbled into a fine silver dust that filled the whole cavern with glittering light.

'Ah!' cried the professor. 'Doesn't that look wonderful? Yet again we see that beauty can arise from the worst of horrors, wouldn't you agree?'

Firedrake nodded. 'What sort of creature was it?' he asked.

'That,' said Barnabas Greenbloom, sitting down on a rock and mopping his brow, 'that, my friend, was a basilisk. A fabulous creature like yourself, but one of the more sinister kind.'

'A basilisk?' The dragon shook his head. 'I've never heard of such a thing.'

'Fortunately such monsters are very, very rare,' explained the professor. 'The mere sound of their voices or one glance from their terrible eyes is usually enough to kill. In your place any mortal would be dead now, but even a basilisk can't destroy a dragon so easily.'

'You destroyed it, though,' said Firedrake. 'With nothing more than a mirror.'

'Oh yes, indeed,' replied Barnabas Greenbloom with an embarrassed smile, and ran a hand through his untidy grey hair. 'There was no great skill in that, you know. A basilisk can't survive the sight of its own reflection. As a matter of fact I've never had a chance to try the theory out in real life until today, but that's what all the books say, and books do sometimes get it right.'

The dragon looked at him thoughtfully. 'I rather think you saved my life,' he said. 'How can I thank you?'

'Don't mention it!' The professor smiled at Firedrake. 'It was an honour. Indeed, an extraordinary honour, I do assure you!' He was looking at the dragon with awe and admiration. 'I could never even have dared to dream of meeting a dragon in my short human life span, you know. This is a very, very happy day for me.' Much moved, the professor rubbed his nose.

'You know a lot about what human beings call fabulous creatures, don't you?' said Firedrake curiously, bending his neck down to Barnabas Greenbloom. 'Most people don't even know that we exist.'

'I've been doing research into the subject for over thirty years,' replied the professor. 'At the age of ten I was fortunate enough to find a woodland fairy caught up in the netting over a fruit tree in our garden. Since then, of course, no one has been able to convince me that fairies exist only in fairy tales. So why, I thought at the time, why shouldn't all the other fabulous creatures exist too? In the end, I made it part of my professional career to seek them out – all the creatures described in the old tales, the most ancient stories of all. I've discussed rare minerals with dwarves, the flavour of tree bark with trolls, immortality with fairies, and enchantment with a fiery salamander. You, however, are the first dragon I've ever met. I was almost sure your species had died out.'

'And what brought you here?' asked Firedrake.

'My search for the winged horse, Pegasus,' replied the professor. 'But instead I found this cavern. The hieroglyphs carved in the rock around its entrance give clear warning of a basilisk. The ancient Egyptians knew about those monsters, you see. They thought the basilisk hatched from a poisoned ibis egg. However, another theory claims that a basilisk is born when a five-year-old cockerel lays an egg, which fortunately doesn't happen very often. Anyway, that's why I'd hidden the mirror outside, but to be honest with you I'd never ventured inside the cave before today.'

Thinking of the basilisk's red eyes, Firedrake could understand the professor's caution only too well.

'You woke it,' said Barnabas Greenbloom. 'Did you realise that?'

'I did?' Firedrake shook his head sceptically. 'That's what the monster said too, but I was only sleeping here. How could I have woken it?'

'Simply by being in the cave,' replied the professor. 'In the course of my research I've discovered a very interesting fact: one fabulous creature attracts another. They sense each other's presence. Sometimes their scalps prickle, sometimes their scales itch. Haven't you ever felt anything like that?'

Firedrake shook his head. 'My scales often itch,' he replied, 'but I never thought anything of it.'

The professor nodded, thoughtfully. 'I assume that the basilisk picked up your scent.'

'It did say I had disturbed its dark dreams,' murmured Firedrake. He shuddered, still feeling sick from the smell given off by the monster.

Professor Greenbloom cleared his throat. 'I do have another request,' he said. 'You see, we humans don't seem able to believe that something is real until we've touched it. So may I stroke your scales?'

Firedrake stretched his long neck out towards the professor. Barnabas Greenbloom reverently passed his hand over the dragon's scales.

'Wonderful!' he whispered. 'Absolutely wonderful! Er . . . by the way, about your tail. I'm really sorry I trod on it. I just didn't know how else to get you to look away from the basilisk.'

Firedrake smiled, and waved his spiny tail back and forth. 'Don't mention it. All it needs is a little of Sorrel's brownie spit—' The dragon stopped short and looked round him. 'But they're not here yet.' Anxiously, he went to the mouth of the cave. 'Where can they be?'

Behind him, the professor cleared his throat again. 'Has your brownie gone missing?'

Surprised, Firedrake turned round. 'Yes, it looks like it.'

Barnabas Greenbloom sighed. 'Just as I feared,' he said. 'They're holding a forest brownie prisoner over in the camp.'

Firedrake lashed his tail so violently that he almost knocked the professor over. 'Sorrel?' he cried. 'They've caught her?' Feeling quite dizzy with rage, he bared his teeth. 'Where is she? I must help her.'

'No, not you,' said Barnabas Greenbloom quickly. 'You'd be in too much danger yourself. I'll get her out. I've been planning to open those cages for some time anyway.' With a determined expression, he tucked the mirror under his arm and strode towards the mouth of the cave. 'I'll be back soon,' he said, 'with your friend Sorrel.'

'Don't bother, she's already here,' a voice grunted from the thorn bushes outside the cave, and Sorrel pushed her way through the dry branches. Ben followed, with Twigleg on his shoulder. They all looked rather the worse for wear, scratched by the thorns, dusty and sweaty. Firedrake went over to them, gave Twigleg a brief and puzzled glance, and then anxiously sniffed Ben and Sorrel all over.

'They caught you?' he asked the brownie.

'Yes, but Ben got me out. Along with that manikin there.' Sorrel looked the professor up and down suspiciously, from his head to his dusty boots. 'And what, in the name of all ferocious fungi, is this human doing here?'

'Your young companion is a human being too, as far as I can see!' Barnabas Greenbloom pointed out, with the hint of a smile.

'He doesn't count,' spat Sorrel, crossly putting her paws on her hips. 'He's a friend. But what about you? Think carefully before you answer, because I'm not feeling too well disposed to humans just now. In fact, I'm feeling very ill-disposed to them – sickeningly, tooth-achingly, green-around-the-gills ill-disposed, if you take my meaning.'

Barnabas Greenbloom smiled. 'I do take your meaning,' he replied. 'The fact is, I—'

'Just a moment,' said Sorrel, taking a wary step towards the professor. 'Didn't I see you back there by the cages?'

'Stop it, Sorrel!' Firedrake interrupted her. 'He saved my life.'

That stopped Sorrel short. Incredulously, she looked first at Firedrake, then at Barnabas Greenbloom. 'Him?' she asked. 'How could he have done that?'

At this moment Twigleg bent down from Ben's shoulder, his pointy nose twitching, and then suddenly raised his head in alarm.

'There's been a basilisk in here!' he whispered, looking

horrified. 'Oh, merciful heavens!'

They all turned to look at the little man in surprise.

'Who's that?' asked Firedrake.

'Oh, him!' Sorrel made a dismissive gesture. 'He's a himin-colossus or something. We picked him up in the human camp and now he's sticking to Ben like a burr.'

Seated on Ben's shoulder, Twigleg put his tongue out at her.

'A homunculus, my dear brownie, he's a homunculus,' said Barnabas Greenbloom. He went over to Ben and carefully shook Twigleg's tiny hand. 'Delighted to meet you. This really is a day full of the most extraordinary encounters.'

The manikin smiled, flattered.

'My name is Twigleg,' he said, bowing to the professor. But when Firedrake stretched his neck to look over Barnabas Greenbloom's shoulder, Twigleg lowered his head in embarrassment.

'*What* was here?' asked Sorrel impatiently. 'What did the little titch say? A basiltwist?'

'Sssh!' Twigleg put a finger to his lips. 'A ba-si-lisk!' he breathed. 'You don't want to speak its name too loud, furry-face.'

Sorrel wrinkled her nose. 'Why not?'

'A basilisk,' whispered Twigleg, 'is the darkest nightmare on earth, a black terror that lurks down wells and in crevices until someone wakes it. It kills brownies like you with a single peck from its hooked beak.'

Ben looked round uneasily. 'You mean one of those things was here?' he asked.

'Yes, one of those things was here,' sighed Professor Greenbloom. 'Fortunately, I was here to help your friend the dragon. But now it's time I showed my face back in the camp, before they decide to send out a search party for me. Oh, and when are you planning to leave again?' he asked when he had reached the entrance of the cave. 'Or are you going to stay here?'

'Stay here? Not likely!' replied Sorrel. 'No, we'll be flying on as soon as the sun has set.'

'Then I'll look in again just before nightfall, if that's all right,' suggested the professor. 'I'm sure you could do with some provisions for the journey, and I have a few more questions to ask.'

'We'll be glad to see you,' said Firedrake, nuzzling Sorrel's back.

'Yes, that's right, we'll be glad to,' she muttered impatiently. 'Okay, can I finally tell the rest of you about my adventure now? Or isn't anyone here even interested to hear how I nearly got stuffed and put on show in a museum?'

CHAPTER FOURTEEN

Professor Greenbloom Explains

The sunset sky was already turning red when Barnabas Greenbloom came back with a big basket in one hand and a large, battered saucepan in the other.

'I thought I'd make us some supper before we part,' he said. 'I'm not as good a cook as my wife, but she's taught me a few things. It's a pity she isn't here to meet you. Forest brownies are one of her special interests.'

'You have a wife, then?' asked Ben, interested. 'And children too?'

'Yes,' replied the professor. 'One daughter, Guinevere. She'd be about your own age. At the moment I'm afraid it's her school term-time, so she can't be here, but the three of us often go on field trips together. My dear dragon,' he added, throwing a handful of dry leaves on the floor of the cave, 'would you be so kind as to let us have a little of your blue fire?'

Firedrake breathed a small tongue of flame at the leaves, which immediately caught light. As the fire flickered up, the professor put a few stones round it and stood his saucepan on them.

'I've made some soup,' he said. 'Chickpea soup with fresh mint, a favourite recipe in these parts. I thought a brownie, a boy and a skinny homunculus could do with a hot meal before setting out again. As for dragons, they live entirely on moonlight, unless I've been misinformed.'

'That's right.' Firedrake nodded, laid his muzzle on his paws and looked into the fire. 'Moonlight is all we need. Our strength waxes and wanes with the moon itself. On nights when the moon is new I'm often too tired to leave my cave.'

'I hope that isn't going to be a problem on your journey,' said the professor, stirring the pan.

Sorrel crouched beside the fire, sniffing hopefully. 'If that's not ready soon,' she muttered, her stomach grumbling, 'I'll have to try one of those prickly plants over there.'

'I wouldn't do that if I were you,' said Barnabas. 'Sandmen often live in cacti, and you don't want to fool around with sandmen. Anyway,' he added, tasting a spoonful of soup, 'this is nearly ready. I think you'll like it. I know a good deal about the tastes of brownies from my wife.' He turned to Ben. 'And do you have a family yourself? Apart from Sorrel and Firedrake, I mean.'

Ben shook his head. 'No,' he mumbled.

The professor looked at him thoughtfully for some time. 'Well, there could be worse company than a dragon and a brownie girl, wouldn't you agree?' he said at last. Searching his basket, he took out three small bowls, three soup spoons, and a tiny sugar spoon for Twigleg. 'But if you do ever happen to feel you'd like human company, I . . . er,' said the professor, rubbing his nose in some embarrassment. 'Listen, I don't even know your name.'

The boy smiled. 'Ben,' he replied. 'My name's Ben.'

'Well then, Ben,' said the professor, filling a bowl with soup and handing it to Sorrel, who was already licking her lips impatiently, 'if you ever fancy you'd like some human company you must visit me and my family.' He took a crumpled and rather dusty visiting card out of his trouser pocket and gave it to Ben. 'There, that's our address. We could have some interesting conversations about brownies and dragons. Your friends might even care to come too. I'm sure you'd like my daughter. She knows a lot about fairies – much more than I do.'

'Th-thanks,' stammered Ben. 'That's really very kind of you.'

'Kind? Not in the least.' The professor gave him a bowl of hot soup. 'What's so kind about it?' He handed Twigleg the tiny spoon. 'Could you share Ben's bowl? I'm afraid I only brought three.'

The homunculus nodded and perched on Ben's arm. Barnabas Greenbloom turned back to the boy.

'On the contrary, Ben, it would be kind of *you* to accept my invitation. You're a nice lad, and I'm sure you'll have some fascinating tales to tell after this journey. Now I come to think of it, I'd call it rather selfish of me to invite you.'

'We'll bring him over as soon as we're back,' said Sorrel, smacking her lips. 'That way we'll be rid of him for a bit. By chanterelles and champignons, this soup tastes good!'

'Really?' Pleased, the professor smiled. 'Well, if a brownie girl says so, it must be true. Wait a moment, you need some of these fresh mint leaves to sprinkle on it. Here you are.'

'Mint! Mmm!' Sorrel rolled her eyes. 'We ought to take you along to cook for us, Professor!'

'Oh, I'd love to come!' sighed the professor. 'But, unfortunately, I get vertigo even at moderate heights, let alone when I fly. And I'm meeting my family soon. We're travelling by ship in search of the winged horse, Pegasus. None the less, I feel deeply honoured by your offer.' He made a small bow, and then helped himself to a bowl of his delicious soup.

'Firedrake told us you think it was his presence that attracted the basilisk,' said Ben. 'Is that right?'

'I'm afraid so, yes.' Professor Greenbloom gave Ben a second helping of soup and a piece of pitta bread. 'I am firmly convinced that one fabulous being attracts another. In my view, the reason Firedrake hasn't noticed the usual signs before is that he always *is* in the company of a fabulous creature – meaning you, my dear Sorrel. But most fabulous creatures start to itch as soon as they come near each other, and curiosity would attract many of them your way.'

'A nice prospect, I must say!' muttered Sorrel. She gave the steaming pan a dark glance. 'Those mountain dwarves weren't so bad, but judging by all I've heard about that basiltwist . . .' She shook her head, gloomily. 'Dear me, what next, I wonder?'

Barnabas Greenbloom's glasses had misted up with the steam from his soup. He took them off his big nose and cleaned them. 'The fact is, there aren't so many fabulous creatures left on this planet. Most of them became extinct centuries ago. Unfortunately, the less friendly specimens have proved best at surviving. So you'd better be ready for anything if you have a journey of any length ahead of you.'

'Professor?' Ben swallowed the last of his soup and put the bowl down in the silver basilisk dust that still covered the cave floor. 'Have you ever heard of the Rim of Heaven?'

Sorrel nudged Ben sharply in the ribs. Firedrake raised his head. Twigleg pricked up his ears.

'Oh yes,' said the professor, wiping out his soup bowl with a piece of pitta bread. 'The Rim of Heaven is a legendary mountain range, said to contain the valley from which dragons first came. But I don't know much more about it.'

'What else *do* you know?' asked Firedrake.

'Well,' said Barnabas Greenbloom, frowning, 'the Rim of Heaven is thought to be in the Himalayas. A defensive ring of nine white peaks, almost all the same height, surround a fabulous valley. My wife, Vita, and I were going to look for it a few years ago, but then we found unicorn tracks. Well . . .' He shook his head. 'Around the same time, a colleague of mine, the famous Zubeida Ghalib, did go looking for the Rim, but unfortunately she didn't find it. However, she knows more about dragons than anyone else in the world.' The professor looked at Firedrake. 'Perhaps you ought to visit her. She's in Pakistan at the moment, and if you're going to the Himalayas that's on your way.'

'Hm.' Sorrel looked hopefully at the steaming pan, and Barnabas Greenbloom made haste to fill her bowl again. 'Firedrake knows all about dragons anyway. I mean, he's a dragon himself.'

The professor smiled. 'Undoubtedly. But Firedrake can't fly unless the moon is shining, am I right?'

Sorrel wrinkled her nose. 'No dragon can.'

'Yes, but was that always the case?' the professor asked. 'Zubeida wrote to me recently to say she'd found something that she thought could replace the power of the moon, at least for a limited period. As for exactly what it is, she was very cagey about that. And of course she can't prove it will work, because she doesn't know any dragons to try it out for her.'

Firedrake, who had been staring thoughtfully at the silver dust left by the basilisk, raised his head.

'That's interesting,' he said. 'Ever since we set off I've been wondering what will happen if we reach the high mountains at the dark time of the moon, before the new moon rises.'

'Well, as I was saying,' repeated the professor, shrugging his shoulders, 'Zubeida is on the track of something, but she didn't want to tell me the details yet. At the moment she's living in a village on the coast of the Arabian Sea, near the estuary of the river Indus. Besides researching into moonlight, she's studying the strange story of an incident said to have taken place near this village over a hundred and fifty years ago.'

'Is the story about dragons?' asked Ben.

'Yes, indeed.' The professor smiled. 'What else? Zubeida is a dracologist – that's a dragon specialist. I believe the story concerns whole flocks of dragons.'

'*Flocks* of dragons?' repeated Firedrake, hardly able to believe his ears.

'That's right.' Barnabas Greenbloom nodded. 'Several of the villagers claim that their grandparents used to see flocks of dragons appearing off the coast every night when the moon was full, flying down from the mountains to swim in the sea. Then something strange happened.' The professor frowned. 'One night, about a century and a half ago, a monster emerged from the sea and attacked the dragons while they were swimming. The creature can only have been a sea serpent. The odd thing is that sea serpents and dragons are distantly related, and I've never heard of a single other case of their fighting each other. However, this sea monster *did* attack the dragons, and after that they disappeared. Zubeida suspects they went back to the Rim of Heaven and never left their hiding place again.'

Firedrake raised his head. 'Taking flight, hiding, being hunted – that's what all dragon stories seem to be about,' he said. 'Aren't there any other stories? Happier ones?'

'Yes, indeed there are!' cried the professor. 'In fact, where

you're going the dragon is regarded as a sacred creature, a bringer of good fortune. But I'm not sure what people would say if a real dragon turned up,' he added, shaking his head. 'You'd better be careful.'

The dragon nodded.

'And we'd better beware of sea serpents too,' said Sorrel gloomily.

'Oh, that was all long ago,' the professor assured her. 'And there's only the one story about it.'

'It wasn't a sea serpent anyway,' muttered Twigleg, and immediately clapped his hand to his mouth in alarm.

Ben turned to him in surprise. 'What was that you just said?'

'Oh...er...nothing!' stammered Twigleg. 'I only said...er ...there can't be any such things as sea serpents these days. Yes, that's what I said.'

'I wouldn't be so sure of that,' said Barnabas Greenbloom thoughtfully. 'But if the story interests you, then you really ought to stop off in Pakistan and visit Zubeida. She might even help you to fly without the power of moonlight, who knows?'

'That's not a bad idea!' Ben put Twigleg down on the ground,

jumped up and went over to the rock where he had spread out Gilbert Greytail's map. It was perfectly dry now, and rustled as Ben unfolded it in front of the professor.

'Can you show me the fishing village where your dracologist friend is at the moment?' he asked.

Barnabas Greenbloom bent over the map in amazement. 'Young man, this is remarkable,' he said. 'A true masterpiece of cartography, I'd call it. Where did you get it?'

'From a rat,' replied Sorrel. 'Not that it's been all that much use to us so far.'

'A rat! Well, well . . .' murmured the professor, examining Gilbert Greytail's masterpiece more closely. 'I wouldn't mind having that rat make a map for me. These areas of yellow shading, for instance, are very interesting. I know some of them. What does the yellow mean? Ah,' he said, reading the key to the colours. 'Yes, I see. Yellow means bad luck, danger. Yes, indeed, I can confirm that. And here, do you see?' He placed a finger on the map. 'This is where we are now. All yellow. Your map should have warned you about this cave.'

'Well, we weren't really supposed to land here at all, you see,'

Ben explained. 'Last night's storm drove us westward and off our course. See that?' He pointed to the golden line that Gilbert Greytail had drawn. 'This is the route we were meant to take. I don't suppose it passes near your friend's village, does it?'

Barnabas Greenbloom shook his head thoughtfully. 'No, but stopping off there wouldn't take you too far out of your way. You'd just have to set a course a few hundred kilometres further south, which wouldn't make much difference to the vast distances you still have to go. Although,' added the professor, frowning, 'as I was saying earlier, Zubeida won't be able to help you in your search for the Rim of Heaven. She's already tried to find it herself, and she got nowhere. No, as for that quest of yours,' said Barnabas Greenbloom, shaking his head, 'I doubt if anyone can help you. The location of the Rim of Heaven is one of the world's great mysteries.'

'We'll just have to look everywhere, then,' said Ben, folding up the map again. 'Even if we have to fly all over the Himalayas.'

'The Himalayas are vast, my boy,' said Barnabas Greenbloom. 'Unimaginably vast.'

He ran his fingers through his grey hair, and then drew some hieroglyphs in the dust with a little stick. One of them looked like a narrow eye.

'What do those signs mean?' asked Ben curiously.

'These? Ah, well . . .' The professor suddenly straightened up and looked at the dragon.

Firedrake returned his gaze in surprise.

'What is it?' asked Ben.

'The djinn!' cried the professor. 'The djinn with the thousand eyes!'

'A thousand eyes?' murmured Sorrel, licking her bowl clean. 'I don't even know anyone with *three* eyes.'

'Listen!' The professor leaned forward in excitement. 'So far the fact that you attract other fabulous creatures has done you more harm than good, right? Or, at least, you haven't reaped any benefits from it?'

The dragon shook his head.

'But suppose,' continued the professor, 'suppose you were to attract a fabulous being who *could* help you in your quest?'

'Meaning this djinn?' asked Ben. 'The kind that comes out of a bottle?'

The professor laughed. 'Asif is unlikely to let anyone put him in a bottle, my boy. He's a rather important djinn. They say he can be as large as the moon or as small as a grain of sand. His skin is blue as the evening sky, and covered with a thousand eyes that reflect a thousand parts of the world. And every time Asif blinks, a thousand different places appear in the pupils of those eyes.'

'Doesn't sound like someone I'd fancy meeting,' growled Sorrel. 'Why would we want to attract his attention?'

The professor lowered his voice. 'Because this djinn knows the answer to every question in the world.'

'*Every* question?' asked Ben, sceptically.

Barnabas Greenbloom nodded. 'Why not fly to see him? Ask him where the Rim of Heaven lies.'

The three companions looked at each other. Twigleg shifted uneasily on Ben's shoulder.

'Where can we find him?' asked Firedrake.

'The way there will take you off your direct route, but I think it could be worth it.' The professor unfolded another section of Gilbert Greytail's map. 'Here. You must go to the very end of the Arabian peninsula,' he said, putting his finger on the map. 'If you follow the coastal road south along the Red Sea, until it turns east here,' he added, pointing, 'then sooner or later you'll come to a gorge called the Wadi Juma'ah. It's so steep and narrow that sunlight reaches the bottom of the ravine for only four hours a day. All the same, huge palm trees grow down there, and a river flows between the rocky walls, even when water has long since evaporated in the hot sun everywhere else in the region. That is the home of Asif, the djinn with the thousand eyes.'

'Have you ever seen him?' asked Ben.

Barnabas Greenbloom shook his head, smiling. 'No, he'd never show himself to me. I'm not nearly interesting enough. But a dragon,' he said, looking at Firedrake, 'a dragon would be a different matter. Firedrake must lure Asif to come out and show himself, and then you must ask the question, Ben.'

'Me?' asked Ben, surprised.

The professor nodded. 'Yes, you. Asif answers questions only if three conditions are met. First: a human being has to ask the question. Second: the djinn must never have been asked that question before. If Asif *has* had the same question put to him before, then the questioner must serve the djinn for the rest of his life.' Ben and Firedrake exchanged glances of alarm. 'And third,' the professor continued, 'the question must be asked in exactly seven words, no more and no less.'

'Then it's no!' Sorrel jumped up, scratching her furry coat. 'No, no, and no again! This doesn't sound good, not good in the least. My own coat itches at the mere idea of meeting this thousand-eyed djinn. I think we'd do better to follow the route that conceited rat recommended.'

Firedrake and Ben said nothing.

'Your rat, yes,' remarked the professor, collecting his bowls and cooking utensils and stowing them in his basket. 'He knew about the djinn too. He shaded in the Wadi Juma'ah gorge with yellow as bright as a quince. I tell you what,' he said, in the silence that followed. 'Sorrel is probably right. Forget the djinn. He's too dangerous.'

Firedrake still remained silent.

'Oh, come on, let's go and see him,' said Ben. 'I'm not afraid. And I'm the one who'll be doing the asking, right?'

He knelt down again beside Barnabas Greenbloom and pored over the map. 'Show me exactly where the ravine is, will you, Professor?'

Barnabas Greenbloom glanced enquiringly first at the boy, then at Firedrake and Sorrel. The brownie girl merely shrugged her shoulders.

'He's right. He'll be doing the asking, after all,' she said. 'And if this djinn really does know the answer then we'll save ourselves no end of time.'

The dragon stood there saying nothing, just flicking his tail uneasily back and forth.

'Oh, come on, Firedrake!' said Ben. 'Don't look like that.'

The dragon sighed. 'Why can't I ask the question myself?' he said fiercely.

'I know what!' cried Sorrel, jumping up. 'We'll get the homunculkiss to ask it. He's a bit small, but otherwise he looks like a human being. This djinn with his thousand eyes must be terribly confused by all the things he sees with them. He's sure to think Twigleg's a real human being. And if anything goes wrong with the question and answer bit, then Twigleg will have a new master and we'll be rid of him.'

'Stop it, Sorrel!' Ben looked round for Twigleg – and found that he had disappeared. 'Where is he?' he asked, sounding worried. 'He was here only a moment ago.' Angrily, he turned to Sorrel. 'He ran away because you keep winding him up!'

'Nonsense!' the brownie girl snapped back. 'That spindly

creature is afraid of the blue-skinned djinn with the thousand eyes, that's why he made off. Well, all I can say is good riddance!'

'You're so mean!' Ben shouted at her. He jumped up, ran to the mouth of the cave and looked out. 'Twigleg!' he called. 'Twigleg, where are you?'

Barnabas Greenbloom laid a hand on his shoulder. 'Perhaps Sorrel is right after all, and the prospect of your journey was too much for the little fellow,' he said. Then he looked up at the sky. 'It's getting dark, dear friends,' he pointed out. 'If you really want to ask the djinn your question, you should set off soon. The way to his ravine leads mainly over desert country, which means hot days and cold nights.' He picked up his basket and smiled at Ben again. 'You're a brave boy, Ben. I'll just hurry down to the camp and get you some provisions for the journey. And a bottle of sun lotion for you, Ben, and an Arab headcloth wouldn't be a bad idea. Don't worry about the homunculus. Such creatures have wills of their own. Who knows, perhaps he simply feels drawn back to the man who made him.'

Then he pushed aside the tangle of thorns at the entrance of the cave and strode off through the evening twilight.

Sorrel went over to Ben and looked round. 'All the same, I wish I knew where that manikin was,' she muttered.

Outside, a raven cawed among the palms.

CHAPTER FIFTEEN

Twigleg's Second Report

Twigleg was hurrying away through the twilight. The sun was sinking red beyond the ruins, and the columns cast long shadows across the sand. The stone faces carved on the old walls looked even eerier at nightfall than by day, but the homunculus took no notice of them. He was used to ferocious stone heads grinning down at him in his master's castle. Just now he had other concerns on his mind.

'Where, for heaven's sake,' he muttered as the hot sand scorched his feet, 'am I supposed to find water around here? There's nothing but ground baked as hard as my master's scales. The sun's sucked up every last drop. Oh dear, he's going to be really furious with me for reporting back so late. Really, truly furious.'

The homunculus ran faster and faster. He hurried into ruined temples, investigated palm groves – and finally found himself sitting in the dry riverbed entirely at a loss. 'And that wretched raven's gone and disappeared too,' he wailed. 'What am I going to do? Oh, whatever am I going to do?'

As the sun sank behind the scorched brown hills, black shadows reached out to Twigleg. Suddenly he clapped his hand to his forehead.

'The sea!' he cried. 'What a fool I am. The sea!'

He jumped up so quickly that he fell over his own feet. Nimble as a squirrel, he raced along the dry riverbed, tumbled and slid down the dunes by the shore, and landed on the fine sand of the beach. The salty waves of the sea lapped the shoreline and the sound of their breakers filled his ears. Surf sprayed in his face. Twigleg clambered up on a rock with the waves washing around it, and spat into the dark water. Slowly, distorted by the movement of the waves, his master's image appeared. It grew larger and larger, spreading over the vast surface of the sea.

'Where've you been all this time?' Nettlebrand roared. He was shaking so violently with fury that the dwarf Gravelbeard kept staggering to and fro on his back.

'I couldn't help it!' cried Twigleg, wringing his hands. 'We got caught in a storm, and then the raven left me in the lurch, and human beings caught me, and . . . and . . .' – his voice broke – 'and . . . then the boy freed me and took me with him, and I couldn't slip away at first, and then I couldn't find any water, and then—'

'And then, and then, and then!' snarled Nettlebrand. 'Stop boring me with your useless twaddle! What have you found out?'

'They're looking for the Rim of Heaven,' said Twigleg.

'Aaaarrgh!' spat Nettlebrand. 'I already knew that, you fool! Did the raven eat what little brain you've got before he flew away? What else?'

Twigleg mopped his damp brow. He was already drenched

with sea-spray. 'What else? Oh, no end of things, but you're getting me all confused, master. I've been under a lot of strain, you know.'

Nettlebrand gave an impatient grunt. 'Carry on cleaning!' he growled at the dwarf, who had just settled down between the spines of his crest hoping for a little nap.

'Well,' said Twigleg, 'there was this other human being who told them a very strange story. All about dragons being attacked by a monster coming up out of the sea. Was that you, master?'

'I don't remember,' growled Nettlebrand, closing his eyes for a moment. 'And I don't want to remember, understand, spider-legs? They got away from me back then. They got away even though I almost had them in my jaws. Forget that story. Never mention it again or I'll eat you up too, the way I ate your eleven brothers.'

'I've forgotten it already,' said Twigleg hastily. 'Completely forgotten it. There's a black hole in my memory, nothing but a black hole, master. Oh, there are so many black holes like that in my head.'

'Shut up!' Nettlebrand furiously slammed his paw down on the cracked flagstones of his castle floor. His image on the shining water grew to such an enormous size that Twigleg ducked his head in terror. The manikin's knees were knocking, and his heart was thumping up and down like a rabbit on the run.

'Well,' said Nettlebrand, in a dangerously soft voice, 'what else did you find out about the Rim of Heaven? *Where* are they going to look for it?'

'Oh, they don't know yet. They're planning to visit a woman who's an expert on dragons and lives on the coast – the coast that I'm not to remind you of. Although she doesn't know where the Rim of Heaven is either, and that's why . . .'

'That's why *what*?' bellowed Nettlebrand.

'That's why they're going to ask a djinn,' Twigleg gabbled. 'A blue djinn with a thousand eyes. Apparently he knows the answer to any question, but he has to be asked by a human being, so the boy will have to do it.'

The homunculus fell silent. To his great surprise, he realised that he was feeling anxious about the human boy. It was a strange, unaccustomed sensation, and Twigleg couldn't understand how it had crept into his heart.

'Aha!' growled Nettlebrand. 'Wonderful! We'll let the little human do the asking for us. How very useful!' He stretched his hideous mouth into a nasty grin. 'So when do we get the answer, spider-legs?'

'Oh, it's probably going to take us a few days to reach the djinn,' Twigleg faltered. 'You'll have to be patient a little longer, master.'

'Huh!' grunted Nettlebrand. 'Patient! Patient! My patience has run out. I want to go hunting properly again. I'm sick of cows and sheep. Follow the boy and his friends and report back whenever you can, do you hear? I want to know exactly where this dragon is. Have you got that?'

'I've got it, master!' murmured Twigleg, pushing the wet hair back from his forehead.

Nettlebrand's image on the sea began to fade.

'Wait!' cried Twigleg. 'Wait a moment, master. *How* am I going to follow them? The raven's made off!'

'Oh, you'll think of something.' Nettlebrand's voice sounded a long way off as his image became more and more blurred. 'You're a clever little fellow.'

All was quiet now except for the roaring of the sea. Twigleg looked at the dark waves unhappily. Then, sighing, he jumped down from the rock, landed on the damp sand and laboriously climbed back up the cliffs. When he finally reached the top, gasping for breath, he saw Firedrake coming along the dry riverbed towards him with Ben, Sorrel and the professor.

The manikin quickly ducked behind a tussock of grass. Now what? What should he say when they asked where he'd been? That brownie girl would definitely ask. Oh, why hadn't they stayed in the cavern just a little longer? Then he could have slipped back, quiet as a mouse, and no one would even have noticed that he'd been away.

Scarcely three human paces from Twigleg's hiding place, the four of them stopped.

'Well, friends,' said the professor, 'here are the provisions I promised you.' He handed Ben a full, bulging bag. 'I'm afraid I didn't have very much left myself, but I'll admit to borrowing a little dried fruit from my colleagues' tents. There's sun cream in there too. You should make sure you keep using it, Ben. And here,' he added, winding a pale cloth round the boy's head, 'this is what they wear in this country to protect themselves from the sun. It's called a keffiyeh, and it ought to keep you from getting sunstroke, as we pale-skinned folk do only too quickly in these parts. As for you two,' he added, turning to Sorrel and the dragon, 'your scales and fur are probably adequate protection. Now, about the route again . . .'

He switched on a torch, and he and Ben bent over the map together. 'From what you tell me of Firedrake's powers of flight, the journey will probably take you about four days. First, as I told you earlier, you must keep flying south. Fortunately you'll be travelling only by night, and by day you must choose the shadiest places you can find to rest in, for the heat will be fierce. There are any number of ruins along your way – tumbledown fortresses and sunken cities. Most of them were buried in the drifting desert sand long ago, but you'll always find somewhere to provide shelter, even for a dragon. Since you'll always be flying along the coast,' he ran his finger down the coastline, 'you'll have a reliable guide even in the dark. And you should be able to see the coastal road clearly with the moon shining as brightly as it is now. The road goes on and on south. On the fourth night of your journey the land will become more mountainous. Cities cling to the rocks there like the nests of giant birds. Then, around midnight, you should reach a place where the road forks, and there's a signpost with Arabic lettering on it, like this.'

The professor wrote on the edge of the map with a ballpoint pen.

'I believe the name is given in English as well, but here's the Arabic, just to be on the safe side. It says "Shibam", the name of a wonderful old city. Follow the road until it turns north. When you reach a ravine, that's the one you're after. It's a good thing Firedrake can fly, because there's no path leading down into the ravine. No humans have even tried to build a bridge over it.' Barnabas smiled. 'Some say that it hides the entrance to hell, but I can tell you that's highly improbable! As soon as you've landed safely, look round for a big car without any windows. Once you find it, hoot the horn, sit down on the ground exactly seventeen paces away from the car, and wait.'

'A car?' said Ben, astonished.

'That's right!' The professor shrugged his shoulders. 'Asif stole it from a rich sheikh, or so the latest tales about him say. It's a mistake to believe that spirits and fabulous creatures always live in caves or ruined buildings. They sometimes have a distinct preference for what might be called modern accommodation. A few years ago, I found two djinns living in plastic bottles in the ruined city where I was looking for unicorns.'

'Amazing!' murmured Ben.

'What's so amazing? Ground-elves like to live in empty cans sunk in the ground!' Sorrel called down from Firedrake's back.

She had climbed up to check whether the safety straps were in good order, for the storm had shown Sorrel that on this journey it was a good idea even for her to lash herself firmly to the spines of the dragon's crest. 'Cans are a wonderful way of terrifying passers-by,' she went on. 'The elves just beat on their insides with acorn hammers,' Sorrel chuckled, 'and you should see how it makes humans jump!'

The professor shook his head, smiling. 'I can well believe that of elves,' he said, folding up the map and giving it back to Ben. 'About elves, by the way: there's a certain elf species you may meet on your way south. Sand-elves swarm by night near the ruined cities that lie buried there. They'll swirl around you and try to drive you off course. Take no notice, but don't be too rude to them. They can be a great nuisance, just like their relations in the cold north.'

'Oh no!' groaned Sorrel from Firedrake's back. 'Elves are the end!' She rolled her eyes. 'The trouble I've had with those pesky creatures! They once shot their nasty itchy arrows at me just because I climbed an elf hill to pick some mushrooms.'

The professor chuckled. 'I'm afraid their Arab relations are no better behaved, so keep away from them if you can.'

'Right.' Ben put the map in his jacket pocket and looked up at the starry sky. The heat of the day had gone and he felt a little chilly, but it was good to breathe cool air.

'Oh, and here's something else, my boy!' Barnabas Greenbloom gave Ben a fat, well-thumbed book. 'Put this in your backpack too. A little goodbye present from me. This book describes almost all the fabulous beings ever said to have existed in this world. It may come in useful on your journey.'

'Oh, thank you, Professor!' Ben accepted the book with a shy smile, stroked the cover reverently and began leafing through it.

'Come on, put it away,' Sorrel urged. 'We can't stay here while you read a book. See how high the moon has risen already.'

'Yes, okay!' Ben took off his backpack and put the map and the professor's book carefully away among his own things.

Twigleg rose cautiously to his feet behind the tussock of grass. The backpacks! That was the solution. Sorrel certainly wouldn't want him going with them, however much the boy might. But if he simply hid in Ben's backpack . . . silent as a shadow, the homunculus stole over to it.

'What was that?' asked Sorrel, leaning down from Firedrake's back. 'Something just shot out of the grass! Are there desert rats here?'

Diving head first in among Ben's clothes, Twigleg disappeared.

'I have something for you too, Sorrel,' said Barnabas Greenbloom, reaching into his basket. 'My wife gave me these to cook with, but I think you'll make better use of them.' He pressed a small bag into Sorrel's paws.

She sniffed it curiously.

'Dried wood blewits!' she cried. 'Girolles, chanterelles, morels!' She stared at Barnabas Greenbloom in amazement. 'Are you really giving me all these?'

'Of course!' The professor smiled. 'No one appreciates mushrooms better than a brownie, am I right?'

'You certainly are.' Sorrel sniffed the bag happily once more and then leaped down off Firedrake's back to stuff it in her backpack, which was lying on the sand beside Ben's. Twigleg hardly dared to breathe as they strapped the two backpacks together, ready for the journey. But Sorrel was too intoxicated by the fragrance of her mushrooms to notice the manikin among Ben's clothes.

Ben looked all around him. 'Twigleg really does seem to have disappeared,' he murmured.

'Thank goodness for that!' said Sorrel, making sure the bag of mushrooms was pushed well down in her backpack, although not before she'd taken one out to nibble. 'He reeked of bad luck, you take my word for it. Any brownie would have spotted that at once, but you humans never notice anything.'

Twigleg would have loved to nip her furry fingers, but he controlled himself and didn't so much as poke the tip of his nose out of his hiding place.

'Perhaps it was just the fact that he's a homunculus you didn't like, Sorrel,' said Professor Greenbloom. 'Such creatures are seldom popular with beings born naturally. In fact they seem sinister to most people. So a homunculus like Twigleg often feels very lonely and rejected, and clings to whoever made him. Although they do usually live much longer than their makers – much, much longer.'

Sorrel shook her head and closed her backpack. 'One way or another,' she said, 'he smelled of bad luck and that's all there is to it.'

'She's stubborn as a mule,' Ben whispered to the professor.

'I'd noticed,' Barnabas Greenbloom whispered back.

Then he went over to Firedrake and looked into his golden eyes once more. 'All I have for you is this,' he said, holding his open hand out to the dragon.

A scale lay on his palm, gleaming, hard and cold – and golden. The dragon bent over it, curious. The professor placed another scale beside it.

'I found these two scales many, many years ago in the northern Alps,' the professor explained. 'Cows and sheep had been disappearing there, and the local people told horror stories of a terrible monster prowling down from the mountains by night. At the time, I'm afraid, I could find nothing but these scales, which look remarkably like your own but feel entirely different. There were some tracks around too, but they'd been blurred by the rain and the angry farmers who'd been milling around.'

In his hiding place, Twigleg pricked up his ears. Those scales could only have come from his master! Nettlebrand had lost three scales in the course of his life, and in spite of sending all his ravens out in search of them he had never recovered any of them. He wasn't going to be at all pleased to hear that a human had found two of the precious scales.

The manikin stuck his nose out of Ben's backpack to get a look at them, but the professor's hand was too far above his head for him to see anything.

'They have no scent,' said Firedrake, 'as if they were made of nothing. Yet they feel as cold as ice.'

'May I see them?' asked Ben, bending over the professor's hand.

Twigleg was listening.

'You can hold them,' said Professor Greenbloom. 'Look at them closely. They're curious things.'

Ben carefully took one of the scales from the professor's hand and ran a finger over its sharp edges. It did feel like metal, yet there was something else about it too.

'I believe they're made of false gold,' the professor told him, 'a metal used by alchemists in the Middle Ages when they were trying to make the real thing. They never succeeded, of course.

But this must be alloyed with something else, because that scale is very, very hard. I couldn't make the slightest scratch on it even with a diamond cutter. Ah, well.' Barnabas Greenbloom shrugged his shoulders. 'Take one with you. You might unravel this mystery too on your travels. I've been carrying those scales around with me for so long that I've given up hope.'

'Shall I put it in with our things?' Ben asked the dragon.

Firedrake nodded. Thoughtfully, he raised his head and looked out to sea. Sorrel scurried up on to the dragon's tail. Ben threw her the backpacks, and she caught them and slung them over Firedrake's back.

'Here we go!' she cried. 'Who knows, tomorrow morning we might even land where we're meant to for a change.'

'The weather is set fair, Sorrel,' said the professor, looking up at the sky.

Ben went over to him and shyly offered his hand. 'Goodbye, Professor,' he said.

Professor Greenbloom took Ben's hand and pressed it hard. 'Goodbye, Ben,' he said. 'I really do hope we shall meet again. Oh yes,' he added, handing Ben a small card, 'I almost forgot this. It's Zubeida's card. If you do visit her after you've stopped off to see the djinn, give her my regards. And should you need more provisions or anything else, I'm sure she'll be happy to help you. If the village where she's working hasn't changed too much, then its people will still be waiting hopefully for the dragons to return. But you'd better make sure of that before Firedrake walks in on them!'

Ben smiled, and put the card away with his other treasures. Then he clambered up on Firedrake's back.

'You've still got my card too, I hope?' said Professor Greenbloom.

Ben nodded.

'The best of luck, then!' cried the professor as Firedrake spread his wings. 'And think hard about the question you ask the djinn. Beware of basilisks. And write to tell me if you do find the dragons!'

'Goodbye!' called Ben, waving.

Then Firedrake rose into the air. The dragon circled once over the professor, breathed a blue flame into the night by way of farewell – and flew away.

CHAPTER SIXTEEN

Flying South

Over the next few nights Firedrake flew faster than the wind. Impatience drove him on. The airstream blew so hard in the faces of his two riders that Sorrel stuffed leaves in her ears, and Ben wound the cloth which the professor had given him tightly round his head for protection.

The nights were cool, but by day it was so hot that they found it hard to sleep. They took the professor's advice and rested among the crumbling walls of ruined cities, far from roads and villages. While Firedrake and Sorrel slept in the shade, Ben often sat for hours among the ancient stones gazing across the hot sand to the horizon, where every now and then a dusty truck drove by, or camels swayed through the heat of the day on their long, thin legs. He would have loved to see more of this strange land, but it was only at night, when Firedrake occasionally flew low over a town, that he caught a few glimpses of domes, slender minarets and flat-roofed white houses crowded together inside old walls.

The Red Sea was always on their right. Below them, the

endless road wound its way south along the foot of an equally
endless mountain range. Beyond it, dry and stony land stretched
to the horizon, with towns and villages scattered like islands, and
deep ravines gaping like vast cracks in the wilderness.

The air was heavy with strange aromas. But on the second
night black clouds came sailing over the mountains, enveloping
Firedrake and his riders in a stinking smog before drifting out to
sea. Barnabas Greenbloom had warned Ben of this too. The dark
clouds were the sooty discharge from oil wells in the east, burning like torches after a war between humans. Just before the sun
rose to blaze down on the land, Firedrake dived into the waters

of the Red Sea to wash off the black filth, but some of it clung fast to his scales. Sorrel spent almost all the next morning cleaning the dragon's wings and her own thick fur, and muttering crossly to herself. It was easier for Ben with his smooth skin.

As he was taking a clean T-shirt out of his backpack he almost touched Twigleg's head.

The manikin was only just in time to duck. Since they set out Twigleg had left the backpack only when he was sure the others were all asleep. Then he would stretch his aching limbs, catch flies and midges to eat – luckily there were plenty of them in this hot country – and creep back into hiding as soon as one of the other three stirred.

He wanted to put off the moment of discovery for as long as possible. Sorrel distrusted him, and that scared him. He did once steal a look at the golden scale the professor had given Ben. The boy kept it in a bag which he wore around his neck, and Twigleg had looked inside while Ben was asleep. It also contained a small photograph, a stone, a shell, and a little of the silvery dust from the basilisk's cave. The scale undoubtedly came from Nettlebrand's armour. Nothing else in the world felt so cold or so hard. When Ben turned over in his sleep the homunculus put it back in the bag with a shudder and sat down beside the boy – as he did whenever the other three were asleep. Then, leaning very, very carefully against the small human being's shoulder, he read the book that the boy always left open at his side. It was the book Barnabas Greenbloom had given Ben. Every day the boy read it until his eyes closed, for it was full of marvels.

It contained everything that humans knew about unicorns and water-sprites, Pegasus the winged horse and the giant roc bird that feeds sheep to its young, about fairies, will-o'-the-wisps, sea serpents and trolls.

Twigleg skipped several chapters. For instance, the one about mountain dwarves – he knew quite enough about them already. But on the third day, while the others were asleep and the light of the afternoon sun was bathing everything in a yellow haze, Twigleg finally came to the chapter about homunculi, artificial man-made creatures of flesh and blood.

His first impulse was to close the book.

He looked around. Ben was murmuring in his dreams, but Sorrel was snoring peacefully, as usual, and Firedrake was sleeping like a log.

Twigleg began reading, his heart beating fast. Oh yes, he knew he had a heart all right, but there was more information on the yellowing pages. *A homunculus usually lives longer than its creator*, he read. He knew that too. But he had never heard what came next. *So far as is known, a homunculus can live almost indefinitely unless it develops a strong affection for a human being. In such cases, the homunculus dies on the same day as the human to whom it has given its heart.*

'Oh-oh! Just think of that! Watch out, Twigleg!' the manikin whispered to himself. 'Keep your heart to yourself if you want to live. You've already survived all your brothers and even your maker. So don't turn foolish in your old age and give your heart to a human being.'

He jumped up and turned back to the page at which Ben had left the book open. Then he looked up at the sun. Yes, it was time he reported to his master. He hadn't done so for two days now. Not that there was anything to report.

Twigleg turned and looked at the small human being. Tomorrow. Tomorrow night they'd reach the ravine where the djinn lived. And if the djinn really knew the answer to the question, the answer his master had been seeking for over a hundred years, then Nettlebrand would set off for the Rim of Heaven and go hunting again at last.

Twigleg shivered. No, he didn't want to think about that. What business was it of his anyway? He was only his master's armour-cleaner. He had been doing what Nettlebrand told him to do ever since he, Twigleg, first slipped out of a small coloured glass test tube like a chick hatching from an egg. What difference did it make that he hated his master? The crucial point was that Nettlebrand would make a single mouthful of him if he didn't come up with what his master had been waiting for so long.

'Just remember to keep your heart to yourself, Twigleg,' the homunculus whispered. 'Now, time to get down to work.'

Just before Firedrake landed that morning, Twigleg had seen light flashing on water somewhere close, in an old cistern that, although disused, still collected precious rainwater. The homunculus was about to set off for the cistern when he felt Ben beginning to stir. He quickly hid behind the nearest rock.

The boy sat up sleepily, yawned and stretched. Then he rose to his feet and climbed the high wall behind which they had camped. This time Firedrake had had to fly some way inland before they found a ruined castle among incense trees growing on a sandy hill. The trees looked half dead. The walls of the castle courtyard still stood, but the buildings behind them had fallen in and were almost buried in drifts of sand. Only lizards and a few snakes lived here, but Sorrel had driven off the snakes by throwing stones at them as soon as they arrived.

Ben sat on the wall, dangling his legs and looking to the south, where high mountains rose into the hot sky, breaking up the line of the horizon.

'It can't be much further now,' Twigleg heard him

murmuring. 'If the professor was right, we'll reach the ravine tomorrow.'

Twigleg peered out from behind his rock. For a moment he felt like revealing himself to the boy as Ben sat staring into the distance, lost in thought. Then he thought better of it. He cast a quick glance at the sleeping Sorrel, then crept over to the backpack without a sound and wriggled in like a lizard among Ben's things. The report for his master would have to wait.

Ben stayed up on the wall for some time, but at last he sighed and jumped down on to the sand. He went over to Sorrel.

'Hey, Sorrel,' he said quietly, shaking the brownie's shoulder. 'Wake up.'

Sorrel stretched and blinked at the sunlight. 'It's still broad daylight!' she hissed, looking at Firedrake, who was sleeping peacefully in the shade of the old castle wall.

'Yes, but you promised me we'd talk about the question to ask the djinn, remember?'

'Oh yes, the question.' Sorrel rubbed her eyes. 'Right, but only if we have something to eat first. This heat makes a person hungry.' She made her way over to her backpack, the sand hot on the furry soles of her paws.

Ben followed, grinning. 'It's the heat now, is it?' he teased her. 'We've had rain and thunderstorms and all kinds of weather since we started out, and you're hungry all the time.'

'So what?' Sorrel took the bag of mushrooms out of her rucksack, sniffed it appreciatively and licked her lips. Then she placed two large leaves on the sand and tipped the mushrooms out on them. 'Hmm . . . which shall I eat first?'

Ben just shook his head. He put a hand into his backpack for his bottle of water and a few of the olives the professor had given him. The bag containing them had slipped to the very bottom. As he rummaged, Ben's fingers felt something hairy. He snatched his hand out in alarm.

'What's up?' asked Sorrel.

'I think there's a mouse in my backpack,' said Ben.

'A mouse?' Sorrel put her mushroom down, bent over the backpack – and pounced, quick as lightning. With one swift movement, she produced the struggling Twigleg.

'Well, take a look at this!' she cried. 'What have we here?'

'Twigleg!' cried Ben, staring at the homunculus in surprise. 'How did you get into my backpack? And why,' he added, baffled, 'have you kept so quiet till now?'

'Oh, young master, because, because . . .' stammered Twigleg, trying to free himself from Sorrel's grasp. But however hard the manikin twisted and turned, the brownie girl held him tight.

'That's stumped you, right?' she growled.

'Let go of me, you furry feline!' squealed Twigleg. 'How can I explain anything with you squeezing me like this?'

'Come on, let him go,' said Ben. 'You're hurting him.'

Reluctantly, Sorrel put the homunculus down on the sand.

'Thanks!' muttered Twigleg. Looking injured, he straightened his jacket.

'So *why* didn't you say anything before?' repeated Ben.

'Why didn't I say anything? Because of her, of course!' Twigleg pointed a trembling finger at Sorrel. 'I know she wants to be rid of me. So I hid in the backpack. And after that,' he added, rubbing his nose and giving Sorrel a nasty look, 'after that I kept quiet because I was afraid she'd throw me into the sea if she found me.'

'Not a bad idea,' growled Sorrel. 'Not a bad idea at all.'

'Sorrel!' Ben dug his elbow into the brownie's ribs. Then,

looking concerned, he turned to the homunculus. 'She'd never do that, Twigleg. Honestly. She's very nice really. She just makes out she's so . . . so . . .' he glanced sideways at Sorrel, 'so hard-hearted all the time, see?'

But Twigleg did not seem convinced. He gave Sorrel another suspicious look. Sorrel responded with a scowl.

'Here.' Ben pushed a few crumbs of pitta bread towards Twigleg. 'You must be hungry.'

'My humble thanks, young master, but I, er . . .' Twigleg cleared his throat, embarrassed. 'I'll just catch myself a few flies.'

'Flies?' Ben looked incredulously at the manikin, who shrugged his shoulders awkwardly.

'Flies! Yuk, putrid panther-caps!' said Sorrel. 'Sounds just like you, you spider-legged fairy-ring champignon!'

'Sorrel!' snapped Ben. 'Stop it, will you? Twigleg's done nothing to hurt you. Okay? He freed you from that cage, remember?'

'Oh, very well.' Sorrel turned back to her mushrooms. 'All right, I promise I won't throw him into the sea. Happy now? So let's think about the question you're going to ask the djinn with the thousand eyes. After all, that's why you woke me up.'

'Okay.' Ben nodded, and took a crumpled piece of paper out of his trouser pocket. 'I've written a few ideas down. Listen.'

'Just a moment,' Sorrel interrupted. 'Do we want the manikin to hear this?'

Ben groaned. 'Here we go again! Why shouldn't he hear it?'

Sorrel looked Twigleg up and down. 'Why *should* he?' she replied tartly. 'If you ask me, as few ears as possible ought to hear our question.'

'I'm off, then,' said Twigleg. 'Don't mind me. I can be gone in a moment.'

But Ben held him back by his jacket. 'You're staying here,' he said. 'I trust you. And I'm the one who has to ask the question. Right, do I finally have your attention, Sorrel?'

The brownie rolled her eyes. 'Just as you like. But you'll land us in trouble, trusting him like that. I'd bet my mushrooms on it.'

'You're nuts, Sorrel,' said Ben. 'Totally nuts.'

Twigleg sat on Ben's knee, hardly knowing where to look. He had often felt small and worthless, but never as small and worthless as he did now. He was so ashamed of himself he felt like confessing everything to the boy there and then. But he couldn't utter a word.

'Right, how about this?' said Ben, smoothing out his paper. '*Where – is – the – Rim – of – Heaven – hidden?* Seven words exactly.'

'Hmm, not bad,' growled Sorrel. 'Sounds kind of funny, though.'

'I've got another one.' Ben turned the piece of paper round. 'Seven words again. *Where – does – the – Rim – of – Heaven – lie?*'

Quietly, Twigleg slipped off Ben's knee and took a couple of steps backwards.

Sorrel instantly turned her eyes on him. 'And where do you think you're going now?' she growled.

'Just for a walk, fur-face,' replied Twigleg. 'Any objections?'

'Going for a walk?' Ben looked at the homunculus in surprise. 'Wouldn't you like me to come too?' he called after him. 'I mean, we don't know what kind of wild animals there may be around here.'

Twigleg's heart sank at the note of concern in Ben's voice.

'No, no, young master,' he called over his shoulder. 'I may be small but I'm not helpless. Anyway, I'm so skinny I don't look very tasty.'

And so saying, he disappeared through a hole in the wall.

CHAPTER SEVENTEEN

The Raven

The hot air felt as thick as cotton wool to Twigleg. He made his way through it, keeping his sharp nose raised to pick up the scent of water. Yes, the old cistern must be right there at the foot of the hill, under that tall incense tree. He could already smell the water distinctly. With difficulty, he made his way through boulders and coarse grass. His arms and legs ached horribly from his days of playing hide-and-seek, shut up inside Ben's backpack.

He had Sorrel to thank for all that – the stuck-up, suspicious brownie! Laughing at him for eating flies, then stuffing her own face with those stinking mushrooms! He just hoped she'd soon pick a poisonous one, a mushroom that would make her stomach ache enough to shut her up for good.

Among a few scrubby bushes Twigleg came upon some tracks, probably made by rabbits going down to the water. He was following their narrow path when a black shadow suddenly loomed over him. The homunculus squealed in alarm and flung himself flat on the ground.

Black claws dug into the dust beside him, and a hooked beak pecked at his jacket.

'Hello, Twigleg,' croaked a familiar voice.

The homunculus cautiously raised his head. 'Raven?'

'In person!' squawked the bird.

Twigleg sat up, sighing, and brushed the untidy hair back from his forehead. Then he folded his arms over his chest and looked reproachfully at the raven.

'You've got a nerve, I must say!' he said. 'I've a good mind to pluck your feathers and stuff a cushion with them. Goodness knows, it's no thanks to you I'm still alive!'

'I know, I know,' the raven cawed apologetically. 'You're right. But what was I to do? They kept throwing stones at me, and you weren't coming out, so I looked for a nice safe tree and kept an eye on you.'

'Oh, kept an eye on me, did you?' Twigleg stood up. 'I didn't get a sight of you for three whole nights going halfway round the world – and now you show up! Come on, I have to find water.' And he set off again without another word.

The raven flapped after him, looking cross.

'All very well for you to talk,' he snapped. 'You think it was easy for me, following that wretched dragon? He flies three times faster than the wind.'

'So what?' Twigleg spat contemptuously into the dust. 'Why do you think our master has been feeding you magic grain ever since you could hop? Now shut up. I've got more important things to do than listen to your squawking.'

The old water cistern lay beyond a low hill, with a narrow flight of stone steps leading down to it. The stone was cracked, and wild flowers grew in the nooks and crannies. Twigleg scurried down the steps, and saw that the water in the old reservoir was cloudy and covered with dust. Taking a deep breath, the homunculus went up to the edge.

'Tell him I couldn't help it, will you?' cawed the raven, flying up into a leafless tree.

But Twigleg ignored him. He spat into the water, and the image of Nettlebrand's head appeared in the cistern, emerging from the depths. Gravelbeard was standing between the dragon's mighty horns, looking very miserable as he dusted them with a bunch of peacock feathers.

'Three – whole – days!' growled Nettlebrand in a menacingly low voice. 'What did I tell you?'

'There was nothing to report, master,' replied Twigleg. 'Sun and dust, that's all we've seen these last few days, nothing but sun and dust. I was hiding in the boy's backpack almost the whole time. I'm all crumpled up.'

'When do you reach the djinn?' Nettlebrand snapped.

'Tomorrow.' Twigleg gulped. 'And master, the raven's turned up again. I suppose I'd better continue the journey on his back now.'

'Nonsense!' Nettlebrand bared his teeth. 'You stay in that boy's backpack. The closer you stick to them the sooner you'll hear the djinn's reply. The raven will follow you, just in case.'

'But that brownie girl!' Twigleg objected. 'She doesn't trust me!'

'What about the dragon and the boy?'

'They do.' Twigleg bent his head. 'In fact the boy even protects me from the brownie.'

Nettlebrand's terrible mouth distorted in a mocking grimace.

'What a stupid child!' he grunted. 'I really ought to thank him. Especially if he finds out where the other dragons are.

Aaah!' He closed his red eyes. 'What a feast that'll be! As soon as you have the answer let me know, understand? I'll set out straight away, and before that fool of a silver dragon is airborne again I'll have reached the Rim of Heaven.'

Surprised, Twigleg stared at the image of his master. He knew very well that Nettlebrand couldn't fly. 'How are you going to do that?' he asked. 'It will be a long journey for you.'

'Oh, I have my ways and means,' growled Nettlebrand, 'but that's none of your business, spindly-legs. Go back now before anyone gets suspicious. I'm off to catch a couple of cows.'

Twigleg nodded. 'At once, master. But there's another thing,' he added, stroking a flower that grew beside the water. 'That tall human, Greenbloom, he had two of your scales.'

Suddenly all was very quiet, apart from a few cicadas chirping in the grass.

'What did you say?' asked Nettlebrand, his red eyes glowing.

Twigleg hunched his head down between his shoulders.

'He had two of your scales,' he repeated. 'He still has one of them. He gave the other to the dragon. The boy is looking after it for him. I've seen it, master. It must be one of the three scales you lost in the mountains long ago.'

Nettlebrand uttered a savage roar. 'So that's where they are! In human hands.' In his anger he shook his head so hard that Gravelbeard only just managed to cling to one of his horns.

'I want those scales back!' roared Nettlebrand. 'No one else is to have them. No one! My skin still crawls where they're missing. Does this human think he can discover the secret of my armour?' Nettlebrand narrowed his red eyes. 'Get that scale away from the boy, do you hear?'

Twigleg nodded hastily.

Nettlebrand licked his lips. 'And as for the scale in the grown-up human's hands, I'll deal with the matter myself,' he growled. 'What was his name again?'

'Greenbloom,' replied Twigleg. 'Professor Barnabas Greenbloom. But he'll soon be leaving the oasis.'

'I move fast,' growled Nettlebrand. 'Very fast.' He shook himself, rattling his scales. 'Now go away. And don't trouble yourself about the suspicious brownie. I'll soon be eating her for starters. And the small human too.'

Twigleg swallowed. His heart was suddenly thudding. 'You're going to eat the boy as well?' he breathed.

'Why not?' Nettlebrand yawned. He was bored now. Twigleg could see right down into his golden jaws. 'Those conceited two-legs don't taste at all bad.'

Then the image of Nettlebrand dissolved, leaving only dust on the surface of the murky water. Twigleg stepped back from the brink of the cistern, turned – and nearly jumped out of his skin.

Sorrel was standing at the top of the steps, holding her empty water bottle.

'Well, well, well,' she said slowly, as she came down the steps. 'And what might you be doing here? I thought you'd gone for a walk.'

The homunculus tried to scurry past, but Sorrel barred his way. He glanced back over his shoulder. The cistern was alarmingly close, and he couldn't swim. Sorrel knelt down beside him and filled her bottle with the dusty water. 'So who were you talking to just now?'

Twigleg edged as far away from the water as he could. If his master reappeared he was done for.

'Talking?' he stammered. 'Um, er . . . oh, just talking to myself. To my reflection in the water. Any objection?'

'Your reflection?' Sorrel shook her head doubtfully. Then, looking round, she saw the raven still perched in the tree, looking down at them with interest.

Twigleg hastily started up the steps, but Sorrel grabbed hold of his jacket.

'Hang on a mo, there's no hurry,' she said. 'Were you by any chance talking to that bird with the black feathers up there?'

'Him?' With an offended expression on his face, Twigleg tugged his jacket out of her grasp. 'Do I look like someone who talks to birds?'

Sorrel shrugged her shoulders. Straightening up, she put the top on her bottle. 'No idea,' she said. 'But you'd better not let me catch you at it. Hey, you there with the black feathers!' She turned and looked up at the raven. 'Do you happen to know this little titch?'

But the raven only flapped his black wings and flew away with a loud croak.

CHAPTER EIGHTEEN

A Visitor for the Professor

Barnabas Greenbloom was packing his bags – not that he had a lot to pack. He travelled light, with only a battered old holdall into which he flung some shirts and underwear, his favourite jumper and a pencil-box. He always packed a camera too, and a thick, much-stained notebook in which he wrote all the stories he came across, illustrating them with photographs, copies of any inscriptions he found, and drawings he had done from descriptions given to him by people who had met fabulous creatures. The professor had already filled almost a hundred such notebooks. They were all in his study at home, neatly sorted according to the species of creatures and the places where they had appeared. This one, thought Barnabas Greenbloom, stroking the current volume lovingly, this one would be given a place of honour, for it contained a photograph of Firedrake. The dragon had allowed him to take his picture out of gratitude for being rescued from the basilisk.

'I can't wait to hear what Vita has to say,' breathed the

professor, stowing the book away in his bag. 'She's always feared that dragons were extinct.' Smiling happily, he picked up a towel and went out into the evening twilight, on his way to wash the dust and sweat off his face before his journey.

His tent was on the outskirts of the camp, close to the only well. A donkey and a few camels, tied to stakes not far away, were dozing in the warm evening air. There were no other human beings in sight. The camp was as good as deserted, for most of its occupants had gone into the nearby town. The rest were in their tents, asleep, writing letters home, or keeping their notes up to date.

Barnabas Greenbloom went over to the big well, hung his towel over the edge of the little wall around it, and drew up a bucket of the wonderfully cool water. As he did so he whistled softly and looked up at the stars. They were as numerous this evening as the grains of sand beneath his feet.

Suddenly the donkey and the camels raised their heads in alarm. They snorted, jumped up and tugged at their ropes. Barnabas didn't notice. He was thinking about his daughter, wondering whether she'd have grown much in the four weeks since he last saw her. Then a noise startled him out of these pleasant thoughts and jolted him back to the present. The noise came from the depths of the well, and it sounded like heavy breathing – the heavy breathing of a very, very large animal.

Alarmed, the professor put the bucket down on the rim of the well and took a step back. No one knew better than he did that the bottom of a well may shelter extremely unpleasant creatures. However, his curiosity was always stronger than his caution, so he did not do the sensible thing, which would have been to turn and run away as fast as he could go. Instead, Barnabas Greenbloom stayed put and waited with interest to see just what was about to crawl out of the well. He did put his left hand to his back trouser pocket, ready to take out the little mirror that he kept there for emergencies. The pocket also held a number of other items which might prove useful in times of danger.

The heavy breathing was getting louder, and a strange rattling noise came from the well, as if a thousand iron rings were scraping against the rough stones.

The professor frowned. What fabulous creature would make a sound like that? Hard as he tried, he couldn't think of a single one, so for safety's sake, he took another step back. Just as the rising moon disappeared for a moment behind wisps of black cloud, a huge, golden, scaly paw emerged from the well.

The animals bleated and rolled their eyes, tore their stakes out of the sand and fled into the desert, dragging the stakes behind them. Barnabas Greenbloom, however, was rooted to the spot.

'Barnabas,' he muttered to himself, 'get out of here, you stupid idiot!' His feet took yet another step backwards – and stopped.

The sturdy wall around the top of the well fell apart like a set of dominoes, and a mighty dragon forced his way out of the shaft. His golden scales shone in the moonlight like a giant's suit of armour. His black claws dug deep into the sand, and his long, spiny tail rattled as it dragged after him. A dwarf holding a huge feather duster was clinging to one of his horns.

Slowly, with steps that seemed to make the desert quake, the monster moved heavily towards Barnabas Greenbloom. His eyes glowed red as blood in the darkness.

'*You* have something that belongs to *me*!' growled Nettlebrand, his voice resounding in the professor's ears.

Professor Greenbloom looked straight up into the monster's open jaws. 'Oh yes, and what might that be?' he enquired, addressing the sharp teeth inside those jaws. As he spoke, he was very slowly putting his left hand inside his back trouser pocket to find a small box which was in there with the mirror.

'My scale, fool!' Nettlebrand snarled. His icy breath made Barnabas Greenbloom shiver. 'Give me back my scale or I'll crush you like a louse.'

'Ah, the scale!' cried the professor, clapping a hand to his brow. 'Of course – the golden scale. So it's yours. How interesting. How *very* interesting. But how did you know I had it?'

'Stop stalling!' roared Nettlebrand, coming so close that one of his black claws touched Barnabas Greenbloom's knee. 'I can tell that you have it. Hand it over to the dwarf. Come on, do it *now*!'

The professor's mind was racing. How had this monster found him? Did he know who had the other scale? Was Ben in danger? How could he warn the boy?

The mountain dwarf began scrambling down from Nettlebrand's head.

At that moment Barnabas Greenbloom dived forward and ducked beneath the gigantic dragon's body. He made for the creature's hind legs, jumped up on one of the mighty feet, and clung to the monster's scaly armour.

'Come on out!' bellowed Nettlebrand, spinning round furiously. 'Where are you?'

The dwarf dropped to the sand like a ripe plum, and quickly took shelter between some rocks to avoid being trampled to death as his master stamped around furiously. Barnabas Greenbloom just held on to Nettlebrand's leg, laughing.

'Where am I?' he called to the monster. 'Where you can't get me, of course.'

Nettlebrand stood still, breathing hard, and tried to reach his muzzle round to his hind leg, but his body wasn't flexible enough. All he could do was put his head down between his front legs and stare furiously at the little human being clinging like a tick to his golden body.

'Give me the scale!' bellowed Nettlebrand again. 'Give me my scale and I won't eat you. My word of honour!'

'Your word of honour? Oh, my word!' Barnabas tapped the giant leg to which he was clinging. The sound was like hitting an iron saucepan. 'You know something? I believe I know who you are. You're the one they call Nettlebrand in the old tales, aren't you?'

Nettlebrand did not reply. He stamped as hard as he could to shake the man off. But his claws only sank into the desert sand, and Barnabas was still clinging firmly to his leg.

'Yes, you're Nettlebrand!' he cried. 'Nettlebrand, the Golden One! How could I ever forget the stories about you? I ought to have remembered them as soon as I saw that golden scale. You're said to be a bloodthirsty, cunning liar, murderous and vain. They even say you ate your maker, but let's face it, he deserved it for creating a monster like you.'

Nettlebrand listened to the professor, his head lowered. His horns bored into the sand.

'Oh yes?' he snarled. 'Talk away! I'll eat *you* any moment now. You can't hang on down there for ever. Armour-cleaner!' He raised his ugly muzzle and looked around. 'Where are you, Gravelbeard?'

Reluctantly, Gravelbeard stuck his head out of his hiding place. 'Yes, Your Goldness?'

'Go and tickle that human with your feather duster!' growled Nettlebrand. 'Perhaps that'll make him fall off.'

The professor gulped. He was still holding on, but his fingers were beginning to hurt and unfortunately he was very ticklish. And there was no hope that any help would come. If the vast dragon's roaring hadn't already brought someone out of a tent to investigate, then it obviously wasn't going to do so in the immediate future. No, he'd have to save himself. But how? Hard as he racked his brains, he just couldn't think of a single good idea.

The mountain dwarf appeared between Nettlebrand's forelegs wearing a sullen expression and a sandy hat, and carrying a peacock-feather duster. He walked unsteadily over the sand towards Barnabas Greenbloom.

Get on with it, think of something, old chap, thought the professor, or your dear wife won't be seeing you again.

And then he did get an idea.

'Here, dwarf!' he whispered to Gravelbeard, who was standing beside his master's paw in his outsize hat, already reaching the peacock feathers out towards the ticklish professor.

Using his teeth, Barnabas Greenbloom took his gold wedding ring off his finger and spat it out at the dwarf's feet. Gravelbeard instantly dropped the duster, picked up the ring, and felt the shining metal with an expert touch.

'Nice piece!' he muttered. 'Solid gold.'

At that moment the professor dropped to the ground, landing in the sand beside the startled dwarf.

'What's going on, Gravelbeard?' boomed Nettlebrand's voice in the darkness. 'Has he let go yet?'

The dwarf was about to reply, but the professor quickly put a hand over his mouth.

'Listen, Gravelbeard,' he whispered into the little creature's ear. 'You can keep this ring if you tell your master I've disappeared, all right?'

The dwarf bit the professor's fingers. 'I'll be getting it anyway,' he said in muffled tones from behind Barnabas Greenbloom's hand.

'Oh no, you won't!' whispered the professor, taking the ring away again. 'If you don't cooperate he'll eat me, ring and all. Well, is it a deal?'

The dwarf hesitated for a moment, then nodded.

'Armour-cleaner!' roared Nettlebrand. 'What's going on?'

He lowered his head again, peering through his front legs with his teeth bared. But by now it was so dark he couldn't make out what was happening back there by his hind legs.

Barnabas Greenbloom threw the ring down in front of the dwarf. 'And don't even think of double-crossing me!' he whispered. 'Because if you do I'll let your master know how easy you are to bribe, understand?'

The dwarf bent to pick up the ring, while the professor, moving as fast as he could, crawled across the sand to Nettlebrand's tail. Gasping for breath, he clambered up on to it and clung to its spines. Gravelbeard watched him, wide-eyed. Then he hid the ring under his stout waistcoat.

'Arrrrmour-cleanerrrr! What's happening?' Nettlebrand roared.

The dwarf picked up his feather duster, looked round one last time – and came out between the dragon's gigantic forepaws, looking crestfallen.

'He's gone, Your Goldness!' he said, shrugging his shoulders as if baffled. 'Vanished. As if the sand had swallowed him up.'

'*What*?' Nettlebrand put his broad muzzle so close to his armour-cleaner that the dwarf flinched back in alarm. 'Then *where* is he, dwarf?' bellowed Nettlebrand, lashing his tail so violently that sand flew up around Barnabas Greenbloom's ears, and it was all he could do to hold on.

The dwarf went pale around the nostrils and pressed his hands to his waistcoat. 'I don't know,' he babbled. 'I really don't know, Your Goldness! He'd gone by the time I went in underneath your golden belly!'

Nettlebrand began to burrow in the sand.

He dug and dug, but however thoroughly he ploughed up the desert sand, there was no sign of Barnabas Greenbloom. Standing on a boulder, Gravelbeard kept putting his hand under his waistcoat to stroke the professor's gold ring.

All this time Barnabas Greenbloom was clinging to the spines on Nettlebrand's tail, waiting for an opportunity to drop off into the sand and crawl away. At first he feared the monster would attack the tents in the camp and devour a couple of his colleagues as substitutes for the professor himself. But Nettlebrand seemed uneasy about facing human beings. When he still didn't find the professor – despite digging up half the desert and uncovering more ruins than all the archaeologists put together – he just stood there in the sand breathing heavily, tail lashing, teeth bared, and looked eastwards.

'Armour-cleaner!' he bellowed. 'Get aboard! We're going back. I want to find out what that djinn said.'

Barnabas Greenbloom jumped. He was so startled that he almost pinched Nettlebrand's tail. Had the monster said '*djinn*'? He leaned a little further forward to hear better.

'Just coming, Your Goldness!' called the dwarf. Grumpily, he trudged towards his master and climbed up on the dragon's back.

'And it'll be too bad if that fool of a spy still has nothing to report,' growled Nettlebrand, as Gravelbeard settled himself between the dragon's horns. 'If I don't find out where the Rim of Heaven is soon, I'm going to eat that silver dragon along with his small human and the shaggy brownie. Yuk! Brownies have a nasty mushroom flavour, and they're far too hairy.'

Professor Greenbloom held his breath. He could hardly believe what he had just heard.

Growling angrily, Nettlebrand turned and marched back towards the well out of which he had clambered. Just before the dragon reached it, the professor dropped to the sand and crawled away as fast as his knees would carry him, to take shelter among the ruins of the wall around the well shaft. At the rim of the shaft, Nettlebrand stopped to look back at the tents, his red eyes surveying the sand he had churned up.

'I'll find you, Greenbloom-human!' the professor heard him growl. 'I'll find you, and next time you won't escape me. But now for the silver dragon.'

With these words he forced his body back into the well, his spiny tail slipping down the dark hole after him. A splash and a snort rose from the depths – and Nettlebrand was gone.

Barnabas Greenbloom sat there by the ruins of the wall, thunderstruck.

'I must warn them!' he murmured. 'I must warn Firedrake and the others about that monster. But how? And who, for heaven's sake, told Nettlebrand the Golden One about the djinn?'

CHAPTER NINETEEN

The Signpost

On the fourth night the country over which Firedrake was flying became more mountainous, just as the professor had said it would. Below the travellers lay a wild and rocky landscape bathed in moonlight. The ground looked like a crumpled grey cloth. The cliffs rose higher and higher, some of them piercing the sky like thorns. Ben watched in amazement as they passed over towns that clung to the steep slopes, their pale mud-brick fortifications rising towards the moon.

'Like the *Thousand and One Nights*!' he murmured.

'Like the what?' asked Sorrel.

'*Thousand and One Nights*,' repeated Ben. 'They're stories – lots of stories – about flying carpets and so on. Some have djinns in them.'

'Fancy that,' muttered Sorrel. She was tired of rocks and sand. All this grey and yellow and brown hurt her eyes. She wanted to see trees. She wanted to hear leaves rustling in the wind – not the eternal chirping of crickets. At her insistence, Firedrake had already come down twice to land by signposts, but neither had pointed the right way. Ben had told her they wouldn't, and held the map in front of her nose, but her impatience was driving her crazy.

'It must be the next one, though,' she said. 'It *must* be the next time the road forks, don't you think?'

Ben nodded. 'Yes, sure.' Suddenly he leaned forward. 'Hey, Sorrel!' He pointed down at the ground in excitement. 'Look at that. Down there. See?'

The slopes of the dark mountains by the roadside were shining brighter than the sea in the moonlight.

'Oh no!' groaned Sorrel. 'It's them. You bet your life it's them.'

'It's who?' Ben leaned so far forward he almost fell off Firedrake's back. 'Who, Sorrel?'

'Elves!' Sorrel hauled on the strap holding her. 'Firedrake!' she cried. 'Firedrake, fly higher! Quick.'

Surprised, the dragon slowed down and looked round. 'What is it?'

'Elves!' cried Sorrel. 'Look! The place is absolutely swarming with elves!'

The dragon immediately rose higher, beating his wings powerfully.

'Oh no!' cried Ben. 'Can't we stay just a little lower? I'd love to see elves at close quarters.'

'Are you out of your mind?' Sorrel shook her head sorrowfully at such human folly. 'No way! They could have love-arrows with them and then, being a stupid little human, you'd be besotted with the next crow we happen to pass. No, no, and no again.'

'For once, Sorrel's right, young master,' Twigleg backed her up. He was nestling inside Ben's jacket, with only his head looking out between two buttons. 'We can thank our lucky stars if they don't notice us.'

Disappointed, Ben looked down at the glittering swarm.

'Oh no!' Sorrel groaned. 'The road forks just ahead. Now of all times! And there's a signpost there too.'

'I'll have to fly lower or Ben won't be able to read it,' called Firedrake.

'Lower?' Sorrel rolled her eyes. 'Oh, wonderful! Now, with those glitterbugs swirling all over the place! Death-caps and destroying angels, there's going to be trouble.'

Firedrake descended slowly, until at last he landed on the asphalt of the road.

But when Ben tried to compare the professor's writing with the lettering on the signpost, he saw that swarms of sand-elves covered the sign. Scarcely any bigger than brimstone yellow butterflies, they were the colour of the sand itself, with shimmering wings and hair dusted with green. They giggled and hummed as they whirred and fluttered around the sign. It made Ben quite dizzy to watch them.

'Now we're in trouble,' muttered Sorrel. 'Big trouble!'

A little group of the featherweight elves left the main swarm and flew towards Firedrake. They settled on his spines, his nose and his horns. Some of them fluttered around Ben and Sorrel too, giggling as they pinched their cheeks, tugged their hair and pulled their ears.

Twigleg drew his head in until only his nose was visible between the buttons of Ben's jacket. 'Young master!' he cried. 'Young master!'

But what with all the twittering and giggling of the elves, Ben couldn't hear the manikin. He sat there entranced and watched the shimmering little creatures.

'Well, do you like them at close quarters?' whispered Sorrel.

Ben nodded. An elf tickled him under the chin, putting out its tiny yellow tongue. Then it settled on his knee, winking at him. Ben marvelled at its brightly coloured wings.

'Hey, you!' Sorrel looked over Ben's shoulder at the elf. 'Would you lot be kind enough to move off that signpost? We have to see if the road down there is the right way for us.'

The sand-elf crossed its legs, folded its wings and grinned at the brownie girl.

'No, it's not the right way,' it twittered. 'Absolutely not.'

Ben looked down at it in surprise. 'How do you know?' he asked.

'Because it's the wrong way,' replied the little creature, winking at him again. 'Undeniably. Onedeniably, twodeniably, threedeniably wrong. See?'

The elf was then overcome by such a fit of the giggles that it almost fell off Ben's knee. Sorrel groaned.

'Which way ought we to go, then?' asked Ben.

'Go any way anyday,' replied the elf. 'Just not that way, no way should you go thataway.'

'Oh,' muttered Ben, baffled.

A second sand-elf flew up and perched on the shoulders of the first, grinning from pointy ear to pointy ear. 'What's up, Mukarrib?'

'They want to go the wrong way,' twittered Mukarrib. 'Tell them it's the wrong way, Bilqis!'

'He's right, it's the wrong way!' twittered Bilqis immediately. 'In fact, I'd say it's the wrongest way of all, no doubt about it.'

'I can't stand this!' growled Sorrel. 'If those silly little flitterbugs don't get off that signpost this minute I'll—'

'What did your friend say?' Mukarrib asked. 'Should we take offence?'

Three more elves flew up and settled on Ben's shoulders, giggling.

'N-no, of course not!' stammered Ben. 'She just meant you have pretty wings.'

Flattered, the sand-elves giggled, and one fluttered down to settle on Ben's hand. Enchanted, he lifted the little creature in the air to look at it more closely. It weighed no more than a feather. But when the boy carefully raised his other hand to touch its iridescent wings, all the elves flew away.

Firedrake turned his head round to them. 'What next, Sorrel?' he asked. The little creatures were turning somersaults all over his spines.

'You could shoo them off with a puff of dragon-fire,' suggested Sorrel. 'I've no idea how they'd react, but we have to get moving.'

The dragon nodded. Then Twigleg suddenly reached his arm out from under Ben's jacket and pinched the boy's hand.

'Ouch!' cried Ben, looking down at the homunculus in surprise.

'Young master!' whispered Twigleg. 'Young master, I know how to get rid of them. Lift me up!'

Luckily, the elves were occupied with sliding down Firedrake's tail. Mukarrib and Bilqis were turning cartwheels in the air, and the three elves who had perched on Ben's shoulders were now dancing round and round in the air above Sorrel's head. Ben took Twigleg out of his jacket and put him on his shoulder.

'Wish me luck,' whispered the manikin. 'I hope they react like the mountain elves I know.' Then he cleared his throat, cupped his hands round his mouth and shouted at the top of his voice:

'*Away, abominable airy apparitions! Begone, beastly blighted banshees! Cease chasing, colourful creatures! Dodge, dire dreadful demons! Escape, evil eager elves!*'

The effect was astonishing. Like a swarm of maddened bumblebees, the elves whirled in confusion and rose into the air like a glittering cloud, scolding furiously in their chirping voices.

'The signpost!' cried Sorrel. 'I can see the signpost!'

But no sooner had she said so than the elves scattered again and then dive-bombed the dragon, screeching angrily. As they shook their green hair, silvery dust drifted down on Ben and Sorrel. It made Firedrake sneeze so hard that blue sparks flashed from his nose.

'You broke the spell, fur-face!' cried Twigleg. 'They're scattering sleepy-dust. Quick, back to the alphabet! F, we'd reached F.'

'F!' stammered Ben, as the elves blew sleepy-dust into his nose and tugged frantically at his hair.

Firedrake sneezed again.

'*Flee, feeble fairy flutterers!*' shouted Ben – only just in time, for two elves had seized Twigleg by the arms and were trying to

DRAGON RIDER

drag him away. Cursing, they let him go, and he fell head first into Ben's lap.

'*Go!*' cried the manikin, shaking his little fists in fury. '*Go, ghastly greedy . . .*'

'*Girolles!*' cried Sorrel, flicking the sleepy-dust out of her fur. '*Go, ghastly, greedy girolles! Horrible, hated, heinous horns-of-plenty!*'

Once more the elves fluttered in frantic confusion. Then, buzzing angrily, they rose above the signpost again and flew away towards the dark mountains. Their glittering light glowed in the dark for a little while until it, too, vanished. No more giggling, no more whirring wings, no more twittering little voices. The only sounds to break the silence of the night were the roaring of the sea, the chirping of cicadas – and the distant rumble of a truck engine on the coastal road.

'A lorry! There's a lorry coming!' cried Sorrel, thumping Ben in the back. 'Quick. What does the sign say?'

Ben compared the characters. 'Yes!' he cried. '*Shibam*! This *is* the right way!'

'Careful. Hold on tight!' called Firedrake, beating his wings and rising into the air. The vehicle came closer, but by the time its headlights lit up the signpost the dragon and his passengers had already disappeared over the mountains.

'Are you all right?' Sorrel asked Firedrake anxiously. 'How much dust did you breathe in?'

'I think I've sneezed it all out,' he called back. 'I don't feel at all tired. How about you back there?'

By way of answer, Sorrel yawned. 'Hey, Twigleg!' Peering over Ben's shoulder, she looked down at the homunculus, who was rubbing his eyes wearily. 'How did you know that trick with the elves?'

'I've had plenty of trouble with elves before,' said Twigleg drowsily. 'But I didn't know if alphabetical order would work with that sort.'

'Well, it did,' muttered Sorrel. 'Luckily. Or that wretched dust of theirs would have sent us to sleep in the middle of the road.' She had to yawn again.

Below them, the road that Firedrake was following wound its way further and further into the mountains. The dragon had to fly very carefully to avoid brushing his wings against the rocky slopes on both sides of it.

'Sometimes I've had to go right through the alphabet,' remembered Twigleg, sleepily, 'but the stupid little things never notice if you leave out X.'

Ben rubbed his itching nose. 'All the same, I wish I could have watched them a bit longer,' he murmured. 'They were so funny. And their wings – they shone like soap bubbles.'

'I tell you what,' Sorrel leaned back on one of Firedrake's spines and closed her eyes. 'If you're so mad about those fluttery little things, you should catch one.'

'Catch one?' Ben looked at her, astounded. 'How?'

'Easy,' murmured Sorrel. 'You mix a little milk, two spoonfuls of honey and some rose petals in a bowl, and then you leave it outside on a warm night when the moon's full.'

Ben glanced back at her, still rather doubtful. 'Then what?' he asked, yawning.

Firedrake's wings rushed on through the dark.

'Then,' said Sorrel softly, 'then you can bet your life one of those stupid creatures will come flying along to lap up your honey-sweet, rose-perfumed milk. Simply drop a cobweb over the bowl and there you are – hey presto!'

'A cobweb?' Ben shook his head, baffled. 'Where would I

get a cobweb?'

'That's your problem,' murmured Sorrel. 'I've told you how to catch an elf. You'll have to do the rest yourself.'

Ben leaned back. 'I don't want to catch an elf anyway,' he said. 'I don't think much of catching things. Do you?'

But Sorrel was already asleep. And on Ben's lap Twigleg was snoring softly, elf-dust still sparkling on his nose.

'Firedrake!' called Ben quietly. 'Are you sure you're not tired?'

'Not a bit,' the dragon called back. 'Who knows, perhaps elf-dust keeps dragons awake?'

'Not humans, though,' murmured Ben as he too fell asleep.

Firedrake flew steadily on through the night, following the road that would lead him to the blue djinn.

CHAPTER TWENTY

The Djinn's Ravine

Ben woke up when Firedrake landed, and looked around him in alarm. The sky was bright, and the mountains were shrouded in morning mist as white as milk. The road stopped dead just beyond a sharp bend, where a cliff fell away as steeply as if the world had snapped in two. There was no bridge over to the other side of the gorge.

This must be it, thought Ben. The blue djinn's ravine.

Firedrake was standing on the edge of the precipice, looking down. A rushing sound rose from the depths below.

Ben turned. Sorrel was still snoring peacefully. Carefully, Ben picked up the sleeping Twigleg and climbed down from Firedrake's back.

'Slept off your elfin hangover?' enquired the dragon when Ben was standing beside him. He nuzzled the boy with gentle mockery. 'Look at that. I do believe we've reached the djinn's home.'

Cautiously, Ben looked over the edge of the ravine.

It was not very wide, hardly twice the breadth of the road they had been following. The sheer drop of the cliffs was bare rock at the top, but only a few metres down dense vegetation grew. Flowers scrambled over the stone, and huge palm trees reached towards the light from the bottom of the ravine. It was dark down there, and the rushing sound came to Ben's ears clearly now. It must be the river the professor had mentioned. But Ben heard other noises too. Animal cries drifted up, and the hoarse calls of strange birds.

'Hey, why didn't you wake me up?' asked Sorrel grumpily, from Firedrake's back.

Twigleg, still asleep in the crook of Ben's arm, gave a sudden start and looked around, feeling dazed.

'You can stay up here if you'd rather, Sorrel,' said Firedrake. 'We're flying down, though landing in all that undergrowth won't be easy.'

The dragon swooped down through the air like a shadow. Palm fronds brushed Ben's face as Firedrake broke through the green canopy of the trees. Beating his wings powerfully a couple of times, the dragon made a soft landing on the bank of a river that flowed sluggishly along the bottom of the ravine. Stray rays of sun fell on the water, and Ben looked up. The sky seemed infinitely far away. They were surrounded by hissing, chirping, grunting and creaking sounds as hundreds of living creatures moved through thousands of leaves. The air was hot and humid, and swarms of midges hovered above the river.

'Merciful morels!' Sorrel climbed off Firedrake's back and sank up to her chest in creepers. 'How are we ever supposed to find anything in this jungle?' She looked around uneasily.

'By starting to look for it,' said Firedrake, making his way on through the thick undergrowth.

'Hang on, wait a minute!' Sorrel clutched his tail. 'It's all very well for you! You're not up to your chin in all these leaves. Although,' she said, taking an experimental bite out of one, 'they taste delicious. Absolutely yummy.'

'Want to get on my back again?' asked Firedrake, turning round.

'No, no,' said Sorrel dismissively. 'It's all right. I'll manage on my own. Yum. Honest I will.' She was pulling leaf after leaf off the plants and stuffing them into her backpack. 'These leaves are very, very tasty.'

Ben put Twigleg on his shoulder and grinned.

'Do come along, Sorrel,' said Firedrake, impatiently swishing his tail back and forth. 'You can stock up on provisions once we've found the djinn.'

He turned and went on. Ben followed, and the two of them had soon disappeared among the trees.

'I call that really mean of him!' said Sorrel crossly, trudging along behind them. 'As if that djinn couldn't wait another five minutes. It's not as if *I* live on nothing but moonlight. Does he want me to get so faint with hunger that I fall off his back?'

Firedrake was making his way along the river. The further they went, the narrower the ravine became. At last a huge, fallen palm tree barred the dragon's way. An untidy tangle of roots stuck up in the air, but its tall trunk rested on a couple of large boulders in the riverbed, so that it was lying like a bridge across the water.

'Wait a moment!' Ben put Twigleg down on Firedrake's tail, climbed up on the trunk of the fallen tree and clambered a little way along it.

'Look!' he called, pointing to the opposite bank. 'There, in among the red flowers!'

Firedrake took a step into the water and stretched his neck.

Yes, there it was. A large grey car overgrown with creepers and covered with fallen flower petals. Lizards basked on its bonnet in the sun.

Ben made his precarious way along the tree trunk and jumped down on the opposite bank. The dragon waded through the shallow water with Sorrel and Twigleg and then waited on the bank with them. Ben pushed the creepers aside and peered cautiously into the car. A large lizard sitting on the front seat hissed at him when he looked through the side window. Ben jumped back in alarm. The lizard rapidly disappeared between the seats.

'No glass in the windows,' said Ben quietly. 'Just as the professor told us.'

Cautiously, he put his head in through the car window again. There was no trace of the lizard now, although two snakes were coiled up on the back seat. Ben tightened his lips, put his hand through the window – and pressed the horn. Then he moved rapidly back.

Flocks of birds flew up, squawking. The lizards shot off the hot metal of the car and disappeared into the twining undergrowth.

All was silent again.

Cautiously, Ben stepped back. The professor had told them to wait seventeen paces away from the car. Ben counted his footsteps. One . . . two . . . three . . . four . . . Seventeen paces were a lot. On purpose, he did not make his steps too large. After the seventeenth he sat down on a rock and waited, while Firedrake lay down behind him among the flowers and leaves. Sorrel and Twigleg sat on the dragon's paws. They all stared at the car as if spellbound.

Asif didn't keep them waiting long.

Blue-tinged smoke billowed out of the car and streamed higher and higher. Ben had to crane his neck to look up at the vast spiral. The drifting wisps merged together among the tree tops, whirling around each other faster and faster until the gigantic pillar of smoke formed into a body, a body as blue as the night sky and so large that its shadow darkened the entire ravine. Asif's thousand eyes, small and bright as jewels, sparkled all over his skin, his shoulders, his arms and his fat belly.

Ben retreated until he felt Firedrake's scales behind him. Sorrel and Twigleg huddled on the dragon's back. Only Firedrake did not move, but raised his head and gazed up at the djinn.

'Well, well! Look at *this*, then!' The djinn bent over them. A thousand eyes with a thousand images in them shone above their heads, and as he spoke Asif's breath blew like the hot desert wind from one end of the ravine to the other.

'So what have we *here*?' boomed the djinn. 'A dragon, a genuine dragon. Well, well, *well*!' His voice was as hollow as an echo, resounding from wall to wall of the rocky ravine. 'So it was *you* making my skin itch so much that a thousand servants had to scratch it for me.'

'I didn't do it on purpose, djinn!' Firedrake called. 'We've come to ask you a question.'

'*Aaaaah*!' The djinn's mouth stretched into a smile. 'I answer only *human* questions.'

'We know!' Ben jumped up, pushed the hair back from his forehead and looked up at the huge djinn. 'I'm going to ask you the question, Asif.'

'*Oooooh*!' breathed the djinn. 'So this little fellow knows *our name*! What *kind* of a question is it? You know the rules?'

'Yes,' replied Ben.

'*Good*.' The djinn leaned a little further down, his breath as hot as the steam rising from a saucepan. Perspiration was dripping off the end of Ben's nose.

'*Ask away!*' breathed Asif. 'I could just *do* with another servant! Someone small to clean my ears, for instance. Now *you* would be the ideal size for that.'

Ben gulped. Asif's face was now directly above his head. Blue hairs as thick as saplings grew in his nostrils, and his pointed ears, rising high above his bald skull, were larger than Firedrake's wings. Two huge eyes, green as the eyes of a giant cat, looked mockingly down on Ben. He saw his own reflection in them, tiny and forlorn. Asif's many, many other eyes showed other scenes: snow fell on strange cities, ships capsized at sea.

Ben mopped the sweat off his nose and said in a loud voice, 'Where does the Rim of Heaven lie?'

Sorrel narrowed her eyes. Firedrake held his breath, and Twigleg began shaking all over. But Ben, heart thumping, waited for the djinn's answer.

'The *Rim of Heaven*!' repeated Asif.

He rose a few more metres into the air, and then laughed so loud that stones broke away from the walls of the ravine and crashed into the depths. His fat belly wobbled above Ben's head as if it might drop on him any moment.

'Oh, little one, little one!' boomed the djinn, bending over the boy again.

Firedrake placed himself protectively in front of Ben, but Asif gently pushed the dragon aside with his huge hand.

'The *Rim of Heaven*!' he repeated. 'You're not putting that question for yourself, are you?'

Ben shook his head. 'No,' he said. 'My friends need to know.

Why ask me that?'

'*Why*?' boomed Asif, so loud that Twigleg put his hands over his ears. 'Because you are the *first*! The *first* not to ask for himself, my beetle-sized little human. The *first* in so many thousands of years that even I can't count them. So I am doubly glad to answer your question. Although I really *could* have used you as a servant.'

'You – you – do you know the answer?' Ben's tongue was sticking to the roof of his mouth.

'Do I know the *answer*?' The djinn laughed again. He knelt down and held his blue thumb in front of Ben's face. 'Look at *that*!' he breathed. 'Look into my two hundred and twenty-third eye. What do you see?'

Ben bent over Asif's thumb.

'I see a river!' he whispered, so quietly that Firedrake had to prick up his ears to hear him. 'It's flowing through green mountains. On and on. Now the mountains are higher. Everything's bare and empty. There are mountains very oddly shaped, like, like . . .' But the picture was changing.

'The river's flowing past a building,' murmured Ben. 'Not an ordinary building. A palace or something like that.'

The djinn nodded. 'Look at it – look at it *hard*,' he breathed. 'Look at it *closely*.'

Ben looked until the picture blurred again. Then Asif held out his forefinger. 'And here is my two hundred and fifty-fifth eye,' he said. 'What do you see *there*?'

'I see a valley,' said Ben. 'A valley surrounded by nine high mountains with snow-capped peaks. They're almost all the same height. The valley is full of mist.'

'*Good*!' Asif blinked. The picture blurred again – like the images in all his other nine hundred and ninety-nine eyes – and a new one appeared.

Ben's eyes opened wide. 'There, oh, look!' He bent excitedly over Asif's gigantic finger. 'Firedrake, there's a dragon there. A dragon like you! In a cave. A gigantic cave!'

Firedrake took a deep breath and stepped forward uneasily. But Asif blinked again, and the picture in his two hundred and fifty-fifth eye blurred, along with all the rest. Disappointed, Ben straightened up. The djinn withdrew his hand, placed it on his mighty knee, and stroked his long moustache with his other hand.

'Did you notice what you saw?' he asked the boy. 'Did you memorise it *carefully*?'

Ben nodded. 'Yes,' he stammered. 'Yes, but—'

'Beware!' Asif crossed his arms over his chest and looked at the boy sternly. 'You have asked your question. But now watch your tongue, or you may yet be my servant.'

Confused, Ben bowed his head. The djinn rose and floated a little way up in the air, as light as a balloon.

'Follow the river Indus and seek the images you saw in my eyes!' boomed Asif. '*Seek the images.* Enter the palace on the mountainside and break the moonlight on the stone dragon's head. When that day comes, twenty fingers will point the way to the Rim of Heaven, and silver will be worth more than gold.'

Speechless, Ben looked up at the vast djinn. Asif smiled.

'*You, you* were the *first*!' he called again.

Then he inflated like a sail in the wind, and his arms and legs turned to blue smoke again. Asif whirled round and round until leaves and flowers were dancing in his wake and he was nothing but a pillar of blue smoke. It dissolved in a gust of wind and disappeared.

'Seek the images,' murmured Ben, and closed his eyes.

CHAPTER TWENTY-ONE
Twigleg's Decision

Firedrake wanted to fly on at once. But the sun was still high in the sky, and although it had soon grown dark in the djinn's ravine there were still many hours to go before night would fall outside. So they found a place far from the djinn's lair, down by the river among the leaves that tasted so good to Sorrel, and waited there for the moon to rise. However, the dragon could not sleep. He paced restlessly up and down the riverbank.

'Firedrake, you really ought to get some sleep,' said Ben, spreading the map out on a sea of white flowers. 'There's still a long way to go before we reach the coast.'

Firedrake craned his neck over Ben's shoulder, his eyes following the boy's finger as it traced their way over mountains, gorges and deserts.

'This is where we ought to reach the sea,' Ben told him. 'See the mark the rat made? I don't think that part of the route looks difficult. But this,' and he indicated the vast expanse of sea between the Arabian peninsula and the delta of the Indus, 'this bothers me. I've no idea where you'll be able to land. Not an island in sight. And it will take us at least two nights to get across.' He shook his head. 'I can't see how we're going to do it without coming down on the water.'

Thoughtfully, Firedrake looked first at the map and then at the boy. 'Where's the village where the woman who knows about dragons lives?'

Ben tapped the map. 'Here. Right at the mouth of the river Indus. So it wouldn't take us far out of our way to visit her. And do you know where the Indus rises?'

The dragon shook his head.

'In the Himalayas!' cried Ben. 'That fits, doesn't it? We only have to find the palace I saw in Asif's eye and then—'

'Then what?' Sorrel sat down beside them in the fragrant flowers. 'Then you break the moonlight on the stone dragon's head. Can you tell me what that's supposed to mean?'

'Not yet,' said Ben. 'But I'll know when it happens.'

'And how about the twenty fingers?' The brownie lowered her voice. 'Always supposing that blue person wasn't just having us on.'

'Oh no.' Twigleg climbed on to Ben's lap. 'That's only the way a djinn talks. The young master's right. The words will explain themselves, you wait and see.'

'I hope you really are right,' muttered Sorrel, rolling up in a ball underneath a huge fern frond.

Firedrake lay down beside her and lowered his head to his paws. 'Break the moonlight,' he murmured. 'Sounds like a riddle to me.' He yawned and closed his eyes.

It was dark and cold under the palms now. Ben and Sorrel pressed close to Firedrake's warm scales, and soon all three of them were asleep.

Only Twigleg remained awake, sitting beside them among the white blossom. The scent of the flowers made him feel dizzy. He listened to Ben's peaceful breathing, looked at Firedrake's silver scales and his friendly face, so different from the face of his master Nettlebrand, and sighed. A single question was buzzing around in his head like a captive bumblebee.

Should he tell his master what the djinn had said? And by doing so betray the silver dragon?

Twigleg's little head was aching so hard as he pondered this question that he pressed his hands to his throbbing temples. He hadn't stolen Nettlebrand's scale back from the boy yet, either. He leaned against Ben's back and closed his eyes. Perhaps his brain would calm down in his sleep. But just as he thought the peaceful breathing of the other three was making him drowsy, something plucked at his sleeve. The homunculus started, and sat up. Was one of those nasty giant lizards that lurked among the creepers trying to take a bite out of him?

But it was the raven sitting in the tangled leaves in front of Twigleg, plucking at his sleeve with his beak.

'Oh, it's you. What do you want?' whispered the homunculus, annoyed.

He rose quietly and beckoned the raven to follow him away from his sleeping companions. The big bird stalked after him.

'You've forgotten your report,' he croaked. 'How much longer are you going to leave it?'

'What business is that of yours?' Twigleg stopped on the other side of a tall bush. 'I – I'm going to wait until we're over the sea.'

'Why?' The raven pecked a caterpillar off the branches of the bush and looked at the manikin suspiciously. 'There's no reason to wait,' he cawed. 'You'll only make our master angry. What did the djinn say?'

'I'll be telling our master,' replied Twigleg, evasively. 'You ought to have listened more carefully.'

'Huh!' croaked the raven. 'That blue creature wouldn't stop growing. I thought I'd better keep out of the way.'

'That's your bad luck.' Scratching his ear, Twigleg peered through the branches at Firedrake. But the dragon and his friends were fast asleep, while the shadows in the ravine grew ever darker.

The raven preened his feathers and gave the homunculus a black look.

'You're getting too uppity, manikin,' he cawed. 'I don't like it. Maybe I ought to tell the master.'

'Go on, then, do! Goodness knows, that won't be news to him,' said Twigleg, but his heart beat faster. 'Anyway, I can set your mind at rest.' He assumed a grave expression. 'I'm going to report to him today. Word of honour. I just have to take another look at the map first. The boy's map, I mean.'

The raven put his head on one side. 'The map? Why?'

Twigleg made a face. 'You wouldn't understand, beaky. Now get out. If that brownie girl sees you she won't believe it if I say we have nothing to do with each other.'

'All right.' The raven caught another caterpillar and flapped his wings. 'But I'm following you. I'll be keeping an eye on you. So you be sure to make that report.'

Twigleg watched the raven until he disappeared among the tops of the palm trees. Then he quickly went over to Ben's backpack, took out the map and opened it. Oh yes, he'd make his report. At once. But it would be a special kind of report, a very special kind indeed. His eyes scanned the seas and mountains until he spotted a large, pale brown area. He knew what brown meant. Ben had explained exactly how to read the wonderful map. Brown meant no water. Not a drop of water far and wide. And that was exactly what Twigleg was looking for.

'I'm sick and tired of it!' he muttered. 'I'm sick and tired of being his spy. I'm going to send him off to the desert. The biggest desert I can find!'

Only a desert could keep Nettlebrand away from the small human being and the silver dragon a little while longer. He couldn't have cared less if his master had only wanted to eat the unfriendly brownie! But not the small human. No. He, Twigleg, wasn't going to help him do that. He'd seen Nettlebrand crunch up his brothers. He'd seen him devour their maker. But Nettlebrand wasn't going to get the little human into his greedy jaws. Ever.

Twigleg noted exactly where the great desert lay. Then he walked deeper and deeper into the ravine, far from the lair of the blue djinn, far from the sleeping dragon.

Leaning over the waters of the river, the manikin reported back to his master.

CHAPTER TWENTY-TWO

The Vanishing Moon

Three days and three long nights later, Firedrake was standing on the shores of the Arabian Sea waiting for night to fall. His scales were dusty with yellow sand. It was a long time since he had set out from his northern valley in search of the Rim of Heaven. His cave at home seemed infinitely far away, and the dark sea ahead of him looked an infinite expanse too.

Firedrake looked up at the sky. The last of the light vanished as if the waves had swallowed it up, and only the round moon, bright as silver, shone over the water. There was still quite a long while to go before the dark time of the moon and the new moon's rising, but would he have found the Rim of Heaven by then?

'Ten more days,' said Ben.

He was standing beside the dragon on the sand and, like Firedrake, looking towards the horizon where sky and sea merged. There lay their journey's end, hidden beyond the waves and mountains. 'We ought to reach the palace I saw in Asif's eye in ten days' time at the latest. It can't be much further after that.'

Firedrake nodded. He looked at the boy. 'Are you homesick?'

Ben shook his head and leaned against the dragon's warm scales. 'No,' he said. 'I could go on flying like this for ever.'

'I'm not homesick either,' said Firedrake. 'But I wish I knew how the others are doing back at home. I'd like to know how close the humans have come, and whether the sound of their machines is already echoing over the dark mountains. But unfortunately,' he sighed, looking out to sea again where patches of silver moonlight floated on the waves, 'unfortunately I don't have a thousand eyes like Asif. Who knows, by the time I reach the Rim of Heaven it may be too late for the others.'

'Oh, come on!' Ben patted the dragon's silver flank affectionately. 'You've made it this far. Once we cross the sea we're almost there.'

'That's right,' said Sorrel. She had been off to fill the water bottles. 'Smell this,' she added, holding a pawful of prickly leaves under Ben's nose. They had a heavy, spicy fragrance. 'These things prickle your tongue, but they taste almost as good as they smell. Where are the backpacks?'

'Here.' Ben handed them over to her. 'But mind you don't squash Twigleg. He's asleep in among my clothes.'

'Don't worry, I won't snap his little legs off,' muttered Sorrel, stowing the aromatic leaves away in her backpack. As she bent over Ben's pack, Twigleg stretched his arms out of it, yawning. He looked around, then hastily tucked his head back inside.

'What's the matter?' asked Ben in surprise.

'Water!' replied the manikin, wriggling down among Ben's now sandy clothes till only the tip of his nose was showing. 'All that water makes me nervous.'

'Just for once we feel the same way,' said Sorrel, putting her backpack over her furry shoulder. 'I'm not too keen on water either. But we have to get across it.'

'You never know who can see you when you're over water,' muttered Twigleg.

Ben glanced down at him in surprise. 'What on earth do you mean? Who'd be looking at you? The fish?'

'Yes, yes, that's what I mean!' Twigleg giggled nervously. 'The fish.'

Shaking her head, Sorrel climbed up on Firedrake's back.

'What utter rubbish he talks!' she growled. 'Even the elves aren't that stupid, and they can natter on all night.'

Twigleg stuck his pointed tongue out at her.

Ben couldn't conceal a grin. 'Want me to leave the backpack open?' he asked the homunculus.

'No, no,' said Twigleg, 'strap it up by all means, young master. I'm used to the dark.'

'If you say so.' Ben closed his backpack, climbed up on the dragon's back with it and strapped himself to Firedrake's spines. Then he took the compass out of his trouser pocket. If they weren't going to rely on Sorrel's instincts they'd be needing it over the next few days and nights. Hundreds of miles of sea water lay ahead of them. There would be no coastline to help them find their way, only the sky above, and none of them knew much about navigating by the stars.

'Ready?' called Firedrake, shaking the desert sand from his scales for the last time and spreading his wings.

'Ready!' Sorrel called.

Firedrake rose into the dark sky and flew towards the moon.

It was a fine, warm, starlit night.

They had soon left the mountainous coast behind. Darkness swallowed up the land, and ahead of them, behind them, to the left and to the right of them stretched nothing but water. Now and then the lights of a ship winked on the waves. Seabirds flew by, squawking in alarm at the sight of Firedrake.

Just after midnight, Sorrel suddenly gave a terrified shriek and bent over the dragon's neck.

'Firedrake!' she called. 'Firedrake! Have you seen the moon?'

'What about it?' asked the dragon.

All this time his eyes had been fixed on the waves below, but now he looked up. What he saw made his wings feel as heavy as lead.

'What is it?' Ben leaned over Sorrel's shoulder in alarm.

'The moon,' she cried frantically. 'It's turning red.'

Now Ben saw it too. The moon was indeed taking on a tinge of coppery-red.

'What does it mean?' he asked, baffled.

'It means it'll disappear any moment now!' cried Sorrel. 'There's going to be an eclipse – a mouldy old eclipse of the moon! Now, of all times!' She gazed down at the crashing, foaming waves in terror.

Firedrake was flying more and more slowly, his wings beating as sluggishly as if invisible weights hung from them.

'You're flying too low, Firedrake!' called Sorrel.

'I can't help it!' the dragon called back to her wearily. 'I'm weak as a duckling, Sorrel!'

Ben looked up at the sky, where the moon now hung like a rusty coin among the stars.

'We've seen eclipses before,' babbled Sorrel, 'but we were always above solid land at the time. What are we going to do now?'

Firedrake dropped lower and lower. Ben could already taste the salt sea-spray on his lips. And then, in the last red glow of light cast on the waves by the fading moon, he suddenly saw a chain of small islands rising from the sea in the distance. Strange islands they were, rising humpbacked from the water like half-submerged hills.

'Firedrake!' shouted Ben, as loud as he could.

The pounding of the waves tore the words from his lips, but the dragon had keen ears.

'Look there, ahead of us!' yelled Ben. 'I can see islands. Try to land on one of them.'

At that very moment the earth's dark shadow engulfed the moon.

Firedrake plummeted from the sky like a bird winged by a shot, but the first of the strange islands was already below him. To Ben and Sorrel, it looked almost as if the island chain were rising towards them from the foaming sea. The dragon fell rather than landed on the island. His riders were almost wrenched from their straps. Ben realised he was trembling all over, and Sorrel wasn't doing much better. But Firedrake let himself sink to the ground with a sigh, folded his wings and licked the salt water off his paws.

'Lawyer's wig and hedgehog fungus!' Weak at the knees, Sorrel slid off Firedrake's back. 'This journey's going to shorten my life by a hundred years – no, more like five hundred or a thousand! Ugh!' Giving herself a shake, she looked down the steep slope of the hilly island to the black waves breaking on its shore. 'We almost took a very nasty dip in the sea!'

'I can't make it out.' Ben slung the backpacks over his shoulders and climbed down Firedrake's tail. 'There weren't any islands marked on the map.'

Narrowing his eyes, he peered into the darkness, where one steep little hill after another rose from the sea.

'That just proves what I keep telling you,' said Sorrel. 'The rat's map is useless.' She looked around her, snuffling. 'There's something fishy about this.'

'Well?' Ben shrugged his shoulders. 'We're in the middle of the sea. There's bound to be fish around.'

'No.' Sorrel shook her head. 'I mean there's something wrong about this island – *and* it smells of fish.'

Firedrake got to his feet and looked rather more closely at the ground. 'Look at that!' he said. 'The island's covered with fish-scales. It's like a—'

'Yes, like a giant fish!' whispered Ben.

'Get on my back!' cried Firedrake. 'Quick!'

At that moment the island quivered.

'Run!' shouted Sorrel, pushing Ben towards the dragon. They scuttled over the damp and scaly mound. Firedrake stretched out his neck, and as the island rose higher and higher from the waves the two of them hauled themselves up by his horns. Clutching his spines, they scrambled on to his back and strapped themselves in place with trembling fingers.

'But the moon!' cried Ben, desperately. 'The moon is dark. How are you going to fly, Firedrake?'

He was right. There was nothing but a black, gaping hole in the sky where the moon ought to have been.

'I must try anyway!' cried the dragon, spreading his wings. But whatever he did, his body wouldn't rise a finger's breadth into the air. Ben and Sorrel exchanged horrified glances.

Suddenly, with a loud snort, a mighty head shot out of the sea in front of them. It had large fins like decorative feathers growing on it. Slanted eyes flashed at them mockingly beneath heavy lids, and a forked tongue flickered between the two sharp, needle-like fangs that emerged from the creature's narrow jaws.

'A sea serpent!' cried Ben. 'We've landed on a sea serpent!'

The serpent's long, long neck rose from the water until its head was hovering directly above Firedrake, who stood on the scaly hump of the creature's back as if he'd taken root there.

'Well, well, look at this!' hissed the serpent in a soft, sing-song voice. 'Such strange visitors to the realm of salt and water where my twin sister and I reign supreme. What brings a fiery dragon, a small human and a shaggy brownie girl out to sea, so far from solid ground? Not just an appetite for a supper of slippery shiny fish, I suppose?' Her tongue flickered like a hungry wild beast in the air above Firedrake's head.

'Get down!' the dragon whispered to Ben and Sorrel. 'Get right down behind my spines.'

Sorrel obeyed at once, but Ben stayed where he was, his mouth wide open, staring at the sea serpent. She was a beautiful sight, an astonishing and enchanting creature. In the absence of

the moon the only light came from the stars, yet every one of her millions of scales shimmered with all the colours of the rainbow. Observing Ben's amazement, the serpent looked down at him with an ironic smile. He was not much bigger than the flickering tip of her tongue.

'Ben, get your head down!' whispered Sorrel. 'Unless you want it bitten off!'

But Ben wasn't listening to her. He felt all Firedrake's muscles tensing as if he were preparing to fight.

'We're not after anything of yours, serpent,' called the dragon, and his voice sounded as it had when he rescued Ben from the men in the old factory building. 'We're searching for a place that lies beyond the sea.'

A quiver ran through the sea serpent's body. To Ben's great relief, he realised that she was laughing.

'Are you indeed?' hissed the serpent. 'Well, if I know your fiery kind you'll need moonlight before you can rise into the air. So until the moon shows its face again, you'll have to stay with

me. But don't worry. I'm here purely out of curiosity, sheer insatiable curiosity. I wanted to find out why my scales have been itching ever since sunset, in a way they haven't itched for over a hundred years. I expect you know the rule: one fabulous creature attracts another, correct?'

'Yes, and a thorough nuisance it is,' replied Firedrake, but Ben felt the dragon's muscles beginning to relax again.

'A nuisance?' The sea serpent's slender body rocked to and fro. 'That rule is what saved you and your two friends from drowning when the moon went dark.' She lowered her pointed muzzle until her face was level with Firedrake's. 'So, where have you come from and where are you going? I haven't seen anyone like you since the day your silver relations were disturbed as they bathed in the sea and vanished from my realm.'

Firedrake straightened up. 'You know that story?' he asked.

The serpent smiled, stretching her huge body in the waves. 'Of course. In fact, I was there at the time.'

'You were there?' Firedrake took a step back. A growl emerged from his chest. 'Then you were the sea monster who chased them away!'

Terrified, Sorrel flung her arms round Ben. 'Oh no, no!' she moaned. 'Careful, it's going to eat us up!'

But the serpent merely looked down at Firedrake with an amused smile. 'Me? Nonsense!' she hissed. 'I only chase ships. The monster was a dragon. A dragon like you, only much, much bigger, with armour made of golden scales.'

Firedrake looked at the creature incredulously.

The serpent nodded. 'His eyes were red like the dying moon, full of murderous greed.' The memory wiped the smile off her face. 'That night,' she said, as the sea rocked her great body, 'that night your relations came down from the mountains to the sea,

as they always did when the moon was round and full in the sky.
My sister and I swam close to the coast, so close that we could see
the faces of the people sitting outside their huts waiting for the
dragons. We submerged our bodies in the water so as not to
alarm them, for human beings fear what they don't know,
especially when it's bigger than they are. Moreover,' said the
creature, smiling, 'we serpents are not popular among them.'

Feeling embarrassed, Ben bowed his head.

'The dragons,' continued the serpent, 'plunged into the foaming waves, looking as if they were made of moonlight.' She
looked at Firedrake. 'The people on the shore smiled. Creatures
of your kind calm the anger that human beings always carry with
them. Dragons banish their sorrow. That's why they believe you
bring good luck. But that night, yes, that night,' hissed the
serpent softly, 'another dragon came to chase the good luck away.
The water boiled around his great muzzle as he surfaced in the
sea. Dead fish floated on the waves. The silver dragons spread
their wet wings in fear, but then, all of a sudden, the light of the
moon was hidden by flocks of black birds. No cloud, however
dark and heavy, can rob the moon of its power, but the birds did.
Their dark feathers quenched the moonlight, and hard as the
dragons tried to beat their wings, they couldn't fly. They would
all have been lost, had my sister and I not been there to attack the
monster.'

The sea serpent fell silent for a moment.

'You killed him?' asked Firedrake.

'We tried to,' replied the serpent. 'We wound our coils around
his armour and kept his jaws shut with our bodies. But his
golden scales were cold as ice and burned us. Before long we had
to let him go, but our attack made the black birds disperse, and
the moonlight gave the dragons enough strength to escape. The

humans, stricken by grief and terror, stood on the shore watching them go as they flew up the river Indus and disappeared into the darkness. The monster plunged beneath the waves, and no matter how hard my sister and I searched the deepest depths of the sea we could find no trace of it. The black birds flew away, cawing. But the silver dragons never returned, although for long afterwards people stood waiting on the seashore on nights when the moon was full.'

When the sea serpent had finished her story no one said a word.

At last Firedrake looked up at the black sky. 'Did you never hear of them again?' he asked.

The serpent swayed back and forth. 'Oh, there are many stories. The mermen and mermaids who swim up the Indus from time to time tell tales of a valley far, far away in the mountains, and say that the shadow of a flying dragon sometimes falls on the valley floor. They believe that brownies have helped the dragons to hide. And looking at your companion here,' she added, glancing at Sorrel, 'I'd say the story is not improbable.'

Firedrake did not reply, but stood there sunk deep in thought.

'I really wish we knew where that monster went,' growled Sorrel. 'I don't like the way he can appear and disappear, just like that.'

The serpent bent her head until her tongue was tickling Sorrel's pointed ears.

'The monster is in league with the powers of the water, brownie,' she hissed. 'All dragons can swim, although they are creatures of fire, but this one is lord of the water. Water is his servant even more than it is mine. I never saw that monster again, but sometimes, when I feel a cold current passing through the depths of the sea, I know that the dragon with golden armour is out hunting.'

Firedrake was still silent. 'Golden,' he murmured at last. 'He was golden. Sorrel, does that remind you of anything?'

The brownie looked at him in surprise. 'No, why should it? Oh, wait a minute—'

'The old dragon at home in the north!' said Firedrake. 'He warned us against the Golden One before we set out. Strange, don't you think?'

Ben suddenly clapped a hand to his forehead.

'Golden!' he cried. 'That's it! Golden scales!' He quickly opened his backpack. 'Sorry, Twigleg,' he said, as the homunculus sleepily put his head out from Ben's things. 'Just looking for my bag with the scale in it.'

'The scale?' All at once the homunculus was wide awake.

'Yes, I want to show it to the serpent.' Ben carefully fished the golden scale out from among his other treasures.

Twigleg emerged anxiously from his warm hiding place.

'What serpent?' he asked, peering out of the backpack – and then, with a shriek of terror, he dived back into Ben's clothes.

'Here, Twigleg!' Ben pulled him out by his collar. 'There's nothing to be frightened of. She's rather large but perfectly friendly. Honest!'

'Friendly?' muttered Twigleg, digging himself in again as far as he could go. 'Anything that size is dangerous, however friendly it may be.'

The sea serpent brought her head closer, looking curious. 'What do you want to show me, little human?' she asked. 'And what's that whispering in your bag?'

'Only Twigleg,' replied Ben. He carefully stood up on Firedrake's back and held the scale out to the serpent on the palm of his hand. 'Look, could this be one of the giant dragon's scales?'

The serpent bent so close to Ben's hand that the tip of her tongue brushed his arm. 'Yes,' she hissed. 'Yes, it could be. Put it against my neck.'

Ben looked at the serpent in surprise, but he did as she asked. When the golden scale touched the serpent's iridescent neck her whole body shuddered so violently that Firedrake almost fell off her back.

'Yes,' she hissed. 'That is one of the monster's scales. It looks like warm gold, but it burns like ice.'

'It's always icy cold,' said Ben. 'Even if you leave it out in the sun. I've experimented.' Carefully, he put the scale back in his little bag. Twigleg had disappeared from view entirely.

'Fair cousin,' said the sea serpent, addressing the dragon politely, 'you must take good care of your little human. Possessing something that belongs to so wild and rapacious a creature is not without its dangers. Perhaps the monster will want its property back one day, even if that property is only a single scale.'

'You're right.' Firedrake turned to Ben, concern in his eyes. 'Maybe you ought to throw that scale into the sea.'

But Ben shook his head. 'No, please!' he said. 'I really want to look after it for you, Firedrake. It was a present, don't you see? Anyway, how would the monster know I have it?'

Firedrake nodded thoughtfully. 'You're right, how would he know?' He looked up at the place of the moon in the sky. A faint rusty-red glow was beginning to return.

'Yes, the moon will soon be back,' said the serpent, following the direction of Firedrake's gaze. 'Do you wish to take to the air again, fiery cousin, or shall I carry you over the sea on my back?

You'd have to tell me where you're going, though.'

Surprised, Firedrake looked at the serpent. His wings were still heavy, and his limbs felt as weary as if he hadn't slept for years.

'Go on, say yes!' said Ben, patting the dragon's scales. 'Let the serpent carry us. She won't get lost, and you could have a good rest, couldn't you?'

Firedrake turned his head to look at Sorrel.

'I expect I'll be seasick,' she muttered. 'All the same – yes, you really could do with a rest.'

Firedrake agreed, and turned back to the serpent. 'We are bound for the village on the coast where the dragons were attacked. Someone we want to visit lives there.'

The sea serpent nodded. 'Then I will take you to the place,' she said.

CHAPTER TWENTY-THREE

The Stone

The great sea serpent carried the dragon and his friends over the Arabian Sea for two days and two nights. She did not fear daylight because she was not afraid of human beings, but at Firedrake's request she steered a course through regions of the sea where no ship ever sailed. Her scaly back was so broad that Firedrake could sleep on it, while Sorrel tucked into her provisions and Ben stretched his legs. When the sea was calm the serpent glided over the water as if it were a green glass mirror. But if the waves surged rough and high, she raised the coils of her body so far into the air that not a drop of spray splashed into the faces of her three passengers.

Sorrel overcame her seasickness by eating the delicious leaves she had picked in the valley where the djinn lived. Firedrake slept almost all through their sea voyage. But Ben spent most of his time sitting behind the high crest on the sea serpent's head, listening to her sing-song voice as she told him about all the creatures hidden from him by the waters of the sea. He was spellbound by her tales of mermaids, of ship-haunting sprites, eight-armed krakens, royal mermen and singing giant rays, luminous fish and coral gnomes, shark-faced demons and the children of the sea who ride on whales. Ben was so captivated by the sea serpent's stories that he quite forgot about Twigleg in his backpack.

The homunculus crouched among Ben's things with his heart thudding, listening to the sounds of Sorrel smacking her lips and the soft hiss of the great serpent's voice, and wondering with every breath he drew where his master might be.

Had Nettlebrand really gone off to the desert? Was he still stuck among the dunes? Had he realised yet that Twigleg had fooled him, or was he still searching for Firedrake's tracks in the hot sand? Twigleg's head was aching fit to burst with all these questions, but worse, much worse, he was tormented by a sound that came to his keen ears on the second day of their voyage with the sea serpent. It was the hoarse croaking of a raven.

Strange and menacing, that sound rang through the roaring of the waves, drowned out the hissing of the serpent and made Twigleg's heart thump frantically. Cautiously, he crawled a little way out of the backpack, which was still hanging from one of Firedrake's spines. The dragon was breathing peacefully, fast asleep. High above them in the blue sky where the sun blazed, a black bird was circling among white seagulls.

Twigleg withdrew his head until only his nose emerged from the coarse fabric of the backpack. That wasn't just any old raven that had lost its way and had been carried by the wind to this part of the world – much as Twigleg wanted to think so. No, it certainly wasn't. If only the gigantic serpent would simply rear up and lick it out of the sky with her tongue, like a frog catching a fly!

But the serpent didn't so much as glance at the sky.

I must think of a good story for Nettlebrand, thought Twigleg. A very good story. Think of something, he told himself, think of something, why can't you?

The manikin was not the only one to notice the raven. Darkness had hidden the black bird during the night, but Sorrel couldn't miss him against the blue sky, and soon she was sure that he was following them. Carefully keeping her balance, she made her way along the serpent's body to Ben, who was sitting in the shade of the creature's shimmering crest and listening to a tale of two warring mermaid queens.

'Have you seen it?' Sorrel asked him, in some agitation.

The sea serpent turned her head in surprise, and Ben reluctantly made himself emerge from the underwater realm into which her stories carried him.

'Seen what?' he asked, watching a shoal of dolphins cross the serpent's path.

'The raven, of course,' hissed Sorrel. 'Look up there. Don't you see it?'

'You're right,' he said in surprise. 'It really is a raven.'

'It's following us,' growled Sorrel. 'It's been following us for quite some time, I'm sure it has. All through this voyage I've had a feeling one of those beaky creatures was after us. I'm beginning to think there was something in what that white rat said. About someone sending out those ravens as scouts. Suppose the golden monster's behind it? Suppose the ravens are his spies?'

'Well, I don't know.' Ben narrowed his eyes. 'Sounds a bit far-fetched.'

'And what about the birds that covered the moon?' asked Sorrel. 'In the old days, when the dragons were trying to escape the monster? Those were ravens, weren't they, serpent?'

The sea serpent nodded, and swam more slowly.

'Black birds with red eyes,' she hissed. 'They're still sometimes seen on the coast to this day.'

'Hear that?' Sorrel bit her lip angrily. 'Oh, mouldy morels! If only I had a stone to throw. I'd soon send that black feathery thing packing.'

'I have a stone,' said Ben. 'In my backpack, in the bag with the scale. The mountain dwarves gave it to me. But it's only a little one.'

'Never mind.' Sorrel jumped up and made her way along the serpent's back to Firedrake.

'But how are you going to throw a stone so high?' asked Ben, when she returned with his backpack.

Sorrel only chuckled. She rummaged around in Ben's back-pack until she found the bag. It really was a small stone, not much bigger than a bird's egg.

'Here!' Alarmed, Twigleg put his sharp nose over the top of the backpack. 'What are you going to do with that stone, fur-face?'

'Get rid of a raven.' Sorrel spat on it a couple of times, rubbed her saliva off it – and then spat again. Ben looked at her, baffled.

'Better not,' whispered Twigleg from the backpack. 'Ravens don't take kindly to that sort of thing.'

'Don't they indeed?' Sorrel shrugged her shoulders and tossed the stone playfully from paw to paw.

'No, honestly they don't!' Twigleg's voice was so shrill that Firedrake raised his head and Ben looked at the homunculus in surprise. Even the sea serpent turned her head to them.

'Ravens,' faltered Twigleg, 'ravens bear a grudge. They're vengeful birds – the ones I know, anyway.'

Sorrel looked at him suspiciously. 'You know a lot of ravens, do you?'

Twigleg jumped nervously.

'N-n-not really,' he stammered. 'But . . . I've heard people say that.'

Sorrel just shook her head scornfully and glanced up at the sky. The raven had come closer, and was circling lower and lower. Ben could see its small eyes quite clearly.

'Look, Sorrel!' he said in surprise. 'That raven has red eyes.'

'Red eyes? Well, well.' Sorrel weighed up the little stone in her paw one last time. 'I really don't like this at all. No. That bird must go.'

Like lightning, she took aim and hurled the stone into the sky.

It flew straight as an arrow to the raven, struck his right wing, and remained stuck to his feathers like a burr. Cawing angrily, the black bird fluttered about, beating his wings violently and lurching about in the sky as if he had lost all sense of direction.

'There!' said Sorrel, pleased. 'That'll keep him occupied for a while.'

Ben watched incredulously as the raven pecked more and more frantically at his wing, and finally flew unsteadily away. Before long he was a mere speck in the distance.

Sorrel chuckled. 'Brownie spit – nothing like it,' she said, going back to have a nap in the shade of the dragon.

The sea serpent lowered her neck into the cool water again, and Ben settled down close to her crest to listen to more of her stories. But Twigleg crouched low in Ben's backpack, his face as white as chalk as he thought despairingly that the raven, too, knew exactly how to summon their master.

CHAPTER TWENTY-FOUR

The Anger of Nettlebrand

Nettlebrand was furious. His spiny tail lashed the desert sand until he was shrouded in clouds of yellow dust, and Gravelbeard, kneeling between the dragon's horns, had a coughing fit.

'Aaargh!' bellowed Nettlebrand, as his huge claws stamped over the dunes of the Great Desert. 'What did that stupid spider-legged creature tell me? Said they were hiding a day's journey away from the oasis, did he? Oh yes? Then how come I've been searching for over two days, running my claws off in this hot sand?'

Snorting, he stopped on the crest of a dune and scrutinised the desert. His red eyes were streaming in the heat, but pitilessly as the sun blazed down from the sky, his armour remained as cold as ice.

'Perhaps the djinn was lying,' suggested Gravelbeard. He kept brushing the sand off Nettlebrand's golden scales, but he couldn't keep up with the work of the desert wind. Nettlebrand's joints were creaking and groaning as if they hadn't been oiled for weeks.

'Perhaps, perhaps!' growled Nettlebrand. 'Or perhaps that fool of a homunculus got the wrong end of the stick.'

He stared up at the burning sun. Vultures wheeled in the sky above them. Nettlebrand opened his jaws and belched his stinking breath up at the great birds. They fell as if struck by lightning and landed in his open mouth. 'Nothing but camels and vultures!' he said, munching noisily. 'When am I going to find something tasty to eat around here?'

'Your Goldness?' Gravelbeard picked a couple of vulture feathers out of Nettlebrand's teeth. 'I know you trust the spider-legged creature, but,' he added, wiping the sweat off his nose, 'just suppose . . .'

'Just suppose what?' asked Nettlebrand.

The dwarf straightened his hat. 'I think that whey-faced creature's been lying to you,' he announced solemnly. 'Yes, that's what I think.'

Nettlebrand stopped as if thunderstruck. '*What?*'

'I bet you anything he's been lying.' Gravelbeard spat on his cloth. 'He sounded peculiar last time he reported back.'

'Nonsense!' Nettlebrand shook the sand off his scales and marched on. 'Old spider-legs wouldn't dare. He's a coward. He's been doing as I tell him ever since he came into the world. No, his fly-sized brain misunderstood something, that's what it is.'

'Just as you say, Your Goldness!' muttered the dwarf into his beard. Grimly, he began polishing again. 'You're always right, Your Goldness. If you say he wouldn't dare, right, then he wouldn't dare. And we'll go on sweating it out in this desert.'

'Shut up.' Nettlebrand ground his teeth and looked around. 'He was a better armour-cleaner than you, anyway. You keep forgetting to cut my claws. And you don't get the stories of my heroic deeds right either.'

He slid down the dune, raising a huge cloud of dust. Tiny will-o'-the-wisps swirled round him like midges, chirping in their little voices, telling Nettlebrand a thousand ways of getting out of the desert. Gravelbeard had his work cut out for him, shooing them away from his master's golden head.

'Don't keep brushing stuff in my eyes, armour-cleaner,' growled Nettlebrand, swallowing a dozen will-o'-the-wisps who had foolishly flown into his jaws. 'How am I supposed to look for water in this pesky desert with you flapping about all the time?'

He stopped again, blinking, and stared across the sand that extended like a yellow sea to the horizon. 'Grrr, I'm so angry I could shed my armoured skin! Not a drop of water for miles around. I'll never get away from here! I never saw such a hopelessly drought-ridden place in my life.'

In his rage Nettlebrand stamped his foot, but the sound it made in the sand wasn't particularly impressive. 'I must devour something this minute!' he bellowed. 'I must devour, destroy, dismantle and despoil something!'

Gravelbeard scanned the desert in alarm. There was nothing to eat for miles around – except Gravelbeard himself. But Nettlebrand seemed to want something larger. Eyes streaming, he glared all about him, until his gaze fell on a cactus growing out of the desert sand like a column. Growling furiously, he marched towards it.

'No, Your Goldness, don't!' cried Gravelbeard, but too late.

Nettlebrand sank his teeth into the cactus with relish, only to flinch back, howling. A thousand tiny thorns were piercing his gums – the only unprotected part of his body.

'Pull them out, armour-cleaner!' he bellowed. 'Pull these sharp, burning things out!'

Hastily, Gravelbeard slid down the huge muzzle, perched on the terrible front teeth and set to work.

'He'll pay for this!' bellowed Nettlebrand. 'He'll pay for every thorn, that stupid homunculus. Thick as two short planks, he is! I must find water. Water! I must get out of this desert!'

Then a fine film of sand suddenly rose in the hot air around the bitten cactus, forming into a creature that seemed to change shape with every breath of the desert wind. Its sandy limbs stretched and grew, until a veiled rider was sitting on a spindly-legged camel in front of Nettlebrand. The rider's billowing cloak, like the rest of him, consisted of a myriad grains of sand.

'You want water?' whispered the rider. Even his voice sounded like sand crunching underfoot.

Gravelbeard shrieked, and fell head first off his master's muzzle. Nettlebrand was so surprised he closed his sore mouth.

'What are you?' he growled at the sandy rider.

The translucent camel pranced up and down in front of the giant dragon, obviously not in the least afraid of him.

'I am a sandman,' whispered the strange being. 'I ask again: do you want water?'

'Yes!' grunted Nettlebrand. 'What a stupid question! Of course I do!'

The sandman blew himself out like a tattered sail in the wind.

'I can give you water,' he breathed, 'but what will you give me in return?'

Nettlebrand was so angry that he spat cactus thorns. 'What will I give you in return? I'll refrain from eating you, that's what.'

The sandman laughed. His mouth was only a hole in his sandy face.

'What will you give me?' he asked again. 'Tell me, you great tinny monster.'

'Promise him something!' Gravelbeard whispered into Nettlebrand's ear. 'Anything!'

But Nettlebrand lowered his horns, snorting furiously. Armour clinking, he leaped forward and snapped. His teeth crunched, and the sandman collapsed. Nettlebrand coughed as grains of sand went down his throat. Then he bared his fangs in a satisfied grin.

'So much for *you*!' he grunted, and he was turning away when Gravelbeard suddenly drummed frantically on his armoured brow.

'Your Goldness!' he croaked. 'Look! Look at that!'

Two more sandmen were rising from the place where the first had just fallen. Bright sunlight shone through the arms they were raising in the air, and a wind suddenly rose over the desert.

'Get away from here, Your Goldness!' cried Gravelbeard, but it was already too late.

The wind howled over the dunes, and wherever it whipped up the sand more and more sandmen rose up. They galloped towards Nettlebrand on their camels and surrounded him. Soon he was enveloped in a vast, impenetrable cloud of sand.

Nettlebrand bit like a mad dog. He snapped at the thin legs of the camels and at their riders' fluttering robes. But for every sandman he managed to get, two more rose from the desert sands. They rode round him in the flying sand, circling faster and faster. Horrified, Gravelbeard put his hat over his eyes. Nettlebrand spat and roared, struck out with his claws, and kept snapping his terrible jaws. But all he got between his teeth was sand – gritty, dusty sand that scratched his nose and throat. Every time the sandmen completed another circle, Nettlebrand sank deeper into the sand – deeper and deeper, until even his snorting, sputtering head disappeared. When the sandy riders finally reined in their camels, there was no sign of the golden dragon and his armour-cleaner, nothing but a huge hill of sand rising among the dunes. For a few moments the camels stood there, breathing hard, while their masters' sandy robes billowed in the breeze. Then the wind blew over the dunes, sighing, and the sandmen disintegrated and became one with the desert again.

A viper winding its way over the hot sand a little later heard a scraping sound inside the strange hill. A small head in an outsize hat emerged from the heap of sand.

'Your Goldness!' called the head, taking off its hat and shaking out enough sand to fill two thimbles. 'I made it! I'm in the open.'

The snake was about to slither silently closer to this apparition to find out whether it was edible when a terrible muzzle emerged from the hill of sand, its stinking breath sweeping the viper away behind the nearest dune.

'Come on, armour-cleaner!' growled Nettlebrand. 'Dig me out. And wipe this filthy sand out of my eyes.'

CHAPTER TWENTY-FIVE
The Indus Delta

Clouds obscured the moon and stars as the sea serpent swam towards the coast of Pakistan. In the darkness Ben could make out huts by the flat beach, boats drawn up on the shore, and the mouth of a mighty river pouring into the sea from countless tributaries.

'Here it is!' the sea serpent hissed to the boy. 'This is where the dragons used to come until the monster drove them away. That is the Indus, also known as the sacred river Sindh. Follow it, and it will take you into the mountains and up to the Himalayas.'

She swam past the village, where lanterns were burning outside several huts, and glided on towards the mouth of the Indus. The land between the branches of the river was flat and muddy. Flocks of white seabirds had settled there, beaks tucked under their wings, but they flew up in alarm when the serpent rested her gigantic head on a sandbank. The cry of birds tore through the silence of the night.

Ben jumped down from the serpent's head, landed in the

damp sand, and glanced in the direction of the village, but it was hidden by low hills.

'Firedrake can hide in the reeds there,' said the sea serpent, darting out her tongue as she arched her neck, 'until you've found out if the villagers are still well disposed towards dragons.'

'Thank you,' said Firedrake, letting Sorrel climb off his back. 'It did me good to rest for a while.'

The serpent bent her head, hissing gently.

'The river is shallow here,' she told Ben. 'You can wade through it when you go to the village. I could drop you off there, but the sight of me would scare the fishermen so badly they wouldn't venture out to sea for days.'

Ben nodded. 'I'd better set off at once.'

'Hey, Twigleg!' he said, opening his backpack. 'You can put your head out again. We've reached land.'

The homunculus crawled sleepily out of his warm nest of human clothing, stuck his head out of the backpack – and pulled it straight back in. 'Land!' he said crossly. 'Land? All I can see is more water everywhere.'

Ben shook his head, smiling. 'Do you want to come to the village with me, or shall I leave you with Firedrake and Sorrel?'

'Leave me with Sorrel? No fear,' said Twigleg hastily. 'I'd rather come with you.'

'Okay.' Ben closed the backpack again.

'We'll hide behind those reeds,' said Sorrel, pointing to a sandbank where they grew particularly densely. 'And this time I won't forget to get rid of our tracks.'

Ben nodded. When he turned to say goodbye to the sea serpent the beach was empty. Far away, three glimmering humps rose from the waves.

'Oh!' he murmured, disappointed. 'She's gone.'

'Easy come, easy go,' said Sorrel, stuffing a reed between her sharp teeth.

Firedrake looked up at the sky, where the moon was just coming out from behind the clouds. 'I hope the human woman really has found a substitute for moonlight,' he murmured. 'Who knows, the moon might leave us in the lurch again as it did over the sea.' He sighed and nudged Sorrel. 'Come on, let's sweep our tracks away.'

Quickly and quietly, they set to work, while Ben set off with Twigleg to look for Zubeida Ghalib the dracologist.

CHAPTER TWENTY-SIX

An Unexpected Reunion

Birds fluttered up into the night sky, squawking loudly as Ben waded through the warm water of the river. Huge turtles were hauling themselves out of the sea and lumbering up over the sandbanks to lay their eggs, but Ben scarcely noticed them.

With a sigh, he looked at the dracologist's card, the one that Barnabas Greenbloom had given him. He didn't think it was going to be much use. There were two addresses on it, one in London and one in Karachi, and her name: Zubeida Ghalib. Ben looked out to sea, and saw a pale streak of light sky just above the horizon. The day's hot fingers were beginning to push the night away.

'Perhaps I'll just show this card to a few children,' murmured Ben, 'and one of them will be able to tell me where she lives.'

Twigleg tugged the lobe of Ben's ear. He had crawled out of the backpack and was making himself comfortable on Ben's shoulder. 'They won't be able to read the card,' he said.

'Why not?' Ben frowned. 'I can read it all right.

Zu-bei-da Gha-lib.'

'Well done!' Twigleg chuckled. 'Then you'd better read the name aloud. There won't be many people around here who can read those characters – if the children in this village can read at all, that is. That's English lettering on the card, young master! People here write quite differently. The dracologist gave the professor a card in his language, not hers, see?'

'Oh.' Ben looked at the homunculus in surprise, and almost fell over a passing turtle. 'What a lot you know, Twigleg.'

'Oh, well.' Twigleg shrugged his shoulders. 'I spent many, many nights in my master's library. I've read books about magic and the history of mankind. I've studied biology, so far as you can from human books, I've studied astronomy, astrology, geography, calligraphy, and any number of foreign languages.'

'You have?' Ben was climbing the low hill that hid the village from sight. Soon he could see the first huts and the fishing nets hung up to dry outside them. The sea was breaking on a wide beach where boats were drawn up side by side. Men wearing turbans were standing among them.

'Do you know the language they speak here?' he asked the manikin.

'Urdu?' Twigleg made a face. 'Yes, of course, young master. I learned it when I was studying the great religions of the world. Urdu isn't my favourite language, but I can get by in it.'

'Marvellous!' That was a load off Ben's mind. If Twigleg understood the local language it wouldn't be too difficult to find the dracologist. 'But I think it would be better if no one saw you for the moment,' he told the homunculus. 'Can you hide among my things somewhere and whisper what they're saying to me?'

Twigleg nodded, and clambered into the backpack.

'How's this?' he said softly. 'Can you hear me, young sir?'

Ben nodded. He climbed down the hill and came to some fields of goats. Chickens were scratching about on the ground. In the morning sunlight, children were playing outside low-roofed huts. They were chasing around the women who were seated outside the huts, laughing together as they cleaned and gutted fish. Hesitantly, Ben approached.

First to notice him were the children, who ran forward and crowded round him, full of curiosity. They spoke to him, grabbed his hands and pulled him along. Most of them were smaller than Ben. Their faces were almost as dark as their eyes, and their hair was as black as coal.

'How do I say "Hello"?' Ben whispered over his shoulder.

The children looked at him in surprise.

'*Salaam aleikum*,' whispered Twigleg. '*Khuea hasiz*!'

'*Salaam aleikum. Khu* – er – *khuea hasiz*,' repeated Ben, trying to get his tongue round the words.

The children laughed, clapped him on the back and talked faster than ever.

Ben raised his hands in protest.

'Stop!' he cried. 'No. I don't understand. Just a moment.' He turned his head. 'How do I say: "I come from far away"?' he hissed over his shoulder.

The puzzled children stared at his backpack. Then, to Ben's horror, Twigleg suddenly crawled out of it. Hauling himself up by Ben's hair and ears, he climbed on top of the boy's head, and bowed low to the children.

'A very good morning to you all!' he called, in less-than-perfect Urdu. 'We come with friendly intentions. There's someone here we want to visit.'

'Twigleg!' whispered Ben. 'Come down at once! Are you crazy?'

Most of the children retreated in fright, but two – a boy and a girl – stayed where they were, staring in amazement at the tiny man standing on top of the foreign boy's head and speaking their own language. By this time some of the grown-ups, too, had realised that something unusual was going on. They left their work, came closer, and then, like the children, they stood staring in astonishment at the sight of the manikin.

'Oh, don't, Twigleg!' Ben groaned. 'This isn't a good idea. I expect they'll take me for a wizard or something.'

But the villagers suddenly began to laugh. They nudged each other, lifted their small children up and pointed to the homunculus as he stood on Ben's head, his chest swelling with pride, bowing again and again.

'Thank you, good people, thank you very much!' he cried in Urdu. 'My master and I are delighted by your kind welcome. Would you now be so good as to show us where the famous dracologist Zubeida Ghalib lives?'

The people frowned, looking puzzled. Twigleg spoke a very old-fashioned Urdu, as old as the books from which he had learned it. Finally, the boy who was still standing close to Ben asked, 'You want to see Zubeida Ghalib?'

Ben was so pleased to hear the dracologist's name that he forgot Twigleg was on his head and nodded vigorously. The homunculus toppled off – and landed on the hand of the foreign boy, who gazed at him with great respect before carefully placing him on Ben's own outstretched palm.

'Oh, really, young master!' whispered Twigleg, straightening his clothes. 'I might have broken my neck!'

'Sorry,' said Ben, putting him on his shoulder.

The little boy who had caught Twigleg took Ben's hand and pulled him along the beach. The villagers all followed them past the huts and the fishing boats, until they reached a hut standing a little way from the others.

A stone statue of a dragon with a wreath of blue flowers round its neck stood beside the door. There was a full moon painted on the wall above the door frame, and flying from the roof were three long-tailed kites shaped like dragons.

'Zubeida Ghalib!' said the little boy, pointing to the doorway, which had only a brightly coloured curtain over it. Then he added something else.

'She works by night and sleeps by day,' translated Twigleg, 'because she's studying the secrets of the dark time of the moon. But she has guests staying with her just now, so she ought to be awake. We only have to ring that little bell.'

Ben nodded. 'Say we thank them very much,' he whispered to Twigleg.

The manikin interpreted. The villagers smiled and retreated a few steps, but they didn't go away. Ben went to the door of the hut with Twigleg and tugged the bell-pull. The tinkling of the tiny bell scared two birds off the roof of the hut and they flew away, croaking.

'Oh no!' cried Ben in alarm. 'Twigleg, those were ravens.'

Someone pulled back the curtain over the doorway – and Ben got a surprise that took his breath right away.

'Professor!' he stammered. 'What are you doing here?'

'Ben, my boy!' cried Barnabas Greenbloom, smiling broadly as he led him into the hut. 'Am I glad to see you! And look at this – why, if it isn't Twigleg. So he turned up again, did he? Well, fancy that! But where are the others?'

'Hiding by the river,' replied Ben, still astonished, and looked around. Seated on cushions at a low table in one corner of the small room were a stocky little woman and a girl of about Ben's age.

'Hello,' murmured Ben, shyly. Twigleg bowed.

'Goodness, what a funny elf you are!' said the girl, looking at him. 'I've never seen an elf like you before.'

Twigleg bowed again, with a flattered smile on his face. 'I'm not an elf, honoured lady. I'm a homunculus.'

'A homunculus?' The girl looked at Barnabas Greenbloom in surprise.

'This is Twigleg, Guinevere,' explained the professor. 'He was made by an alchemist.'

'Really?' Guinevere looked at the homunculus in amazement. 'My word, I never met a homunculus before. What creature did the alchemist use to make you?'

Twigleg shrugged his shoulders regretfully. 'I'm afraid I don't know, noble lady.'

'Guinevere,' the professor interrupted them, putting his arm round Ben's shoulders, 'let me introduce my young friend Ben. I've already told you a good deal about him. Ben, this is my daughter Guinevere.'

Ben blushed red as a beetroot. 'Hello,' he murmured.

Guinevere smiled at him. 'Then you must be the dragon rider,' she said.

'The dragon rider!' The woman sitting at the low table next to Guinevere folded her arms. 'My dear Barnabas, would you be good enough to introduce me to this remarkable young man?'

'Of course!' Barnabas Greenbloom handed Ben a spare cushion and then sat down beside him at the table. 'This, dear Zubeida, is my friend Ben the dragon rider. I've already told you a great deal about him. And this, dear Ben,' he added, indicating the stout little woman in her brightly coloured sari, with her grey hair in a long braid hanging down to her waist, 'this is the famous dracologist Dr Zubeida Ghalib.'

Dr Ghalib bowed her head, smiling.

'It is a great honour to meet you, dragon rider,' she told Ben in his own language. 'Barnabas has told me some remarkable things about you. He says you are not just a dragon rider but a friend of brownies, too, and I can see for myself that there's a genuine homunculus sitting on your shoulder. I am very glad to see you. Barnabas wasn't sure if you and your companions would come, so we've been waiting for you anxiously ever since he arrived a couple of days ago. And where,' she said, looking at Ben hopefully, 'is your friend the dragon?'

'Quite close,' said Ben. 'He and Sorrel are hiding by the river. I came into the village first to see if it would be safe for them.' He added, looking at Barnabas Greenbloom, 'That's what the professor advised.'

Zubeida Ghalib nodded. 'Sensible of you, although I don't think they'll be in any danger in this village. The fact is, you're not the first dragon rider the place has known. But more about that later.' She looked at the boy, smiling. 'I'm glad you acted as you did. The arrival of a dragon would have created so much excitement you'd probably never have reached my hut at all. You see,' said Zubeida Ghalib, pouring Ben a cup of tea, her bangles jingling like the little bells at her door, 'I expect by now you take the dragon for granted, but my heart flutters like a young girl's at the thought of meeting one at last, and I'm sure it would be just the same for the people of this village.'

'Well, knowing a dragon is still rather exciting for me too,' murmured Ben, casting a quick glance at Guinevere, who was smiling at Twigleg. Much flattered, the homunculus kissed his hand to her.

'You'd better get Firedrake here as soon as possible,' said Professor Greenbloom. 'I have some news for the three of you.' He rubbed his nose. 'I'm afraid it's no coincidence that we meet again so soon. I came here on purpose to warn you.'

Ben looked at him in surprise. 'Warn us?'

The professor nodded. 'Yes, indeed.' He took off his glasses and cleaned them. 'I have had an extremely unpleasant encounter with Nettlebrand the Golden One.'

Twigleg almost stopped breathing.

'The Golden One?' said Ben. 'The dragon who lost the golden scales? Did you know he was the one who drove the dragons away from the sea? It wasn't a sea monster after all!'

'Yes, Zubeida's already told me about that.' Professor Greenbloom nodded. 'His name should have occurred to me much sooner. Nettlebrand the Golden One. Terrible tales are told of him, although they are all hundreds of years old – except for the one about that attack on the dragons just off the coast here.'

Twigleg fidgeted uneasily on Ben's shoulder.

'I must admit, my boy,' the professor went on, 'I still feel weak at the knees when I think of that monster. I owe it only to my knowledge of mountain dwarves that I'm sitting here now. Do you still have that golden scale I gave you to look after for Firedrake?'

Ben nodded. 'It *is* one of his, isn't it – the monster's?'

'Yes, and I'm not sure you ought to keep it. But I'll tell you the whole story when Sorrel and Firedrake are with us. I'd say you should fetch them now. What do you think, Zubeida?' said the professor, with an enquiring look at the dracologist.

Zubeida nodded. 'The dragon is certainly in no danger from

the people of this village,' she said, 'and strangers seldom come here.'

'But what about the ravens?' asked Twigleg.

The others looked at him in surprise.

'Oh yes, that's right, the ravens!' cried Ben. 'I'd forgotten all about them. There were two of them up on the roof of this hut. We think they're spies. Spying for that – what did you call him?'

'Nettlebrand,' said Professor Greenbloom. He and Zubeida exchanged concerned glances.

'Yes, those ravens.' The dracologist folded her hands. Ben saw that every finger of her left hand wore a ring with a different gemstone in it. 'I've been worried about them myself for some time. They were here when I arrived. Usually they roost up by the tomb, but I sometimes feel they're following me about. Of course, I immediately thought of the old tale of the black birds darkening the moon to prevent the dragons from escaping the monster. I've tried to chase them away, but every time I shoo them off they're back within minutes.'

'Sorrel has a special method,' said Ben, rising from his cushion. 'They don't come back after she's had a go at them. Right, I'll get the other two.'

'It's a dangerous method,' muttered Twigleg.

The rest of them looked at him in surprise, and the homunculus hunched his head down between his shoulders, scared.

'My dear Twigleg,' said the professor, 'do you have any inside knowledge of those ravens?'

'No, why would I?' Twigleg made himself as small as possible. 'No, no! I just think it's better not to provoke them. Ravens can be very nasty birds,' he added, clearing his throat. ''Specially ravens with red eyes.'

'Yes,' the professor nodded. 'Yes, I've heard that myself. As for your suspecting that they're spies,' he said, leading Ben to the door with him, 'Nettlebrand knew you had been to see the djinn. I had the clear impression that someone close to you has been telling him about everything you do. I was racking my brains to think who it might be, and then—'

'The ravens?' Ben interrupted, horrified. 'You think the ravens told him what we were doing? But I didn't see any ravens in the djinn's ravine.'

Twigleg went first red, and then white as a sheet. He began trembling all over.

'What's the matter, Twigleg?' asked Ben, looking at him in concern.

'Um . . . er . . .' Twigleg steadied his shaking hands on his knees, not daring to meet Ben's eyes. 'I did see one,' he stammered. 'A s-sp – a raven, yes. Yes, definitely. A raven roosting up in the palm trees when the rest of you were asleep. I didn't want to wake you.' Thank goodness no one could hear his heart thumping.

'Well, that's unfortunate,' murmured Barnabas Greenbloom. 'But if Sorrel knows a way of shooing them off, perhaps we needn't worry too much, even if our friend the homunculus here doesn't think much of brownie methods. Brownies and homunculi tend not to get on too well, isn't that right, Twigleg?'

Twigleg managed a feeble smile. What could he say? That enchanted ravens are vengeful birds? That Sorrel might already have thrown one stone too many? That his master had an endless supply of ravens?

Ben shrugged his shoulders and pulled back the door curtain. 'I'll go and fetch Firedrake,' he said. 'If the ravens are here, they're going to notice him sometime anyway.'

Zubeida Ghalib rose from her cushions. 'We'll get the village cats to go up on the rooftops,' she said, 'and under all the trees. Perhaps they'll keep the ravens away so that they can't hear what we're discussing.'

'Good idea.' Ben made her a shy little bow, glanced again at Guinevere, and hurried off. The villagers, still waiting outside the hut, looked at him expectantly.

'Tell them we'll be back soon,' Ben whispered to Twigleg. 'And tell them we'll be bringing a dragon with us.'

'If you say so,' said the manikin, and translated it into Urdu.

A murmur of astonishment rose in the air, the villagers drew back, and Ben and Twigleg set off.

CHAPTER TWENTY-SEVEN

The Dragon

The sky was radiant in the mild morning light as Firedrake approached the village with Ben and Sorrel, and the sun was not yet too hot for comfort. Flocks of white seabirds circled above the dragon, announcing his arrival with excited cries.

The villagers were waiting for him, standing outside their huts with children in their arms. The beach had been sprinkled with flower petals. Paper kites flew above the roofs of the huts, and even the smallest children were wearing their best clothes. Ben felt like a king sitting high above them on the dragon's back. He looked for the ravens, but there wasn't one in sight. However, the village cats – white, ginger, tabby, black-and-white and tortoiseshell – were all over the place: on rooftops, outside huts, in the branches of trees. Firedrake walked over the flower petals and past the cats and the people until he saw Barnabas Greenbloom. When he stopped in front of the professor, the onlookers respectfully retreated a few steps. Only Zubeida and Guinevere stayed put.

'My dear Firedrake,' said Barnabas, bowing low. 'The sight of you makes me almost as joyful today as it did when we first met. You will meet my wife later, but let me introduce my daughter Guinevere. And this lady is Dr Zubeida Ghalib, the most famous dracologist in the world, who will help you to fly at the dark time of the moon.'

Firedrake turned his head to her. 'Can you really do that?' he asked.

'I think so, *Asdaha*.' Zubeida bowed, smiling. '*Asdaha* would be the word for you in our language. *Khuea hasiz* – God be with you. Do you know, I imagined your eyes exactly as they are?' Tentatively, she raised her hand to touch Firedrake's scales.

At that, the children lost the last of their fear. They clambered down from their parents' arms, surrounded the dragon and patted him. Firedrake patiently put up with it, nuzzling them gently one by one. The giggling children hid between his legs, and the bravest made their way up the spines of his tail to sit on his back. Unsettled by all this, Sorrel had been watching the crowd of humans uneasily. Her ears were twitching, and even nibbling a mushroom couldn't calm her down. She was used to avoiding human beings and hiding whenever she smelled or heard them. Ben had changed that, but so many humans all at once made her brownie heart beat alarmingly fast.

When the first small boy appeared behind her, she was so startled that she dropped her mushroom.

'Hey, you, small human!' she snapped at the boy. 'Get down!'

Frightened, the boy ducked into shelter behind Firedrake's spines.

'Leave him alone, Sorrel,' said Ben, soothingly. 'You can see Firedrake doesn't mind, can't you?'

Sorrel just growled, clutching her backpack tight.

But the boy wasn't interested in the backpack. He was staring at the furry brownie girl, asking a question in a soft voice. Two more children appeared behind him.

'What's he after?' growled Sorrel. 'I don't understand much of this human language of theirs.'

'He wants to know,' interpreted Twigleg, who was sitting between Ben's legs, 'if you're a small demon.'

'A what?'

Ben grinned. 'A kind of evil spirit.'

'Oh, thanks a lot.' Sorrel pulled a ferocious face at the children. 'No, I'm not! I'm a brownie. A forest brownie.'

'*Dubidai*?' asked a girl, pointing at Sorrel's furry coat.

'Now what are they on about?' asked the brownie girl, wrinkling her nose.

'It seems to be the word for brownie or woodland spirit in these parts,' said Twigleg. 'But they wonder why you've only got two arms.'

'*Only* two?' Sorrel shook her head. 'So people around here have more than two, do they?'

One brave little boy reached out his hand, hesitated for a moment and then patted Sorrel's paw. She flinched at first, but decided to put up with it. The boy said something quietly.

'Hmm,' said Sorrel. 'I understood that bit! The little human with skin like a bay boletus mushroom says I look like a cat goddess. How about that, then?' Feeling flattered, she preened and stroked her spotted coat.

'Come on, Sorrel,' said Ben. 'Let's give them a bit more space up here. We can sit on Firedrake's back any time, but it's a new experience for these children.'

Sorrel shook her head vigorously.

'What, get down there? No way!' She clung tight to

Firedrake's spines. 'No, I'm staying up here. *You* get down and let your own kind trample you underfoot.'

'Oh, very well – stay put then, you furry grumbleguts.' Ben put Twigleg in his backpack, and clambered past the children to climb down from Firedrake's back.

A little girl had hung a garland of flowers over the dragon's horns, and he was licking the tip of her nose. More and more children climbed up on Firedrake's back, clutched his spines, tugged at the dragon riders' leather straps and stroked the dragon's warm silver scales. Sorrel sat in the middle of this throng with her arms folded, keeping a tight grip on her backpack.

'Sorrel's in a temper,' Ben whispered in the dragon's ear.

Firedrake glanced over his shoulder, and nodded in amusement.

The grown-ups were crowding round the dragon too, touching him and trying to catch his eye. Firedrake turned to Zubeida, who was watching the children on his back and smiling.

'Tell me,' he said, 'how can I fly at the dark time of the moon?'

'We need a quieter place to discuss that,' replied the dracologist. 'Let me show you where I found the answer to the secret.'

She raised her hands, bangles jingling, the rings on her fingers flashing in the sunlight. Immediately all was still. The excited voices died away. The children slid off Firedrake's back, and there was no sound to be heard but the roaring of the sea. Zubeida addressed the villagers.

'I am taking the dragon to the tomb of the dragon rider now,' Twigleg translated. 'I have important matters to discuss with him, matters that must not come to the wrong ears.'

The people of the village looked up at the sky. Zubeida had told them about the ravens, but apart from a flock of white seabirds making for the river the air was empty. An old man stepped forward and said something.

'They're going to prepare the feast now,' Twigleg translated. 'A feast to celebrate the return of the dragons and the dragon rider.'

'A feast?' asked Ben. 'For us?'

Zubeida turned to him, smiling. 'Of course. They won't want you to leave before they give a party for you. These people believe that a dragon brings a year of good luck – good luck *and* rain, which is the best luck of all in these parts.'

Ben looked up at the blue sky. 'It doesn't look much like rain,' he said.

'Who knows? Dragon's luck can come as suddenly as the wind,' replied Zubeida. 'But follow me.' She turned, beckoning Firedrake with her ringed fingers.

The dragon was about to set off after her when Guinevere shyly tapped his foreleg. 'Please,' she said, 'do you think I'd be too heavy for you? I mean, I was just wondering, could you possibly . . .?'

Firedrake bent his neck. 'Climb on,' he said. 'I could carry ten people your size and hardly notice!'

'What about people my size?' enquired Zubeida, putting her hands on her hips. 'Too much even for a dragon, I fear?'

Smiling, Firedrake lowered his neck once more. Zubeida gathered in the full skirt of her sari and nimbly scrambled up on the dragon's back, holding on to his spines.

Sorrel gave the girl and the woman a dark look. But when Guinevere held out her hand, saying, 'Hi! I can't say how pleased I am to meet you!', even the brownie's furry face softened in a smile.

And while Firedrake carried the three of them to the hill beyond the huts where the tomb of the dragon rider stood, Ben followed on foot with Barnabas Greenbloom and Twigleg.

'As you see,' said the professor, as Firedrake's tail dragged through the sand in front of them, 'Guinevere loves riding anything – elephants and camels too. Personally, I'm happy if I can stay on a donkey's back for five minutes. Oh, by the way,' he added, putting his arm round Ben's shoulders, 'my wife is waiting for us at the tomb, where I hope you'll tell us what's happened to you all since we last met. Vita is particularly looking forward to meeting you and Sorrel – and she will be delighted to see Twigleg too. She knows some other brownies, but she's been wanting to meet a homunculus for ages.'

'Hear that, Twigleg?' Ben asked, turning his head to the manikin on his shoulder.

But the homunculus was lost in thought. In his mind's eye he could still see the happy faces of the villagers as Firedrake approached their huts. Twice in the past he and his master had entered a village of humans, but Nettlebrand certainly hadn't made any of them feel happy. Fear was all his master ever brought, and he relished doing it.

'Is something wrong, Twigleg?' asked Ben.

'No, no, nothing, young master,' replied the homunculus, mopping his forehead.

The professor put his arm round Ben's shoulders again. 'I'm so keen to hear your news I can hardly wait! But tell me one thing first.' He glanced up at the sky – there was still no sign of any ravens. Even so, he lowered his voice. 'Did the djinn know the answer? Did you manage to ask the right question?'

Ben grinned. 'Yes, but his answer was rather mysterious, like a riddle.'

'Like a riddle, eh? Typical of a djinn, but—' The professor shook his head. 'No, no, tell me what he said later, when Vita's with us. She ought to hear it too. But for her I'd never have ventured to board the wretched plane that brought us here. And besides, ever since this business about a spy came up, I've been feeling very cautious.'

Twigleg couldn't help flinching when he heard the word 'spy'.

'My dear Twigleg,' said the professor, 'you really don't look at all well. Perhaps flying doesn't agree with you either?'

'I don't think he looks too good either,' agreed Ben, examining Twigleg with concern.

'N-no, really,' stammered the manikin. 'Honestly, I'm fine. I just don't like this heat. I'm not used to it.' He mopped the sweat from his brow. 'I was meant to live in the cold. In the cold and the dark.'

Ben looked at him in surprise. 'Why, I thought you came from Egypt! At least, that's where we first met you.'

Twigleg glanced at him, alarmed. 'Egypt? I . . . er . . . yes, right, but . . .'

Barnabas Greenbloom spared the homunculus the problem of finding a plausible answer. 'Sorry to interrupt,' he said, pointing ahead, 'but we've nearly reached the tomb. It's up there. And there's Vita!' He waved – and then suddenly let his hand drop, horrified. 'Oh, good heavens! Do you see that, my boy?'

'Yes,' replied Ben, frowning. 'Two fat ravens, waiting for us.'

CHAPTER TWENTY-EIGHT

The Tomb of the Dragon Rider

The tomb of the dragon rider stood on the top of a low hill. It had grey columns and looked like a small temple. A flight of steps led up to it from each of the four points of the compass. Firedrake's three riders got down at the foot of the northern flight, and Zubeida led the dragon up the steps, which were worn smooth. As Guinevere helped Sorrel up the steep stairs she waved to her mother, who was standing at the top between the columns waiting for them expectantly. Three cats were rubbing themselves around her legs, but they ran away when they saw the dragon.

The tomb looked very old. The stone dome resting on the columns was still well preserved, but there was some damage to the burial chamber underneath it, and here and there the walls had fallen in. Carvings of flowers and tendrils of leaves adorned the white stone.

When Firedrake came up the steps the two ravens perched on the dome rose and flew away, cawing. But they stayed quite close, two black dots in the cloudless sky. The monkeys sitting on the top steps ran away, screeching, and climbed the trees at the foot of the hill. Firedrake stepped between the columns of the tomb, accompanied by Zubeida, and bent his neck low before the professor's wife.

Vita Greenbloom returned his bow. She was almost as tall and thin as her husband, and her dark hair was turning grey. Smiling, she put her arms round her daughter, and looked first at the dragon, then at Sorrel.·

'How wonderful to see you all,' she said. 'And where is the dragon rider?'

'Here, my dear. This is Ben,' said Barnabas Greenbloom, coming up the steps with him. 'He was just asking me why this place is known as the tomb of the dragon rider. Would you like to tell him?'

'No, I think Zubeida should do that,' replied Vita Greenbloom. Then, smiling at Ben, she sat down with him on the back of a stone dragon that stood guard outside the tomb. 'The story of the dragon rider had almost been forgotten, you see,' she told the boy quietly, 'until Zubeida rediscovered it.'

'Yes, that's right, but it's a true story all the same.' Zubeida glanced up at the sky. 'We must keep an eye on those ravens,' she murmured. 'They weren't at all scared of the cats. But now for the story.' She stood leaning against the head of the stone dragon, and looked at Ben. 'Well, about three hundred years ago,' she began, 'a boy lived down there in the village, a boy no older than you. Every night when the moon was full, he sat on the beach and watched the dragons come down from the mountains to bathe in the moonlight. Then one night the boy jumped into the sea, swam out to the dragons and climbed on to the back of one of them. The dragon didn't mind, and the boy sat there until it rose from the water and flew away with him. His family were very sad at first, but whenever the dragons came back so did the boy, year after year until he was a grown man, and he lived to be so old that his hair turned white. Only then did he come back to visit his brothers and sisters in the village, and see their children and grandchildren. But no sooner was he back than he fell ill – so ill that no one could help him. On a night when the dragon rider's fever was particularly bad, a solitary dragon came down from the mountains, even though there was no moon. He settled outside the dragon rider's hut and breathed gentle blue fire all over it. When morning came, the dragon flew away again. But the dragon rider was cured, and he lived for many, many more years – so many that there came a time when everyone had lost count of them. And as long as he lived, enough rain fell on the village fields every year, and the fishermen's nets were always full. When finally he died, the villagers built this tomb in honour of the dragon rider and the dragons. And once more, the night after his funeral, a solitary dragon came down from the mountains and breathed dragon-fire over these white walls. Since then, they say, any sick person who touches the stones of these walls will be cured too. When the land is cold by night and people are freezing, they can find a warm place here, for the stones are always as warm as if the dragon-fire lived on in them.'

'Is that really true?' asked Ben. 'The bit about the warm stones, I mean? Have you tried it out?'

Zubeida Ghalib smiled. 'Of course,' she said. 'It's just as the story says.'

Ben touched the ancient wall and put his hand inside one of the carved stone flowers. Then he looked at Firedrake. 'You never told me you had such powers,' he said. 'Have you ever cured anyone, Firedrake?'

The dragon nodded, bending his head down to the boy. 'Of course. I've cured brownies, injured animals, and anyone else I've breathed dragon-fire on. Never humans, though. Where Sorrel and I come from, human beings believe that dragon-fire will burn and destroy them. You thought so yourself, didn't you?'

Ben nodded.

'I don't want to break up this cosy story-telling session,' growled Sorrel, 'but take a look at the sky, will you?'

The ravens had come closer, and were circling above the stone dome of the tomb, croaking hoarsely.

'Time to drive those two away.' Sorrel sat down beside Ben on the stone dragon and put a hand inside her backpack. 'Ever since we had to get rid of that raven over the sea, I've gone nowhere without a good pawful of suitable stones.'

'Ah, you're going to try the brownie saliva trick,' said

Vita Greenbloom.

Sorrel grinned at her. 'Dead right I am. Watch this.'

She was about to spit on the stones she held in her paw when Twigleg suddenly jumped off Ben's shoulder and landed on hers.

'Sorrel!' he cried in agitation. 'Let Firedrake breathe dragon-fire on the stone.'

'Why?' Sorrel looked at him in surprise, and wrinkled her nose suspiciously. 'What do you mean, little titch? Don't meddle with what you don't understand. This is brownie magic, get it?' And she pursed her lips again to spit on her stones.

'Oh, you pig-headed pointy-eared brownie!' cried Twigleg desperately. 'Can't you see those are no ordinary ravens? Or do you only ever open your eyes to tell one mushroom from another?'

Sorrel growled at him angrily. 'What are you going on about? A raven is a raven is a raven.'

'Oh no, it's not!' cried Twigleg, flailing his arms about so excitedly that he almost fell off her shoulder. 'A raven is not always just a raven, Miss Cleverclogs! And your silly little stones will only put those birds up there in a bad temper. Then they'll fly away and tell their master. They'll tell him where we are, and he'll find us, and—'

'Calm down, Twigleg,' said Ben, patting the homunculus soothingly on the back. 'What do you suggest we do, then?'

'The dragon-fire!' cried Twigleg. 'I read about it in that book. The book the professor gave you. It can—'

'It can turn enchanted creatures back into their real shapes,' said Barnabas Greenbloom, looking thoughtfully up at the sky. 'Yes, so they say. But what makes you think those are enchanted ravens, my dear Twigleg?'

'I . . . I . . .' Twigleg sensed Sorrel looking at him distrustfully.

He made haste to climb back on Ben's shoulder.

But the boy too was looking at him curiously.

'Yes, what makes you think so, Twigleg?' he asked. 'Is it just their red eyes?'

'Exactly!' cried the homunculus, in relief. 'Their red eyes. Precisely. Everyone knows that enchanted creatures have red eyes.'

'Really?' Vita Greenbloom looked at her husband. 'Have you ever heard such a thing, Barnabas?'

The professor shook his head.

'You have red eyes yourself,' growled Sorrel, looking at the manikin.

'Of course I do!' Twigleg snapped back at her. 'A homunculus is an enchanted creature, right?'

Sorrel was still looking at him suspiciously.

'Why not try it, instead of just rabbiting on?' said Guinevere. 'Those really are very peculiar ravens. Twigleg could be right.'

Firedrake looked thoughtfully at the girl, then at the ravens.

'Yes, let's try it,' he said, putting his head over Sorrel's shoulder and blowing a shower of blue sparks very gently over the little stones in her paws.

Sorrel watched, frowning, as the sparks went out, leaving only a pale blue shimmer on the stones. 'Brownie spit and dragon-fire,' she murmured. 'Okay, let's see what happens.' She spat on each stone, rubbing the saliva well in.

The ravens had come even closer.

'Just you wait!' cried Sorrel. 'Here goes. A present from a brownie.' She jumped up on the stone dragon's head, put her arm back, aimed, and threw. First one stone, then the other.

Both hit their mark.

This time, however, they did not cling for long. The ravens

shook the stones out of their feathers with a cry of fury and dive-bombed Sorrel.

'Help!' she cried, leaping down and landing in safety behind the stone dragon. 'Oh, by death-cap and yellow stainer, I'll get you for this, Twigleg!'

Firedrake bared his teeth and moved in front of the humans to protect them. The ravens shot through the air above the temple dome – and suddenly began to tumble and fall.

'They're changing!' cried Guinevere, peering out from behind Firedrake's back. 'They're changing shape! Look at that!'

They all saw it.

The birds' hooked beaks were shrinking. Black wings turned into pincers, snapping frantically in the air. A small body wriggled inside each armoured shell as the relentless force of gravity pulled them down to earth. They landed on one of the flights of crumbling steps, rolled down them, and disappeared into the thorny undergrowth at the foot of the hill.

'By slippery jack and yellow oyster!' whispered Sorrel. 'The homunculus was right!' Dazed, she struggled to her feet.

'They turned into crabs!' Ben looked incredulously at the professor.

Barnabas Greenbloom nodded thoughtfully. 'They were crabs all along,' he said. 'Before someone turned them into ravens. Interesting, really most interesting, don't you agree, Vita?'

'Yes, indeed,' replied his wife, standing up with a sigh.

'What shall we do with them?' asked Sorrel, going to the top of the steps down which the enchanted ravens had tumbled. 'Shall I catch them?'

'No need for that,' said Zubeida. 'All memory of their master will have vanished when the magic spell was broken. They've become perfectly normal crabs. Dragon-fire brings out the true nature of any creature, isn't that so, Firedrake?'

Firedrake had raised his head, and was looking up at the blue sky. 'Yes,' he replied. 'Yes, that's right. My parents told me so, long, long ago, but this is the first time I've ever seen it happen. There are not so many enchanted creatures in the world these days.'

Twigleg's hands were trembling so badly that he hid them under his jacket. What would *he* turn into if dragon-fire fell on him? Sensing his gaze, the dragon looked at him. Twigleg quickly turned away. But Firedrake hadn't noticed how frightened the manikin was; he was too deep in thought.

'If those ravens were Nettlebrand's spies,' Firedrake said, 'he must have cast a spell on them. A dragon who can turn a water creature into a bird of the air!' he mused, looking enquiringly at Zubeida.

The dracologist twisted one of her rings thoughtfully. 'I know of no story that speaks of a dragon with such powers,' she replied. 'This is really very, very strange.'

'Nettlebrand is a very strange being anyway,' said Professor Greenbloom. He leaned against a column. 'I've only told Vita and Zubeida this, but when he came after me in Egypt he crawled up out of a well. Out of water. Odd for a creature associated with fire, don't you think? Where does he really come from?'

They were all silent, baffled.

'And do you know the strangest thing of all?' continued Barnabas Greenbloom. 'Nettlebrand hasn't turned up here!'

The others all looked at him in alarm.

'I mean, that's why I came myself!' said the professor. 'The monster tracked me down to get his scale back, so I thought his next move would be to find Ben. I assumed he might attack Firedrake too, because he likes to hunt other dragons. But he hasn't done any of that. Instead, he's getting his spies to eavesdrop on you. He's having this village and Zubeida watched. What's his plan?'

'I think I know,' said Firedrake.

He looked down the hill to where the sea lay in the sunlight. 'Nettlebrand is hoping we will lead him to the Rim of Heaven. He wants us to find him the dragons who escaped him in the past.'

Ben looked at Firedrake, horrified.

'Of course!' cried Sorrel. 'He doesn't know where they are. When he took the dragons by surprise in the sea here, the sea serpents helped them to get away, and since then he's lost all trace of them.'

Firedrake shook his head. He looked at the humans, a question in his eyes. 'What am I to do? We're so close to our journey's end, but how can I be sure Nettlebrand's not following us? How can I be certain one of his ravens won't be following me under cover of dark if I fly on?'

Ben was transfixed.

'That's right,' he murmured. 'He's probably known for ages what the djinn said. And Twigleg saw a raven back there in the ravine, didn't he? Oh no!' Ben brought his hand down on the back of the stone dragon. 'We've probably been a great help to the monster. He was just waiting for us. And I even asked the djinn his question for him.'

No one said anything. The Greenblooms exchanged anxious glances.

Then, very quietly, so quietly that Ben could hardly hear him, Twigleg said, 'Nettlebrand doesn't know what the djinn told you, young master.'

The words had come out of Twigleg's mouth as if of their own accord. As if they were tired of being held back and swallowed all the time.

All the others looked at him. All of them.

Sorrel narrowed her eyes like a hungry cat.

'So, just how do you know that, little titch?' she growled in a menacingly low voice. 'How come you're so certain of what you say?'

Twigleg did not look at her. He didn't look at anyone. His heart was beating as if it would burst out of his narrow chest.

'Because *I* was his spy,' he replied. '*I* was Nettlebrand's spy.'

CHAPTER TWENTY-NINE

Twigleg the Traitor

Twigleg closed his eyes. He was waiting for Ben to brush him off his shoulder, or Firedrake to breathe dragon-fire over him and turn him into some kind of bug – but nothing happened. It was very silent among the old columns, that was all. A hot wind, blowing off the land to the sea, ruffled the manikin's hair.

When still nothing happened, Twigleg opened his eyes and glanced sideways at Ben. The boy was staring at him with such horror and disappointment that his gaze cut the homunculus to the heart.

'You!' stammered Ben. 'You? But . . . but what about the ravens?'

Twigleg looked down at his thin, spindly legs. They were all blurred because his eyes were full of tears. The tears ran down his sharp nose, dripping on to his hand and into his lap.

'The ravens are his eyes,' sobbed the homunculus, 'but I . . . I'm his ears. I'm the spy the professor heard about. I gave everything away. I told him that the professor had two of his scales, and that you were looking for the Rim of Heaven and were going to ask the blue djinn the way, but . . . but . . .'

He could say no more.

'I might have known it!' snapped Sorrel. And in a single bound she turned on the homunculus, reaching for him with her sharp claws.

'Leave him alone!' said Ben, pushing her away.

'What?' Sorrel's coat was bristling with rage. 'You're not still standing up for him, are you? Even when he tells you himself how he's betrayed us to that monster?' She growled, bared her teeth and took another step forward. 'I felt all along there was something not quite right about this little creep. But you and Firedrake were so crazy about him. I ought to bite his head off, that's what!'

'You'll do nothing of the kind, Sorrel!' said Ben, putting his hand protectively in front of Twigleg. 'Stop carrying on like that. You can see he's sorry.' Carefully, he lifted Twigleg down from his shoulder and set him on the palm of his hand. Tears were still running down the manikin's nose. Ben took a dusty handkerchief out of his pocket and gently dabbed Twigleg's face dry.

'Nettlebrand was my master,' stammered the homunculus. 'I polished his scales and cut his claws, and I had to tell him a thousand and one tales about his heroic deeds. He could never hear enough of them. I've been his armour-cleaner ever since I was made – though what I was made *from* I don't know.' He sobbed again. 'Maybe I'm only a crab with snapping pincers myself. Who knows? Anyway, the man who created Nettlebrand brought me into the world as well. That was hundreds of years ago – and dark, cold, lonely years they've been too. I had eleven brothers, and Nettlebrand ate them all.' Twigleg buried his face in his hands. 'He ate the man who made us, and he'll eat you too. You and all the dragons. Every last one of them.'

Guinevere suddenly went over to Ben. Pushing her long hair back from her forehead, she looked at the homunculus sympathetically. 'But why does he want to eat all the dragons?' she asked. 'He's a dragon himself, isn't he?'

'He's not a real dragon!' replied Twigleg, sobbing. 'He just looks like one. He hunts dragons because that's what he was made to do. Like a cat that's born to catch mice.'

'What?' Incredulous, Barnabas Greenbloom looked over Ben's shoulder. 'Nettlebrand isn't a dragon? What is he, then?'

'I don't know,' whispered Twigleg. 'I don't know what kind of creature the alchemist made him from. His armour is some kind of indestructible metal, but no one knows what's underneath it. Our maker gave Nettlebrand the appearance of a dragon so that he could get close to them more easily when he went hunting. All dragons know it's best to avoid humans, but no dragon would flee from one of its own kind.'

'That's true.' Zubeida Ghalib nodded thoughtfully. 'But why did the alchemist need a monster to kill dragons in the first place?'

'For his experiments.' Twigleg mopped the tears from his eyes with the hem of his jacket. 'He was a very gifted alchemist. As you can see, he'd discovered the secret of creating life, and I'm the proof of it. But he wanted more. Like every alchemist of his time, he wanted to make gold. Human beings are absolutely mad about gold, aren't they?'

Vita Greenbloom stroked Guinevere's hair and nodded. 'Yes, some of them,' she said.

'Well,' Twigleg continued in a trembling voice, 'my maker discovered that the essential ingredient for making gold is the ground-up horns of dragons, a material even rarer than ivory. In the old days he paid knights to go hunting dragons and bring back their horns for him – but the knights weren't killing enough. He needed more horns for his experiments – many, many more. So he created Nettlebrand, his own dragon-killer.' Twigleg looked at Firedrake. 'He gave him the shape of a real dragon but made him much, much bigger and stronger. The one thing Nettlebrand couldn't do was fly, because the alchemist had made his armour from an indestructible heavy metal that even dragon-fire couldn't melt. Then he sent Nettlebrand out hunting.'

Twigleg fell silent for a moment, looking out to sea where the fishing boats rocked gently on the water.

'He caught them all,' the homunculus whispered. 'He came down on them like a terrible storm. My maker was carrying out experiments day and night. And then the dragons suddenly disappeared. Nettlebrand searched high and low, until his claws were blunt and his limbs ached with walking. But they were nowhere to be found. My maker was furious. He had to give up his experiments – but he soon discovered that was the least of his worries. Nettlebrand began to get bored, and the more bored he was, the more violent and evil-tempered he grew. My maker created enchanted ravens to search the world for the missing dragons, but in vain. Then Nettlebrand, in his rage, ate all my brothers. He spared me only because he needed someone to clean his armour.' Twigleg's eyes closed as he remembered.

'And then,' he went on quietly, 'on a day when yet another raven came back without news of any dragons, Nettlebrand, the Golden One, ate our maker too, and with him the secret of his own origin. But,' said Twigleg, raising his head and looking at Firedrake, 'he's still searching for dragons. The last lot he found escaped when two sea serpents and his own impatience robbed him of his prey. However, he's learned his lesson. This time he's waiting patiently for *you* to lead him to the dragons he's been searching for all these years.'

The manikin fell silent, and the others did not speak.

A fly settled on Twigleg's thin legs, and he brushed it away wearily.

'Where is he now?' asked Ben at last. 'Is Nettlebrand somewhere close?'

Sorrel looked round uneasily. None of them had stopped to think that the golden monster might be quite near them already. But Twigleg shook his head.

'No,' he said. 'Nettlebrand is far, far away. I did tell him about the djinn's answer, but,' he added, a small smile appearing on his tear-stained face, 'but I was lying to him. For the first time ever.' He looked at them proudly. 'For the very first time in my life I, Twigleg, lied to Nettlebrand, the Golden One!'

'You did, did you?' enquired Sorrel suspiciously. 'And you expect us to believe you? Why would you suddenly lie to him when you've been such a fabulous spy, fooling the whole lot of us?'

Twigleg looked crossly at her. 'Certainly not to save your shaggy skin!' he said nastily. 'I wouldn't shed a tear if he ate you!'

'Huh, it's *you* he'll be eating!' Sorrel snapped back furiously. 'Always supposing you really did lie to him.'

'I did, I did!' cried Twigleg, his voice trembling. 'I sent him off to the Great Desert, far, far away, because . . . because . . .' he added, clearing his throat and glancing shyly at Ben, 'because he was going to eat the little human here too. And the young master was kind to me. For no reason at all. He was kind and friendly, just like that. No one was ever friendly to me before.' Twigleg sniffed, rubbed his nose and looked down at his sharp, bony knees. Very quietly, he said, 'So I decided he can be my master from now on. If he likes.' The homunculus looked anxiously at the boy.

'Your master! Oh, orange birch boletus!' Sorrel gave a scornful laugh. 'What an honour! And when are you planning to betray *him*?'

Ben sat down on the stone dragon and put Twigleg on his knee.

'Never mind all this nonsense about masters,' he said. 'And don't keep calling me young master either! We can be friends, can't we? Just ordinary friends, okay?'

Twigleg smiled. A tear ran down his nose again, but this time it was a tear of joy. 'Friends,' he repeated. 'Oh yes, friends!'

Barnabas Greenbloom cleared his throat and leaned over the pair of them.

'Twigleg,' he said, 'what did you mean just now about sending Nettlebrand into the desert? What desert?'

'The biggest desert I could find on the map,' replied the homunculus. 'Only a desert can hold Nettlebrand prisoner for a while, you see. Because,' Twigleg lowered his voice, as if his old master were lurking in the dark shadows cast by the stone dome, 'he speaks and sees through water. Only water gives him the power to move instantly from one place to another. So I sent him where there's less of it than anywhere else.'

'He is Lord of the Water,' said Firedrake softly.

'What did you say?' Barnabas Greenbloom looked at him in surprise.

'It's something we were told by a sea serpent we met on the way here,' explained the dragon. 'She said Nettlebrand has more power over water than she does herself.'

'But how does he do it?' asked Guinevere, looking enquiringly at the homunculus. 'Do you know, Twigleg?'

Twigleg shook his head. 'I'm afraid I don't know all the secrets the alchemist told him. When one of his servants spits or throws a stone into water, the image of Nettlebrand appears. He talks to us as if he were actually there, even if he's at the other end of the earth. But no, I don't know how it's done.'

'Oh, so that's what you were up to beside that water cistern,' said Sorrel. 'When you tried to make me think you were talking to your reflection. You treacherous little locust! You—'

'Stop it, Sorrel!' Firedrake interrupted her. He looked at the homunculus.

Ashamed, Twigleg bent his head. 'She's right,' he murmured. 'I was talking to my master.'

'And I think you'd better carry on doing just that,' said Zubeida.

Twigleg turned to look at her in surprise.

'You may yet be able to make amends for your treachery,' said the dracologist.

'Exactly the same thing occurred to me, Zubeida!' Barnabas Greenbloom struck the palm of one hand with his fist. 'Twigleg could be a kind of double agent. What do you think, Vita?'

His wife nodded. 'Not a bad idea.'

'What exactly does a trouble agent do?' asked Sorrel.

'Simple! Twigleg just has to act as if he were still spying for Nettlebrand,' Ben explained. 'But he'll really be spying for us. Get it?'

Sorrel wrinkled her nose.

'Yes, of course! Twigleg could go on fooling him!' cried Guinevere. She looked intently at the homunculus. 'Would you do it? I mean, wouldn't it be too dangerous?'

Twigleg shook his head. 'I wouldn't mind that,' he replied. 'But I'm afraid Nettlebrand will have found out by now that I betrayed him. You're forgetting the ravens.'

'Oh, they turned back into crabs,' said Sorrel airily.

'He has more than just those two ravens, fur-face,' snapped Twigleg. 'For instance, there was the one out at sea when you played that trick with the stone on him. He was the bird I used to ride on, and he was already suspicious. Your stone will have annoyed him no end.'

'So?' growled Sorrel.

'Don't you have anything but fur inside your head as well as on it?' cried Twigleg. 'Doesn't it strike you he may have been so furious that he rushed off to see my old master? Don't you think Nettlebrand will suspect something if the raven tells him we were crossing the Arabian Sea on the back of a sea serpent? Although I told him the dragons were hiding in a desert thousands of kilometres further west?'

'Oh, I see,' muttered Sorrel, scratching herself behind the ears.

'No.' Twigleg shook his head. 'I don't know if it's such a good idea for me to report back to him. You mustn't underestimate Nettlebrand!' The homunculus shuddered, and looked at Firedrake, who was gazing down at him anxiously. 'I don't know why you're looking for the Rim of Heaven, but I think you ought to turn back, for fear of leading your worst enemy exactly where he wants to go in his wicked dreams.'

Firedrake returned Twigleg's gaze in silence. Then he said, 'I set out on this long journey to find a new home – for me and the other dragons who flew north long, long ago to escape Nettlebrand and the human race. We had a place there in the north, a remote valley – it was damp and cold, but we could live there in peace. Now that human beings want that valley, the Rim of Heaven is our only hope. Where else shall we find a refuge that doesn't belong to mankind?'

'So that's why you're here,' said Zubeida quietly. 'That, as Barnabas has told me, is why you're looking for the Rim of Heaven.' She nodded. 'It's true that the Himalayas, where that mysterious place is believed to lie hidden, are no place for human beings. Perhaps that's why I've never discovered the Rim of Heaven myself – because I'm human. I think *you* might well find it, Firedrake. But how can we keep Nettlebrand from following you?'

Barnabas Greenbloom shook his head, at a loss. 'Firedrake can't go back home either,' he murmured, 'or he'll lead Nettlebrand straight to the dragons in the north. We're in a real fix, my friend.'

'Yes, no doubt about it!' Zubeida sighed. 'But I think some such thing was bound to happen. You haven't yet heard the end of the old story of the dragon rider. Follow me, all of you. I want to show you something – particularly you, dragon rider.'

So saying, she took Ben's hand and led him into the ruins of the tomb.

CHAPTER THIRTY

All is Revealed to Nettlebrand

'Spit!' snapped Nettlebrand. 'Go on, spit, you useless dwarf!' Tail twitching, he was sitting among the dunes, surrounded by the mountains of sand from which Gravelbeard had finally freed him. It was lucky for Nettlebrand that mountain dwarves are good at digging.

With difficulty, Gravelbeard collected a little saliva in his dry mouth, pursed his lips, and spat into the bowl he had carved from the cactus which Nettlebrand had incautiously tried to eat.

'It's not going to work, Your Goldness!' he said fretfully. 'Look, the sun's going to roast us alive before we have enough liquid in this.'

'Spit!' Nettlebrand growled, and contributed a pool of bright green saliva himself.

'Wow!' Gravelbeard leaned over the bowl with such enthusiasm his hat almost fell in. 'That was amazing, Your Goldness! A whole pondful – no, a lakeful of spit! It works! Amazing! Look, the sun's reflected in it. Let's hope it doesn't all evaporate.'

'Then stand where your shadow falls on it, fool!' snapped Nettlebrand. He spat again. Splish! A puddle of green hit the hollowed-out cactus flesh. Splat, splosh! Gravelbeard added his bit. They kept spitting until even Nettlebrand's mouth was dry.

'Stand aside!' he hissed, pushing the dwarf down in the hot sand and peering with one red eye into the little pool they had made. For a moment, the green goo remained clouded, but then it suddenly shone like a mirror, and the dark figure of a raven appeared in the cactus-flesh bowl.

'At last!' cawed the raven, dropping the stone he had been holding in his beak. 'Where were you, master? I've thrown more stones into this sea than there are stars in the sky. You've got to get that brownie and eat her. At once! Look at this!' Indignantly, he raised his left wing, where the stone Sorrel had thrown at him still clung. Brownie saliva lasts a long time.

'Don't make such a fuss!' growled Nettlebrand. 'And forget the brownie. Where's Twigleg? What was he doing when he eavesdropped on the djinn? Had his ears plugged with raisins, did he? I haven't seen so much as the tip of a dragon's tail in this ghastly desert where he sent me.'

The raven opened his beak, shut it, and then opened it again.

'Desert? What desert?' he cawed in surprise. 'What are you talking about, master? The silver dragon flew over the sea ages ago – taking Twigleg with him. I last saw them riding a sea serpent. Didn't he tell you about that?' The raven shook his wing again, accusingly. 'And then the brownie cast her magic spell with the stone. That's what I've been trying to tell you. Twigleg didn't lift a finger to stop that little fur-faced brute.'

Nettlebrand frowned. 'Flew over the sea?' he grunted.

The raven leaned forward a little way. 'Master?' he said. 'Master, I don't have a very clear view of you.'

Nettlebrand spat impatiently into the cactus bowl.

'Yes!' cried the raven. 'I can see you better now.'

'Over what sea?' Nettlebrand shouted at him.

'You know the sea, master!' cried the raven. 'You know the serpent too. Remember the night of the full moon when you hunted the dragons as they swam? I'm sure it was one of the serpents that thwarted you then.'

'Shut up!' bellowed Nettlebrand. He was so angry he could have smashed the cactus bowl with one blow of his paw. Snorting, he dug his claws into the sand. 'No, I don't remember, and you'd better not either. Go away now. I have to think.'

The startled raven retreated. 'Yes, but that brownie,' he squawked in a small voice. 'What about that brownie?'

'Get out, I said!' Nettlebrand roared.

Straightening up and growling, he lashed the sand with his tail. 'That stinking flea! That spidery monstrosity! That sharp-nosed bird-brain! He actually dared to lie to me! *Me*!' Nettlebrand's eyes were blazing. 'I'll trample him to death!' he snarled at the desert sands. 'I'll crack him like a nut, I'll eat him alive the way I ate his brothers! Aaaargh!' Opening his jaws, he roared so loud that Gravelbeard threw himself on to the sand, trembling, and pulled his hat down over his ears.

'Up on my back, armour-cleaner!' snapped Nettlebrand.

'Yes, Your Goldness!' stammered the dwarf. Weak at the knees, he ran to his master's tail and clambered up it so fast that he almost lost his hat. 'Are we going home at last, Your Goldness?' he asked.

'Going home?' Nettlebrand gave a hoarse laugh. 'We're going hunting. But first you'll tell that treacherous spindly homunculus how I perished miserably in the desert.'

'You what?' asked Gravelbeard, bewildered.

'I rusted up, you fool,' Nettlebrand snapped. 'I rusted, I got sand in the works, I was buried alive, all seized up – oh, invent any story you like. Only make it sound good, make it sound so likely that the little traitor, suspecting nothing, will jump for joy and lead us to our prey.'

'But,' said Gravelbeard, gasping for breath as he hauled himself up on his master's gigantic head, 'but how are you going to find him?'

'Leave that to me,' replied Nettlebrand. 'I have a very good idea where the silver dragon was going. But now we need a nice big stretch of water for you to deliver your made-up story. And if you don't manage to make him believe every word of it,' said Nettlebrand, his muzzle distorting into a terrible smile, 'then I shall eat you alive, dwarf.'

Gravelbeard trembled nervously.

Nettlebrand dipped a black claw into the puddle of spit – and disappeared like one of the ghostly apparitions of the Great Desert. Only the prints of his mighty paws were left in the sand, together with Gravelbeard's feather duster, but the desert wind soon covered them up for ever.

CHAPTER THIRTY-ONE

Return of the Dragon Rider

It was dark inside the tomb of the dragon rider, although the noonday sun was blazing down on the land outside. Only a few dusty sunbeams made their way through the crumbling walls and fell on the strange carved patterns adorning the walls of the tomb. There was enough space under the stone dome for even Firedrake to turn round easily. A strange, heavy fragrance rose from some faded flowers lying on the floor around a stone sarcophagus.

'Look,' said Zubeida Ghalib, taking Ben over to it. The dry petals crackled under their feet. 'Do you see this writing?' The dracologist put her hand on the stone slab covering the sarcophagus.

Ben nodded.

'It took me a long time to decipher it,' Zubeida went on. 'Many of the characters had been eroded by the salt wind blowing in from the sea, and no one down in the village knew what they said. None of them remembered the old stories clearly.

Only with the help of two very old women whose grandmothers had told them tales of the dragon rider did I manage to decipher the forgotten words – and this morning, when I saw you and Sorrel riding into the village on Firedrake's back, it was as if they had come to life.'

'Why, what do they say?' asked Ben. His heart had been thumping when Dr Ghalib had led him into the burial chamber. He didn't like cemeteries. They frightened him – and now here he was inside a tomb. But the fragrance rising from the dry petals was reassuring.

'It says here,' replied Zubeida, passing her ringed fingers over the weather-worn characters, 'that the dragon rider will return in the shape of a boy with skin as pale as the full moon, coming to save his friends the dragons from a terrible enemy.'

Incredulous, Ben examined the sarcophagus. 'Is that really what it says? But . . .' Baffled, he looked at the professor.

'Did some soothsayer say so at the time, Zubeida?' asked Barnabas Greenbloom.

Zubeida Ghalib nodded. 'Yes, a woman who was present at the dragon rider's deathbed. Some even say that those were his own words.'

'He said he'd return? But he was a human being, right?' asked Sorrel. She laughed. 'Oh, come on! You humans don't return from the World Beyond. You lose yourselves there. Either you lose yourselves or you forget the world you came from.'

'How do you know if that's true of all human beings?' asked Zubeida Ghalib. 'I know you can enter the other world whenever you like, Sorrel. All fabulous creatures can, except for those who die a violent death. But there are some humans beings who believe we too have only to become a little better acquainted with death to be able to return, if we want to. So who knows, perhaps there really is something of the old dragon rider in Ben.'

The boy looked down at his feet uncomfortably.

'Oh, come on!' Sorrel chuckled sceptically. 'We found him in a pile of old packing cases. A stack of crates and cardboard cartons, on the other side of the world, and he didn't know a thing about dragons and brownies, not a single thing.'

'That's true,' said Firedrake. He bent his neck over Ben's shoulder. 'But he has become a dragon rider now, Sorrel, a true dragon rider. There aren't many of those in the world. There never were many, even when dragons could still roam free and didn't have to hide. In my view,' he said, raising his head and looking round, 'whether or not there's something of the old dragon rider in him, here he is, and perhaps he really can help us to defeat Nettlebrand. One thing fits, anyway.' Firedrake nudged Ben and gently blew the hair back from his face. 'He's as pale as the moon. In fact, rather paler at the moment, I'd say.'

Feeling rather embarrassed, Ben grinned at the dragon.

'Huh!' Sorrel picked up one of the fragrant petals and held it under her nose. 'I'm a dragon rider too, you know! I've been a dragon rider ever since I can remember. But no one's making a big fuss about me.'

'You're not exactly as pale as the moon, are you?' said Twigleg, scrutinising her furry face. 'More the colour of storm clouds, if you ask me.'

Sorrel put her tongue out at him. 'No one did ask you,' she snapped.

Professor Greenbloom cleared his throat and leaned against the old sarcophagus, evidently thinking hard.

'My dear Zubeida,' he said, 'I assume you showed us this old inscription because you think Firedrake ought not to turn back, despite his sinister pursuer. Right?'

The dracologist nodded. 'Right. Firedrake has come so far, and so many people have helped him along the way – I just can't believe all that was for nothing. And I think it's time for the dragons to fight back and banish Nettlebrand for ever, instead of hiding away from him. Could there be a better opportunity?' She looked round at them. 'We have a dragon with nothing more to lose, a brownie girl who can bring enchanted ravens falling from the sky, a human boy who's a true dragon rider and is even mentioned in an old prophecy, a homunculus who knows almost all his master's secrets,' her bangles jingled as she raised her arms, 'and a great many people who long to see dragons flying in the sky again. Oh yes, I think Firedrake should continue his quest, but first I must tell him how to fly at the dark time of the moon.'

It was very quiet in the tomb of the dragon rider. They were all gazing intently at the dragon. Thoughtfully, Firedrake looked down at the ground. At last he raised his head, looked steadily at

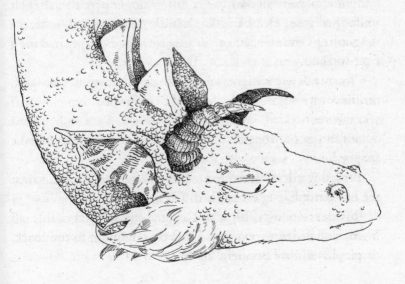

them all – and nodded.

'I'll fly on,' he said. 'Perhaps what the writing on the stone says *is* true. Perhaps the prophecy really does mean us. But before we go on, I'd like Twigleg to see if he can find out where his master is now.' He looked at the homunculus, a question in his eyes. 'Will you do that, Twigleg?'

Twigleg felt his legs beginning to tremble, but he nodded. 'I'll try,' he whispered. 'As true as my name's Twigleg and I was born in a test tube.'

When they returned to the village it looked like it had been deserted. The midday heat beat down on men and animals, and the air seemed too thick to breathe. Even the children were out of sight. But the villagers were busy in their huts, cooking and baking, and their excited voices could be heard behind the colourful curtains.

'The whole village is expecting you to bring us luck,' Zubeida told Firedrake on the way to her hut. 'They believe that dragon scales shed good luck like gold dust; they think it will settle on our rooftops and the nets of our fishermen and stay with us long after you and your friends have flown away again.'

'We must leave tonight,' said Firedrake. 'The sooner we start, the harder it will be for Nettlebrand to follow us.'

Zubeida nodded. 'Yes, you're right. But if I am to help you outwit the moon when it's dark, you must wait until it is high in the sky tonight. Come with me.'

She led Firedrake and the others round behind her hut, where she had fenced in a plot of land. She had been growing flowers there, flowers with prickly leaves and tightly closed buds.

'As you all know,' explained Zubeida, leaning on the fence, 'most plants need sunlight to live and grow. This flower is different. It lives on the light of the moon.'

'Extraordinary,' murmured Barnabas Greenbloom.

Vita leaned over the fence for a closer view of the strange plants. 'I've never seen a flower like that before, Zubeida,' she said. 'Where did you find it?'

The dracologist smiled. 'I found the seeds up there in the dragon rider's tomb. The plants that must once have lain there fell to dust long ago, but the seeds were still scattered round the sarcophagus. So I collected them, soaked them in water for a few days, and then sowed them here. You see the results before you. The petals we walked on in the tomb are the remains of my last harvest. I dry the flowers up there to get new seed. I've called them dragon-flowers – what else?' Zubeida Ghalib smiled, and stroked one of the tightly closed buds. 'They open only in moon-light, and then the blue flowers are so fragrant that moths come flying around them as if they were lamps. But most wonderful of all: the longer the moon shines down on them the brighter they glow, until the moonlight collects on their petals and leaves like dewdrops.'

'Amazing!' Barnabas Greenbloom looked at the dragon-flowers, fascinated. 'Did you discover that by chance, or did someone tell you about these plants?'

'Can you say exactly what chance means, Barnabas?' replied Zubeida. 'I remembered the age-old stories in which dragons once flew through the sky even by day. But only the oldest stories of all tell that tale. Why, I asked myself? How was it that a time came when dragons could fly only by moonlight? I looked for an answer in the inscriptions up at the tomb, and it was there – call it chance if you like – that I found the seeds. I believe the dragon rider was on the track of the secret himself. After all, the dragon who cured him with dragon-fire came on a moonless night, didn't he?' She looked into Firedrake's golden eyes. 'I believe these flowers gave that dragon the strength to fly, and the dew that collects on them has the power of the moon in it.'

'You *think* so?' Sorrel scrambled under the fence and sniffed the prickly leaves. 'But you've never tried it out, have you?'

The dracologist shook her head. 'How could I? Firedrake is the first live dragon I've ever met. And there's no other creature that can rise in the air only with the aid of moonlight.'

'Hear that?' Sorrel turned to Firedrake. 'You might just as easily fall out of the sky like a stone if you put your faith in these prickly things.'

Firedrake shook his wings. 'Perhaps we won't need their help, Sorrel. Perhaps we shall have reached the Rim of Heaven long before the next dark time of the moon. But suppose there's another eclipse, like the one over the sea? Suppose the moon disappears while we're above mountains?'

Sorrel shook herself. 'Oh, all right. You have a point.' She plucked a leaf from a flower and nibbled the tip of it suspiciously. 'Doesn't taste bad. More like catmint than moonlight, though, if you ask me.'

'Do I have to eat them?' Firedrake asked the dracologist.

Zubeida shook her head. 'No, you just have to lick the dew off their leaves and petals. But as I can't give you the flowers to take with you, I've been collecting moon-dew from them ever since Barnabas told me about you. I'll collect more tonight, and then I can give you a full bottle to take on your flight. If the moon deserts you, one of your friends must put a few drops on your tongue. I think you'll be able to tell how much you need. The dew will stay clear as water until the next full moon, when it will turn cloudy. So if you need any more for your flight home to the north you must visit me again on the way.'

Firedrake nodded. He looked at the horizon thoughtfully. 'I can hardly wait,' he said quietly. 'I long to see the Rim of Heaven at last.'

CHAPTER THIRTY-TWO

All Lies

Twigleg enjoyed the party very much – all the singing and laughing and dancing, and the children chasing each other over the sand while the moon cast a broad ribbon of bright light over the sea.

The homunculus sat outside Zubeida Ghalib's hut with Ben, Sorrel and the Greenblooms. Firedrake was lying on the beach. The villagers were crowding around him so eagerly that most of the time all the others could see of him was his head. Everyone in the village wanted to stroke his scales, climb on his crested back or sit between his paws. The dragon took it all kindly, but Sorrel knew him well enough to sense his impatience.

'See how his ears are twitching?' she said, stuffing a pawful of rice into her mouth. There were raisins in the rice, and sweet almonds and such delicious spices that, for the first time in her long life, Sorrel was really enjoying human food.

'When Firedrake's ears twitch like that,' she said, licking her lips, 'it means he's impatient. In fact, very impatient. See that frown on his face? What he really wants to do is get up and fly away.'

'And so he can, very soon,' said Zubeida, sitting down beside the brownie. She was holding a small red glass flask containing a silvery liquid. 'I've collected every drop I could from the petals of the dragon-flowers. I'm afraid that's all I can do for you. Here you are, dragon rider,' she said, giving Ben the bottle. 'Look after it carefully. I hope you won't need it, but in case you do I feel sure it could help Firedrake.'

Ben nodded, and tucked the moon-dew away in his back-pack, where he had the rat's map ready to hand too. He had discussed the djinn's instructions with Barnabas Greenbloom. The professor thought that the palace Ben had seen in the djinn's eye sounded very like a monastery the Greenblooms had once visited on a field trip. It was not far from the place where the Indus changed course deep in the Himalayas, and the way to its source went east. Gilbert Greytail's map showed a great many blank patches in those parts.

'Zubeida,' said Sorrel, 'do you think a hungry brownie could take some of this human food along for the journey?'

Zubeida Ghalib laughed. 'I'm sure she could,' she said. 'After all, you must keep your strength up. Who knows how many more enchanted ravens you'll have to drive out of the sky?'

'Yes, who knows?' murmured Sorrel, looking up. Her sharp eyes couldn't make out the smallest black speck among the stars, but she didn't trust this lull in hostilities. Night was a good disguise for black feathers.

'Hey, Twigleg,' she said, tugging the manikin by the sleeve, 'find yourself a pool of water. It's time you had a word with your master.'

Twigleg jumped. He had been sitting on Ben's knee, dreamily

watching the people enjoying themselves. 'What did you say?'

'Nettlebrand!' repeated Sorrel impatiently. 'Your *old* master! Find out if he's still in the desert. We're leaving soon.'

'Oh, yes.' Twigleg's shoulders slumped.

'Shall I come with you?' asked Ben.

'Would you really, young master?' Twigleg gazed at the boy gratefully.

'Of course.' Ben put the manikin on his shoulder and stood up. 'But if you say "young master" once more, I shall go away and you can talk to the monster on your own.'

Twigleg nodded, clutching the boy's jumper.

'Good. While you two do that,' Professor Greenbloom called after them, 'Zubeida and I will rescue Firedrake from his admirers.'

Ben carried Twigleg to the field of dragon-flowers, where a shallow water basin had been dug in the ground near the fence. Zubeida watered the flowers from it when the heat made their leaves droop. It was covered with black plastic to keep the precious water from evaporating in the sun.

Ben put Twigleg down on the ground, pulled the plastic cover off the basin and sat on the fence. The dragon-flowers were wide open now, and their prickly leaves shone in the dark.

'Suppose he really is still in the desert?' asked Ben. 'Can he answer you all the same?'

Twigleg shook his head. 'Not without water. But I don't think Nettlebrand will be in the desert any more.'

'Why not?'

'I just feel it,' murmured Twigleg. He picked up a small stone.

Ben shifted uncomfortably on the fence. 'If he does turn up in the water,' he said, 'do you think he'll be able to see me here?'

Twigleg shook his head. Weak at the knees, he went to the rim of the basin. His reflection was paler than the moon, but the fragrance of the flowers filled the night and calmed the frantic beating of his heart.

'Stay as you are, please!' whispered the homunculus. 'Stay dark, water!'

Then he threw the stone. Splash! Shimmering circles rippled over the surface of the water. Twigleg held his breath. An image appeared in the dark pool, but it was not the image of Nettlebrand.

'Gravelbeard!' Twigleg stepped back in surprise.

'Oh, Twigleg, there you are at last!' The mountain dwarf pushed his outsize hat back on his head. Large tears were trickling down his nose. 'His Goldness, our master,' he gulped, raising his short little arms and then letting them sink again, 'our master, he's . . . he's . . .'

'He's what?' stammered Twigleg.

Ben leaned over from the fence to hear better.

'He's buried in the sand!' moaned Gravelbeard. 'Gone, just like that! Oh!' He rolled his eyes and went on, hoarsely. 'It was terrible, Twigleg. The crunching. The squealing. And then suddenly,' the dwarf bent double, until it looked as if his nose would come up through the water, 'suddenly everything was still. Perfectly still.' He stood up again, shrugging his shoulders. 'What was I to do? I couldn't dig him out. I'm much too small!'

Twigleg scrutinised the sobbing dwarf thoughtfully. He didn't believe Gravelbeard's story. Was it really possible that the source of all their troubles lay buried in the sand of a distant desert?

'Where are you now, Gravelbeard?' Twigleg asked the snivelling dwarf.

'Me?' Gravelbeard wiped his nose on the sleeve of his jacket. 'I was lucky. A camel caravan happened to pass by soon after His Goldness,' here, he started sobbing again, 'soon after His Goldness sank into the sand. I managed to cling to a camel's leg and ride with them. And so I came to a city, a human city full of gold and diamonds. A wonderful place, I can tell you, an absolutely wonderful place.'

Twigleg nodded. Deep in thought, he stared into the water.

'What about you?' asked the dwarf. 'Where are you now?'

Twigleg opened his mouth, but at the last minute he bit back what he had been about to say. 'We only got out of the desert ourselves yesterday,' he said instead. 'We didn't find dragons any more than you did. That wretched djinn lied to us.'

'Yes, by tin and iron ore, what a villain!' Gravelbeard looked at Twigleg, but the homunculus could scarcely make out the dwarf's eyes under the huge brim of his hat. 'So what are you going to do now?' asked Gravelbeard. 'Where will the silver dragon look next?'

Twigleg shrugged his shoulders and looked as indifferent as he could. 'No idea. He seems very depressed. Have you seen the raven lately?'

Gravelbeard shook his head. 'No, why?' He looked around. 'I must go now,' he whispered. 'Good luck, Twigleg. Maybe we'll meet again.'

'Maybe,' murmured Twigleg, as the image of Gravelbeard blurred in the dark water.

'Hooray!' Ben jumped off the fence, swung Twigleg up on to his head, and danced around the dragon-flowers with him.

'We're rid of him!' he chanted. 'Goodbye, Nettlebrand! He sank into the sand in a desert land. Not so clever, he's gone for ever! Oh, wow!' He leaned on the fence, laughing. 'Hear that?

I'm a poet, I am!'

He took Twigleg off his head and held him in front of his face. 'Why don't you say something? You're not looking too happy either. You weren't actually fond of that dragon-eater, were you?'

'No!' Twigleg shook his head indignantly. 'It's just,' he said, rubbing his pointed nose, 'it's just that it sounds *too* good to be true, see? I've had such a terrible time with him for so long, I've been afraid of him for so many hundreds of years, and now,' he concluded, looking at the boy, 'now do you think he's really sunk into the sand, just like that? Not him!' He shook his head. 'No, I don't believe it.'

'Oh, come on!' Ben poked his narrow chest with one finger. 'That dwarf sounded as if he was telling the truth. There's no end of quicksands in the desert. I saw something about them once on TV. A quicksand can swallow up a whole camel as if it were no bigger than a sand-flea, honest.'

Twigleg nodded. 'Yes, yes, I've heard that too. All the same—'

'Never mind *all the same*!' said Ben, putting the homunculus on his shoulder. 'You've saved us. After all, it was you who sent him off into the desert. Imagine Sorrel's face when we tell her! I just can't wait.'

And he ran back down to the beach to tell everyone the good news.

CHAPTER THIRTY-THREE

Face to Face

'Good!' growled Nettlebrand. 'You did really well there, dwarf. That pathetic stick-insect creature really believed you.'

He raised his muzzle from the water and hauled his gigantic body up on to the bank, panting and snorting. A flock of birds fluttered into the night sky, screeching raucously. Gravelbeard clung to one of Nettlebrand's horns and looked anxiously down at the great river, which was black as ink as it lapped around his master's scales.

'How about a little reward?' he suggested. 'Give me just one of your scales, Your Goldness!'

'What, for a few little lies? Shut up!' grunted Nettlebrand.

Gravelbeard muttered crossly into his beard.

'I'm going to pick up his scent now,' growled Nettlebrand.

'Whose scent?'

'The silver dragon's, you pebble-brained idiot.'

'But there are human beings there.' The dwarf adjusted his

hat nervously. 'Lots and lots of them. Suppose they see you? Your scales shine in the moonlight, Your Goldness!'

'Shut your gob!' Nettlebrand waded on through the mud of the riverbank towards the hill beyond which the village lay. The party was still going on, and the sound of music and laughter drifted their way on the wind, drowning out the roaring of the sea. Nettlebrand pricked up his ears and made his way to the top of the hill, still snorting.

And there he was. There was the silver dragon.

Firedrake was standing on the seashore, surrounded by people, and Ben and Sorrel were just climbing on his back.

Nettlebrand greedily inhaled the night air, snuffling and grunting. 'Ah yes, I have his scent,' he breathed. 'He can't escape me now. At long, long last, the hunt is up!'

He licked his dreadful lips. The thrill of the chase was running through him like wildfire, and he trod restlessly from one paw to the other.

'How are you going to follow him?' asked the dwarf, wiping a few splashes of mud off Nettlebrand's armoured brow. 'He can fly and you can't.'

'Huh!' Nettlebrand shook his head scornfully. 'There's only one way from here into the mountains, and that's up the river. If he can fly, I can swim. We'll be going the same way. And now that I have his scent I can always find him again. The whispering wind will tell me where he is.'

Down on the beach, Firedrake was moving. He turned his back to the sea, which gleamed silver in the moonlight, and looked north. The crowd around him stepped back, leaving only four of them standing there: a tall, thin man, two women, one short and the other tall, and a child. The dragon leaned down to them.

'It's that professor,' growled Nettlebrand. 'The one who has my scale. How the devil did he get here?'

'No idea, Your Goldness,' said Gravelbeard, nervously putting a hand under his shirt to touch Barnabas Greenbloom's wedding ring, which hung on a ribbon round his neck.

'I'll deal with him later,' grunted Nettlebrand. 'I can't stop now. Yes, I'll save some of the fun for later.'

'Look, Your Goldness,' whispered Gravelbeard, 'the dragon is taking off.'

Firedrake was spreading his wings. They shone like spun moonlight.

'At last!' whispered Nettlebrand. 'Off you go to the Rim of Heaven, my little silver sleuth-hound, and find the other dragons for me.'

At that moment the boy glanced up at the hills.

Nettlebrand's scales flashed in the moonlight so brightly that Ben narrowed his eyes. Next moment the glint of gold was gone. A large rain cloud had drifted in front of the moon, casting a dark shadow over the hilltops. Puzzled, the boy stared into the night.

Nettlebrand laughed hoarsely. 'You see, dwarf?' he growled. 'Even the clouds are on our side.'

The silver dragon beat his wings and rose into the night sky, light as a bird. He circled a couple of times over the huts, while the people down on the beach waved to him, and then flew off into the night.

Nettlebrand watched him for a moment. Then, grunting, he slid back down the hill and into the river. He swam soundlessly through the dark water, startling pelicans and flamingos out of their sleep, and snapping at everything that flew past his muzzle.

'Your Goldness!' whispered Gravelbeard. 'I can't swim.'

'You won't have to.' Sniffing loudly, Nettlebrand raised his nose from the water. 'Ah, he's above us,' he growled. 'He's going quite slowly. The wind's against him, blowing from the mountains. Good.'

'Your Goldness!' Gravelbeard clung to Nettlebrand's horn.

'Now what is it?'

'Do you know this river? Have you ever swum up it before?'

'Yes,' growled Nettlebrand. 'When I lost the dragons because of those wretched sea serpents. I swam up and down this river, wearing my claws out on the mountains from which it flows. Not a trace of them. Nothing. Not the tip of a dragon's tail, not a single scale. They might have vanished into thin air. But now,' he said, his tail lashing the water so violently that waves slapped against the far bank, 'this dragon will lead me to them. And if he can't find them either, then I'll have him anyway. That'll be better than nothing.'

Gravelbeard was only half listening to what his master said. All was quiet on the mighty river except for the sound of the water as it splashed and slurped, slapped and lapped against Nettlebrand's scales. 'Do you know what it's like inside the mountains where the river comes from?' asked the dwarf. 'Is there gold there? Gold and precious stones?'

'I've no idea,' snarled Nettlebrand, snapping at a fat fish which had been foolish enough to jump out of the water in front of him. 'Only humans and dwarves are interested in that kind of thing.'

They spent the rest of the night swimming upstream in silence. Firedrake was already some way ahead, but that didn't bother Nettlebrand. The moon would soon fade in the light of dawn, and the silver dragon would have to find a hiding place for the day. Meanwhile he, Nettlebrand, would plunge down into the waters of the river – leaving his horns sticking out just far enough for the dwarf to get a breath of air – and then he would wait until the dragon's scent came to his nostrils again.

No, Firedrake could not escape him now.

CHAPTER THIRTY-FOUR

Snatched Away

'There they are!' cried Ben. 'I saw them in Asif's eye! I'm sure I did. Do you see them, Firedrake?'

He pointed excitedly to the east, where the red light of the rising sun fell on a strangely shaped mountain range. They had been flying for the last two nights above hot, flat land, lakes with birds swimming on them, and ancient fortresses set among green mountains, places that looked as if time had stood still there. Some of them looked familiar to Ben, who thought he had seen them in the eyes of the djinn. And he remembered these mountains very clearly, for they resembled the spiny crest of a sleeping dragon.

'Careful, you'll break the straps the way you're bouncing about!' said Sorrel crossly as Firedrake slowly flew lower.

'I'm sure of it, Sorrel!' cried Ben. 'The monastery must lie beyond those mountains!'

'They're still a long way off,' said Firedrake. 'But we can make it to the foothills.'

Beating his wings a couple of times, he crossed the river where it made its way between rocky banks, foaming fast. The moon was already turning pale, but Firedrake flew on until the foothills of the dragon mountains lay beneath him like rocky paws. He circled above the slopes looking for a landing place, and came down on a rocky outcrop.

The river rushed along in the depths behind them. Ahead, the mountains rose first gently and then ever more steeply to the sky. Peak after peak soared up like the spines of a giant dragon. The mountain range beyond was higher still, its snow-covered slopes glittering in the morning sunlight.

Firedrake came down among the rocks, yawned, stretched his weary limbs, and let Ben and Sorrel clamber down from his back.

'We seem to be going the right way,' said Sorrel, looking around. 'Not a sign of any human beings. Only the road down there by the river, and it looks as if no one's been along that for hundreds of years.'

'Am I tired!' murmured Firedrake, settling down in the shade of a large boulder and yawning. 'I've done too little sleeping and too much talking these last few days.'

'We'll wake you up when it gets dark again,' said Ben. He looked across to the dragon-shaped mountains, and all the pictures he had seen in the djinn's eyes suddenly came back into his mind. 'It can't be far now,' he murmured. 'I'm sure it can't. Funny, it feels almost as if I've been here before.'

'Well, of course you have,' said Sorrel sarcastically. 'You're the old dragon rider come back to life, right?'

'Oh, pack it in!' Ben took out the map and two of the delicious chapatti breads Zubeida Ghalib had given him for the journey, and sat down beside Firedrake. The dragon was already asleep.

'Hmm, that part's all marked yellow,' murmured Ben, taking a bite of bread. 'I wonder what we'll find there.' Thoughtfully, he brushed some crumbs off the map. 'Never mind, we'll just stick close to the river.'

Sleepily, Twigleg put his head out of the backpack and looked round. 'Where are we?' he asked.

'Going the right way,' said Sorrel, rummaging in her own backpack. 'Oh, bother! One of the water bottles is empty, and there's not much left in the other.' She nudged Ben, who was still poring over the map. 'Hey, dragon rider, if this place seems so familiar to you I expect you'll know where to find water, right?'

'Water?' Ben looked up, frowning, folded the map, put it in his backpack and glanced round. 'I'll look for some,' he said. 'How about it, Twigleg? Want to come with me?'

'Yes, count me in.' The manikin crawled out of the backpack. 'You wait and see, I'm brilliant at finding water.'

'And we all know why,' growled Sorrel.

'Oh, stop it, Sorrel. Don't start squabbling again.' Ben put Twigleg on his shoulder, slung the water bottles round his neck, and wound the keffiyeh the professor had given him round his head. 'See you,' he said.

'See you,' murmured Sorrel, curling up like a ball beside Firedrake. 'And don't bother looking for mushrooms. Not a hope of the least little boletus growing in this wilderness.'

She smacked her lips at the thought of mushrooms and then began to snore.

'What's a boletus?' Ben whispered to Twigleg. 'I wouldn't know one if it walked up to me and shook hands.'

'It's a particularly tasty sort of mushroom,' Twigleg whispered back. 'There are many sub-species.'

'There are?' Ben looked at him admiringly. 'You're an expert on mushrooms too? I can't imagine how everything you know fits into your little head. Mine's as empty as this water bottle. Tell me about the sub-species!'

Twigleg enumerated them as they walked along, describing the bay boletus, the cep or penny bun, the slippery jack pine boletus or sticky bun, the orange birch boletus and many more.

Ben found a slope that didn't have too steep a drop, then relied on Twigleg's nose. They soon found a spring where the water bubbled up among stones before running down the mountainside. Ben put Twigleg down on a rock, knelt beside the spring and dipped the bottles in the clear water.

'I wish I knew why the rat shaded everything over there in yellow on his map,' he murmured. There was not a living creature to be seen on the mountains across the valley.

'I don't know, young master,' said Twigleg, getting down from the rock where he was sitting, 'but I have a feeling we ought to get back to the others as quickly as possible.'

'Oh no!' Ben screwed the tops on the water bottles and hung them round his neck. 'You went and said "young master" again. Next time, I'm going to pull your nose!'

Just as Ben was about to put Twigleg on his shoulder, he heard a sudden rushing sound above him. Ben looked up at the sky – and shrank back in horror.

A huge bird was diving down on him, claws outstretched. It plucked him off the rocks as easily as if he were a beetle.

'Young master!' screamed Twigleg. 'Oh, young master!'

Ben tried to bite the giant bird's claws. He twisted and turned like a worm, but it was no good. Uttering a hoarse screech, the bird rose into the air with its prey.

'Twigleg!' Ben shouted. 'Twigleg, get Firedrake! Get Firedrake!' And then the giant bird carried him away.

It flew towards the dragon mountains.

Twigleg stood rooted to the spot for a moment or so, breathless with horror as he watched the giant bird soar into the sky. A sob rose from his chest. Then he pulled himself together and scrambled up the rocks as nimbly as a spider.

'Faster, Twigleg, faster!' he told himself, panting. He was so scared of the abyss behind him that he felt sick. He kept slipping, losing his grip, sliding back down the slope. His thin fingers were soon grazed, his bony knees scratched. His heart was thumping faster and faster, but he hardly noticed. He could think of nothing but that enormous bird carrying Ben further and further away with every beat of its wings. When Twigleg finally saw the tip of Firedrake's tail among the rocks before him he uttered a sob of relief.

'Help!' he cried with what little breath he had left. 'Quick, help!'

His little hands tugged at the sleeping dragon's tail, and he pulled at Sorrel's furry coat until he had a tuft of her hairs in his fingers. Firedrake opened his eyes sleepily. Sorrel jumped as if a snake had bitten her.

'Are you crazy?' she spat at the homunculus. 'What the—?' But she got no further.

'It's the young master!' cried Twigleg shrilly. 'Please, come quick! Quick! A bird – a giant bird has carried him off.'

Firedrake was on his feet at once. 'Where to?' he asked.

'It flew towards the dragon mountains,' said Twigleg. 'You must follow it!'

'But we can't,' groaned Sorrel, pointing to the sky. 'Firedrake can't fly now. The moon set ages ago.'

'Find that little flask!' said Firedrake. 'And hurry.'

Her paws trembling, Sorrel found the flask of moon-dew in Ben's backpack and put three drops of it on Firedrake's tongue. Holding their breath, she and Twigleg stared at the dragon. He closed his eyes, opened them again, and went to the edge of the precipice.

'Quick, climb aboard,' he called, as the wind blew beneath his wings, raising them in the air. 'We must try it.'

Sorrel grabbed Twigleg and the backpacks and climbed up on Firedrake's back. The dragon spread his wings, took off – and flew.

'It works!' cried Twigleg, clutching Sorrel's furry arms. 'Thank goodness!'

Firedrake felt as strong as if the full moon were in the sky. He shot past the rocks, rising higher and higher, his shadow passing over the mountains in the full light of day. They soon reached the mountain range that looked like a dragon's back. Five peaks rose into the blue sky, casting their shadows on the valleys and ravines below. Firedrake looked around, searching for some sign.

'Oh, beastly blewits!' groaned Sorrel. 'A giant bird will be even harder to spot here than a truffle in the forest.'

'But we must find him!' wailed Twigleg, wringing his little hands. 'Oh, please!'

Firedrake flew into the first ravine.

'Ben!' shouted Sorrel. 'Ben, can you hear us?'

'Answer us, do, young master!' cried Twigleg.

Firedrake put his head back and uttered a roar such as Sorrel had never heard from him before. The dragon's cry resounded from the rocks, echoed through the ravines, and died away only in the far distance. But not even Sorrel's keen ears could hear any answer.

'I've read about that bird!' moaned Twigleg. 'In the

professor's book. It's the giant roc. We've attracted it the way we attracted the basilisk and the sea serpent! Oh, what terrible luck!'

'You talk too much, little titch!' Sorrel snapped at him. 'Knowing the bird's name isn't going to help us. We must find it, so shut your mouth and keep your eyes open.'

'Yes, yes!' wailed Twigleg. 'But suppose it's already eaten the young master?'

No one answered that question.

CHAPTER THIRTY-FIVE

The Nest of the Giant Roc

But the bird had not eaten Ben yet. It carried him further and further into the mountains. Ben hardly dared to look down. At first he had fought against the sharp claws, but now he was clinging to them for dear life, terrified that the bird might see some juicier prey and let go of him.

He had never felt dizzy on Firedrake's back, but it was a completely different feeling to be dangling helplessly in the air with nothing below him, nothing but empty sky between him and the ground.

He was bird-food. This was not the way he had imagined the end of his journey. Ben gritted his teeth, but they kept on chattering, whether because of the wind or his terror he couldn't have said. Suddenly the giant bird was flying towards a rugged rock wall. It rose higher and higher, and let Ben drop.

Screaming, Ben plummeted down to land in a mighty nest perched on top of a peak like an untidy crown. The nest was made of uprooted tree trunks. In the middle of it, on a thick cushion of feathers, sat a huge chick. It greeted its mother with a hoarse caw and opened its beak wide, but she was already spreading her wings to fly off in search of more prey.

The chick turned its head, which was covered with little more than fluffy down, and glared hungrily at Ben.

'No!' Ben murmured. 'Oh no!'

He looked desperately around. There was only one way to save himself from that hungry beak. He jumped up and struggled through the feathers towards the edge of the nest.

Seeing its meal trying to get away, the chick squawked angrily. Its giant beak pecked at Ben, but he managed to throw himself aside just in time. Desperately, he burrowed under the feathers and kept crawling until his fingers came up against the side of the nest. Just as he was trying to wriggle in among the tree trunks to take shelter, the chick caught hold of his leg. With the last of his strength Ben managed to pull it free, and he scrambled in among the tangle of branches.

The chick jerked its head in surprise, straightened up clumsily, and started pecking at the side of the nest. But Ben had crawled so far into the branches that its beak couldn't reach him. The chick pecked more and more furiously. It tore away whole tree trunks, but every time it came close to Ben's hiding place he thrust his way into the next gap. The twigs and branches were almost impaling him. They tore his clothes and scratched his face, but anything was better than ending up in that hungry beak.

The furious chick had already pecked half the side of the nest to pieces when Ben suddenly heard a mighty roar echoing through the ravines, so loud and angry a roar that the monstrous chick turned its scrawny neck in alarm. It's Firedrake! thought

Ben. I'm sure it is! His heart beat faster – this time for joy. Then he heard someone calling his name.

'Sorrel!' he cried. 'I'm here, Sorrel. Up here!'

The young roc bird swung its head to look his way again, but Ben managed to wriggle out through the branches until he could peer down into the ravine. Firedrake was coming. Wings rushing, he shot towards the giant nest with Sorrel crouched on his back, waving her fists in the air.

'Here we come!' she shouted. 'Don't let it eat you!'

Beating his wings vigorously, Firedrake landed on the edge of the nest, as close as possible to where Ben was sheltering. The huge chick retreated in fright. It uttered a hoarse croak and opened its beak menacingly. Ben was alarmed to see that Firedrake wasn't much bigger than the chick. But when it tried lunging at Ben again, the dragon bared his teeth and roared so threateningly that it flinched back in terror.

Ben made his way through the branches until his head emerged beside Firedrake's paws.

'Oh, young master!' cried Twigleg, bending down anxiously from Firedrake's neck. 'Are you all right?'

'Yes, he is, but not for long!' Sorrel made her way down Firedrake's neck and seized Ben's hand. Twigs kept catching in the boy's clothes, but Sorrel managed to pull him free of the branches and heave him up on Firedrake's back. Twigleg clung to Ben's jacket and scanned the sky anxiously. But there was no sign of the mother roc.

Firedrake growled threateningly at the chick one last time, then spread his wings and rose into the air. He shot away like an arrow, flying in an arc down the ravine. But he did not get far.

'There!' cried Twigleg, pointing ahead with trembling fingers. 'Look! Mama Roc is coming back.'

With a mountain goat in her talons, the huge mother roc was making straight for them, the tips of her mighty wings brushing the sides of the ravine.

'Turn round!' Ben shouted to Firedrake. 'Turn round – she's much, much bigger than you.'

But the dragon hesitated.

'Firedrake, turn round!' cried Sorrel. 'Or are you planning to pick us up from the ground in pieces after you've fought the bird?'

Behind them, the young roc screeched. Its mother responded with a furious cry. Dropping her prey, she made for the dragon, feathers bristling, claws braced to attack. Ben could see the whites of her eyes.

At last, Firedrake turned. 'Hold on tight!' he called.

Letting himself drop like a stone, he plunged deep into the ravine until it was so narrow the giant bird couldn't follow him.

Twigleg looked up anxiously. The great roc bird was directly above them. Her dark shadow fell on Firedrake. She too dropped through the air, but her wings struck the rocky walls of the ravine. Screeching furiously, she rose once more and tried again. With each attempt to dive-bomb the fleeing dragon she came a little closer.

Firedrake felt his strength fading. His wings were heavy; he was spinning round and round.

'It's stopped working!' cried Sorrel. Desperately, she reached behind her. 'Quick, quick! The flask of moon-dew!'

Ben plunged his hand into his backpack and put the flask into her paw. Undoing her strap, Sorrel inched her way forward. 'I'm coming!' she cried, wriggling down the dragon's long neck. 'Turn your head to me, Firedrake!'

Ben heard the giant roc chick in the distance, its screeches sounding increasingly desperate. Once more its mother tried to dive into the ravine, but in vain. Cawing hoarsely, she turned.

'She's flying back!' cried Ben. 'She's going back to her chick, Sorrel!'

'Huh!' Sorrel shouted back. 'She might have thought of that before!' Arms trembling, she hung from the spiralling dragon's neck and let a drop of moon-dew fall on his tongue.

Firedrake felt his strength return at once. 'Can you hold on, Sorrel?' he gasped, slowly descending.

'Yes, yes!' the brownie girl called back. 'Just get us away from that horrible bird!'

The ravine narrowed yet further, until it was a mere cleft between the walls of rock. Firedrake shot along it like a thread passing through the eye of a needle. At the far end it opened out into a wide, desolate valley lying among the mountains like a shallow bowl filled with stones. No foot seemed ever to have trodden here. Only the wind blew through the scanty grass.

Firedrake landed at the foot of a mountain as round as a cat's arched back. Other mountains rose behind it. Snow-covered peaks shone, glittering white in the sun.

With a sigh of relief, Sorrel dropped from Firedrake's neck and fell into the grass.

'I wouldn't want to do that again in a hurry!' she groaned. 'Not on your life! Puffballs and penny buns, do I feel sick!' She sat on the ground, picked some grass from between the stones and stuffed it rapidly into her mouth.

Ben slipped off Firedrake's back, carrying Twigleg. He could still hear the screeching of the young roc in his ears. His trousers were torn, his hands were scratched, and he had lost his Arab headcloth in the tangled branches of the giant roc's nest.

'My word!' said Sorrel, giggling at the sight of him. 'You look as if you've been trying to steal blackberries from the fairies.'

Ben plucked a few dead leaves out of his hair and grinned. 'Wow, was I glad to see you three!'

'It's Twigleg you have to thank,' said Sorrel, putting the little flask of moon-dew away among Ben's things. 'Twigleg and the dracologist. Without her moon-dew, Firedrake would have had to go in search of you on foot.'

Ben put Twigleg on his arm and tapped his nose. 'Thank you very much indeed!' he said. Then he patted Firedrake's long neck and nudged Sorrel in the ribs. 'Thank you all,' he repeated. 'I really did think I was going to end up as bird-food.'

'We'd never have let that happen!' said Sorrel, swallowing noisily and wiping her mouth. 'Now, take a look at that clever map of yours and tell us where we are.' She pointed to the mountains around them. 'Do you think you've been here before, too?'

Ben looked round and, smiling, shook his head. 'Can you still hear the river?' he asked anxiously.

Sorrel pricked up her ears. 'No, I haven't heard it for quite some time. But unless I'm much mistaken,' she said, pointing to the snow-covered peaks, 'those are quite a bit closer.'

'You're right,' murmured Ben.

Beside him, Firedrake stretched and yawned.

'Oh dear!' said Ben. 'Now you've missed your sleep again.'

'Never mind,' said Firedrake, yawning once more.

'What do you mean, never mind?' Sorrel shook her head. 'You have to sleep. Who knows how many more mountains we'll have to cross? We've probably got the worst of the journey still to come, and how are you going to manage if you're yawning all the time?'

Sorrel clambered a little way up the slope to look around. 'Hey!' she suddenly called down to the others. 'I've found a cave.

Come on up.'

Wearily, Firedrake and Ben climbed up to join her.

'Let's hope it doesn't have another of those horrible basilisks living in it,' murmured the dragon, as Sorrel disappeared into the dark mouth of the cave. 'Or do any of you happen to have a mirror with you?'

CHAPTER THIRTY-SIX

Losing the Trail

'Where is he?' growled Nettlebrand, raising his head from the turbulent waters. Dark grey mountains rose into the sky, and the river foamed against their rocky slopes as if trying to wash them away. Its dark waters lapped over Nettlebrand's scales and almost swept Gravelbeard off his master's armoured brow.

'Your Goldness!' spluttered the dwarf, spitting out icy water. 'When can we get out onto the riverbank? Dwarves aren't fish, you know.' He was wet through to his woollen shirt, his teeth were chattering, and he'd already had to pull his hat out of the river seven times.

'The riverbank?' snorted Nettlebrand. 'This is no time for me to mix with human beings.'

Shivering, Gravelbeard looked ahead of them. A suspension bridge spanned the foaming torrent. Houses clustered at the foot of the mountain slopes, and a road led along the bank between huge boulders, almost buried under the mud and stones of a landslide that had fallen during the last rainy season. There was no one on the bridge, but two birds were perched on its fragile cables. A solitary bus was driving along the road, and people were bustling about among the houses.

'Where is he?' growled Nettlebrand again. 'He can't have gone on – that's impossible!' He sniffed the cool evening air. Days here on the roof of the world were boiling hot, but as soon as the sun had set an icy chill, like the snowy breath of the mountains, descended on the valleys.

'It's quite some time since you last scented him, Your Goldness,' said Gravelbeard, tipping water out of the brim of his hat. 'In fact, it's a very long time.'

'I know, I know,' snarled Nettlebrand, swimming on until he was in the shadow of the bridge. 'Everything was fine until we reached these mountains, then the trail suddenly vanished. Aaaargh!' Furious, he spat into the turbulent water.

'He's probably not following the river any more.' Gravelbeard sneezed, and rubbed his cold hands. 'You were wrong, Your Goldness, and he's flying over the mountains. How are you going to follow him there?'

'Oh, shut up!' Nettlebrand dipped his head in the water, spuffling, and turned to let the current carry him downstream and back south. The place where he had lost Firedrake's scent was not too far behind him.

'Your Goldness!' the dwarf suddenly cried. 'Watch out! There's a boat coming upstream straight towards us.'

Nettlebrand jerked his muzzle up. 'Ah! Just what I fancy!' he growled. 'I'll push it about a bit. Batter it, bash it, capsize it! Hold tight, armour-cleaner. This is going to be fun. I do like to hear those two-legs squeal.' Bracing himself in the current, he plunged his head deep into the water. 'One little shove should do it!' he whispered. 'Humans are such helpless little things on the water.'

The narrow boat was making its way upstream with difficulty. When it was quite close, Nettlebrand raised his head and gazed up at the humans. Most of them were looking at the houses on the bank, but a tall thin man and the girl with him had raised their eyes to the mountains, indistinct outlines in the evening twilight.

'Well, look at that, dwarf!' Nettlebrand submerged his head and laughed until he shook all over. 'What have we here? That's the professor who stole my scale. Oh, what a surprise!' Flipping his tail a couple of times, he drifted sideways until his armour clunked against the stony bank.

The boat glided past him, and the people on board had no idea of the danger they had barely escaped. Only the girl glanced at the place where Nettlebrand was lurking in the water. She tugged at her father's sleeve and said something, but the roaring of the river drowned out her words. Barnabas Greenbloom just stroked his daughter's hair absent-mindedly as he continued looking up at the mountains.

'Not going to capsize it after all?' sighed Gravelbeard, who had been clinging as tightly as he could to one of the dragon's horns. 'Very wise. Very wise, Your Goldness! It would only have made trouble.' Then he realised that his master was changing direction yet again. 'Hey, where are we going this time?' he called, crossly wringing the water out of his beard. 'I thought we were going back, Your Goldness! Back to where you lost the scent!'

'Not now,' replied Nettlebrand, swimming upstream against the current as if he felt none of its force. 'A good hunter follows his nose, and my nose tells me I shall find the silver dragon again if I follow that thin human. Get it?'

'No,' grumbled Gravelbeard, sneezing three times in rapid succession.

'Well, never mind,' growled Nettlebrand. 'You dwarves are burrowers, not hunters. I doubt if you can even catch woodlice. Keep quiet and make sure the river doesn't wash you off my head. I may still need you.'

And, as night fell, he set off to follow the boat carrying the humans.

'I really did see him!' Guinevere told her father, who was still standing by the rail and looking at the mountains.

'It's easy to imagine you see things in rough water, my dear,' replied Barnabas Greenbloom, glancing at her with a smile. 'Especially on a sacred river like this.'

'But he looked exactly as you described him!' cried Guinevere. 'With golden scales and horrible red eyes!'

Barnabas Greenbloom sighed. 'Which just proves that your mother's right and I've told you too many tales about that dreadful monster.'

'Nonsense!' snapped Guinevere, bringing her hand angrily down on the rail. 'You've always told me stories about all sorts of things. Does that mean I go imagining fairies or giants or basilisks all over the place?'

Barnabas looked at her thoughtfully. 'No, that's true, you don't,' he admitted.

The stars were shining above the snow-covered mountains, and it was growing bitterly cold. The professor wrapped his daughter's scarf more snugly round her neck and looked into her eyes gravely.

'Right, tell me again, what exactly did you see?'

'He was peering out of the water,' said Guinevere. 'Very close to the riverbank. His eyes glowed like fiery globes and,' she continued, raising her hands, 'and he had two horrible horns with a dwarf clutching one of them! The dwarf was sopping wet!'

Her father took a deep breath. 'You're sure you saw all that?'

Guinevere nodded proudly. 'You always taught me to observe things in detail.'

Barnabas Greenbloom nodded. 'Yes, and you were a good pupil. Always the first to spot the fairies in our garden.' He looked thoughtfully down at the river. 'If you're right, it means that Nettlebrand wasn't buried in the sand after all,' he murmured. 'Which, goodness only knows, is not good news. We'll have to warn Firedrake the moment we meet him at the monastery.'

'Do you think he's following *us*?' asked Guinevere.

'Who?'

'Nettlebrand.'

'Following *us*?' Her father looked at her in alarm. 'I sincerely hope not.'

They spent all night on watch, looking over the rail and down at the river, but the darkness hid Nettlebrand from sight.

CHAPTER THIRTY-SEVEN

An Old Campfire

'Sorry,' said Ben, poring over the rat's map with a sigh, 'but I've no idea where we are. As long as we were flying upstream along the river it was clear enough, but now,' he shrugged his shoulders, 'we could be anywhere.'

He pointed to the many white patches on the map east of the river Indus. They were like gaping holes in the landscape.

'This is a nice prospect!' groaned Sorrel. 'What will the professor think when we don't show up at the monastery on time?'

'It's all my fault,' murmured Ben, folding up the map. 'If you hadn't gone looking for me, you might have reached it by now.'

'Yes, and you'd be bird-food, remember,' Sorrel pointed out.

'Lie down and get some sleep,' said Firedrake from the darkest corner of the cave. He had curled up in a ball, muzzle on the tip of his tail, eyes tightly closed. Flying in the sunlight was more exhausting than three nights of flight in a row. Even his anxiety about their route couldn't keep his eyelids open.

'Yes, good idea,' murmured Ben, stretching out on the cool floor of the cave with his head on his backpack. Twigleg lay down beside him, using the boy's hand as a pillow.

Only Sorrel remained on her paws, undecided and snuffling. 'Can't you smell that?' she asked.

'Smell what?' muttered Firedrake drowsily. 'Mushrooms?'

'No, I smell fire.'

'So what?' Ben opened one eye. 'There are the sites of old campfires all over this cave, you can see there are. It seems to be a popular place for people to take shelter.'

Sorrel shook her head. 'And some of them aren't all that old,' she said. 'This one, for instance.' She pushed the charred branches apart with her paw. 'It's from two days ago at the most, and that one over there is still quite fresh. Only a few hours old.'

'All right, you'd better keep watch, then,' sighed Firedrake sleepily. 'And wake me up if anyone comes.' Then he was asleep.

'A few hours old. Are you sure?' Ben rubbed the drowsiness from his eyes and sat up.

Twigleg leaned against his arm, yawning. 'Which fire do you mean, fur-face?' he asked.

'This one, of course!' Sorrel pointed to a tiny heap of ashes.

'Good heavens,' groaned Ben, lying down once more. 'That could only have been a campfire for a worm, Sorrel.' He rolled over on his side, and next moment he was as fast asleep as Firedrake.

'Campfire for a worm – huh!' Crossly, Sorrel picked up her backpack and went to sit at the mouth of the cave.

Twigleg followed her. 'I can't sleep either,' he said. 'I've slept enough recently to last me the next hundred years.' He sat down beside Sorrel. 'Are you seriously worried about that campfire?'

'I'm keeping my eyes and ears open, anyway,' growled Sorrel, taking the professor's bag of dried mushrooms out of her backpack.

Cautiously, Twigleg stepped out of the cave. The wide valley was bright in the midday sun, and there was not a sound to be heard.

'It must look like this on the moon,' said the homunculus.

'The moon?' Sorrel nibbled a puffball. 'I imagine the moon quite differently. Damp and misty. All cold.'

'Ah.' Twigleg looked round thoughtfully.

'I just hope the fireplace has nothing to do with sand-elves,' muttered Sorrel. 'But no, that's out of the question – sand-elves never light fires. How about trolls, though? Are there any mountain trolls about your size?'

'Not that I know of.' Twigleg caught a passing fly and popped it into his mouth behind a politely raised hand.

Then, suddenly, Sorrel put a warning finger to her lips. She threw her backpack into the cave behind her, grabbed Twigleg and hid behind the rocks with him.

Twigleg heard a quiet humming sound, then a loud rattle – and a small, dusty aeroplane taxied to a halt at the mouth of the cave. It was bright green and covered from nose to tail with black paw-prints. Each wing bore a sign that seemed curiously familiar to Sorrel.

The cockpit opened with a jerk, and out climbed a grey rat. She was so fat that in her flying suit she looked like a sausage bursting out of its skin.

'Nice landing!' Sorrel and Twigleg heard her comment. 'Flawless! You're an ace airwoman, Lola Greytail, that's what you are.'

The rat turned her back to the cave and took several rolls of paper, some poles and a telescope out of the plane. 'Where did I put that book?' she muttered. 'Oh, thunder and lightning, where is the dratted thing?'

Sorrel picked Twigleg up, put a finger to his lips, and made her way out of hiding.

'Did you say your name was Greytail?' she asked.

The rat swung around, dropping all her things in her fright. 'What? Who? How?' she stammered. Then she jumped back into her plane and tried to start it.

'Wait!' cried Sorrel, standing in front of the small aircraft and holding on to the propeller. 'Not so fast! Where are you going? Are you by any chance related to a rat called Gilbert who's as white as a cultivated mushroom?'

Taken aback, the rat stared at the brownie girl. Then she switched the engine of her plane off again and stuck her whiskered nose out of the cockpit. 'You know Gilbert?' she asked.

'We bought a map from him,' replied Sorrel. 'His rubber stamp looks just like the sign on your wings. Not that the map's prevented us from getting lost in these parts.'

'A map?' The rat climbed out of her aircraft again and jumped down to the ground. 'A map of the countryside round here?' She glanced at the cave, and then at Sorrel. 'You don't by any chance have a dragon in there?'

Sorrel grinned. 'Yes, I do.'

Lola Greytail rolled her eyes and said, through gritted teeth, 'Then it's all your fault I'm surveying these godforsaken parts!' she snapped. 'Oh, thanks! Thank you very, very much indeed!'

'Our fault?' said Sorrel. 'Why?'

'Ever since you visited Gilbert,' said the rat, picking up the things she had dropped when Sorrel had suddenly appeared, 'he's been obsessed with the blank patches on his map! So he rings me up just as I'm having a nice little holiday visiting my brother in India and goes on and on at me. "Lola, you must fly to the Himalayas! Lola, do your old uncle a little favour! Lola, I simply *must* find out about the blank patches on my map. Please, Lola!" So here I am.'

The rat groaned under the weight of the equipment she was hauling into the shelter of the cave. 'Can't you make yourself useful instead of just gawping at me?' she snapped at Sorrel. 'Push the plane into the cave or it'll soon be hot enough to fry ostrich eggs on it.'

'Just like her uncle!' growled Sorrel, putting Twigleg down and fetching the plane. It weighed so little that she could tuck it under her arm. When she brought it into the cave she found Lola Greytail standing transfixed in front of the sleeping Firedrake.

'Wind and weather!' she whispered. 'It really is a dragon.'

'What did you expect? Don't wake him up, he needs a good sleep or we'll never get out of here.' Sorrel put the plane down and looked at it rather more closely. 'Where did you get this aeroplane?' she asked, lowering her voice.

'From a toy shop,' murmured Lola Greytail without taking her eyes off the dragon. 'Of course, I did a conversion job on it. It flies really well. Even the mountains around here were no problem.' She took another cautious step towards the dragon. Standing on her hind legs, she was hardly any bigger than one of Firedrake's paws. 'Beautiful,' she whispered. 'But what does he eat?' She turned to Sorrel, looking anxious. 'Not rats, I hope?'

Sorrel chuckled. 'No, don't worry. Nothing but moonlight, that's all he needs.'

'Ah, moonlight.' The rat nodded. 'Interesting source of energy, that. I've tried building moonlight batteries. Never got them to work yet, though.' She turned to look at Ben, who was asleep near the mouth of the cave, still exhausted after his adventure with the giant roc.

'You've got a human with you, too?' she whispered. 'My uncle only mentioned you and the dragon.' Pointing at Twigleg, she added, 'He didn't say anything about that little creature either.'

Sorrel shrugged her shoulders and twirled the propeller of Lola's plane with her paw. It whirred round. 'Those two sort of just came along,' she said. 'We have a bit of trouble with them now and then, but they're not so bad really. The little one's a homincolossus.'

'Homunculus!' Twigleg corrected her, and bowed to Lola Greytail.

'Ah,' she said, examining him from head to foot. 'No offence meant, but you look like some kind of toy human.'

Twigleg smiled shyly. 'Well, in a way you're right,' he said. 'May I ask how far you've got with surveying and mapping these parts?'

'I'm almost through,' replied Lola, smoothing her whiskers. 'Just dropped in here to write up my records for today.'

Sorrel looked at her in surprise. 'Then you know your way around here?'

'Of course.' The rat twitched her shoulders. 'I know every dratted stick and stone in these parts by now.'

'You do?' Sorrel ran over to Ben and shook him.

'Wake up!' she whispered into his ear. 'Wake up – there's someone here who can show us the way. The way to the monastery!'

Ben turned over sleepily, and blinked at Sorrel. 'What is it? Who's here?'

Sorrel pointed to Lola. The fat rat took a step back, for

safety's sake, but she put her paws on her hips and stared the human bravely in the face. Ben sat up in surprise and looked down at her.

'Where did this character spring from, then?' he asked in amazement.

'This *character*? You see before you Lola Greytail,' said the rat, insulted.

'She's that white rat's niece,' hissed Sorrel. 'Gilbert sent her here to survey the terrain for him.' She pulled Ben's sleeve. 'Come on. Let's discuss the rest of it outside the cave, or we'll wake Firedrake.'

It was still uncomfortably hot outside, but the temperature was bearable in the shade of a large boulder near the mouth of the cave.

'Get the map out,' said Sorrel.

Ben did as she said, opened it and showed it to the rat.

'Can you tell us where we are?' Sorrel asked Lola, holding her breath in suspense.

The rat padded over her uncle's map looking at it closely, her brow wrinkled. 'Let's see,' she murmured. 'Yes, that's clear

enough.' Raising her paw, she tapped a place south-east of the Indus. 'You're here, among these mountains, in what I call the Rocky Valley.'

'We're looking for a monastery,' explained Ben. 'It's on a mountainside overlooking a wide, green part of the Indus valley. A large place with a lot of buildings, and banners fluttering in the wind.'

'Hmm.' Lola nodded, and looked at the boy. 'Yes, I know it. Good description. Been there before, have you?'

'No.' Ben shook his head. 'I saw it in a djinn's two hundred and twenty-third eye.'

Lola Greytail's jaw dropped. She gaped at the boy for a moment. 'Really?' she said at last. 'Well, like I said, I know the place. Full of monks with bald heads. Little monks and big ones. Very friendly human species, monks. Really hospitable. But their tea is something awful.'

Ben looked at her hopefully. 'Can you take us there?'

'Sure.' Lola shrugged her shoulders. 'But my plane will never keep up with the dragon.'

'I dare say it won't!' Firedrake reached his long neck out of the cave, yawned, and looked curiously down at the fat rat.

He gave Lola such a shock that she suddenly sat down. 'He . . . he's bigger than I expected,' she stammered.

'Actually, he's about average for a dragon,' Sorrel told her. 'Some come bigger and some come smaller.'

'Firedrake, this is Lola,' explained Ben, 'Gilbert Greytail's niece. Isn't that a wonderful coincidence? Lola can show us the way to the monastery.'

'Coincidence! That's a good one!' muttered Lola, still unable to take her eyes off the dragon. 'It's all your fault that I'm in these mountains at all.'

'You're right,' said Twigleg. 'It's not a coincidence at all. It's a disposition of providence.'

'A what?' asked Sorrel.

'A preordained meeting,' said Twigleg. 'Something that was bound to happen. I can only call it a good omen. A very good omen.'

'Oh.' Sorrel shrugged her shoulders. 'Call it what you like, so long as Lola can get us out of here.' She looked up at the sky. 'We ought to set off as soon as possible – we ought to keep the moon-dew for emergencies. So we'll fly at moonrise, right?'

Firedrake nodded. 'Do you know Rosa Greytail?' he asked Lola. 'She'd be your aunt.'

'Of course I know her.' Lola hopped off her uncle's map so that Ben could fold it up again. 'Met her once at a family party. First time I ever heard of dragons.'

'And what about here?' asked Ben, leaning forward in suspense. 'Have you seen any dragons in these mountains?'

'Here?' Lola Greytail shook her head. 'Not so much as the tip of a dragon's tail. Though I've flown all over these mountains, believe you me. I know why you ask. Gilbert told me. You're looking for the Rim of Heaven. I can only say I've never seen any such place. No end of white peaks, of course. But no dragons, no sign of them at all.'

'Th-that must be wrong!' Ben stammered. 'I saw the valley. And a dragon in a huge cave.'

Lola Greytail looked at him incredulously. 'Saw it! Where?' she asked. 'In your djinn's eye? No, take my word for it, there are no dragons here. Monasteries, shaggy cattle, a few human beings, that's it. Nothing else at all.'

'There was a misty valley enclosed by a rim of white peaks, and a wonderful cave!' said Ben.

But Lola only shook her head again. 'There are hundreds of valleys here, and so many white peaks you'd go crazy trying to count them. But dragons, no. Sorry. I'll be telling Uncle Gilbert so, too. The Rim of Heaven doesn't exist, and there's no hidden valley of the dragons. It's nothing but a pretty fairy tale.'

CHAPTER THIRTY-EIGHT

The Monastery

It was just on midnight when Firedrake reached the river Indus again. Its waters glittered in the starlight. The river valley here was wide and fertile, and even in the dark, Ben could make out fields and huts. High above them stood the monastery, clinging to the steep slope of a mountain on the other side of the river. In the light of the waning moon, its pale walls shone like white paper.

'That's it!' whispered Ben. 'That's what it looked like. Exactly like that.'

Lola Greytail's plane was humming along beside him. The rat opened the cockpit and leaned out.

'Hey!' she shouted over the noise of the propeller. 'Is that the place?'

Ben nodded.

Satisfied, Lola closed the cockpit and flew on ahead. Her plane made much better speed than the others had expected, but for the dragon, this was the easiest flight of the whole journey anyway. He soared silently over the wide valley, left the river behind, and rose towards the high monastery walls.

There were several buildings, both large and small, clustering together on the cliff. Ben saw tall, windowless stone turrets rising upwards, dark and narrow windows, shallow roofs, high walls, and pathways winding like ribbons of rock down the mountainside.

'Where should I land?' Firedrake called to the rat.

'On the courtyard in front of the main building,' Lola called back. 'You'll have nothing to fear from these people. Anyway, they'll all be asleep at this time of night. I'll go first.'

With a loud humming noise, the little plane swooped down.

'Look, look!' cried Sorrel as Firedrake circled above the courtyard in front of the largest building. 'There's the professor!'

The dragon descended through the night air. As they landed, a tall figure rose from the steps leading up to the main monastery building and strode towards Firedrake.

'My word, have I been worried!' cried Professor Greenbloom. 'Where've you been all this time?' His voice echoed around the ancient walls, but still nothing stirred, apart from a few mice scurrying over the stones.

'We were delayed – had to save our little human here from ending up inside a giant bird,' Sorrel told him as she clambered off Firedrake's back with her backpack.

'What?' The professor looked up at Ben in alarm.

'It wasn't so bad,' said Ben, sliding down the dragon's tail.

'Not so bad?' cried the professor when he and Ben were face to face. 'Good heavens, you're scratched all over.'

'Scratched, but not eaten alive,' Sorrel pointed out. 'That's something, right?'

'Well, yes, if you look at it that way.' Barnabas Greenbloom took a step backwards and almost trod on the rat's plane.

'Hey, look out!' squeaked Lola shrilly. 'Watch where you're stepping, can't you, you great clumsy lump.'

The startled professor turned round. Lola Greytail clambered out of her cockpit and jumped down in front of him, landing heavily.

'Hello, Professor. I've heard a lot about you!' she said.

'You have? I hope it was all good.' Professor Greenbloom went down on one knee and shook the rat's paw gently. 'And whom do I have the pleasure of meeting?' he asked.

Feeling flattered, Lola giggled. 'Greytail,' she replied. 'Lola Greytail, pilot, cartographer, and on this occasion foreign tourist guide.'

'We flew slightly off course,' explained Sorrel, joining the two of them. 'How was your own journey, Professor?'

'Oh, peaceful enough.' Barnabas Greenbloom stood up, with a sigh. 'But Guinevere says,' he added, scratching his head and looking up at the dark windows of the monastery, 'although to be honest I don't know if I ought to tell you this . . .'

'Guinevere says what?' asked Ben. Twigleg leaned against his cheek, yawning.

'Guinevere says,' continued the professor, clearing his throat, 'well, she claims she saw Nettlebrand.'

'Where?' cried Sorrel.

The professor's remark gave Twigleg such a shock that he stopped yawning and Firedrake and Ben exchanged anxious glances.

'What's up?' Lola threaded her way between all the long legs around her and looked enquiringly from one to another of the companions.

'There's someone after us,' growled Sorrel. 'We thought we

were rid of him, but we could have been wrong.'

'Why don't I make a little reconnaissance flight?' asked Lola helpfully. 'Just tell me what the person who's after you looks like and roughly where he might be, and I'll be off in a jiffy.'

'Would you really scout around for us?' asked Firedrake.

'Yes, of course.' The rat passed a paw over her ears. 'Glad to. Makes a nice change from measuring stupid mountains and boring old valleys for Uncle Gilbert. Right, what am I looking for? A brownie, human, dragon, or maybe something like the little homunculpus thingummy there?'

Firedrake shook his head. 'It's a dragon,' he said, 'but a much bigger dragon than me. With golden scales.'

'And he has a mountain dwarf with him,' added Barnabas Greenbloom. 'A dwarf wearing an outsize hat. My daughter thinks she saw them both in the river down near the large suspension bridge where a landslide has fallen on the road.'

'I know it,' said Lola Greytail casually. 'I'll be off – take a look around.'

Quick as lightning, the fat rat was back in her plane. The engine purred, and the little aircraft shot up into the starlit sky. Soon it had disappeared even from Sorrel's keen sight.

'That rat moves fast,' said the professor admiringly. 'It's a load off my mind to have her scouting for us. How did you meet her?'

'Oh, rats get everywhere,' replied Sorrel, looking round her. 'You just have to wait around and a rat is sure to cross your path.'

'She's the niece of Gilbert Greytail who sold us the map,' Ben explained. 'Her uncle sent her to survey some of the mountain regions that are still blank on his map.' He looked at the professor. 'Lola says there's no such place as the Rim of Heaven.'

Barnabas Greenbloom returned Ben's gaze thoughtfully. 'Does she? Well, in your place I'd put my faith in what the djinn showed you. Let's have a go at deciphering his directions. Come on!' Putting an arm around Ben's shoulders, he led him towards the great flight of steps leading up to the main monastery building. 'I want to introduce you to someone. I've told him all about your quest, and he's been expecting you for some time.'

Firedrake and Sorrel followed the two of them up the long flight of steps.

'This is the Dhu-Khang,' explained Barnabas Greenbloom, when they reached the heavy front door. It was painted with strange figures, and the handle was skilfully made of wrought iron. 'It's the monks' prayer and assembly hall, although it's not very much like our churches at home. There's a lot of laughter here – it's a cheerful place.'

Then he pushed the heavy door open.

The hall they entered was so high that even Firedrake could stand upright in it. Although it was dark, countless lamps burned in the great room, their flames flickering. Tall columns supported the ceiling. The walls were painted, and large pictures hung among shelves full of ancient books. The pictures were so strange and brightly coloured that Ben would have liked to stop and study each of them, but the professor led them on. Rows of low seats stood among the columns, and a small man with short grey hair was waiting for them in the front row. He wore a bright red robe, and he smiled as the professor and Ben approached him.

Firedrake followed, more hesitantly, for this was only the second time in his life that he had ever been inside a building made by humans. The light of all the little lamps made his scales shimmer. His claws scraped on the floor, and his tail dragged after him with a soft rustling sound. Sorrel kept close to Firedrake, her paws on his warm scales while her ears twitched nervously and her eyes flicked from column to column.

'Trees,' she whispered to Firedrake. 'Look, they grow stone trees here.'

When they stopped in front of the monk, he bowed to them.

'May I introduce the venerable lama of this monastery?' said Barnabas Greenbloom. 'He's the highest-ranking monk here.'

The lama spoke in a soft voice.

'Welcome to the monastery of the moonstones,' Twigleg translated for Ben. 'We are very glad to see you. According to our beliefs, the arrival of a dragon announces a great and happy event. And we are equally glad to see a dragon rider under our roof again after so long a time.'

Surprised, Ben looked from the monk to the professor.

Barnabas Greenbloom nodded. 'Yes, that's what he said. The dragon rider, whose tomb Zubeida showed us, visited this place. Indeed, he paid it several visits, if I understood my friend the lama correctly. They even have a picture of him hanging over there.'

Ben turned and went over to the niche in the wall indicated by the professor. A large pictorial scroll hanging between two bookshelves showed a dragon in flight with a boy riding it. There was another small figure sitting behind the boy.

'Sorrel!' said Ben, excitedly beckoning for the brownie girl to join him. 'Don't you think that looks almost like you?'

Firedrake came closer too, and put his head over Ben's shoulder curiously. 'He's right, Sorrel,' said the dragon in surprise. 'That figure does look like you.'

'Ah, well,' said Sorrel, shrugging her shoulders, although she couldn't suppress a proud smile, 'dragons have always had a special liking for brownies. Everyone knows that.'

'I can see one difference, though,' whispered Twigleg from his perch on Ben's shoulder. 'The brownie in the picture has four arms.'

'Four arms?' Sorrel took a closer look. 'So it does,' she murmured. 'But I don't think that means much. Take a look at the rest of the pictures – almost everyone in them has any number of arms.'

'You're right, they do,' said Ben, looking round. Many of the pictures on the walls did indeed show figures with several arms apiece. 'What do you think that means?'

'Come and look at this!' cried the professor. 'The dragon rider left something here long ago.'

The lama led them to a small wooden shrine standing in a niche beside the altar of the prayer hall.

'These,' Twigleg translated again, 'are the sacred moonstones given to the monastery by the dragon rider. They bring health and happiness, and keep evil spirits away from this valley.'

The stones were white as milk, and not much bigger than Ben's fist. They glowed as if moonlight were caught inside them. 'Break the moonlight!' whispered Ben, looking at Firedrake. 'Remember? Do you think the djinn meant us to break one of these stones?'

The dragon thoughtfully nodded his head. Barnabas Greenbloom translated what Ben had said to the lama. The monk smiled and replied, looking steadily at the boy.

'He says,' Twigleg whispered in Ben's ear, 'that after the morning meal he will give the dragon rider back his property, and he can do with it what he came here to do.'

'Does that mean he's going to give me one of the sacred stones?' Ben looked first at Firedrake, then at the lama.

The monk nodded.

'Yes, I think you've got the general idea,' said Barnabas Greenbloom.

Ben made a shy bow to the monk. 'Thank you. That's very

kind of you. But don't you think the luck may be lost if I break one of these moonstones?'

The professor translated Ben's question to the lama, who laughed out loud, and took Ben's hand.

'Dragon rider,' Twigleg translated the lama's answer, 'no stone can bring as much luck as the visit of a dragon. But you must strike hard to shatter the moonstone, for those you wish to conjure up like to sleep soundly and long. After breakfast I will show you the stone dragon's head.'

Ben looked at the monk in surprise. 'Did you tell him all that?' he asked the professor quietly. 'What the djinn said, I mean?'

'I didn't have to,' Barnabas Greenbloom whispered. 'He already knew. You seem to have the knack of fulfilling prophecies, my boy. You're right in the middle of an ancient legend.'

'Amazing,' murmured Ben, looking round once more at the shrine containing the moonstones. Then he and the others followed the lama outside. The sun was rising in a red glow above the snow-covered peaks, and the courtyards of the monastery buildings were now swarming with monks. To his surprise, Ben saw that some of them were even younger than him.

'Look, they have child monks here!' he whispered to Barnabas Greenbloom.

The professor nodded. 'Yes, of course. These people believe that we all live many lives on this planet. So any one of these children could really be older than the oldest of the grown-up monks. Intriguing idea, don't you think?'

Ben nodded, feeling confused.

Suddenly the peaceful activity in the monastery courtyard was interrupted. Firedrake had put his long neck out of the door of the Dhu-Khang. Most of the monks were transfixed by the sight. Raising his hands, the lama spoke a few words.

'He says,' Twigleg whispered to Ben, 'that luck will fall like moonlit snow from Firedrake's scales, and you and Sorrel are dragon riders who need their help.'

Ben nodded, and looked down at all the faces gazing up at the dragon in amazement, but without fear.

'Ben,' whispered Barnabas Greenbloom, 'breakfast will be *tsampa*, roasted barley flour, and hot tea with butter. It's very healthy and good for you at these altitudes, but you may not like it much when you first taste it. Shall I make your excuses and say you'll keep Guinevere company instead? I'm sure she can rustle up something you'd prefer to eat.'

Ben looked at the lama, who returned his glance and smiled. Then he whispered something into Twigleg's ear.

'The lama says,' translated the homunculus, 'that he understands a few words of our language and will by no means think it uncivil of you, dragon rider, to seek the company of the professor's clever daughter instead of enjoying *tsampa* and buttered tea.'

'Th-thank you,' stammered Ben, returning the lama's smile. 'Twigleg, tell him I like it here very much, and say,' he added, looking at the mountains rising on the other side of the valley, 'say I somehow feel at home here, even though it's very different from where I come from. Very, very different. Tell him that, would you? Only put it better, please.'

Twigleg nodded, and turned back to translate Ben's words for the lama, who listened attentively to the homunculus before replying with his customary slight smile.

'The lama says,' Twigleg told Ben, 'that in his opinion it is quite possible you have indeed been here before. In another life.'

'Come on, dragon rider,' said Barnabas Greenbloom, 'I'll take you to Guinevere before your head bursts with all this wisdom. And I'll come back for you when breakfast is over.'

'What do you think Sorrel and I should do, Professor?' asked Firedrake, putting his muzzle gently over the man's shoulder.

'Oh, these people will go along with anything you want, Firedrake,' replied Professor Greenbloom. 'Why not have a nice sleep in the Dhu-Khang? No one will disturb you – in fact they'll say so many prayers for you that you'll be sure to find the Rim of Heaven.'

'And what about me?' asked Sorrel. 'What do I do while Firedrake's asleep and the rest of you are drinking buttered tea? I don't like tea and I don't like butter, so I'm hardly going to like tea with butter in it.'

'I'll leave you with Guinevere, too,' said the professor. 'There's a nice soft bed in our room, and she brought some biscuits which I expect you *will* like.'

Then he led the two of them down the steps, through the crowd of monks standing respectfully in the courtyard, and over to a small building nestling below the high wall of the Dhu-Khang.

As for Firedrake, he followed the lama into the great prayer hall, coiled up among the columns and slept a deep, sound sleep, while the monks sat around him quietly murmuring prayers, wishing all the good fortune of earth and sky to descend upon the dragon's scales.

CHAPTER THIRTY-NINE

The Rat's Report

Sorrel enjoyed Guinevere's breakfast so much that she ate almost half of it all by herself. Ben didn't mind. He wasn't very hungry anyway. All the excitement of the last few days and the thought of what still lay ahead had taken away his appetite. He never felt hungry when he was excited.

When Sorrel, having eaten to her heart's content, curled up in a ball on Guinevere's bed and started snoring loudly, Ben and Guinevere tiptoed out of the room, perched on one of the low monastery walls and looked down at the river. Morning mist still clung to the mountainside, but as the sun rose over the snowy peaks the cold air slowly warmed.

'It's lovely here, isn't it?' said Guinevere.

Ben nodded. Twigleg was sitting on his knee, dozing off. People were working in the green fields down in the valley. They looked no bigger than beetles from up here.

'Where's your mother?' asked Ben.

'In the Temple of the Angry Gods,' Guinevere told him. She

pointed to a red-painted building to the left of the Dhu-Khang. 'Every monastery in this country has one. The building next to it is the Temple of the Kindly Gods, but the angry gods are considered particularly useful because they look so terrifying that they keep evil spirits away. The mountains around here are said to be full of evil spirits.'

'Goodness!' Ben looked admiringly at the girl. 'What a lot you know.'

'Oh, well,' said Guinevere dismissively, 'that's hardly surprising with parents like mine, is it? My mother's copying the pictures on the temple walls at the moment. When we're back home she shows them to rich people and gets them to give money to have the pictures restored. The monks can't afford that kind of thing, and the pictures are already very old, you see.'

'Goodness!' said Ben again, covering the sleeping Twigleg with his jacket. 'You're lucky to have parents like that.'

Guinevere cast him a questioning glance. 'Dad says you don't have any parents yourself.'

Ben picked a little stone off the wall and fiddled with it. 'That's right. I never did.'

Guinevere looked at him thoughtfully. 'But you have Firedrake now,' she said. 'Firedrake and Sorrel and,' she added, smiling and pointing to the little homunculus, 'and you have Twigleg.'

'So I do,' agreed Ben. 'But that's different.' Suddenly, he narrowed his eyes and looked westward to where the river disappeared into the mountains. 'Hey, I think Lola's coming back! There, see?' He threw the stone over the wall and leaned forward.

'Lola?' asked Guinevere. 'Is that the rat you were talking about?'

Ben nodded. A faint humming could be heard. It grew louder and louder, until the little plane landed in expert style on the wall beside them. Lola Greytail opened the cockpit and got out.

'Nothing!' she announced, clambering up on one of the wings and making her way down to the top of the wall. 'Nothing, absolutely not a sign of anything. All clear, I'd say.'

Twigleg woke up, rubbed his eyes and looked at the rat, confused. 'Oh, it's you, Lola,' he muttered drowsily.

'That's right, humblecuss,' replied the rat, and turned to Guinevere. 'And who, may I ask, is this?'

'This is Guinevere,' said Ben, introducing her. 'She's the daughter of the professor who almost trod on your plane, and she thinks she saw Nettlebrand.'

'I *know* I saw him,' said Guinevere. 'I'm a squillion per cent certain I did.'

'Could be.' Lola Greytail opened a flap under the wing of her plane and took out a miniature lunchbox. 'But the creature's disappeared now, anyway. I flew upstream and downstream, keeping so low over the river the fish thought I was a midge and water kept splashing into the cockpit. But I didn't see any sign of a golden dragon with a dwarf. Not a thing. Not a single golden dragon scale.'

'Well, that's good!' said Ben, sighing with relief. 'I really thought we had him after us again. Thanks, Lola!'

'You're welcome,' replied the rat. 'Glad to be of service.' She crammed a few breadcrumbs into her mouth and stretched out on the wall. 'Oh, I do like lazing about!' she sighed, raising her pointed nose to the sun. 'Good thing Uncle Gilbert can't see me. He'd really get his tail in a twist.'

Guinevere was still silent. Frowning, she looked down at the river. 'All the same, I bet that monster's down there somewhere, lying in wait for us,' she said.

'Oh, come off it, he's buried in the sand,' said Ben. 'We know he is. You should have heard that dwarf – I'm sure he wasn't lying. Come on!' He nudged her with his elbow. 'Tell me more about the temple.'

'What temple?' muttered Guinevere, without looking at him.

'The one your mother's looking at,' replied Ben. 'The Temple of the Angry Gods.'

'The Gon-Khang,' murmured Guinevere. 'That's its Tibetan name. Okay, if you really want to know . . .'

When Barnabas Greenbloom came down the steps of the great prayer hall with Firedrake and the lama, he found Ben and his daughter still on the wall. Between them were Lola Greytail and Twigleg, both snoring. The children were so deep in conversation that they hadn't heard the others coming.

'I don't like to disturb you two,' said Barnabas Greenbloom, coming up behind them, 'but Ben could try breaking the moonlight now. The lama has brought him one of the sacred stones.'

The monk opened his hands to reveal the white stone. It had a radiant glow even in the daylight. Ben got off the wall and carefully took the moonstone.

'Where's Sorrel?' asked Firedrake, looking round for her.

'In bed,' replied Guinevere. 'Full of breakfast and snoring.'

'You astonish me!' Her father grinned. 'And what has our friend the rat to report?'

'Not a sign of Nettlebrand,' replied Ben, looking at the moonstone, which he thought seemed darker in the sunlight.

'Well, that's a relief.' Barnabas Greenbloom looked at his daughter. 'Don't you think so, Guinevere?'

Guinevere frowned. 'I don't know.'

'Oh, come on,' he said, taking his daughter and Ben by their arms. 'Let's go and find Sorrel and Vita, and then our dragon rider can see about solving the puzzle the djinn set him. I haven't been in such suspense for ages. I wonder what sort of creature will appear when Ben breaks that stone?'

CHAPTER FORTY

Work for Gravelbeard

But Lola Greytail was wrong. Nettlebrand was lurking on the bed of the river Indus, sunk deep in the mud, just where the shadow of the monastery buildings fell on the water. The river ran so deep there that not the faintest reflection of Nettlebrand's golden scales could reach the surface. He lay waiting patiently for his armour-cleaner to return.

Before Nettlebrand had dived deep into the river, Gravelbeard had jumped to the bank and hidden among some tussocks of grass. And when, all of a long day and half a night later, Firedrake came flying out of the mountains to land behind the white walls of the monastery, the mountain dwarf set off. He trudged on, through fields and past huts, until at last he reached the mountain with the monastery on its slope.

Then Gravelbeard climbed.

The mountain was high, very high, but not for nothing was Gravelbeard a mountain dwarf. He loved climbing almost as much as he loved gold. The solid rock of the mountain whispered and spoke under Gravelbeard's fingers as if it had been waiting all this time for him, and him alone. It told him tales of vast caverns with columns made of precious stones and veins of gold ore, and caves where strange creatures lived. Gravelbeard chuckled with delight as he scaled the rocky slope. He could have climbed for ever, but by the time day slowly dawned above the peaks he was hauling himself over the top of the low wall surrounding the monastery. Cautiously, he peered down into the courtyard.

Gravelbeard had arrived just in time to see Firedrake and his friends disappear into the Dhu-Khang. The dwarf even followed them up the steps, but the heavy door of the hall was already closed before he reached the top, and hard as he tried to prise it open just a crack with his short, strong fingers, it wouldn't budge.

'Too bad,' muttered the dwarf, looking round, 'but they'll have to come out again some time.' He looked around the court-yard for a hiding place where he could keep watch on the steps and the courtyard unobserved. It wasn't difficult to find a suitable gap in the old walls.

'Just the job,' whispered Gravelbeard as he pushed in among the stones. 'Could have been made for me.' And then he waited.

He had chosen his hiding place well. Admittedly, when Firedrake and the others came out of the prayer hall, Gravelbeard couldn't see much apart from the feet of countless monks in their well-worn sandals. But when all the monks were up in the Dhu-Khang praying, Ben and Guinevere came and sat down on the wall only a stone's throw away from him.

So now Gravelbeard learned that a flying rat had been out looking for his master, but had failed to find him; and he discovered that the boy really did believe Nettlebrand had been buried in the desert sand. The dwarf saw the stone in the lama's hand and heard about the djinn's riddle. He saw Ben take the stone, and when Firedrake and his dragon riders went with the monk to try solving the riddle, Gravelbeard stole after them.

CHAPTER FORTY-ONE

Burr-Burr-Chan

The lama led his guests to the other side of the monastery grounds and the place where the Gon-Khang and the Lha-Khang stood, one the Temple of the Angry Gods and the other the Temple of the Kindly Gods. And scurrying from wall to wall Gravelbeard, Nettlebrand's spy, came after them.

As they were passing the red temple, the lama stopped. Vita Greenbloom had joined her husband.

'This,' she said, translating what the lama said, 'is the Temple of the Angry Gods who are said to keep all evil from the monastery and the village.'

'What sort of evil?' asked Sorrel, looking around uneasily.

'Evil spirits,' replied the lama, 'and snowstorms, avalanches, rockfalls, disease—'

'Starvation?' added Sorrel.

The lama smiled. 'Starvation too.'

A strange shivery feeling came over Gravelbeard. Weak at the knees, he crept past the dark red walls. His breath was coming faster, and he felt as if hands were reaching out to him from the temple, hands ready to seize him and drag him into the darkness.

Involuntarily, he leaped forward with a little shriek, and almost collided with Barnabas Greenbloom's heels.

'What was that?' asked the professor, turning round. 'Did you hear it, Vita?'

His wife nodded. 'Sounded as if you trod on some poor cat's tail, Barnabas.'

The professor shook his head and looked round again, but by now Gravelbeard had hidden in a crevice in the wall.

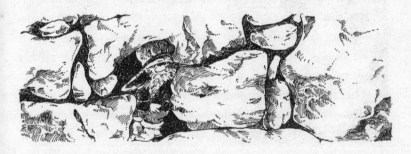

'Perhaps it was the evil spirits,' said Guinevere.

'Very likely,' said her father. 'Come on, I think the lama's reached our destination.'

The old monk had stopped where the slope of the mountain met the monastery walls. The rock here was like a Swiss cheese full of holes. Ben and Sorrel tilted their heads back. Yes, there were niches everywhere in the rock, all of them large enough for either the boy or the brownie to fit into one comfortably.

'What's that?' asked Ben, looking enquiringly at the lama.

Twigleg interpreted for him.

'These are dwellings,' replied the lama. 'The dwellings of those from whom you are about to seek help. They do not often show themselves. Very few of us have ever seen them face to face, but they are said to be friendly beings, and they were here long, long before we came.'

The lama went up to the rock wall, taking Ben with him. Ben hadn't noticed them earlier, but he now saw the heads of two stone dragons jutting out from the rock.

'They look like Firedrake,' whispered Ben. 'Just like Firedrake.' He felt the dragon's warm breath on his back.

'They are the Dragon of the Beginning and the Dragon of the End,' the lama explained. 'For what you have in mind, you should choose the Dragon of the Beginning.'

Ben nodded.

'Go on, dragon rider, hit it,' whispered Sorrel.

Raising the moonstone, Ben brought it down with all his might on the horns of the stone dragon.

The moonstone smashed into a myriad splinters, and it seemed to all of them that they heard a deep rumble slowly dying away in the heart of the mountain. Then all was still. Very still. They waited.

As the sun slowly rose behind the mountains, they cast their shadows on the monastery. A cold wind was blowing from the snowy peaks as a figure suddenly appeared in one of the holes in the rock, high above the heads of those waiting below.

It was a brownie. He looked almost like Sorrel, except that his coat was paler and thicker. And he had four arms. He was resting their paws on the rock where he stood.

'Twenty fingers, Twigleg,' whispered Ben. 'He has twenty fingers, just as the djinn said.'

The homunculus could only nod.

The strange brownie looked down suspiciously, inspected the humans briefly, and then stared long and hard at the dragon.

'Well, fancy that!' he cried in the language of fabulous creatures, which can be understood at once by any other living creature, man or beast. 'Thought better of it after all, have you? After so many years! I thought you'd all mouldered away in your hiding place by now!' The strange brownie spat scornfully on the rock. 'So what's happened for them to send you here all of a sudden to ask us for help? And what weird kind of brownie is that you have with you? What's it done with its other arms?'

'I've only got two arms,' snapped Sorrel, looking up at him. 'Which is quite enough for any self-respecting brownie, you pathetic puffball, you. And no one sent us. We came of our own free will. The other dragons didn't dare come, but they haven't mouldered away.'

'Ooh!' said the strange brownie, grinning. 'Pathetic puffball, eh? At least you know your mushrooms. My name is Burr-Burr-Chan. What's yours?'

'She's Sorrel,' replied Firedrake, taking a step forward, 'and you're right about one thing: we're here because we need help. We have come a long, long way to find the Rim of Heaven, and a djinn told us you could guide us there.'

'A long, long way?' Burr-Burr-Chan wrinkled his furry brow. 'What do you mean by that?'

'We mean,' said Sorrel, 'that we've flown half way round the world just to listen to your bare-faced cheek.'

'Calm down, Sorrel,' said Firedrake, nudging her aside with his nose. Then he looked up at Burr-Burr-Chan again.

'We come from a valley far away to the north-west, a place where my kind went many hundreds of years ago when human beings were beginning to take over the world. Now they are reaching out their greedy hands to steal our valley too, and we must find a new home. So I set out to seek the Rim of Heaven, the home of all dragons. I am here to ask if you know it.'

'Of course I know it!' replied Burr-Burr-Chan. 'I know it as well as I know my own fur, although it's a long time since I was last there.'

Ben held his breath.

'Then it exists?' cried Sorrel. 'The Rim of Heaven really exists?'

'What did you think?' Burr-Burr-Chan wrinkled his nose, and looked distrustfully at Firedrake. 'Are you sure you don't come from the Rim of Heaven yourself? Are there really other dragons in the world?'

Firedrake nodded. 'Will you guide us?' he asked. 'Will you show us where to find the Rim of Heaven?'

For a few long moments the four-armed brownie did not answer. Sighing, he sat down in the niche in the rock where he had appeared and dangled his legs.

'Well, why not?' he said at last. 'But I can tell you now, you won't get much joy out of your relations.'

'What's that supposed to mean?' asked Sorrel.

Burr-Burr-Chan shrugged his shoulders and crossed his four arms over his chest. 'It means they've turned into pathetic, snivelling, cowardly weaklings. It's over fifty winters since I was there, but that's how it was when last I saw them.' He bent down towards Sorrel. 'Imagine, they don't leave their cave any more! Not even by night! When I last saw them they were limp as withered leaves for want of moonlight. Their eyes were cloudy as puddles because of the darkness, their wings were dusty for lack of use, and they had fat bellies from eating lichen instead of drinking moonlight. Yes, you may well look shocked.' Burr-Burr-Chan nodded. 'It's very sad to see what's become of the dragons.' The brownie leaned forward and lowered his voice. 'Do you know who they're hiding from? Not from human beings, no, they're hiding from the golden dragon. They've been hiding ever since the night he came up out of the sea to hunt them.'

'We know that story,' said Ben, stepping up beside Firedrake. 'But where are they hiding? In a cave, you said?'

Burr-Burr-Chan turned to him in surprise. 'And what sort of creature are you? White as a milk-cap, and in the company of a dragon. Don't tell me you rode here on his back!'

'Yes, indeed he did,' replied Firedrake, nuzzling Ben.

Burr-Burr-Chan whistled through his teeth. 'So you're the dragon rider! It was you who broke the moonstone that summoned me?'

Ben nodded. The lama said something in a quiet voice.

'Yes, yes, I know.' Burr-Burr-Chan scratched his head. 'That old story: silver will be worth more than gold when the dragon rider returns.' The brownie narrowed his slanting eyes and looked Ben up and down. 'Yes, the dragons are hiding in a cave,' he said slowly. 'A wonderful cave deep within the mountain range known as the Rim of Heaven. We dug that cave for them

– we, the Dubidai, the brownies of these mountains. But we never meant them to bury themselves alive in it. When they hid there after the golden dragon had hunted them, we withdrew our friendship and came back here. As we left, we told them there was only one way to make up the quarrel: we would return to them on the day they summoned us with a moonstone to help them overcome the golden dragon.' He looked at Firedrake. 'I will take you to them, but I will not stay, for they still haven't summoned us.'

'The golden dragon is dead,' replied Firedrake. 'Dead and buried in the sand of a distant desert. They needn't hide any more.'

'No, no, he isn't dead!' cried Guinevere.

Everyone turned to look at her. Burr-Burr-Chan pricked up his furry ears.

'You have no proof of that, Guinevere!' said Barnabas Greenbloom.

'I tell you, I saw him!' Guinevere stuck her chin out obstinately. 'With my own eyes. I didn't imagine a single scale of him. And I don't care what you all say, I didn't dream up the dwarf perched on his head either. The golden dragon is *not* buried in the sand. He followed us along the river. And I bet you my collection of fairy shoes he's somewhere very close, waiting to see what we do next.'

'Interesting!' said Burr-Burr-Chan. With one bound he jumped down from his hole in the rock and landed on the stone dragon's head.

'Listen,' he said, raising all four paws, 'I will take you to the Rim of Heaven. It's closer than you may think. We have only to fly over this mountain,' he continued, tapping the rock, 'and then ahead of you, just where the sun rises, you will see a chain of mountains as beautiful as white field mushrooms in the moon-dew. The dragons are hiding in the valley beyond those mountains. You wouldn't spot the entrance to their cave even if your nose was right up against it. Only the dragons and the Dubidai know where it is, but I will show you. All of a sudden I have a very strange itch in my fur. The kind of itch I get only when some great deed lies ahead, something adventurous and exciting.' Burr-Burr-Chan licked his lips and looked at the sky. 'Right, we'll set off as soon as the sun sets.'

Then he leaped into the nearest hole in the rock – and was gone.

CHAPTER FORTY-TWO

A Farewell and a Departure

'Dubidai! Huh!' muttered Sorrel as soon as Burr-Burr-Chan had disappeared. 'Calls himself a brownie, does he? I'm not so sure about him. He might lead us straight into Nettlebrand's jaws.'

'Oh, nonsense!' Ben pulled her pointy ears. 'Cheer up and stop moaning! We've done it! He's going to take us to the Rim of Heaven! And if Nettlebrand shows his ugly mug there we'll chase him back to the sea!'

'Oh yes?' Sorrel wrinkled her nose. 'You know something, little human? You're crazy.'

The lama whispered something to the Greenblooms.

'What did he say, Twigleg?' Ben asked.

'The small will defeat the great,' replied the homunculus, 'and the gentle will defeat the cruel.'

'Well, let's hope so,' muttered Sorrel. Suddenly, she turned her head and sniffed. 'Yuk, what a disgusting whiff of mountain dwarf. You can't get away from it! Go to any mountain in the world and you'll find dwarves in their silly hats hammering away.'

'What did you say?' asked Guinevere in alarm.

'I said the place smells of dwarf,' repeated Sorrel. 'Why?'

'Where?' asked Ben, grabbing her arm. 'Where exactly did you pick up the scent?'

At that very moment, a small figure shot out of a rocky crevice and scurried away like lightning.

'Gravelbeard!' screeched Twigleg, almost falling head first off Ben's shoulder. 'It's Gravelbeard! Nettlebrand's new armour-cleaner! Catch him! Quick, catch him! He'll give everything away!'

They all dashed off in hot pursuit, falling over one another and getting in each other's way, but by the time they reached the courtyard outside the prayer hall the dwarf had vanished.

Sorrel snuffled around in every nook and cranny, muttering crossly. A couple of monks coming back from gathering firewood looked at her in amazement. When the lama asked if they had seen a small creature running away they just pointed at Lola Greytail, who was still asleep on the wall, snoring beside her plane.

Ben and Guinevere ran to the wall, leaned over it side by side and peered down into the depths below. But there was no suspicious movement on the steep mountainside.

'Oh no!' groaned Ben. 'He's got away!'

'Who?' asked Lola, sitting up drowsily.

'A spy,' replied Ben. He turned to Firedrake. 'Now what? What are we going to do? He'll tell Nettlebrand everything.'

'A spy?' asked the rat disbelievingly. 'What sort of a spy?'

'The one you failed to spot on your famous reconnaissance flight,' snapped Sorrel, raising her nose to the wind. 'But I can't seem to pick up the scent of that poisonous panther-cap. There's something much stronger blocking my sense of smell.' She looked about her, and pointed to a pile of brown things like cowpats stacked by the wall. 'What's that?'

'Dung,' said Barnabas Greenbloom. 'Dried yak dung, to be precise.'

The lama nodded and said something.

'He says,' Twigleg translated, 'that they burn the dung for heating because wood is scarce here.'

Sorrel groaned. 'Then how am I supposed to pick up a scent?' she said crossly. 'How do you expect me to get on the trail of that wretched dwarf if the whole place stinks of yak dung? Whatever a yak may be.'

'Shall I climb down the rocks, young master?' asked Twigleg.

But Ben shook his head. 'No, far too dangerous.' He sighed. 'He's got away, and there's nothing we can do about it.'

'Imagine anyone being able to run so fast on such short legs,' said Vita Greenbloom. 'Amazing. Well, dwarves are certainly quick on their feet, especially in the mountains.'

'So long as no one takes their hats away.' Twigleg crawled up on the wall and looked down. For a split second he thought he heard a soft panting sound, but the sight of the abyss below made him giddy, and he withdrew his head quickly.

'What happens if you take their hats away?' asked Ben, curious.

'They get all dizzy,' replied Twigleg, climbing back on to Ben's arm.

'This is what comes of not believing one's children!' muttered Barnabas Greenbloom gloomily. He put an arm around his daughter's shoulders. 'I apologise, Guinevere. You were right, and I'm an old fool.'

'That's okay,' replied Guinevere. 'I only wish I *hadn't* been right.'

Firedrake stretched his neck out over the wall and looked down at the river. The sun was reflected in its brown waters. 'We must move faster than Nettlebrand, then,' he said. 'That dwarf must have heard everything Burr-Burr-Chan said, and they'll be setting off at once.'

'You mean you've found out where the Rim of Heaven is and that spy overheard!' Lola Greytail jumped up. 'Well, so what? Didn't you say this golden dragon can't fly? It will be child's play for Firedrake to shake him off.'

But Twigleg shook his head, looking unhappy. 'You needn't think it will be as easy as that. Nettlebrand knows many cunning tricks.' Angrily, he slapped his bony knee. 'Oh, why did Burr-Burr-Chan have to go and describe the place where the dragons live in such detail?'

'He won't be able to find the entrance to the cave,' Guinevere pointed out. 'Burr-Burr-Chan said no one could.'

'Just so long as *we* don't lead Nettlebrand to it,' Sorrel growled grimly.

They all fell silent.

'It would have been really good if he *had* been buried in the sand,' muttered Ben, looking downcast.

The lama put a hand on his shoulder and said something. Ben looked enquiringly at Twigleg.

'That would have been too easy, dragon rider,' the homunculus translated.

Ben shook his head. 'Maybe,' he said, 'but I wouldn't mind having it easy for once.'

Ben and the others had become acclimatised quite quickly to the thin air of the Himalayas, the roof of the world, but the monks insisted on giving them provisions and warm clothing for their flight. Even Sorrel realised that she would have to wear human clothes over her fur to keep out the cold above the clouds. A boy of Ben's own age took him and the professor to a building on the outskirts of the monastery where the monks kept food and clothing. Only on the way there did Ben realise how large the monastery complex was, and how many people lived in it.

'We'd love to come with you,' said Barnabas Greenbloom, as they followed the young monk. 'Vita, Guinevere and me, I mean. But I'm afraid human beings have no part to play in this adventure.' He patted Ben on the shoulder. 'Except the dragon rider, of course.'

Ben smiled shyly. The dragon rider. Every monk they met bowed to him. He hardly knew where to look.

'Have you thought what you're going to do afterwards?' asked the professor, without looking at Ben. 'I mean, when you've found the Rim of Heaven, and if everything goes well, and . . .' He cleared his throat, running a hand through his grey hair. 'And if Firedrake flies back to the north to fetch his relations. Will you stay with the dragons for good?'

He looked at the boy almost shyly.

Ben shrugged his shoulders. 'I don't know. I haven't thought. At the moment there's no before and no after, if you see what I mean.'

The professor nodded. 'Yes, I know the feeling. It's common at moments of crisis. But,' he said, clearing his throat again, 'but if you should feel like – I mean,' he added, wiping his nose with a large handkerchief, 'I mean, if you'd like to be back with ordinary people after all these adventures . . .' He looked up at the sky. 'Vita is very fond of you, and Guinevere's often told me she wished she had a brother. Perhaps,' he concluded, looking at Ben and turning quite red in the face, 'perhaps you'd like to think of us as your family for a while. What do you say?'

Ben stared at Barnabas Greenbloom, speechless.

'Only a suggestion,' the professor made haste to say. 'Just one of my eccentric ideas. But we would—'

'Oh, I'd like to,' Ben interrupted. 'In fact, I'd love to!'

'You would?' Barnabas Greenbloom sighed with relief. 'I'm so glad. Well, that'll make the wait here even harder for us. You may remember,' he said, smiling down at the boy, 'that on our next field trip we're going to search for Pegasus.'

Ben nodded. 'I'd love to come along and search too,' he said, and shook the professor's hand.

All was ready for their departure by the time darkness fell over the mountains. Ben and Sorrel were well muffled up, with warm caps on their heads, gloves and fleecy jackets. Twigleg sat on Ben's lap, wrapped in a piece of lambskin, with the thumb-piece of a glove on his head for a cap. Sorrel's backpack contained dried apricots and a thermos flask of 'hot buttered tea – just in case,' as the lama said with a smile when Sorrel sniffed it suspiciously.

Firedrake did not mind the cold, and the monks didn't seem to feel it either. Wearing only their thin robes, they accompanied the dragon through the bitter cold of the night to the Dubidai caves. In the light of their torches, Firedrake shone as brightly as the light of the moon. Lola Greytail flew just ahead of him, her plane buzzing along. The rat had decided to accompany the dragon, and was now waving to the monks as if she were the centre of all the excitement.

Burr-Burr-Chan was waiting for Firedrake in the same niche in the rockface from which he had emerged earlier, but this time he was not alone. More Dubidai were peering out of other niches. They had all come out to see the strange dragon, and when Firedrake stopped beneath the caves and looked up, an excited whispering arose. Furry heads, both large and small, gazed at the silver dragon.

Burr-Burr-Chan swung a sack over his shoulder, scrambled down the rocks and climbed on to Firedrake's crest as if he had been doing it all his life.

'Any room left for my luggage?' he asked as he sat down in front of Sorrel.

'Hand it over,' grunted Sorrel, hanging his sack beside her own backpack. 'What on earth have you got in there? Stones?'

'Mushrooms,' Burr-Burr-Chan whispered in her ear. 'The most delicious mushrooms in the world. I bet you've never tasted anything like them.'

'Oh yeah, I can just imagine,' sniffed Sorrel, strapping herself into place. 'If they grow on these mountains they'll probably taste of grit.'

Burr-Burr-Chan just grinned.

'Here,' he said, pressing some tiny mushrooms into Sorrel's paw. 'They may not be particularly tasty, but they're good for altitude sickness. Give one to the small human, and let the two little creatures have one each too. The dragon won't need anything of that kind, but the rest of you definitely ought to eat them, understand?'

Sorrel nodded, and put a mushroom in her mouth. 'You're right, this is nothing special,' she muttered, but she handed the rest of the mushrooms on to the others.

Burr-Burr-Chan rested all four paws on Firedrake's warm scales. 'I'd quite forgotten how wonderful it is to ride a dragon,' he whispered.

Firedrake turned to him. 'Ready?' he asked.

Burr-Burr-Chan nodded.

'We fixed another strap on for you,' called Ben from behind the Dubidai. 'Strap yourself in.' And so Burr-Burr-Chan buckled the strap round his furry stomach.

'Oh, and by the way,' said Sorrel, tapping him on the shoulder, 'it seems we may not have seen the last of that golden dragon after all. His mountain dwarf was eavesdropping on us yesterday just as you gave such a wonderfully detailed description of the way to the Rim of Heaven. You realise what that means?'

Burr-Burr-Chan scratched his stomach thoughtfully. 'Yes, we have to get there ahead of him, right?' He leaned forward over Firedrake's neck. 'What are you going to do,' he asked the dragon, 'what are you going to do if the Golden One turns up at the Rim of Heaven? Are you planning to hide along with the others?'

Firedrake turned his head to him. 'No, I shall never hide again,' he said.

'But of course you will!' cried Sorrel in alarm. 'Of course you must hide! Until he's gone away again, I mean. What else can you do?'

Firedrake did not reply. 'Ready?' he called to the riders on his back.

'Ready!' cried Burr-Burr-Chan, moving a little further forward. 'Let's wake the dragons from their slumber!'

The monks holding torches stepped back, and Firedrake spread his wings. The moon was waning, so he had drunk a little moon-dew to be on the safe side. His wings felt as light as the feathers of a bird.

'Good luck!' cried Barnabas Greenbloom.

'Come back soon!' called Vita, and Guinevere threw Ben a chocolate bar.

He just managed to catch it before it fell into Sorrel's lap. Lola Greytail started the engine of her plane, and Firedrake rose into the sky above the monastery. He flew up and over the mountainside to which its buildings clung, and made for the white peaks rimming the sky to the east.

CHAPTER FORTY-THREE

The Pursuers

Gravelbeard had hidden among the rocks less than a metre below the wall, in a crevice so narrow that he'd had to duck his head between his shoulders to force himself into it. There he had crouched as they looked for him, trembling, holding his breath, and pressing his back to the cold stone. He had felt the dragon's warm breath on his nose, and he ground his teeth with fury when the treacherous homunculus suggested climbing down the rocks. If that spindly creature had tried it, he'd have pushed him down the mountain to where Nettlebrand was waiting in the mud. But Twigleg didn't come. The skinny little coward wouldn't dare.

By the time Gravelbeard could finally hear no more sounds from above it was pitch dark. The mountain still whispered in his ear, telling him its wonderful stories, but the dwarf tore himself away, crawled out of the crevice that had saved him, and climbed down into the valley. It was more difficult in the dark than by daylight, but Gravelbeard found his way.

Once down at the foot of the mountain he ran past the huts. Would it be worth stopping to steal in and look for rings, gold chains, coins, beautiful precious stones? But these huts didn't smell like rich places, so Gravelbeard hurried on, past sheds full of sheep and goats, over the fields to the river where Nettlebrand was lurking in the brown water.

On the bank, the dwarf looked round again. All was still. The people were asleep, weary after their hard day's work in the fields. Their animals were safe from cold in the stables, and the wild beasts roaming around had nothing but prey in mind. Gravelbeard picked a twig from the nearest bush and struck the water with it.

'Your Goldness!' he called softly. 'Your Goldness, I'm back.'

Snorting, Nettlebrand rose from the river.

'Well, what did you find out?' he growled, shaking the mud off his scales.

'Everything!' replied Gravelbeard proudly. 'The dragons have been hiding, Your Goldness! That's why you couldn't find them all these years! They hid away in a cave inside a mountain. You ought to have taken a mountain dwarf along when you went looking for them before. We can find any cave anywhere!'

'So where is this cave, then?' Nettlebrand asked impatiently.

'You have to cross that mountain,' replied Gravelbeard portentously. 'The one with the monastery built on its side. Then you turn east, and then,' he said, grinning triumphantly, 'then you come to the mountain range they call the Rim of Heaven. The entrance to the cave is in the valley beyond it.'

Nettlebrand reared up, hardly able to believe it, and water dripped from his huge body. 'In *that* valley, you say?' he roared. 'But I know the place. I've searched and searched it until my claws were worn right down. Huh!' He licked his lips, and chortled. 'The fools – they couldn't have chosen a better place!'

'What do you mean, Your Goldness?' asked Gravelbeard curiously.

'You'll soon see!' Nettlebrand snorted happily. 'Has the silver dragon set off yet?'

Gravelbeard shrugged his shoulders and looked at Nettlebrand's muddy scales, frowning. 'Probably. He was planning to take off as soon as darkness fell. But you'll soon find him. Just let me clean your scales first, Your Goldness. I can hardly see their beautiful golden glow.'

'Forget the golden glow!' Nettlebrand snapped. 'Come here and get into my mouth.' He laid his terrible muzzle on the bank and opened his jaws wide.

'Oh no!' Gravelbeard retreated defiantly. 'You want to swallow me again.'

'Of course I do!' growled Nettlebrand. 'I have to dive deep, a long, long way down, so get a move on, will you?'

'But I don't like it in there!' whimpered Gravelbeard as he approached Nettlebrand's mighty teeth, his knees shaking.

'Why not? I thought you mountain dwarves liked caves, and what's my stomach but a large cave?' replied Nettlebrand nastily. 'Come on, jump!'

'Don't want to!' repeated Gravelbeard.

But then he held tight to his hat and jumped in – between those terrible teeth and on to that gigantic tongue. And Nettlebrand swallowed him.

CHAPTER FORTY-FOUR
The Rim of Heaven

Firedrake flew on. The nine white peaks forming the Rim of Heaven shimmered in the distance as if starlight clung to them. The rat flew her plane on the leeward side of the dragon, where she was out of the wind.

Firedrake felt strong, as if moonlight were flowing through his veins. And he felt light, as if he were made of the same elements as the night itself. At last he was approaching his journey's end. His heart was beating fast in anticipation, driving him across the sky faster than he had ever flown before, so fast that soon the rat couldn't keep up and landed her plane on his tail.

'Whee!' cried Burr-Burr-Chan. 'Whoo! I'd forgotten how great it feels to ride a dragon!'

He clung to the straps with two of his paws, and used the other two to rummage in his sack and bring out a mushroom. It was so wonderfully fragrant that Sorrel forgot all her anxiety about what lay ahead of them and leaned over Burr-Burr-Chan's shoulder, sniffing. 'By chanterelles and truffles!' she said, licking her lips. 'What kind of a mushroom is that? It smells of leeks and—'

'It's a shitake,' replied Burr-Burr-Chan, smacking his own lips. 'A genuine Japanese shitake. Want to try one?' Putting a paw into his sack, he brought out another and dropped it over his shoulder into Sorrel's lap.

'Quite useful, those four arms of yours,' she murmured, sniffing the strange mushroom before taking a cautious bite.

'Very useful,' agreed Burr-Burr-Chan. He looked ahead to where the Rim of Heaven was rising higher and higher into the night sky. 'Well done, we're almost there. My word, your dragon is a strong flyer.'

'He's had plenty of practice these last few weeks,' said Sorrel, chewing noisily. She rolled her eyes appreciatively. 'Do mushrooms like these really grow on rocks?'

'Good heavens, no!' Burr-Burr-Chan laughed so heartily that Firedrake turned in surprise to look at him.

'Your brownie girl here is a real comic,' gasped Burr-Burr-Chan. 'Very amusing indeed!'

'So amusing she's liable to bite off a couple of your twenty fingers!' snapped Sorrel.

Burr-Burr-Chan turned to look at her, grinning broadly. 'No mushroom can grow on stone,' he said. 'This species grows on wood. We cultivate it in our caves. Don't you cultivate mushrooms yourself?'

'No,' growled Sorrel. 'So what if I don't?' she added crossly, thumping the other brownie's back.

'Stop squabbling, Sorrel!' Firedrake called back to her. 'I have to think.'

Looking offended, Sorrel bent her head and went on nibbling

her mushroom. 'Has to think, does he?' she muttered. 'Too right. Like what's he going to do if that monster comes after us? There won't be much time to think then. Is he planning to fight him or what?' Uneasily, she spat into the depths below.

'What do you mean, Sorrel, fight?' Ben put his head over her shoulder.

'Oh, forget it,' growled Sorrel. 'Only thinking out loud.' She stared gloomily at the mountains as they came closer and closer.

Ben pulled Twigleg's little cap made from the glove thumb-piece down over his ears and wrapped him a little more snugly in his lambskin. It was getting colder and colder the higher Firedrake climbed, and Ben was very grateful for the warm clothing the monks had given them. He wished he could feel glad they were so close to their journey's end, but he kept thinking of Nettlebrand.

Suddenly, Ben felt something touch his shoulder. Whipping round in alarm, he was just in time to catch Lola Greytail by her long tail. 'Hey, what are you doing here, Lola?' he asked.

'Thinking of throwing me overboard, were you?' replied the rat, her teeth chattering. 'It's too cold in my plane. The heating only works when I'm flying. Any space for me in your backpack, by any chance?'

'Of course.' Ben tucked the shivering rat in among his things. 'What about the plane, though?'

'It's lashed well into place on Firedrake's tail,' replied Lola. With a sigh of relief she snuggled down inside the backpack until only her ears and pointed nose were sticking out.

'Must I fly higher, Burr-Burr-Chan?' called Firedrake, as the wind blew more strongly than ever around their heads.

'Yes,' Burr-Burr-Chan called back. 'The pass we have to cross is a little further up, and there's no other way into the valley.'

Ben felt his heartbeat thudding in his ears as Firedrake rose yet higher. Night pressed its dark fists against his temples. Breathing was difficult, and Sorrel was curled up like a little cat. Only Burr-Burr-Chan sat upright and at ease. He was used to these high altitudes, for he had been born in the mountains known to humans as the roof of the world.

The white summits were so close now that Ben felt as if he could put out his hand and touch the snow on their slopes. Firedrake was flying towards a narrow pass between the two most pointed mountain peaks. Dark rocks merged with the darkness of the night, and needles of stone rose menacingly in the air, barring the dragon's way. When Firedrake was right between the two peaks, the wind fell on him like a hungry wolf. Howling, it roared beneath the dragon's wings, and sent him whirling like a leaf towards the rocks.

'Watch out!' shouted Burr-Burr-Chan, but Firedrake had already regained control. Bracing himself against the wind with all his might, he shook off its invisible clutches. Snow drove down on them, covering the dragon and the heads and shoulders of his riders. Ben's teeth were chattering.

'We're going to make it!' shouted Burr-Burr-Chan. 'See that? There's the highest ridge, ahead of us!'

Firedrake shot through the pass and over it, leaving the howling wind behind at last – and flew into the Valley of the Dragons.

A lake lay among the mountains, as round as the moon, and Zubeida Ghalib's blue flowers grew on its banks. They glowed in the darkness of the night, making the valley look as if the stars had fallen into it from the sky above.

'By St George's mushroom! And by Caesar's cap too!' breathed Sorrel.

'We call that lake the Eye of the Moon!' called Burr-Burr-Chan as Firedrake made for the shimmering water. 'Fly over it! Fly to where—'

But Twigleg interrupted. 'No! Don't – don't fly over the water!' he shouted shrilly.

He struggled out of the lambskin. 'You furry great fool!' he shouted at Burr-Burr-Chan. 'You didn't say anything about a lake! You didn't breathe a word!'

'Who are you calling a furry great fool?' Burr-Burr-Chan turned round crossly, but the homunculus ignored him.

'Fly higher, Firedrake!' he croaked, tugging at the straps. 'This lake is a gateway – an open gateway!'

But Firedrake had realised what he meant. Beating his wings strongly, he rose and made for the opposite bank. He looked down anxiously, but nothing seemed to be moving. Only a few snowflakes melted into the black waters. With a sudden jolt, the dragon landed on a rocky ledge many hundreds of metres above the shimmering flowers. Trembling, he folded his silver wings.

'I don't see anything, Firedrake,' said Sorrel, looking intently into the night. 'I really don't.'

Annoyed, she turned to Twigleg, who was huddled in Ben's lap, shivering. 'That manikin will drive us crazy! How could his old master possibly get here so fast, may I ask?'

'Leave him alone,' said Ben brusquely. 'Can't you see he's frozen?'

With stiff fingers that even the monks' gloves could not keep warm, Ben reached for the thermos flask of tea and carefully gave Twigleg a sip. Then he had a sip himself. The peculiar taste almost turned his stomach, but a comfortable warmth spread through him.

Firedrake stood there, never taking his eyes off the surface of the lake.

'At any rate we have a head start on the monster,' whispered Sorrel. 'He can't fly.'

'We'd only have a head start if there wasn't any water here, you stupid pointy-eared nitwit!' snapped Twigleg. He was not trembling quite so badly now he had drunk a little hot tea. 'Are you telling me that lake down there isn't water? I warn you, he's probably here already, watching us.'

For a moment they were all silenced by shock.

'Then we have a problem,' growled Burr-Burr-Chan. 'I ought not to show you the way into the dragons' cave if the Golden One is watching, ought I?'

'No.' Firedrake shook his head. 'He's learned too much from us already. We can approach the cave only when we know for certain that Nettlebrand isn't around.' Anxiously, he looked down at the lake. 'Have we really led him here?' he murmured.

The valley was even more beautiful than he had imagined it in his dreams. Firedrake gazed at the Rim of Heaven, looking down at the sea of blue flowers covered with moon-dew and breathing in the fragrance that rose from them. Then he closed his eyes – and felt the presence of other dragons nearby. He sensed it clearly, as clearly as the scent of the flowers, as clearly as the cold night air.

Firedrake opened his eyes again, and they were dark with anger. A growl emerged from his throat. Alarmed, his friends looked at him.

'I will fly down,' said the dragon. 'By myself. If Nettlebrand is there then he'll come out.'

'Nonsense!' cried Sorrel, horrified. 'What are you talking about? Even if he does come out, are you planning to tackle him on your own? He'd make a single mouthful of you, and we'll be stuck here on this rock to the end of our days without any mushrooms. Is that what we flew half way round the world for? No, if anyone's going down it must be someone he won't notice!'

'She's right, Firedrake,' said Ben. 'One of us must find out whether Nettlebrand's lurking down there, and if he really is then we must distract his attention so that you and Burr-Burr-Chan can reach the dragons' cave unobserved.'

'Ex-act-ly!' Lola Greytail jumped out of Ben's backpack, hopped up on his knee and spread her short forelegs wide. 'I volunteer! No problem, rat's honour! This is the ideal job for me!'

'Huh!' Sorrel poked her scornfully in the chest. 'So you can come back and tell us he isn't there, same as last time?'

The rat gave her a nasty look. 'Anyone can make a mistake, fur-face,' she hissed. 'But this time I'll take the humpleklumpus with me. He must know his old master's tricksy ways better than anyone, right?'

Twigleg gulped. 'Me?' he asked. 'Me, go in that plane? But—'

'It's a good idea, Twigleg,' said Ben. 'The two of you are so small I'm sure he won't notice you.'

Twigleg shivered. 'And suppose we see him?' he asked in a trembling voice. 'Suppose he really is down there? Who's going to distract his attention?'

'Don't you worry, hummlecuss!' said Lola. Her eyes were positively shining. 'If we spot him I'll give the signal by looping the loop. Then we'll divert the monster and Firedrake will fly to the cave as fast as he can and disappear into it.'

'Divert him!' said Twigleg faintly. 'How?'

'Wait and see!' Lola clapped him so hard on the shoulder that he almost fell head first off Firedrake's back. 'All you have to do is keep your eyes open. I'll do the flying.'

'That's a great comfort, I'm sure!' murmured Twigleg. 'Okay, only one more question: what's looping the loop?'

'Turning the plane upside down in the air,' replied Lola. 'Gives you a lovely tingly feeling in your tummy. Absolutely indescribable.'

'Oh, really?' Twigleg nervously rubbed his nose.

'Not a bad plan,' muttered Burr-Burr-Chan. 'It could just work.'

'I don't know,' growled Sorrel. 'I don't like leaving everything to these two little titches.'

'Oh, you don't? Fancy flying down there yourself, fur-face?' enquired Lola. 'Come on, let's go, humblecuss!' She took Twigleg's hand. 'We're going to make ourselves useful,' she said, and turned to Firedrake. 'Comes in handy having a couple of really small people along, right?'

Firedrake nodded. 'Very handy,' he replied. 'I'll tell you something, Lola. I believe the world will belong to small people one of these days.'

'That's okay by me,' said Lola.

Then, with Twigleg in tow, she climbed over Ben's knees, scuttled along Firedrake's back, and guided the homunculus down to where her plane was still safely lashed on to the dragon's tail. They undid the thin chains, Lola opened the cockpit, and the two of them climbed in.

With a faint smile, Twigleg cast a last glance at Ben, and the boy waved to him. Then Lola Greytail started the engine. Its hum filled the night air like the chirping of crickets as the little plane took off with the two scouts on board, swooping down towards the Eye of the Moon.

CHAPTER FORTY-FIVE

The Eye of the Moon

'Pretty big, this lake!' shouted Lola through the noise of the engine.

'Yes,' whispered Twigleg. 'As big as a sea.' Looking out of the window, he could hear his teeth chattering. The sound of the engine rang in his ears, and his knees were knocking. Flying in a tinny little plane! What a horrible thought. Nothing but a bit of metal and a whirring contraption between him and empty air. He wished he was still on Firedrake's strong back, on Ben's warm lap, in the backpack, anywhere but in this infernal machine.

'Come on, let's have your report. See anything suspicious, homuncupus?' asked the rat.

Twigleg swallowed. But you can't get rid of fear by swallowing. 'No,' he said in a trembling voice. 'Nothing. Only the stars.'

They were reflected in the water like tiny fireflies.

'Fly closer to the bank,' Twigleg told the rat. 'That's the kind of place where he likes to hide, lurking in the mud.'

Lola immediately turned and flew towards the bank.

Twigleg's stomach was doing somersaults.

The lake lay below them like a mirror of black glass. Humming, the plane flew over the water. All was dark. Only the flowers on the bank glowed a mysterious blue.

Twigleg looked over his shoulder to where Firedrake had landed, but there was no sign of the dragon. He had probably hidden, and was watching for their signal from a cranny in the rock. Twigleg turned again and glanced down at the water. Suddenly, as if coming out of nowhere, a strange trembling shook his chest.

'He's here!' he cried in terror.

'Where?' Lola clutched her joystick and peered into the dark, but she could see nothing suspicious.

'I don't know where,' cried Twigleg, 'but I can feel it. Quite clearly.'

'Could be something in what you say.' Lola pressed her sharp nose to the cockpit window. 'There's kind of a suspicious ripple on the water there ahead. As if a large stone had just dropped into it.' She throttled back the engine. 'I'll turn off the lights,' she whispered. 'We want to get a closer view of this.'

Twigleg's knees were knocking again. The mere idea of seeing his old master once more froze his blood. Lola flew in an arc towards the suspect spot. She didn't need lights; like Twigleg, she had the eyes of a nocturnal creature, and starlight was enough for her.

Where the ripples were curling and little waves lapped the shore, the stems of the flowers were bent as if someone had been making his way through them. It must have been some small creature. No bigger than a dwarf.

'There!' Twigleg jumped up from his seat and hit his head on the roof of the aircraft. 'It's Gravelbeard – running along ahead of us!'

Lola steered her plane towards the bank. The startled dwarf stuck his head out of the glowing flowers and saw the buzzing aircraft making straight for him. Gravelbeard didn't stop to think twice. He ran back to the water like lightning.

Lola Greytail wrenched the plane around.

She caught up with the dwarf on the shoreline, where Gravelbeard was still running as fast as his short legs would carry him.

'Grab hold of him, humpusklumpus!' shouted Lola.

Opening the cockpit, she flew so low that the undercarriage of the plane brushed the flowers. Twigleg summoned up all his courage, leaned right out of the plane and tried to seize Gravelbeard by the collar. But the waters of the lake suddenly erupted, foaming. A mighty muzzle emerged from the waves – and snapped at the fleeing dwarf.

One gulp and he was gone.

Lola turned the plane with a sudden jolt, and Twigleg dropped back into his seat.

'He ate him!' cried the rat incredulously. 'He just ate him!'

'Get out of here!' moaned Twigleg. 'Get out of here, quick!'

'Easier said than done,' cried Lola, struggling desperately to control the little aircraft with her joystick as it staggered and spun in the air. Surely it couldn't escape Nettlebrand's gnashing teeth as he snapped, and snapped again. He was crawling further and further out of the water, driven on by his fury with the whirring little nuisance.

With a hunted expression on his face, Twigleg looked out of the back window. What had happened to Firedrake? Was he flying away?

'You didn't loop the loop!' he wailed. 'That was the signal.'

'They could hardly miss seeing the monster down here,' Lola shouted back. 'They'll have noticed him without our dratted signal!'

The plane juddered as the engine coughed and spluttered.

Twigleg was shaking all over. Once again he glanced through the back window, and saw a gleam of silver on the black mountainside.

'Fly away!' cried Twigleg, as if the dragon could hear him. 'Fly away before he sees you!'

And Firedrake flew, spreading his wings wide – but instead of escaping he came diving down towards the lake.

'No!' shrieked the terrified Twigleg. 'Lola, Lola – Firedrake is flying this way!'

'Oh, bother it all!' said the rat crossly as she narrowly avoided another swipe of Nettlebrand's claw. 'He thinks he has to help us! Hold on tight, Twigleg!'

Wrenching the nose of the plane upwards, Lola looped the loop right above Nettlebrand's open jaws. Then she rose higher and looped the loop again, and yet again, until Twigleg felt his stomach was in his throat. The homunculus stared down at his old master flailing about in the water. Then he looked the other way – and saw Firedrake hovering motionless in the air.

'Fly, oh please, please fly to the cave!' whispered Twigleg, although his heart was racing with his fear of Nettlebrand, and his eardrums ached with the monster's roaring.

'What's going on? Has he seen our signal? Is he turning away?' shouted Lola, flying in a spiral round Nettlebrand's neck with death-defying daring.

Now Firedrake did turn in the air.

He shot off like an arrow, while the golden dragon had eyes for nothing but the little aircraft, the silly little thing that had the impertinence to pester him.

'Yes, he's flying away,' cried Twigleg, his voice almost breaking with delight. 'He's flying back towards the mountains.'

'Excellent,' replied Lola, stepping on the gas and whizzing right between Nettlebrand's legs. He struck out at the plane with both forepaws, but the weight of his armour made him drop back into the water, snorting.

Twigleg saw Firedrake rise higher and higher until he landed on a snowy slope – and then suddenly disappeared! As if he had simply been wiped off the face of the earth.

'Rat!' cried the homunculus. 'We've done it. Firedrake's gone. He must be in the cave.' He dropped back into his seat with a sigh. 'You can fly away now!'

'Fly away?' cried Lola. 'Just when we're having such fun? Not likely! Here goes!' And she brought the plane round in a wide arc and made for Nettlebrand's horns.

'What on earth are you doing?' cried the horrified Twigleg.

Disbelievingly, Nettlebrand raised his head, narrowed his eyes, and stared at the whirring widget coming back towards him like an angry hornet.

'Once more unto the breach, dear friends, once more!' cried Lola. 'Full throttle ahead!'

She whirred past Nettlebrand, so close to his armoured brow that Twigleg slid down between the seats with his hands over his eyes.

'Yoohoo!' shouted the rat as she flew round Nettlebrand's horns. 'This is better than surveying mountains! This is something else! Yoohoo!'

Snorting, the golden dragon whipped round. He turned, he snapped, he snapped again and again and again – and never got anything but empty air between his teeth.

'Whoo!' cried Lola, flying around Nettlebrand until he was twisting and turning in the water like a dancing bear. 'Whoo! Your old master must be getting on in years a bit, humpleclups, right? Not as quick off the mark as he might be, anyway.' She waved through the windscreen. 'Bye-bye for now! Why not just lie back down in the mud and rust away, stupid?'

Then she pulled out of her circling manoeuvre and took the plane up steeply, until Twigleg didn't know whether he was on his head or his feet.

'Tantantara, tantantara, gone awaaay!' The rat tapped the instrument panel of her plane appreciatively. 'Well done, my old Tin Lizzie! I'd call that something special.'

Behind them, Nettlebrand was bellowing so loud that Twigleg put his hands over his ears. But the aircraft was already well out of the monster's reach.

'Well, what about it, hompelclompus?' said Lola, drumming happily on the joystick. 'Think we've earned our breakfast?'

'Oh yes!' murmured Twigleg. He looked back at his old master. Nettlebrand's blood-red eyes were following them as if his fierce glare alone could blast them out of the sky. Had he recognised Twigleg when he tried to grab Gravelbeard?

The homunculus sat there all hunched up. 'I never want to see him again,' he whispered, clenching his fists. 'I never, ever want to see him again.'

Even if he flew around Nettlebrand's nose a hundred times, even if he escaped those teeth two hundred times, even if he spat three hundred times on his armoured head – Twigleg would always, always be afraid of him.

'I'm going to land where we came down before,' said Lola. 'Okay by you?'

'Okay by me,' murmured Twigleg, heaving a deep sigh. 'But

then what? How will we find the others?'

'Oh,' said Lola, flying a couple of arcs and grinning, 'they'll come and find us. But first, we'll have breakfast. If you ask me,' she said, smoothing her ears with satisfaction, 'we've worked enough for a whole week, don't you think, hinclecompulsus?'

Twigleg nodded.

Down in the lake, however, Nettlebrand dropped back into the water, dived and disappeared from sight as if he had been nothing but a nightmare.

CHAPTER FORTY-SIX

The Dragons' Cave

Firedrake stood in the snow, looking down at the lake. It was far beneath them now, but his keen dragon eyes could see Nettlebrand reeling about in the foaming water, striking out at the tiny aircraft as it whirred round and round the thrashing monster, taunting him.

'Come on,' said Burr-Burr-Chan, climbing off Firedrake's back. 'You saw the rat's signal. She'll manage. And we must hurry, or that monster may look our way again.'

The Dubidai marched rapidly through the snowfield. Ben and Sorrel followed him to a high wall of rock, white with snow too. Burr-Burr-Chan stopped in front of it.

Firedrake came up beside him and glanced at him enquiringly. 'Well?'

Burr-Burr-Chan chuckled. 'I told you. You can look straight at it and never see it.' He pressed one furry finger to a certain spot on the smooth rock, a place that he could only just reach. 'See that groove? Lean your shoulder against it and brace yourself against the rock.'

Firedrake did as he was told. As soon as he pushed at the icy stone the rock swung aside, revealing the entrance to a dark tunnel. Cautiously, the dragon leaned forward to look inside.

'Come on, hurry up and get in there!' Burr-Burr-Chan pushed Ben and Sorrel into the darkness.

Firedrake cast one last glance down at the lake, where Lola Greytail was still infuriating Nettlebrand. Then he turned and disappeared down the tunnel.

A familiar odour met him. It was quite faint in the cold air, which was getting warmer with every step they took into the heart of the mountain. It was Firedrake's own aroma, sharp and fresh as the air above the clouds – it was the scent of dragons. All of a sudden, he felt as if he had come home.

The tunnel led downwards. Sometimes it turned left, sometimes right. Several times narrow passages forked off it, passages just high enough for brownies. A tempting smell of mushrooms wafted out of some of these passageways. Sorrel's stomach rumbled, but she resolutely walked on.

'It's not at all dark in here,' said Ben when they were deep inside the mountain. 'Why not?'

'Moonstone,' replied Burr-Burr-Chan. 'We made the walls of moonstone. It soaks up light like a sponge. You only have to let moonlight in now and then, or blow a little dragon-fire down the tunnel, and it'll last for years. Even so, the place is much darker than when I was last here.' He looked up at the shimmering walls and shrugged his shoulders. 'They've probably stopped letting any moonlight in for fear of the golden dragon. I can't wait to hear what they say when they know he's paddling about right down there in the lake!'

'They'll be furious, that's what,' muttered Sorrel, nervously tugging at her ears. 'Simply furious. They probably won't even bother to ask what we've come for.'

'We can't fight human beings,' said Firedrake. 'If we drive away a hundred, then a thousand will return. But we can deal with Nettlebrand.'

'What?' Sorrel barred his way. She looked uneasy. 'Are you on about that again – fighting and so forth? When we set out, it was to find somewhere you dragons could live at peace! Now you're planning to fight that monster? Huh!'

'The Golden One is rather cumbersome in a fight,' said Burr-Burr-Chan behind her. 'With his heavy armour, he soon gets out of breath. And he doesn't seem to be especially clever. Look how the rat flew rings around him.'

'Nonsense!' Sorrel turned on him angrily. 'Absolute rot, rubbish, garbage! He's twenty times larger than Firedrake!'

'Larger, yes.' Burr-Burr-Chan shrugged his shoulders. 'So what?'

'Don't upset yourself, Sorrel,' said Firedrake, gently pushing the brownie girl aside. 'Let's go on.'

'Okay!' growled Sorrel crossly. 'But no more nonsense about fighting, right?'

They went on in silence. For a while the tunnel continued downwards, but then it turned a sharp bend and a huge cavern opened out before them. The ceiling glittered faintly with thousands of moonstones. Stalactites hung from it in the dark like frozen sea-spray, and stalagmites grew upwards from floor to roof.

Ben took a couple of steps forward in astonishment. He had never seen such a place before. Here, far inside the mountain, the rock seemed to have come to life. He felt as if he were standing among strange plants and trees and hills, all made of shimmering silver stone.

'Well?' said Sorrel behind him. 'Where are the other dragons, then?'

'Crawled away into hiding, you bet your life,' replied Burr-Burr-Chan.

Hesitantly, Firedrake stepped into the cavern. Sorrel followed him. Burr-Burr-Chan and Ben came slowly after them. In the middle of the cave, among mounds of stone shaped like spiny dragon crests, Firedrake stopped.

'Where are you?' he called.

There was no answer but the echo of his own voice.

'Hi there! Hello!' shouted Sorrel. 'Look, dragons, we've flown half way round the world – you might at least show your faces and welcome us.' But she got no answer either.

There was nothing to be heard but a faint rustling from a thicket of stalactites and stalagmites at the very back of the cave.

Sorrel pricked up her ears. 'Hear that?' she whispered to Firedrake.

Firedrake nodded.

'It's too dark in here,' he said. 'I'll give us a bit more light.' Arching his long neck, he breathed fire. It ran hissing among the stones, licked its way up the dark walls and blazed blue all the way to the roof. The whole dragon cave began to shine so brightly that for a moment Ben had to half-close his eyes. The moonstones shone down from the roof, the walls glowed, and dragon-fire collected in crackling flames on the tips of the stalactites and stalagmites.

'Yes!' cried Burr-Burr-Chan, raising his four arms in the air. 'Yes, that's just how it ought to look!'

Firedrake closed his muzzle and looked around.

'Firedrake,' whispered Ben, placing a hand on his scales, 'there's something back there. Do you see those eyes?'

'I know,' replied the dragon quietly. 'They've been there for some time. Let's wait.'

All was still for a few moments. Firedrake's dragon-fire still burned among the stones, crackling and hissing. Then, suddenly,

a dragon emerged from the stalactites and stalagmites at the back of the cave. This one was rather smaller than Firedrake, with more delicate limbs, but its scales shone with just the same silvery gleam.

'It's a she-dragon,' whispered Sorrel. 'You can tell by the horns. They're straight, not curved like Firedrake's.'

Ben nodded.

The she-dragon snuffled, and moved tentatively towards Firedrake. For a moment or so, they stood looking at each other in silence.

'You're not golden,' the she-dragon said at last, in a hoarse voice.

Firedrake shook his head. 'No,' he replied. 'I'm like you.'

'I . . . I wasn't sure,' said the she-dragon uncertainly. 'I've never seen the Golden One myself, but I've heard terrible tales of him. He's said to be very cunning, and sometimes he has small creatures with him.' She looked curiously first at Sorrel, then at Burr-Burr-Chan.

'These are brownies,' said Firedrake. 'You must have heard of them too.'

The she-dragon frowned. 'The stories say they let us down when we most needed their help.'

'What?' cried Burr-Burr-Chan indignantly. 'We never—'

Firedrake looked at him and shook his head. 'Don't upset yourself,' he said. 'There'll be time for explanations later.'

'Where are the others?' asked Ben, stepping out of Firedrake's shadow.

The she-dragon retreated in surprise. 'The dragon rider,' she whispered. 'The dragon rider is back!'

Ben bowed his head shyly.

'You ask where the others are?' The she-dragon bent over

him until the tip of her muzzle almost touched his nose. 'They're here. Look around you.'

Baffled, Ben looked past her. 'Where?'

'There,' replied the she-dragon, nodding towards the cave behind him.

Sorrel whistled. 'Yes,' she whispered. 'She's right. There they are.' She climbed up on one of the mounds of rock that looked like crested dragon backs, and patted the scaly stone. For once, she was speechless. Firedrake and the others looked up at her incredulously.

Ben put out his hand and touched the rocky grey tails and bowed necks of the dragons. The she-dragon came up behind him.

'There were twenty-three of us,' she said, 'but I am the only one left. Maia the Reckless, they always called me. Moonstruck Maia.' She shook her head sadly.

Firedrake turned to her. 'What happened?'

'They didn't go out any more,' replied Maia in a low voice. 'They stopped flying in the moonlight. And very slowly, they changed. I warned them. I said: forgetting the moon is more dangerous than the golden dragon. But they wouldn't listen to me. They became tired, sluggish, bad-tempered. They laughed at me when I went out in the moonlight or flew over the lake on nights when the moon was full. They were forever repeating the old tale of the golden dragon who would destroy us all if we didn't hide from him. "Careful," they used to say, when I wanted to go out, "he's out there. He's lying in wait for us." But he never was. I told them so. "Remember," I said, "remember there's another story, the tale of the dragon rider who will come back on the day when silver is worth more than gold, and with his aid we'll defeat the golden dragon." But they only shook their heads

- 357 -

and said the dragon rider was dead and gone and would never return.' She looked at Ben. 'I was right, though. The dragon rider has come back.'

'Perhaps,' said Firedrake, looking at the dragons now turned to stone. 'But someone else is back too. Nettlebrand is here as well. Nettlebrand, the golden dragon.'

'He followed us,' added Sorrel. 'He's down there in the lake.'

Horrified, Maia looked at them. 'The golden dragon?' she asked blankly. 'So he really exists? And he's here?'

'He's been here often enough,' said Burr-Burr-Chan. 'But he never found the way into this cave, and he won't find it now either.'

Firedrake nodded. 'Nonetheless, we brought him here. I'm sorry.' He bowed his head. 'I was so anxious to find this place that, without meaning to, I have led Nettlebrand to your door. But I won't hide from him any longer. I will—'

'You'll do what?' asked Maia. A shudder ran over her scales.

'I will fight him,' replied Firedrake. 'I'll chase him away from here. I will hunt him. I'll rid you of him for ever, for I am tired of hiding.'

Ben and the two brownies looked at each other in alarm.

'Fight him?' Maia looked at Firedrake. 'I've wanted to do that a hundred times – a thousand times – when the others told me how he hunted them. The dragon-eater, protected by his golden skin, armed with a thousand ravenous teeth. Is he as terrible as they said?'

'They weren't exactly exaggerating,' growled Sorrel.

Firedrake nodded. 'Yes, he is terrible indeed, but I will fight him.'

'Yes,' murmured Maia. She fell silent again, looking round at the cave that was suddenly so bright once more. 'I'll help you,' she said. 'Together, perhaps we can do it. That's what I always told the others: united we're stronger than he is. But they were too frightened to try.' Sadly, she shook her head. 'See what fear does to you.' She pointed with her head to the petrified dragons. 'See how they cower there, motionless and lifeless. I don't want to end up like that. You know what I think?' She came close to Firedrake. 'I think you were meant to bring him here. It was bound to be so, and the two of us will overcome him. Just as the old stories say: when the dragon rider returns, silver will be worth more than gold.'

'Just the two of you? Oh, wonderful!' Insulted, Sorrel wrinkled her nose. 'Don't you think you could use a bit of help with all this fighting?'

'Er . . . they didn't count me in either,' said Ben.

'Don't be silly – we can do with all the help we can get,' said Firedrake, nuzzling Sorrel in her furry stomach.

'Right, that makes five of us. Or no,' said Sorrel, perching on the tail of a stone dragon, 'no, seven! Twigleg and the rat too.'

'Twigleg and Lola!' cried Firedrake 'They're still out there somewhere!'

'Oh, mouldy matsutakes!' Burr-Burr-Chan jumped up. 'They'll be waiting for us where we first landed. There's a mushroom cultivation tunnel that leads there. Come on, Sorrel, let's find them.'

'Just a moment, I have to get out of these human clothes!' Sorrel quickly stripped off the clothing the monks had given her for the flight, and then the two brownies raced off together.

Ben stayed in the cave with the two dragons.

'A rat and a – er – a twigleg?' asked Maia curiously.

Firedrake nodded. 'Neither of them is much bigger than one of your ears, but they are very brave.'

For a few moments they stood in silence, looking at the dragons who had turned to stone.

'Could they be revived?' asked Ben.

Maia shook her head. 'How could you bring the moon down here?'

'Perhaps moon-dew would help?' Ben looked enquiringly at Firedrake.

'Moon-dew?' asked Maia.

'Yes. You know what we mean,' replied Firedrake. 'The dew that on any moonlit night gathers on the blue flowers growing down by the lake. If you lick it off the petals and leaves you can fly by day as well as by night. Didn't you know?'

Maia shook her head.

'Forget it,' said Ben. 'How are we going to collect dew from the flowers with Nettlebrand lurking down there in the lake?'

'I have a few drops left,' said Firedrake, 'but they would hardly be enough. And who knows, we may yet need them ourselves.'

'You're right,' murmured Ben, disappointed, and he patted the scaly backs of the stone dragons.

CHAPTER FORTY-SEVEN

No, No and No Again

'No, I'm not coming out, so there!' said Gravelbeard.

He was in the great cavern of his master's belly, sitting on the golden casket that held Nettlebrand's heart, and staring crossly down at the fermenting brew of the golden dragon's digestive juices. Acrid vapours wafted up from them, stinging his nose.

'Come on out, armour-cleaner!' bellowed the voice from above.

'No, no and no again!' Gravelbeard shouted up the huge throat. 'Not unless you promise never to swallow me again! I'm sick and tired of being swallowed. Suppose I go down the wrong pipe? Suppose I land in all the muck down there next time?' Shuddering, he stared at the bubbling, hissing, filthy liquid below him.

'Don't talk rot!' came Nettlebrand's furious voice from above. 'I swallowed that treacherous Twigleg a thousand times, and he never went down the wrong pipe.'

'Oh yes,' muttered Gravelbeard, straightening his hat. 'All very well for you to talk! And I'm all shaken up from splashing about in the water too!' he shouted up. 'Did you catch that tinny hornet thing? I don't see it swimming around down here.'

'It got away!' growled Nettlebrand. Gravelbeard felt the vast body quivering with rage. 'It flew up to the mountains and landed where the silver dragon had been sitting.'

'Oh yes?' In a thoroughly bad temper, Gravelbeard scratched his chin. 'And where's *he* now? Did he show you where the other dragons are hiding?'

'No!' Nettlebrand spat. 'He's disappeared. Come up out of there this minute! I want you to climb up to where the tin hornet landed. You saw who was in it, didn't you? That spider-legged traitor! Aaarrgh! I'm going to crush him like a woodlouse, but he must lead us to his new master first.'

'Oh yes?' Gravelbeard was still sulking. 'And what do I get if I find him? Him and the tin hornet?' Putting his hand under his shirt, he felt Barnabas Greenbloom's wedding ring.

'You dare ask that?' bellowed Nettlebrand. 'Come on up, or I'll shake myself so hard you really will fall into my guts.'

'Oh, all right.' Gravelbeard rose to his feet and climbed up his master's throat, muttering crossly into his beard.

'I can understand why that Twigleg took off,' he grumbled. 'Oh yes, I can understand it very well indeed.'

CHAPTER FORTY-EIGHT

The Captive Dwarf

'They've forgotten us!' wailed Twigleg, pacing restlessly up and down. 'Talk about ingratitude!'

'Oh, come off it!' said the rat, stirring the pan on her tiny camping stove.

As the sun climbed slowly in the cloudy sky, a thick mist clung to the mountain slopes. Its white vapour hid everything: the flowers, the lake – and Nettlebrand. If he was still around. Lola tasted the concoction bubbling in her pan, licked her whiskers and went on stirring. 'Oh, do sit down, humpelcuss!' she said. 'This is about the hundredth time I've told you, they'll come back – when it gets dark, if not before. I really don't know why you're making all this fuss. We have all we need – something to eat, a nice hot drink. I even have sleeping bags. Two, luckily.'

'But I'm so worried,' wailed Twigleg. 'Who knows what those other dragons are like? Maybe they're the sort of dragons you read about in fairy tales. Maybe they're particularly fond of eating human boys!'

The rat chuckled. 'Oh, honestly! Believe you me, that boy can look after himself. And if he doesn't, well, Firedrake's there. Not to mention those furry-faced brownies.'

Twigleg sighed, and looked down into the mist.

'Are all hompulkisses like you?' enquired Lola.

'What do you mean?' murmured Twigleg.

'Well, so pessimistic.' Lola took a spoonful of soup from the pan and tasted it. 'Oh, yuk!' she muttered. 'I've put too much salt in again.'

Suddenly, she raised her pointed nose and sniffed. Her ears twitched.

Twigleg looked at her in alarm.

'Would you like some soup?' Lola asked in a strangely loud voice. As she spoke, she discreetly pointed one paw to the place behind her where the plane was parked, wedged in place with a couple of large stones. Something was moving behind its wheels.

Twigleg held his breath. 'Soup?' he faltered. 'Er, yes, yes, I'd love some.' He took a quiet step towards the plane.

'Right, I'll get the soup bowls,' announced the rat, standing up.

Then, with a sudden leap, she dived between the wheels and tugged at a stout leg. Twigleg came to her aid. Together, they dragged a struggling dwarf out from under the plane.

'Gravelbeard!' cried the startled Twigleg. 'It's that mountain dwarf again!'

Gravelbeard ignored him. He bit, kicked and hit out, almost pushing Lola down the mountainside. Dwarves are strong, much stronger than a rat or a pale little homunculus. But just as Gravelbeard broke free of Lola's clutches, Twigleg knocked the hat off his head.

Immediately the dwarf stopped struggling. He narrowed his

eyes, staggered back from the edge of the abyss, and sat down abruptly, groaning. Twigleg snatched the hat just before it started rolling downhill and put it on his own head. It slipped almost down to his nose, but he didn't feel bad wearing it. Quite the contrary. He went to stand on the very edge of the precipice, the toes of his shoes projecting into empty space – and he didn't feel the least bit dizzy.

'Astonishing,' he murmured, turning and lifting the hat far enough back for him to see out from under its brim. The mountains suddenly looked quite different, glittering and shimmering in a thousand hues. Amazed, Twigleg stared around him.

'Hey, hummelcuss, give me a hand, will you?' Lola took a length of string out of her flying suit. 'We must tie this dwarf up, unless you want him running back to his master. Good thing you remembered that trick with the hat. I'd forgotten it completely.'

'Hello there, Gravelbeard,' said Twigleg, sitting on the dwarf's stomach while Lola tied up her prisoner. 'What a busy little spy you are. Much busier than I ever was in all the three hundred years I served Nettlebrand.'

'Traitor!' growled the dwarf, spitting at Twigleg. 'Give me back my hat!'

Twigleg merely shrugged his shoulders. 'No, why should I?' He bent over the dwarf. 'I know exactly why you're so keen to serve my old master. It's because you're blinded by greed for his golden scales. Only how are you going to get at them without being eaten? Thinking of pulling some off while he's asleep, are you? I really wouldn't advise it. You know how he treasures every single one of them. Have you forgotten he was going to eat the professor just for having a single one of his precious scales? What do you think?' He put his head a little closer to the dwarf's. 'Is he afraid someone will discover what his armour's made of? Or is he even more afraid of anyone finding out what's inside that casket he calls his heart?'

Gravelbeard bit his lips furiously and glared into the fire.

'What are we going to do with him?' asked Lola. 'Any bright ideas, homompulos?'

'Take him with us, what else?' said a voice behind them.

Lola and Twigleg shot round in alarm. But it was only Sorrel. She had suddenly appeared in front of the rocks, and Burr-Burr-Chan was grinning at them over her shoulder.

'How did you get here?' asked Twigleg in surprise. 'Did you find the dragons' cave?'

'We did,' replied Sorrel. 'And I see you've caught the little spy. Not bad. And guess what,' she added, biting the shrivelled mushroom she had in her paw. 'On the way back to you we found some old mushroom beds from way back when the Dubidai still lived here. The mountain's full of the passages they made.' Licking her lips, she cocked an eyebrow at Twigleg. 'Got a new hat, little titch?'

The homunculus felt its brim. 'It's a very special hat,' he said.

'The way you two fooled Nettlebrand was something special too,' said Burr-Burr-Chan. 'Shitake and matsutake, not bad at all. And now you've caught his spy too!'

Flattered, Lola smoothed her ears. 'Oh, it was nothing,' she said.

'Nothing or not, I'll carry him back. The rest of you can bring the other things,' said Burr-Burr-Chan, looking down into the valley. The mist was slowly lifting. Black birds were circling among the white wisps of vapour – countless black birds. Whole flocks of them emerged from the mist and then disappeared into it again. 'That's odd,' muttered Burr-Burr-Chan. 'I never saw black birds like those before. Where did they spring from?'

Sorrel and Twigleg were beside him in a twinkling.

'The ravens!' growled Sorrel. 'I knew they'd turn up again.'

'He's summoned them all!' groaned Twigleg, taking shelter behind her. 'Oh no! Now we're done for. They'll see us! They'll pick us off the rocks, one by one.'

'What are you carrying on about?' The rat joined him, and suddenly gave such a shrill whistle that it made Twigleg jump. 'Goodness, you're right! Ravens, any number of them. My uncle told me about some rather nasty specimens of his acquaintance. Are those down there the same sort?'

Twigleg nodded. 'Enchanted ravens. And this time there are too many for Sorrel to drive them off with a few well-aimed stones.'

'We'd better get out of here before they spot us,' said Sorrel, pulling Burr-Burr-Chan back from the edge of the abyss.

'Nettlebrand, the Golden One, will gobble up the whole blasted bunch of you!' croaked Gravelbeard, trying to bite Burr-Burr-Chan's furry foot. But the Dubidai brownie only chuckled.

'He'll have to drag his heavy armour all the way up here first,' he said, throwing the dwarf over his shoulder like a sack.

'And your clever master doesn't know where the secret entrance is either,' added Sorrel.

'He'll find out!' bellowed the mountain dwarf, kicking and struggling. 'He'll squash you like cockroaches. He'll—'

Burr-Burr-Chan gagged the dwarf by stuffing his beard into his mouth. Then, carrying their prisoner, he disappeared down the passage along which he had just come.

'Come on, titch!' said Sorrel, picking up Twigleg. 'Or the ravens really will get you.'

Lola put out the fire, handed the tiny pan of soup to Sorrel and packed the rest of her things into the plane. 'You can fly with me, hommelcuss!' she said, climbing into the cockpit and starting the engine.

'No thanks,' said Twigleg, clutching Sorrel's arm tightly. 'One flight with you will do me for the rest of my life.'

'Just as you like!' The rat closed the cockpit and flew the whirring little aircraft over their heads and into the passage.

Sorrel cast a final anxious glance at the circling ravens. Then she too stepped into the passage, pushed the stone slab across the entrance, and now there was nothing of the Dubidai tunnel to be seen from the outside.

CHAPTER FORTY-NINE

Making Plans

Burr-Burr-Chan took Gravel-beard, still well and truly trussed up, to a small cave so far from the dragons' huge cavern that even the dwarf wouldn't be able to overhear the plans they were hatching to outwit his master. When he was dumped alone there, Gravelbeard soon spat his beard out of his mouth and shouted loud insults after the retreating brownie, but Burr-Burr-Chan only chuckled.

On returning to the great cavern he found the others sitting in a circle, silent and obviously at a loss. Burr-Burr-Chan sat down beside Sorrel.

'Well?' he whispered to her. 'Looks as if you haven't yet thought up a good plan, right?'

Sorrel shook her head.

'We can't attack him down in the valley,' said Lola Greytail. 'He can disappear into the lake at any time.'

'Maybe we could try tackling him on the mountainside,' suggested Twigleg. 'His armour would be a drawback there.'

But Firedrake shook his head. 'The approach flight would be tricky,' he said. 'We could crash among the rocks.'

Sorrel sighed.

'Then we must lure him to a valley where there isn't any water!' said Burr-Burr-Chan.

'I'm not sure how we'd do that,' muttered Ben.

They talked and talked. How could they best attack Nettlebrand? Dragon-fire could not harm his armour, as they knew only too well. Sorrel suggested luring him up the mountains so that they could push him off a precipice, but Firedrake just shook his head. Nettlebrand was much too big and heavy. Even he and Maia working as a team couldn't do it. Lola made a daring suggestion: she volunteered to fly her plane down his throat and destroy him from the inside. But the others wouldn't hear of it, and Twigleg told her that Nettlebrand carried his heart in an armoured metal casket anyway. Idea after idea was suggested and turned down, until they were sitting round in frustrated silence again.

Thoughtfully, Ben put his fingers into the little bag hanging round his neck and brought out Nettlebrand's golden scale. It lay there in his hand, cool and shining.

'What's that?' asked Burr-Burr-Chan, looking at it curiously.

'One of Nettlebrand's scales,' replied Ben, stroking the cold metal. 'The professor found it – Professor Greenbloom. He has one too.' Ben shook his head. 'I've tried scratching it with my penknife, I've tried bashing it with stones, I've even thrown it in the fire, but nothing happened. It didn't get so much as a scratch on it.' He sighed, and laid the scale on the palm of his hand again. 'And Nettlebrand is armoured with these things from head to foot. How could we ever pierce such armour? He'd just laugh at us.'

Lola Greytail jumped out of her plane and climbed up on Ben's knee. Twigleg was sitting on the other knee. 'You're sure you've tried dragon-fire?' she asked.

Ben nodded. 'Firedrake and Maia breathed some fire on the scale when you were outside. Nothing. No effect at all. It didn't even warm up.'

'Of course not,' said Twigleg, rubbing the tip of his nose. 'Nettlebrand was made on purpose to kill dragons. Do you think he'd wear armour that could be harmed by dragon-fire? No, believe you me,' he said, shaking his head, 'I polished that armour for three hundred years and there's nothing, absolutely nothing that can penetrate it.'

'But there must be something we can do,' said Firedrake, pacing restlessly up and down between the silent dragons who had turned to stone.

Ben was still holding the scale, turning it this way and that.

'Put the stupid thing away,' growled Sorrel. 'I bet it brings bad luck.' Then she spat on it.

'Oh, don't be so disgusting, Sorrel!' Ben wiped the scale with his sleeve, but the brownie saliva was not to be so easily removed. A thin film of it clung to the metal.

'Wait a minute!' All at once, Firedrake was standing behind Ben. He looked at the golden scale.

'It's gone all cloudy,' Twigleg pointed out. 'Nettlebrand wouldn't like that a bit. You should just see how he admires his reflection in the water when his scales have been polished. Specially when he's going hunting. You wouldn't believe how hard I had to clean him then. I rubbed till my fingers bled!'

'Brownie saliva and dragon-fire,' murmured Firedrake. He raised his head. 'Sorrel, remember those ravens?'

Sorrel looked puzzled, but she nodded.

'Brownie saliva mixed with dragon-fire broke the spell on them, correct?'

'Yes, but . . .'

Firedrake pushed forward between Ben and the brownie. 'Put the scale on the ground, Ben,' he said, 'and the rest of you stand well away. You in particular, Twigleg.'

The homunculus hastily clambered off Ben's knee and took shelter behind Maia's tail.

'What are you going to do?' asked Maia, surprised.

But Firedrake did not reply. He was gazing at Nettlebrand's scale as if transfixed. Then he opened his mouth and blew dragon-fire over it. Very gently. The blue flame licked its way over the metal.

And it melted.

Nettlebrand's scale melted like butter in the sun. It liquified, leaving a golden puddle on the grey rock of the cave floor.

Raising his head, Firedrake looked round triumphantly.

Speechless, the others came closer. Twigleg knelt down beside the small puddle and cautiously dipped a finger into it. Lola joined him, and drew her tail through the liquid gold.

'Look at that!' she chuckled. 'I'll be called Goldtail instead of Greytail now!'

Ben laid his hand on Firedrake's flank. 'That's it!' he breathed. 'You've found the solution, Firedrake. That's how we can destroy him.'

'Oh yeah?' said Sorrel mockingly. 'And just how are we going to dip Nettlebrand's armour in brownie spit?'

The others couldn't tell her.

Then Twigleg rose to his feet. 'Nothing simpler,' he said, wiping his gold-stained finger on his jacket.

They all stared at him.

'Sorrel,' said Twigleg, 'please would you bring me our prisoner's things?'

'Anything else you fancy?' muttered Sorrel. But she fetched Gravelbeard's backpack and put it down in front of Twigleg's feet.

'My humble thanks,' said the homunculus. He opened the backpack, reached into it and brought out a hammer, matches, candles, the comb the dwarf used on his beard, a hat-brush, two dusters – and a green glass bottle.

'There we are,' said Twigleg, holding up the bottle. 'Still more than half full.'

'What's that?' asked Ben.

'Polish for my old master's armour,' explained Twigleg. 'He has it specially mixed for him by an ancient mountain dwarf. A few drops in a bucket of water, and hey presto, his scales gleam like a mirror.' Twigleg opened the bottle and tipped its contents out on the rocky ground.

'Right,' he said, holding the empty bottle out to Sorrel. 'Spit in it. You and Burr-Burr-Chan can take turns. We need it to be just over half full.'

Burr-Burr-Chan took the bottle from the homunculus's hand. 'A little bottle like this – we'll do the job in no time, right, Sorrel?'

Chuckling, the pair of them sat down on the back of a petrified dragon and set to work.

'Won't the dwarf notice?' Firedrake asked the homunculus anxiously.

'Yes, of course he will.' Twigleg carefully repacked the backpack with Gravelbeard's things. 'He'll notice when he applies it to the very first scale. So he'll add more and more brownie spit to the water, hoping to get the scales shiny. Which is just what

- 373 -

we want, right?'

Firedrake nodded thoughtfully.

'Let's hope it still works with so much water added,' said Maia.

Ben shrugged his shoulder. 'We have to try.'

'Yes,' said Firedrake. 'We must let the dwarf go as soon as the brownies have finished, so that he can get straight back to his master.'

'No, we don't want to just let him go,' said Twigleg, shaking his head firmly. 'He'd suspect something at once. We'll allow him to escape, that's the way.'

'Escape?' asked Sorrel, horrified. She and Burr-Burr-Chan had finished their work.

'One good helping of brownie gob!' laughed the Dubidai, placing the bottle in Twigleg's thin fingers. The homunculus carefully put it back where it had come from.

'Yes, we'll allow him to escape,' he said, closing the backpack. 'We'll even show him the entrance to the cave.'

'Little titch here really has gone crazy!' groaned Sorrel. 'I knew he would. It was only a question of time.'

'Let him finish, Sorrel,' said Firedrake.

'We *have* to lure Nettlebrand up here!' said Twigleg. 'Or do you want him to escape through the water when he realises that his armour is dissolving? He won't bring the ravens with him, they'd be too close to the dragon-fire. But once he's in this cavern he can't escape except down the tunnel, and we can bar his way.'

'You're right,' muttered Sorrel.

'It still won't work,' said Maia. 'You've forgotten the moon. We can't fly inside the cave.'

'You can't fly outside it either!' Twigleg pointed out. 'We told you about the ravens. They'll cover the moon the way they did back then over the sea, and you'd be helpless to do anything but fall into Nettlebrand's jaws.'

'Twigleg is right,' Firedrake told Maia. 'We must lure him in here. And we *can* fly in the cave. I have a little moon-dew left, enough for the two of us.'

The she-dragon looked at him doubtfully, but finally she nodded. 'Very well, we'll lure him here. But surely he'll destroy the whole place?' She looked around her.

'Oh, you two won't let it come to that!' cried Lola. 'Now, let the hommlecuss explain properly. I want to know what he's planning to do with the dwarf.'

Twigleg looked round importantly. 'As soon as the moon rises, our prisoner will escape,' he said. 'With all the information Nettlebrand wants and that bottle of brownie spit. He'll tell his master where to find the entrance to the cave and how to open it. He'll polish Nettlebrand's armour with brownie spit, and then,' concluded Twigleg, smiling, 'then he'll lead him to his doom.'

'How are you going to make sure he doesn't see through the whole plan?' asked Ben.

'You leave that to me, young master,' replied Twigleg, looking at his finger, which still shone golden from the metal of the molten scale. 'This is going to be my revenge for three hundred years of misery and the death of eleven brothers.'

CHAPTER FIFTY

Deceiving the Spy

Gravelbeard had done his best to loosen his bonds. He had thrashed around on the cave floor like a fish on dry land, rubbing his bound wrists against sharp stones and trying to get at the knife in his pocket. It was no use. The rat had tied some very professional knots. So he lay there for hours on the hard, rocky floor like a sack of potatoes, grinding his teeth, while thousands of wonderful stones glittered down at him in the dark and he dreamed of tearing the spidery legs off that treacherous homunculus.

When at long last he heard steps approaching, Gravelbeard expected to see the fat rat or one of those hairy brownies coming back. But much to his surprise it was Twigleg who emerged from the dark passage along which he himself had been dragged. That traitor Twigleg was still wearing Gravelbeard's hat.

'What are *you* doing here?' spat Gravelbeard, wriggling like an eel in his bonds. 'Come to question me, have you? Get out! Go back to your friends. But you can give me my hat back first, you revolting spider-legged traitor.'

'Shut up!' hissed Twigleg. He knelt down beside the dwarf and, to Gravelbeard's terror, took a knife out of his pocket.

'Help!' shrieked the dwarf. 'Help, Your Goldness, he's going to murder me!'

'Nonsense!' Twigleg began sawing at Gravelbeard's bonds. 'Although if you go on squirming like that I may well accidentally cut off one of your fingers. And if you keep shouting, Sorrel will have you for breakfast.'

Gravelbeard closed his mouth again. 'Brownies don't eat dwarves!' he growled.

'Oh, they do sometimes,' said Twigleg, cutting through the last knot. 'Once I even heard a brownie say that dwarves were nice and crunchy.'

'Crunchy?' Gravelbeard struggled up. He listened. Only the eternal whispering of the stones.

Twigleg handed him his backpack. 'Here are your things, and now let's get out of here.'

'Get out of here?' The dwarf looked suspiciously at the homunculus. 'What's the big idea? Is this some kind of trap?'

'Don't be silly!' hissed Twigleg, hauling the dwarf along after him. 'You nearly ruined my wonderful plan, but even so, I'm not going to let the brownies get you. Anyway, I need you as a messenger.'

'What are you talking about?' Reluctantly, the mountain dwarf followed Twigleg down the dark passages. 'What plan? You cheated us! You sent Nettlebrand off to the desert. Do you know I spent days and days there digging him out of the hot sand? All thanks to you!'

'Nonsense!' whispered Twigleg. 'Pure rot. I'm not a traitor. I've been Nettlebrand's faithful armour-cleaner for over three hundred years, longer than you've spent tapping away at your stones, you half-wit. You think I'd turn traitor just like that? No, it's all the ravens' fault! Those ravens have been telling lies about me. They never did like me. But I'm the one who'll make sure Nettlebrand can go hunting again at long last. I, Twigleg, not those miserable birds with their crooked beaks. And you'll help me.'

'I will?' Dazed, Gravelbeard was stumbling along after him. 'How? What—?'

'Psst!' Twigleg put a hand in front of his mouth. 'Not a squeak out of you now. Understand?'

Gravelbeard nodded – and then his jaw dropped and his eyes popped, for they had reached the great cave.

Never in his entire dwarfish life had Gravelbeard seen such wonders. The stones dazzled him. Their voices sang in his ears, countless beautiful voices speaking in tones such as he had never heard before. When the homunculus dragged him roughly on, Gravelbeard woke as if from a dream that had held him spellbound.

'What's the matter? Planning to hang around here and turn to stone?' hissed Twigleg, dragging the dwarf on through the glittering heart of the mountain. He led Gravelbeard past the sleeping brownies, past the rat lying beside her plane and snoring, past the human boy who was curled up like a cat. Gravelbeard noticed none of them. He saw only the glowing moonstones, he followed the bright pattern they traced on the cave walls – and then he stumbled over the tail of a sleeping dragon. He stopped short and gasped.

Two silver dragons lay before him, so close to one another that you could hardly tell where one ended and the other began.

'Two?' he whispered to the homunculus. 'Only two? Where

are the others?'

'In another cave,' whispered Twigleg. 'Now, do come on! Or do you want to be here when they wake up?'

Gravelbeard hastily stumbled on. 'How many are there?' he whispered. 'Tell me, Twigleg. His Goldness is sure to ask me.'

'Twenty,' hissed Twigleg over his shoulder. 'Maybe more. Come *on*.'

'Twenty,' murmured Gravelbeard, looking back once more at the sleeping dragons. 'That's a lot.'

'The more the merrier,' Twigleg whispered back. 'Bet you that's what he'll say.'

'Yes, you're right. He certainly will.' Gravelbeard nodded, and tried to take his eyes off the stones, but with such marvels surrounding him he kept forgetting that he was escaping. Only when they had left the cavern behind was the spell broken. The homunculus guided him down a long tunnel that led upwards and ended in front of a great slab of stone. Gravelbeard looked round, confused, but without a word Twigleg led him out through a narrow side-passage.

The moon was already in the sky. A last streak of sunset light was fading beyond the white peaks. The lake where Nettlebrand lurked lay dark among the mountains, with ravens circling above its waters.

'Here, your hat.' Twigleg put the hat on the mountain dwarf's shaggy hair. 'Will you be able to find your way back here on your own?'

Gravelbeard looked round and nodded. 'Of course,' he replied. 'Wonderful stones. I've never seen anything like them! Unique!'

'If you say so.' Twigleg shrugged his shoulders and pointed to the rock on their left. 'This is the stone slab you just saw from inside. It swings open when a dragon pushes it. So it shouldn't be any problem for our master to get into the mountain, and the tunnel on the other side is wide enough even for him. Rather stupid of those brownies to make it that big, eh?' He chuckled gleefully.

'He'll want me to polish him up before the great hunt.' Gravelbeard put the backpack over his shoulders. 'And he's all muddy right now, so don't expect him to attack too soon.'

The homunculus nodded, and gave the dwarf a strange look. 'Mind you polish him up better than ever before,' he said. 'This will be his greatest hunt for over a hundred years!'

'Yes, I know.' Gravelbeard began his downward climb. 'I wish the hunt were over and I had my reward at last. He's promised me two of his scales for my services.'

'Has he indeed? Two whole scales!' murmured Twigleg as the dwarf climbed down. 'What generosity!'

The homunculus stood there a moment or so longer, watching Nettlebrand's new armour-cleaner go on his way, and then the cold of the night drove him back into the mountain.

CHAPTER FIFTY-ONE

Polishing Nettlebrand
for the Hunt

'Haven't you finished yet, armour-cleaner?' growled Nettlebrand.

He was standing in the dark water up to his knees, looking at his shimmering reflection. Gravelbeard crouched on his head, polishing his armoured brow. The dwarf was working so hard that sweat ran down into his beard, even though the night was bitterly cold.

'Oh, nickel and gypsum!' he said through clenched teeth. 'What's the matter with them? They're as dull as ditchwater, however hard I polish.'

'What are you going on about?' grumbled Nettlebrand, lashing the water impatiently with his tail. 'I'm sure you've polished that place four times already. Isn't it shiny yet?'

Distrustfully, he lowered his head and stared at the water, but in the darkness of the night his reflection was scarcely more than a golden shadow distorted by the ripples.

'Master!' cawed a raven, landing on one of Nettlebrand's crest spines.

Reluctantly, the golden dragon turned to him. 'What is it?' he grunted.

'Shouldn't at least a couple of us go up to the cave with you?'

'Nonsense.' Nettlebrand shook his head. 'You'd fall from the air like fried fish if the dragon-fire hit you. No, I'll be needing you again later, so stay here for now, understand?'

'We obey, master!' croaked the raven, lowering its beak respectfully before flying back to the others, who were circling over the lake in a black cloud.

'Let's hope those dragons are in good fighting fettle,' growled Nettlebrand when the raven had left, 'or hunting them won't be any fun. What did they look like, armour-cleaner?'

'I only saw two of them,' replied Gravelbeard sulkily, and slipped a couple of scales down his master's back. 'They're smaller than you. Much smaller.'

'Only two?' Nettlebrand squinted up at the dwarf. 'How come you only saw two?'

'The rest were in another cave,' replied Gravelbeard, scrubbing away until his knuckles ached. But there was still a dull film on Nettlebrand's scales. With a sigh, the dwarf put his cloth down, and threw it and the bucket to the bank.

'There we are, Your Goldness! Finished!' he cried, mopping the sweat from his brow with his beard and straightening his hat.

'About time, too!' grunted Nettlebrand.

He took a last look at his reflection, stretched, licked his terrible teeth and lumbered out of the water, snorting. His paws crushed the blue flowers. Then he scraped the mud from his claws, sharpened them on his teeth one last time – and marched towards the mountains.

'Well, where is it?' he panted. 'Come on, tell me, armour-cleaner. In that mountain there?'

'Yes, Your Goldness.' Gravelbeard nodded and crouched down on his master's back. The cold was digging its icy fangs into his plump cheeks. Sure of victory ahead, Nettlebrand marched through the fragrant flowers. Gravelbeard heard him grinding his teeth, smacking his lips and laughing hoarsely to himself. No doubt this was what people called the thrill of the chase. The dwarf yawned nervously and thought of the huge cavern. What lovely stones it held: treasures such as no one had ever seen before! But how about the fight? Those twenty dragons weren't just going to lie down meekly to be eaten. Gravelbeard frowned, his nose running with the cold. Such fights were dangerous for little folk like him. You could easily get trampled by the dragons' claws.

'Er, Your Goldness!' he called. 'I think I'd better stay here, don't you? I'll only be in the way during your great battle.'

But Nettlebrand took no notice of him. He was trembling with eagerness for the fray. Snorting, he began to heave himself up the mountainside.

I could jump off, thought Gravelbeard. He wouldn't even notice. And then I could join him when it's all over.

He peered down, but the ground was a long, long way off. The dwarf shifted uneasily. Fine snowflakes were falling from the sky and settling on his hat. The wind blew over the rocks, filling the night with groaning and sighing. Nettlebrand liked that. He loved the cold; it made him feel strong. He climbed higher and higher, snorting and snuffling with the weight of his armour. His claws dug deep into the newly fallen snow.

'That manikin,' he grunted, as the white peaks came slowly closer. 'I knew he'd never dare betray me. He's a clever little thing, not a gold-digging fool like you, dwarf.'

Gravelbeard frowned, secretly making a face at Nettlebrand.

'All the same,' added the huge dragon, hauling himself up the rocks, 'I think I'm going to eat him. He's too impertinent for an armour-cleaner. I'll keep you to do the job instead.'

'What?' Gravelbeard sat upright in horror. '*What* did you say?'

Nettlebrand uttered a horrible laugh. 'You can go on being my armour-cleaner, that's what I said. Now shut up. I have to concentrate on the hunt. Aha!' Licking his lips, he rammed his claws into the mountainside, getting a firm grip. 'They're so close now – so close at last. I'm going to pick them off the roof of their cave like pigeons.'

The furious Gravelbeard clung to one of the dragon's horns. 'But I don't want to be your armour-cleaner any more!' he shouted in Nettlebrand's ear. 'I want my reward, and then I want to go back to prospecting for stones.'

'Oh, stuff and nonsense!' Nettlebrand gave a menacing growl. 'Hold your tongue, or I'll eat you before I eat the homunculus, and then where am I going to get another armour-cleaner?' He stopped on a rocky ledge, groaning. 'Where is it?' he asked, putting his head back. 'Can't be much further now, can it?'

Gravelbeard snivelled. His horny fists were clenched in anger. 'You promised me!' he shouted into the icy wind. 'You promised!'

'Where – is – it?' bellowed Nettlebrand. 'Show me, armour-cleaner, or do you want me to eat you here and now?'

'There!' Gravelbeard raised a trembling finger and pointed. 'Up there where the snow's settling in that big hollow.'

'Good,' growled Nettlebrand, snarling as he made his way up the last few metres.

Gravelbeard sat between his horns, chewing his beard in fury. If he wasn't going to get his reward after all, he had no intention of ever cleaning Nettlebrand's armour again.

Soundlessly and slowly, very slowly, he began sliding down Nettlebrand's neck, using all the skill he had learned from climbing mountains. As Nettlebrand braced his weight against the slab of stone that stood between him and his prey, the armour-cleaner jumped down into the snow. And when the stone slab slid aside and Nettlebrand forced his way into the tunnel, Gravelbeard scurried silently along behind him – on his own two feet and at a safe distance. Not to watch the dragon-hunt, no. He just wanted to be back in that wonderful cavern.

CHAPTER FIFTY-TWO
Nettlebrand's End

Sorrel ran. She ran back along the endless tunnel. 'He's coming!' she cried. 'He's coming!'

Swift as an arrow, she shot into the cave, ran straight over to Firedrake and hauled herself up by his tail. Ben was already on the dragon's back with Twigleg perched on his lap, the way they had ridden through so many nights of their journey. Burr-Burr-Chan sat astride Maia, crouching between two of the she-dragon's crest spines.

'He's rolling up the mountain like one of those machines humans use!' gasped Sorrel, buckling the straps around her waist. 'He's snorting and grunting and he's as big as, as big as . . .'

'Bigger than any of us,' the rat interrupted, starting the engine of her plane. 'Come on, then. Time to put our plan into action.' She closed her cockpit, took off immediately, and flew in a wide arc to a ledge above the entrance to the tunnel, where she waited for Nettlebrand to appear.

'Good luck,' cried Firedrake to Maia, flexing his wings. 'Or do you think a dragon brings luck only to human beings?'

'Who knows?' replied Maia. 'But anyway, we need as much of it as we can get.'

'Twigleg,' said Ben, checking the straps one last time, 'mind you hold on tight, won't you?'

The homunculus nodded, and stared at the tunnel entrance. His heart was thumping as if he were a mouse in a trap. Suppose that stupid dwarf had diluted the brownie saliva so much that it wouldn't work?

'Sure you wouldn't rather stay in the backpack?' Ben whispered to him.

But Twigleg shook his head vigorously. He didn't want to miss a minute of this. He wanted to see Nettlebrand perish. He wanted to see the golden armour he had polished for so many years melt as the dragon-fire turned Nettlebrand back into whatever creature he was made from.

Suddenly, Sorrel sat up very straight. 'Hear that?' she said, hoarsely.

They had all heard it, even Ben with his feeble human ears. A hollow stamping sound echoed along the tunnel. It was coming closer at a menacingly slow pace. Nettlebrand had tracked down his prey. He was on the trail.

Ben and Sorrel clutched the straps. Twigleg leaned back hard against the boy's stomach. The two dragons spread their wings and rose into the air. Side by side, they flew up to the roof of the cave, where they circled in the dark, waiting.

The stamping came closer and closer. The whole cave seemed to shake. Then Nettlebrand's golden head emerged from the tunnel.

*

He was crouching. It was the only way his gigantic body could fit into the tunnel carved through the rock by the Dubidai. Slowly, with eyes that glowed as red as blood, he looked around him. He snuffled, greedily drawing in the dragon scent.

Ben heard him breathing heavily after his long climb. An aura of malice and cruelty filled the cavern like a dark miasma. Little by little, Nettlebrand forced his massive body through the narrow confines of the tunnel, until at last his whole awesome, mighty figure stood there in the cave.

His legs were bent with the weight of the armour covering every last part of his dreadful body. His tail, dragging heavily over the ground behind him, bristled with sharp spikes. Snorting, teeth bared, the monster looked around, and an impatient roar rose from his chest.

Lola Greytail took off from the ledge, bringing the plane whizzing down toward Nettlebrand's armoured skull, whirring in circles round his horns, racing past his eyes.

Taken by surprise, Nettlebrand flung up his head and snapped at the plane as if it were a bothersome fly.

'Not so close!' breathed Ben. 'Don't get so close to him, Lola!'

But the rat was an ace airwoman. Unpredictable and fast as lightning, she whirred round the monster's head, dipped under his chin and raced between his legs. She landed on his back, took off again just as he was going to snap her up – and gradually lured him further and further into the cave.

The game the rat was playing infuriated the Golden One. He struck out, roared and snorted, trying to crush this annoying little nuisance, stamp on it, bite it. It was keeping him from his real prey. When Nettlebrand had come to a halt in the middle of the cavern, right in front of the stone dragons, Firedrake swooped down from the roof, wings rushing and neck outstretched. He flew at Nettlebrand from the front, while Maia came at him from one side.

Surprised, the monster flung up his head, spitting and baring his terrible fangs. His foul breath almost made the dragons falter. Lola turned her plane and landed neatly on the head of one of the stone dragons. She had done her work for the moment. Now it was Firedrake and Maia's turn.

The two dragons circled above their enemy's head.

'Aaaargh!' growled Nettlebrand, salivating as he followed them with his red eyes. 'So here are two of you.'

His voice shook the stone columns. It was deep and hollow, as if it were booming down an iron pipe. 'And with your brownies on board too. Not bad! Brownies always make a nice pudding!'

'Pudding?' Sorrel leaned so far down from Firedrake's back that Nettlebrand's hot breath singed her whiskers. 'You're the one on the menu today, you great golden meatball!'

Nettlebrand didn't so much as look at her. He cast Firedrake and Maia a brief glance, licked his lips and reared up menacingly.

'Where are the others?' he snarled, looking around impatiently. His whole body was quivering with greed as his claws scraped fitfully over the stony ground. 'Come out!' he bellowed, horns thrusting at the empty air. 'Come on out! I want to hunt you all together. I want to see you scatter like a flock of frightened ducks when I bring one of you down.'

Bellowing, he raised one claw and smashed a stalactite as if it were made of glass. Splinters of stone shot around the cavern. But the two dragons, flying as steadily as ever, kept on circling above his head.

'There *are* no others!' called Firedrake, diving so low that his wings almost brushed Nettlebrand's nose.

Ben and Sorrel both felt their hearts miss a beat as they came so close to the monster. Clutching their straps, they cowered down behind Firedrake's spines.

'We're the only dragons here,' cried Maia, skimming over Nettlebrand's back, 'but we will overcome you, wait and see. He and I will defeat you with our dragon riders.'

Furiously, Nettlebrand whipped round.

'Dragon riders – huh!' He twisted his muzzle, taunting them. 'Trying to scare me with those old stories, are you? Where – are – the – others?'

Ben didn't notice Twigleg slipping out of his strap. Inconspicuous as a tiny mouse, the homunculus clambered up the boy's jacket and stood on his shoulder.

'Twigleg!' cried Ben, horrified.

But the homunculus wasn't looking at him. Cupping his hands round his mouth, he shouted in a shrill voice, 'Hey, yoohoo, look who's here, master!'

Nettlebrand's head shot up in surprise.

'Here I am, master!' shouted Twigleg. 'On the dragon rider's shoulder. There aren't any other dragons. Get it? I lied to the dwarf! I lied to you too! You're going to melt, and I'm going to stand by and watch!'

'Twigleg!' cried Ben. 'Get down.'

He tried to pluck the homunculus off his shoulder, but Twigleg clung to his hair, shaking his tiny fist.

'This is my revenge!' he screeched. 'This is my revenge, master!'

Nettlebrand's mouth creased into an ugly grin. 'Well, look at that!' he growled. 'Our spidery friend riding the silver dragon. My old armour-cleaner. Look at the fool up there, Gravelbeard, and let what I'm about to do to him be a lesson to you.'

'Gravelbeard?' Twigleg yelled, almost toppling off Ben's shoulder. 'Haven't you noticed? Gravelbeard isn't with you any more. He's abandoned you, just like me. You don't have an armour-cleaner any more, and pretty soon you won't be needing one either.'

'Quiet, Twigleg!' Firedrake called back to him.

Nettlebrand suddenly reared up on his hind legs, snarling. His claw struck out with terrible force at the circling dragon. Firedrake only just avoided it. But Twigleg uttered a shrill scream, tried desperately to find something to hang on to – and fell head first into the depths below.

'Twigleg!' shouted Ben, leaning forward. But his out-stretched hand caught only empty air.

The homunculus came straight down on Nettlebrand's armoured brow, slid along the monster's thick neck, and was caught, struggling, between two spines.

Nettlebrand lowered himself back on all four paws, with a grunt. 'Got you now, spider-legs!' he growled, snapping at the place where his treacherous servant was clinging on for dear life, his thin legs flailing in the air.

'Firedrake!' cried Ben. 'Firedrake, we must help Twigleg!'

But both dragons were already swooping down on Nettlebrand, one from each side. They were just opening their mouths to breathe fire at him when Twigleg uttered a shrill cry.

'No!' he pleaded. 'No, not dragon-fire! It'll disenchant me! No, oh, please, no!'

The dragons braked in their flight.

'Are you crazy, Twigleg?' cried Sorrel. 'He's going to eat you!'

Nettlebrand turned with a grunt and snapped at the manikin's legs again. Once more Firedrake and Maia set out to distract him, striking at his armour with their claws, but

Nettlebrand shook them off like troublesome flies. Ben's heart almost stopped in despair. For a moment, he simply shut his eyes. And then he suddenly heard a buzzing sound.

The rat was coming.

Her plane raced towards Nettlebrand's back. The roof of the cockpit opened, and Lola leaned out.

'Come on, humplecuss, jump in!' she shouted.

With a manoeuvre of breakneck daring, she flew alongside the struggling Twigleg.

'Jump, Twigleg!' shouted Firedrake. 'Jump!' And he dug his claws into Nettlebrand's armoured neck to divert his attention from the manikin for a few precious seconds. As the golden dragon snapped and spat at Firedrake, the homunculus let go of Nettlebrand's spine and dropped on to the back seat of Lola's plane. The rat stepped on the gas at once, and the plane shot up to the roof of the cave with its cockpit still open and the trembling Twigleg safe inside it.

Nettlebrand bellowed so loud that the brownies had to put their paws over their sensitive ears. Hissing, the Golden One reared up again and struck out at both dragons. His claws only just missed Maia's wings. But instead of turning to escape, the she-dragon flew at him like a furious cat. She opened her mouth – and spat blue fire.

Firedrake attacked him from the other side. A mighty flame shot from his jaws and came down on Nettlebrand's head. Then Maia's dragon-fire engulfed Nettlebrand's golden back, making its way along his tail and licking down his legs.

The golden dragon bared his teeth and laughed. He laughed so loud that stones fell clattering down from the roof of the cave.

Dragon-fire! Huh!

How often it had licked around him before! It would

evaporate the moment it touched his armour. The chill he gave off would devour the blue flames. And then, when the two dragons were exhausted and discouraged, he, Nettlebrand, could pluck them from the air like helpless bats. He smacked his lips, and grunted in anticipation.

Then he suddenly felt something running down his forehead and dripping into his eyes. Instinctively, he raised a paw to wipe it away – and froze rigid.

His claws were distorting, losing their shape. His scales looked like withering leaves. Nettlebrand blinked. The stuff running down his forehead and blinding him was liquid gold.

Once again the dragons swooped towards him. Once again their blue fire licked at him, burning his limbs. Nettlebrand stared down at himself. His armour was melting into a sticky golden sludge. Gold dripped from his paws. Nettlebrand spat and gasped. The dragons were flying down at him again. He snapped at them, and slipped in a puddle of molten gold.

Then, for the first time in his long and wicked life, he felt fear – dark, hot fear. Brought to bay, he looked around him. Where could he flee? Where could he go to escape the fire eating at his armour? He felt hotter all the time – hotter and hotter. His strength was leaving him even as his scales dissolved. He must get to the water. Back to the water.

Nettlebrand stared at the tunnel down which he had come so infinitely long ago, when he was still Nettlebrand, the Golden One, Nettlebrand, the invincible. But the silver dragons were circling in front of the entrance with blue fire still leaping from their mouths, melting his precious armour. Nettlebrand crouched down. Grunting, he tried to raise his paws, but they were stuck in the golden puddles spreading out around him. And deep inside him, Nettlebrand felt his heart crack.

White vapour, damp and cold as ice, surged from his jaws. Hissing, the chill escaped his body until he collapsed like a punctured balloon. The icy vapour drifted through the cavern, hanging like clouds above the stone dragons.

Firedrake and Maia stopped, and hovered motionless in the white mist. It was getting cold in the cave, very cold. Shivering, Ben and Sorrel pressed close to one another, narrowing their eyes as they looked down. But the mists hid Nettlebrand from them, and there was little left of him to be seen now, only a hunched shadow.

Cautiously, Firedrake and Maia flew down through the chilly mist. Snowflakes settled on Sorrel's coat and stung Ben's face with cold. There was no sound except for the buzzing of Lola's plane somewhere in the fog.

'There!' whispered Burr-Burr-Chan as Maia and Firedrake landed on the ground, which was now covered with molten gold. 'There he is.'

CHAPTER FIFTY-THREE

The Dwarf's Request

Nettlebrand's armour lay in a huge pool of gold, looking like a cast-off snake-skin. Snowflakes hissed as they melted on its surface. Greenish fumes drifted out past the teeth in the monster's half-open jaws. His eyes were dark now, like extinguished lamps.

Stepping carefully, the two dragons waded through the liquid gold to see what was left of their enemy. Lola whirred past them and landed on the molten armour. When the rat opened her cockpit with a sudden jerk, Twigleg put his head out from his shelter behind the back seat, and gazed incredulously at what had once been his master.

'Well, take a look at that!' said Lola, hopping out on to one wing. 'Nothing but tin, that creature. Like one of the humans' machines, right?' She tapped the gold, which was still warm. 'Sounds hollow.'

Twigleg, wide-eyed, peered out of the cockpit. 'It'll show itself now!' he whispered.

'What will show itself?' Lola sat on the side of the wing,

dangling her legs.

But the homunculus did not answer. Transfixed, he was staring at Nettlebrand's open mouth, from which green vapours were still rising.

'What are you waiting for, Twigleg?' asked Firedrake, slowly coming closer. 'Nettlebrand is dead.'

The homunculus looked at him.

'Were the ravens dead?' he asked. 'No. They turned back into what they'd been all along. What kind of creature did the alchemist use to make Nettlebrand? He couldn't give him life, because he couldn't really create life. He could only borrow it – from some other living creature.'

'Some other living creature?' Sorrel shifted uncomfortably on Firedrake's back. 'You mean something's about to crawl out of there?' She pulled at the straps. 'Come on, Firedrake, we can watch this from a safe distance, can't we?'

But the dragon did not move. 'What kind of creature, Twigleg?' he asked.

'Oh, there aren't many creatures whose life you can borrow as you might a warm jacket,' said the homunculus, never taking his eyes off Nettlebrand's muzzle.

The others looked at each other, puzzled.

'Well, don't keep us in suspense, homplecuss,' said Lola, rising to her paws. 'Is the fight over or not?'

'There!' whispered Twigleg, without looking at her. He leaned forward and pointed. 'Look at that! Here comes Nettlebrand's life.'

A toad hopped out of the half-open mouth.

It landed with a splash in the pool of gold, jumped out again in alarm and hopped up on a snow-covered stone.

'A toad?' Sorrel leaned down from Firedrake's back, an

incredulous expression on her face. The toad looked at her with golden eyes, and began croaking uneasily to itself.

'Nonsense, humplecuss,' said Lola. 'You're having us on. The monster swallowed that toad at some point, that's all it is.'

But Twigleg shook his head. 'Believe me or not, as you like, but the alchemist was good at making something terrible out of a tiny creature.'

'Had we better catch it, Twigleg?' asked Firedrake.

'Oh no.' The homunculus shook his head again. 'The toad's harmless. Nettlebrand's wickedness came from our creator, not the toad itself.'

Sorrel wrinkled her forehead. 'A toad! Fancy that!' Suddenly, she grinned at Twigleg. 'So that's why you didn't want the dragon-fire to touch you. You were made from a hoppity old toad like that, right?'

Twigleg looked at her with annoyance. 'No,' he replied, sounding hurt. 'I was probably made from something much smaller, if you must know. The alchemist preferred woodlice or spiders for beings of my size.' So saying, he turned his back on Sorrel.

Firedrake and Maia carried their riders out over the pool of liquid gold. The toad watched them go. It didn't move, not even when Ben and the brownies climbed down from the dragons and went to the edge of the golden pond for one last look at what remained of Nettlebrand's armour. The toad hopped away only when Lola revved the engine of her plane.

Sorrel was going to follow it, but Firedrake gently held her back with his muzzle.

'Let it go,' he said – and turned around.

Something small was scurrying through the snow towards him, something stout with a large hat and a shaggy beard. It threw itself flat on the floor in front of Firedrake and Maia, wailing pitifully. 'Have mercy, silver dragons, have mercy on me. Grant me one wish. The greatest wish of my life. Grant me my wish, or my heart will be eaten away by longing for the rest of my wretched days.'

'Isn't this Nettlebrand's little spy?' asked Maia in surprise.

'Yes, yes, I admit it!' Gravelbeard struggled to his knees and looked timidly up at her. 'But I didn't spy of my own free will. He made me do it, honest!'

'Huh! Liar!' said Twigleg, clambering out of the rat's plane. 'You sneaked off to him of your own free will in the first place. Out of pure greed for gold. But for you he'd never have heard of Firedrake!'

'Well, okay,' muttered Gravelbeard, tugging at his beard. 'Maybe. But—'

'Look around you!' Twigleg interrupted him. 'You can bathe in his gold now. How about that?'

'Is that your wish?' Firedrake stretched and looked down at the dwarf, frowning. 'Come on, out with it. We're all tired.'

But Gravelbeard shook his head so hard that his hat almost fell off.

'No, no, I'm not interested in the gold any more,' he cried. 'Not a bit. I couldn't care less about it. What I want,' he said, spreading his stumpy arms wide, 'what I want is to stay in this cave. That's my wish.' He looked hopefully at the two dragons.

'What for?' asked Burr-Burr-Chan suspiciously.

'I'd like to make it even more beautiful,' whispered Gravelbeard. He looked around him reverently. 'I'd like to bring the stones hidden here to light, very carefully, very slowly. I can see them, you know. I can hear them whispering. On the walls, inside the columns. A tiny tap here, a thin shaving taken off the rock there – and they'd be shining and sparkling in all the colours of the rainbow.' He sighed, and closed his eyes. 'It would be wonderful.'

'Hmm,' murmured Burr-Burr-Chan. 'Doesn't sound a bad idea. But the dragons must decide.'

Firedrake yawned, and looked at Maia. The she-dragon was so tired that she could scarcely keep on her feet. She had breathed out so much fire that for the first time in her life she felt cold.

'I don't know,' she said, glancing at the stone dragons. 'I don't need this cave any more, now I don't have to hide from the Golden One. But what about *them*? Won't his hammering disturb them?'

Gravelbeard looked round.

'Who do you mean?' he asked uneasily.

'Come with me,' said Firedrake, offering the dwarf his tail. Hesitantly, Gravelbeard settled between the spines, and Firedrake carried him round the huge pool of gold and over to the dragons who had turned to stone. Maia and the others followed them.

'These,' explained Firedrake, when Gravelbeard jumped down from his tail to land on the paw of a stone dragon, 'these are the other twenty dragons Nettlebrand was after. Twigleg lied to you so as to keep Nettlebrand eager for the hunt. We wanted to lure him here.'

The dwarf inspected the petrified bodies with interest.

'They stopped drinking moonlight,' said Maia.

She settled on the floor. The snow was melting in the warmth of the cave, and bright pools of water were forming on the ground, but it was too late now for Nettlebrand to disappear into them.

'Yes, such things can happen quickly,' murmured Gravelbeard, tapping an expert finger against one stone paw. 'Stone grows fast. People don't realise that.'

No one was really listening to him. Firedrake settled drowsily on the floor beside Maia. Burr-Burr-Chan and Sorrel were preparing a mushroom picnic. Lola was wiping splashes of gold off her plane. They were all weary after the battle that was now behind them. Only Ben really listened to Gravelbeard's remark.

'What do you mean?' he asked, crouching down beside the dwarf. Twigleg clambered up on Ben's knee. 'Have you ever seen anything like this before? Something live that turned to stone?'

'Certainly.' Gravelbeard laid his hand on the dragon's stony scales. 'It happens to fabulous creatures very easily. Your castles are full of them. Dragons, winged lions, unicorns, demons, all turned to stone. Human beings find them and put them on display thinking they're stone all through. Which of course they aren't. Usually there's a breath of life left in them somewhere. But humans don't know that. They display them as if they'd actually made them. Huh!' The dwarf wrinkled his nose scornfully. 'Conceited folk, human beings. Now with these,' added Gravelbeard, pushing back his hat and looking up at the stone dragons, 'the shell isn't very thick yet. It could easily be cracked open.'

'Cracked open?' Ben looked at the dwarf incredulously.

'That's right.' Gravelbeard straightened his hat. 'But personally I like them better turned to stone.'

'Firedrake!' cried Ben, jumping up so suddenly that Twigleg slipped off his knee. 'Firedrake, listen to this.'

The dragon sleepily raised his head, and Maia woke with a start.

Gravelbeard grasped Twigleg's arm in fright. 'What does the

little human want?' he whispered. 'I haven't done a thing! You're my witness! I didn't even take my hammer out.'

'The dwarf says he can bring them back to life!' cried Ben excitedly.

'Bring who back to life?' muttered Firedrake, yawning.

'The dragons!' said Ben. 'The stone dragons. He says the stone is only a thin layer and can be cracked open like a shell, understand?'

Sorrel and Burr-Burr-Chan looked up from their picnic.

'If you ask me, the dwarf just wants our permission to hammer at the rocks around here,' said Sorrel, biting the stalk off a mushroom. 'Cracked open like a shell? Nonsense!'

'It's not nonsense!' Gravelbeard, looking insulted, planted himself in front of the claws of one of the stone dragons. 'I can prove it.' Taking the hammer from his backpack, the dwarf climbed up a spiny tail until he was standing on the petrified dragon's back. 'It will take a bit of time,' he called down, 'but you just wait and see!'

The dragons looked at him doubtfully.

'Can we help?' asked Maia.

The mountain dwarf merely shook his head scornfully. 'You? With your great big paws? No fear! Even that little human doesn't have enough feeling in his fingers to do that.' Looking important, Gravelbeard straightened his hat. 'We mountain dwarves are the only people who can do this sort of thing.'

'Goodnight, then,' muttered Sorrel, turning back to her mushrooms. 'By the time one of them hatches out of his stone shell I'll probably be toothless.'

'A day!' called Gravelbeard, waving his hammer excitedly in their direction. 'I'll need a day, perhaps less. You wait and see.'

Twigleg sighed and made himself comfortable on Ben's lap.

'Terribly conceited, these mountain dwarves,' he whispered to the boy. 'They always have to know best. But he just might do it. They really do have a lot of experience of stone.'

'A day?' Firedrake yawned, and looked down at the little dwarf, still doubtful. 'You certainly talk big, don't you? Well, wake us if you really do find any sign of life, all right?'

'Yes, yes,' replied Gravelbeard. He knelt down, passed a hand experimentally over the stone scales and began tapping very carefully, wielding his hammer with tiny strokes that made scarcely any more noise than the ticking of a clock.

For a while Ben watched the dwarf at work, although his eyelids kept closing. But at some point, when the dragons and the brownies had been asleep for a long time and faint snoring was coming from Lola's plane, he too fell asleep, and so did Twigleg.

All was still in the great cavern. Only Gravelbeard went on tapping away tirelessly with his hammer. Every now and then he cast a glance at the remains of Nettlebrand's armour, lying in the slowly solidifying pool of gold. Then he chuckled gleefully, and returned to his work.

and groaning were coming from the stone.

'Firedrake!' Ben grabbed Twigleg and Gravelbeard and leaped back. 'Firedrake, wake up! He's moving!'

The others all woke with a start.

'What's up?' cried Lola, jumping out of her plane.

'He's hatching out!' cried Ben. With two bounds, the rat was on his shoulder.

The grey stone into which Gravelbeard had driven his hammer cracked, crumbled, crunched open – and burst into a thousand pieces.

They all retreated in alarm.

Dusty and coughing, limbs stiff, a dragon crept out of the ruins. His eyes were still half closed. He struggled out with faltering steps, shaking a few stones off his scales – and opened his eyes. Confused, he looked about him, like someone waking from a dream.

Maia took a step towards him. 'Shimmertail,' she said. 'Do you recognise me?'

For a few moments, the dragon just looked at her. Then, slowly, he stretched out his neck and sniffed.

'Maia,' he said. 'What's happened?'

He turned his head to Firedrake, who was standing behind Maia. 'Who are you, and,' he added, staring at the brownies and Ben, who had Gravelbeard, Twigleg and Lola all on his shoulders, 'and who are these?'

'One of us is a Dubidai!' replied Burr-Burr-Chan, crossing his four arms. 'Remember us, Shimmertail?'

Shimmertail nodded, still confused. Then his gaze fell on the molten remains of Nettlebrand's armour, and he flinched back in alarm.

'He's here!' he whispered. 'The Golden One is here too!'

'No, he *was* here!' said Sorrel, scratching her stomach. 'But we melted him down.'

'Well, not us exactly,' added Burr-Burr-Chan. 'Firedrake and Maia did it.'

Shimmertail took another cautious step towards Maia. 'You defeated the Golden One? Just the two of you?' He shook his head and closed his eyes in disbelief. 'This is a dream,' he murmured. 'A beautiful dream. It must be.'

'No, it isn't,' said Maia, nudging him until he opened his eyes again. 'The golden dragon is dead.'

'Or sort of dead, anyway,' added Ben.

Shimmertail turned to the boy in amazement. 'The dragon rider!' he whispered.

Maia nodded, and blew the stone dust off Shimmertail's forehead. 'The dragon rider has come back, and the Golden One is defeated.'

'Just like the old stories,' murmured Shimmertail, gazing at Nettlebrand's molten armour. 'Like the stories you always used to tell, Maia.'

'But it wasn't the stories that defeated him,' said Ben, putting Lola and the dwarf down on the ground.

'No, it wasn't, it was us!' cried Sorrel, spreading her arms wide. 'All of us together. Brownies, dragons, the little human, the homunculus, the rat, the mountain dwarf. A story to melt anyone's heart!' She chuckled. 'Sad to say, you slept through the whole thing. Like them.'

She pointed to the other dragons, still crouching motionless inside their stony skins. Shimmertail went over to them. He stood among the ruins of his own stone shell, unable to take it all in.

'What happened?' he asked softly. 'Tell me, Maia. What's all this if it isn't a dream?'

The she-dragon went over to him and gently nuzzled his dusty flank. 'Does that feel like a dream? No, you're awake. The mountain dwarf there woke you.'

Gravelbeard proudly thrust out his chest.

'Will he wake the others too?' asked Shimmertail.

The dwarf crossed his arms and grinned. 'Of course. If we can do a little deal.'

'Just like you!' called Twigleg from Ben's shoulder. 'Exactly what I expected you to say, slate-brain. A dwarf never does anything for free. What do you want? Gold? Jewels?'

'No!' cried Gravelbeard indignantly. 'Nothing like that, you spidery-legged homunculus. Like I said before, I want to stay in this cave, tap at its walls just a little. Clean and polish up its beauty. And maybe pick out a tiny little stone now and then. That's all.'

Maia looked down at him with an ironic smile. 'You'll pick out more than one little stone, dwarf,' she said. 'You're greedy. All the same, we'll let you stay here if you wake the other dragons.'

Gravelbeard bowed so low to her that he had to hold his hat on.

'I'll wake them!' he cried. 'All of them, Your Silverness, all of them. I'll set to work at once.'

And with his hammer already in his hand again, he climbed the nearest petrified dragon's tail and started chipping away as if his old master were breathing down his neck.

Firedrake and Maia took the dusty Shimmertail between them and led him down the long tunnel to the outside world, where he had not set paw for over a thousand nights. The black ravens had disappeared. The three dragons flew over the valley in the light of the thin sickle of the waning moon, and Shimmertail washed the dust off his scales in the lake.

The toad that had lent Nettlebrand its life sat on the bank, watching. And with every moonbeam that fell on the scales of the silver dragons, its dark memories faded.

CHAPTER FIFTY-FIVE

What Now?

At noon the next day, Firedrake was perched on a rocky outcrop high above the valley, unable to sleep. Gravelbeard's tapping and hammering had driven him out of the great cavern. The light and warmth of the sun usually made him sleepy, but it wasn't working today. Firedrake kept raising his head from his paws, looking at the surrounding peaks and sighing.

After a while Ben joined him. He climbed the rocks, sat down beside the dragon, and looked at him anxiously. 'What's the matter?' he asked. 'Why aren't you asleep?'

'I can't seem to drop off,' said Firedrake. 'What are the others doing?'

Ben shrugged his shoulders. 'Oh, nothing special. Well, no one's asleep. Sorrel is getting Burr-Burr-Chan to explain the Dubidai method of cultivating mushrooms. Maia is telling Shimmertail all about what happened while he was asleep. Gravelbeard is tapping away, and Twigleg's flying on a sightsee-

– 408 –

ing trip with Lola.'

'Really?' Firedrake nodded, and then sighed again.

'What are you going to do now?' Ben looked enquiringly at the dragon. 'I mean, are you going straight home to the north now you've found this valley?'

'I wish I knew,' replied Firedrake, looking up at the white peaks. 'I thought of nothing else on our way here. Suppose I fly home and find that the others don't want to come back here with me after all?'

Ben looked at him in surprise. 'Why wouldn't they? I thought they *had* to leave? You told me human beings were going to flood your valley.'

Firedrake nodded. 'Yes, but when I left, the others wouldn't believe it might really happen. They wanted to try driving the humans off. The way the fairies do, you know. Fairies know how to prevent humans building roads over their fairy mounds.'

'They do?' Ben stared at Firedrake. 'How?'

'They sprinkle magic dust on the engines that work the machinery,' replied the dragon. 'They pinch and nip, they blow itching powder into safety helmets and up noses, and they conjure up so much rain that the humans and their machines get stuck in the mud. Fairies are so tiny they can even make themselves invisible for a moment or so. Humans can never catch them. It's different with us dragons.'

'It is indeed,' murmured Ben, admiring Firedrake's silver scales. He still never tired of gazing at the dragon. As far as he was concerned, there was no more magical creature in the whole world.

'What do you advise?' asked Firedrake, looking at the boy. 'Shall I just stay here? Or shall I fly back all that way, back to the others who may not want to come? Who may just think I'm a young fool?' At a loss, Firedrake shook his head. 'Perhaps they won't even believe I've found the Rim of Heaven.'

Ben leaned against Firedrake's warm scales and looked down at the lake.

'I think you'll have to go back,' he said after a while. 'Or you'd always be wondering what had happened to them. Whether the humans destroyed them. Whether they would have followed you here. It would always be going round in your head, driving you crazy.'

Firedrake said nothing for quite a long time, then he nodded slowly. 'You're right, dragon rider,' he said, nuzzling Ben affectionately with his nose. 'Yes, you're right. Much as I like it here, I must go back. And it will be best if I set off this very night.'

He rose, shook himself, and looked round once more. 'I'll tell Sorrel and the others. What about you? Will you come with us, or shall I take you to the monastery? The Greenblooms will be there.'

Now it was Ben who was stuck for an answer.

'I don't know,' he said. 'What would you do?'

Firedrake looked at him. 'I'll take you to the Greenblooms,' he said. 'You need human beings, the way I need the other dragons, the way Sorrel isn't happy without other brownies to quarrel with. Without human beings, you'd get to feel very lonely.'

'I'll feel lonely without you dragons too,' said Ben, looking away from Firedrake.

'No, no!' Firedrake rubbed his head very gently against the boy's. 'Believe me, we shall meet again. I'll visit you as often as your short human life allows.'

'Oh yes, please,' replied Ben. 'Visit me often.' And he put his arms round the dragon's neck and hugged him as if he would never let him go.

CHAPTER FIFTY-SIX

The Way Back

The moon had risen over the valley when Firedrake emerged from the Dubidai tunnel with Ben and Sorrel on his back. Lola's plane was whirring round the dragon's horns, and Twigleg was sitting on the back seat. He and Lola had been inseparable ever since the rat saved him from Nettlebrand's jaws.

Maia had Burr-Burr-Chan on her back. She was planning to accompany Firedrake to the monastery. By now Gravelbeard's hammer had brought two more dragons back to life, and they too came out with Shimmertail to say goodbye to Firedrake and Maia – and to set eyes on the moon again. Only Gravelbeard had stayed in the cave. He was so busy tapping away that he just nodded when the dragons said goodbye to him.

'Come back soon,' Shimmertail told Firedrake as they stood at the entrance to the tunnel. 'And bring the others with you. This valley is much too large for just us, even if the dwarf does wake all the others.'

Firedrake nodded. 'I'll try to bring them,' he replied. 'And if they don't want to come, I'll fly back on my own.'

He looked round one last time, taking in the white mountains and the black lake, and then gazing up at the starry sky. Then he spread his wings and took off from the rocky slope of the mountainside. Maia caught up and flew beside him until they reached the pass which Firedrake had crossed so short and yet so long a time ago.

He enjoyed flying through the mountains with another dragon beside him. Sometimes, when he was not sure of the best way, Maia flew ahead with Burr-Burr-Chan so that the Dubidai brownie could guide them. But most of the time the two dragons travelled side by side. Firedrake flew more slowly than usual so that Maia could get used to the unaccustomed winds.

As they soared above the mountain with the monastery on its steep slope, they saw the dull gleam of the river Indus below. The rat was first to land in the courtyard outside the prayer hall.

This time there was no one waiting for them. But before they set off for the Rim of Heaven, Ben had made a special promise to Barnabas Greenbloom and the lama. No sooner had Firedrake folded his wings than Ben jumped off his back and ran over to a long row of bells swaying gently in the wind beside the flight of steps leading to the Dhu-Khang. Then he rang the largest of them. Its deep, full sound echoed through the night, and soon doors and windows were opening everywhere, and the monks came pouring out of their little cells.

They surrounded the two dragons, all laughing and calling out at once. Ben could hardly manage to get back to Firedrake through the crowd. When he had finally made his way over to the dragon, he quickly climbed on his back again to keep watch for the Greenblooms.

Maia was staying very close to Firedrake's side. Her ears twitched nervously as she looked timidly down at the thronging humans. Burr-Burr-Chan patted her scales soothingly.

At last, Ben saw the professor and his family hurrying towards the dragons, together with the lama. Guinevere was waving wildly. Ben waved back shyly.

'Welcome!' cried Barnabas Greenbloom. 'My word, are we glad to see you!'

He was so excited that he almost fell over a couple of young monks who were standing in front of Firedrake, beaming up at him. When the lama whispered something to them they nodded, and busily set about clearing a path for the dragon up the steps to the Dhu-Khang. First Barnabas Greenbloom flung his arms around Firedrake's neck, then he shook Sorrel's furry paw, and finally he grinned broadly up at Ben.

'Well, dragon rider?' he shouted above the hubbub of voices. 'Shall I make a guess? Between you all, you did it, am I right? You defeated Nettlebrand, the Golden One!'

Ben nodded. What with all this excitement, he couldn't get any words out. The little monks – the youngest was perhaps just half Ben's age – had made a way through the crowd for the dragons, and the lama himself led them up the wide flight of steps to the prayer hall. Maia was glad to disappear into the cool darkness. The lama said a few more words to the monks, who suddenly stood quite still down in the moonlight. Then he closed the heavy door behind the dragons and turned to them with a smile.

'Two dragons at once,' the professor translated. 'Which means great good luck for our monastery and the valley! Did it all turn out as the prophecy foretold? Has the return of the dragon rider brought us back the dragons?'

Ben climbed off Firedrake's back and went over to the professor, a shy smile on his face. 'Yes, I think the dragons will come back,' he said. 'Nettlebrand's gone for ever.'

Barnabas Greenbloom took the boy's hand and shook it vigorously. Guinevere smiled at him. Ben couldn't remember ever having felt happier in his life – or more embarrassed.

'But – but it was all of us working together,' he stammered.

'With brownie spit and dragon-fire!' Sorrel slipped off Firedrake's back. 'With homunculus cunning, human reason, an aviator-ace rat and even the help of a dwarf, although that wasn't exactly what the dwarf intended.'

'It sounds as if you have a great deal to tell us,' said Vita Greenbloom.

Ben nodded. 'A very great deal.'

'Good.' Rubbing his hands, Barnabas Greenbloom exchanged a few words with the lama. Then he turned back to the dragons. 'The people here love a good story,' he said. 'Do you think there'll be time to tell them yours before Firedrake sets off on the journey home? They would be very glad to hear it.'

The dragons exchanged glances before they both nodded.

'Would you like to rest a little first?' asked Barnabas Greenbloom solicitously. 'Would anyone like something to eat and drink?'

'Sounds like a good idea!' cried Sorrel and Burr-Burr-Chan in unison.

So the two brownies had mushrooms to eat, while Ben polished off a whole mountain of rice, and two chocolate bars that Guinevere had given him. Now that all the excitement was over, his appetite had returned.

The dragons lay down on the wooden floor at the far end of the hall, with Firedrake resting his head on Maia's back. In the light of the many little lamps illuminating the hall, they looked as if they had just climbed out of one of the pictures on the wall. Then the lama opened the door again, and the monks streamed in. The sight of the dragons rooted them to the spot among the columns.

Only when Firedrake raised his head and the professor beckoned them forward did the monks approach, slowly and with hesitant steps. They squatted on the floor at a respectful distance from the dragons. The oldest monks pushed the youngest ones to the front, where they could kneel close to the creatures' silver claws.

The Greenblooms joined the monks, but Ben and the brownies, Twigleg and Lola sat on the crests of Firedrake and Maia's tails.

When all was still in the hall, and the only sound was the rustling of the monks' robes, Firedrake cleared his throat and began to tell the story – in the language of fabulous animals, the language that everyone can understand.

As the moon set outside and the sun began its daily journey across the sky, he told the tale of his quest from the very beginning. His words filled the hall with pictures. He spoke of a clever white rat, enchanted ravens and mountain dwarves, sand-elves and Dubidai. As he went on with his story, the basilisk fell to dust once more, the blue djinn opened his thousand eyes. The sea serpent swam through the waves, and the great roc bird snatched Ben away. Finally, as the sun outside was sinking in the sky, Nettlebrand climbed the dragons' mountain. His armour melted in blue dragon-fire, and a toad hopped out of his mouth.

Finally, Firedrake fell silent, stretched, and looked round him.

'The story ends here,' he said, 'the story of Sorrel and Ben, the dragon rider, of Firedrake and Nettlebrand, the Golden One, whose servants were his doom. Tomorrow night a new story begins. I don't yet know how it will end, and I will not tell it to you until I do.'

Then the lama rose, bowed to Firedrake and said, 'We thank you. We will write down all we have heard, and we wish you luck on the journey that still lies ahead of you. Now we will go and leave you to gather strength for the journey home.'

As if at a signal, the monks rose quietly to leave the hall. At the door they all turned to look once more at the dragons sitting between the columns, for they were not sure whether they would ever again in their lives be fortunate enough to see a dragon.

'Ben,' said Barnabas Greenbloom, when the hall was empty and only the lama was still with them, 'we'll have to leave tomorrow too. Guinevere's school term is about to begin. I was wondering,' he continued awkwardly, running his hand through his grey hair, 'if the dragon rider has decided what to do yet?'

Ben looked at Firedrake and Sorrel and Twigleg, who was sitting on the floor next to Lola. 'Yes, please. I'd like to come too,' he said. 'With you, I mean.'

'Wonderful!' cried Barnabas Greenbloom, shaking Ben's hand so hard it almost hurt. 'Hear that, Vita? Hear that, Guinevere?'

Vita Greenbloom and her daughter smiled.

'Yes, Barnabas, we did,' said Vita, 'but however pleased you may be, you mustn't crush my future son's fingers.'

Guinevere leaned over to Ben and whispered, 'You know, I've always wished I had a brother. It can sometimes be a real pain being an only child.'

'Yes, I can imagine,' Ben whispered back, although at the moment he could imagine nothing but the most wonderful things in the world when he thought of his new family.

'See them whispering together?' said Barnabas Greenbloom to his wife. 'They have secrets from us already. This could be interesting!'

Then they suddenly heard a sob.

Twigleg was sitting on the floor with his face buried in his hands. Tiny tears trickled through his fingers and dripped onto his bony knees.

'Twigleg!' Ben knelt down beside the homunculus, concerned. 'But you knew I wanted to stay with the Greenblooms.'

'Yes, yes,' the homunculus sobbed even louder, 'but what's to become of me? Where am I to go now, young master?'

Ben quickly picked him up and put him on his arm. 'Why, you'll stay with me, of course!' He glanced enquiringly at his new mother. 'That'll be all right, won't it?'

'Of course,' replied Vita. 'We could really use your talents as an interpreter, Twigleg.'

'Indeed we could!' cried the professor. 'How many languages do you speak?'

'Ninety-three,' murmured the homunculus, and he stopped sobbing.

'I tell you what!' Guinevere tapped his knee. 'You can live in my doll's house.'

'Doll's house?' The homunculus removed his hands from his face and looked at the girl indignantly. 'I am not a doll! No, a nice cool corner of the cellar, surrounded by a few books, that's what I'd really like.'

'Well, that shouldn't be any problem,' said Barnabas Greenbloom, smiling. 'We have a big old house with a large old cellar. But we'll be away a good deal on our travels, as you know. I hope you can live with that too.'

'Oh yes!' Twigleg took a handkerchief out of his sleeve and

blew his nose. 'I've actually enjoyed getting to know the world.'

'Good, then that's settled.' said the professor happily. 'Let's start packing.' He turned to Firedrake. 'Is there anything else we can do for you? When do you mean to set off?'

The dragon put his head on one side. 'As soon as the moon has risen in the sky. Admittedly I haven't had much sleep recently, but I'll make up for that later. Now I just want to start the journey. How about you, Sorrel?'

'No problem,' muttered Sorrel, scratching her stomach. 'Or rather, yes, there is just a tiny little problem.'

Firedrake looked at her in surprise. 'What is it?'

Burr-Burr-Chan cleared his throat. 'I'd like to come too,' he said. 'I could teach my two-armed relations how to grow cultivated mushrooms.'

Firedrake nodded. 'Then I'll have two dragon riders again,' he said. 'All the better.' He turned to the she-dragon, who was standing beside him licking her scales. 'But what about you, Maia?' asked Firedrake. 'Can you find your way back to the Rim of Heaven on your own?'

'Of course.' Maia raised her head and looked at him. 'But I'm not going back. Shimmertail is there to look after the others. I'm coming with you.'

Firedrake's heart leaped with joy. All of a sudden, he hardly minded what might be waiting for him on his return.

'After all, suppose they don't believe you at home in the north?' asked Maia, as if she had read his thoughts. 'If I'm there too I'll be living proof that you found us and the Rim of Heaven. And together I'm sure we can persuade them to come back with us.'

'Two dragons!' Barnabas Greenbloom frowned anxiously. 'That's not without its dangers, my dear Firedrake. It will be harder for two dragons to find places to hide during the day.'

'Don't worry about that!' Lola Greytail scampered in among all the huge feet and claws. 'You see before you the best pilot they could possibly have! And as it happens I'm going the same way. The dragons will have to adjust to my speed now and then, that's all.'

'Are you going back already?' asked Twigleg in surprise, looking down from Ben's arm. 'I mean, have you finished your surveying?'

'Surveying? Huh!' The rat waved a dismissive paw. 'You know what I'm going to do? I'm going to invent things. I'm going to fake the map of these parts so cleverly that no one will ever find the Rim of Heaven.' She smoothed her ears with satisfaction. 'What do you say to that?'

Firedrake bent his neck down to the little rat and gently nuzzled her fat hindquarters. 'We say *thank you*. And we'd be even more grateful to you and your uncle if such a map were widely distributed.'

'Oh, it will be,' replied Lola. 'You bet it will. Uncle Gilbert has a very select circle of customers and a large extended family.'

'That's wonderful!' With a sigh, Firedrake straightened up again. 'Then may I invite the smallest monks to go for a farewell flight on my back? Will you come too, Maia?'

'Of course,' replied the she-dragon. 'I'll even carry some of the older ones if they like.'

And so it was that the farmers down by the river, walking through their fields in the dusk, saw two dragons circling above the mountains. On their spiny crested backs, laughing like little children, sat the monks of the monastery. Even the very oldest of them.

CHAPTER FIFTY-SEVEN

Good News

Two months later, the Greenblooms were having breakfast. Ben had just helped himself to a second roll when Barnabas suddenly spoke up from behind his newspaper.

'Good heavens!'

'Really?' said Twigleg who, as usual, was sitting on the table next to Ben's plate. 'You mean the weather forecast's still set fair?'

'No, no!' cried the professor, lowering his newspaper. 'I didn't mean the weather, my dear Twigleg. There's a news story here which ought to interest you all.'

'About Pegasus, perhaps?' asked his wife, stirring milk into her coffee.

Barnabas Greenbloom shook his head.

'Some fairies have got another digger stuck in the mud?' suggested Guinevere, licking marmalade off her fingers.

'Wrong again,' replied her father.

'Oh, come on, Barnabas, don't keep us in suspense,' said Vita.

'What is it?'

Ben looked intently at the professor. 'Something about the dragons?'

'Ex-act-ly!' cried Barnabas Greenbloom. 'The boy's hit the nail on the head again. Listen to this!' And he read aloud:

'"A strange phenomenon was observed two days ago in the night sky over a Scottish valley. A large flock of gigantic birds, or some have described them as creatures resembling giant bats, rose into the sky and flew south in the light of the full moon. Unfortunately all trace of them was lost over the open sea, but scientists are still trying to identify the species of bird concerned."'

Guinevere and Ben looked at each other.

'That was them,' murmured Ben. 'Firedrake really did manage to convince the others.'

He looked out of the window, where there was nothing to be seen but empty grey sky.

'You miss them, don't you?' Vita leaned over the table and took his hand.

Ben nodded.

'Well,' said Barnabas Greenbloom, pouring himself more coffee, 'the school holidays begin in eight weeks' time, and we'll be setting out in search of Pegasus. I've found an interesting clue near the ancient city of Persepolis. And it's not too far from there to the village where Zubeida lives. I assume that if all goes well, Firedrake and the other dragons will reach the Himalayas within a month. Why don't we ask our good friend Lola Greytail to carry news to the Rim of Heaven, asking if he can meet us at Zubeida's in two months' time?' The professor turned to Ben.

'You know his travelling speed – do you think he'll do it?'

'Perhaps.' In his excitement Ben almost spilled his cocoa. 'Yes, probably! Hear that, Twigleg? We may be seeing Firedrake again in a couple of months' time.'

'That's good,' replied the homunculus, sipping tea from his thimble mug. 'But I'm afraid it means seeing Sorrel too, and she'll start needling me horribly again.'

'Oh, we'll tell her not to,' said Guinevere, giving him a fragment of biscuit. 'The moment she starts winding you up we'll take away the mushrooms we've been collecting for her.'

Ben went to the window and looked up at the sky.

Two months. He might be riding on Firedrake's back again in just two months.

He sighed.

Two months can be a long time. A very long time.

'Come on,' said Guinevere, leaning against him on the window seat. 'Let's go out and look for fairy tracks, okay?'

Ben tore himself away from the sight of the empty sky and nodded. 'I saw some down by the pond yesterday,' he said.

'Good.' Guinevere led the way to the garden gate. 'We'll try there first, then.'

'Wrap up warm,' Vita Greenbloom called after them. 'There's a smell of autumn in the air this morning.'

'Wait a minute, I'm coming too!' cried Twigleg, scrambling hastily down the table leg.

'But this time you must translate everything they say to us,' said Guinevere, putting his knitted jacket on him. 'Promise?'

'Even if those fairies just talk more nonsense?' snapped Twigleg.

'Yes, even then,' replied Guinevere. 'I want to hear their nonsense too.'

Ben grinned. Then he picked Twigleg up and followed her outside.

Yes, two months could be a long time. But not with a sister like Guinevere.